WILD

WILD

KIM PRITEKEL
&
ALEX ROSS

SAPPHIRE BOOKS

SALINAS, CALIFORNIA

Wild

Copyright © 2014 by Kim Pritekel **&** Alex Ross. All rights reserved.

ISBN - 978-1-939062-34-5

This is a work of fiction - names, characters, places, and incidents are the product of the author's imagination or are used fictitiously. Any resemblance to actual persons living or dead, business, events or locales is entirely coincidental.

All rights reserved. No part of this publication may be reproduced, distributed, or transmitted in any form or by any means, including photocopying, recording, or other electronic or mechanical methods, without written permission of the publisher.

Cover - Christine Svendsen
Editor - Margaret Martin
Book Designer - LJ Reynolds

Sapphire Books Publishing
P.O. Box 8142
Salinas, CA 93912
www.sapphirebooks.com

Printed in the United States of America
First Edition – May 2014

This and other Sapphire Books titles can be found at
www.sapphirebooks.com

Kim's Dedication

For Roxy, an incredible little girl who has a very special place in my heart.

Alex's Dedication

To Lea, with love.

This Grad School application is about the one person who changed my life. I imagine you've gotten plenty of good answers over the years to that question. Some people may have written about their moms, dads, a sibling, perhaps a neighbor, a professor, or maybe a friendly neighborhood police officer.
That's not my story.
I write about Abel Cohen. Though her namesake was murdered in legend and lore, in this story, she is sent as an angel to earth to show me what real freedom is all about. This is my story; her story; and most importantly, our story.

Prologue

The small blonde child walked on, green eyes growing large with apprehension and fear. As she wandered through the woods, one tree began to look like the next in the maze of unending forest. Worried now, she resorted to chewing on her fingernails as tension filled her body. Her long golden hair grew damp with sweat against her skull, and her tiny hand clutched into a fist to try to keep herself under control. She didn't want to call for help because her mommy would be angry at her for wandering so far off.

She stopped, suddenly feeling eyes on her. In her childish mind, she imagined all sorts of monsters hiding in the shadows of the trees. Monsters who wanted to eat her up, and never let her play with her baby brother again, or see her mommy and daddy. Whimpering in fear, she looked in all directions, her tiny white teeth still chewing painfully on her fingernails, gnawing them to the quick. "Hello?" she called, her high voice causing a bird to take flight from a nearby branch, startling her. She looked up, following its progress above the tree tops, wishing she could fly like that.

"Hi."

The little blonde whipped around, eyes the size of saucers, immediately letting out a sigh of relief when she saw a child standing before her. "Who are you?"

She knitted her dark blonde brow, glad it was a child, but suspicious all the same. Her mommy taught her not to trust strangers.

"I'm Zac," the child with short, dark hair said, an impish grin on her face. The strange blue color of her eyes seemed to glow under the canopy of trees.

"You have pretty eyes, Zac."

Zac seemed taken aback, but shook it off. "Thanks. What's your name?"

"Abel. Nice to meet you, Zac," the little blonde said, remembering her mother's constant teachings of politeness and manners.

"Nice to meet you too, Abel. I think you're lost." Zac nodded at the woods surrounding them.

"Yes. Can you help me?" Abel hoped beyond hope that Zac knew where to go.

"Sure! Are you from that house with the green dock?" At Abel's nod, Zac smiled. "Come on." Zac led the way through the trees, glancing often at her smaller companion. "I've never seen any kids roaming around here before." She noticed a fleeting smile on Abel's lips.

Chapter One

Fourteen Years Later...
Abel Cohen grinned as she sang to the song "Who Let The Dogs Out?" by the Baha Men, her blonde locks bouncing back and forth as she bobbed her head to the beat. She drove her two-door Jetta through the winding roads toward Maine's Wachiva Forest.

With finals over, she loaded her car and began the drive from the family home in Greenwich, Connecticut, to their cabin. She promised to air it out and get it cleaned and ready for a fun summer, until her younger siblings finished school and her family could join her.

As she tapped the wheel with dancing fingers, she looked at her surroundings, watching the trees pass. The extensive wooded area was coming back to life after a harsh winter that lasted far into spring, leaving plants and trees shocked and frozen when they should have been blooming. Although late May, Abel would be taking a hot bubble bath tonight.

She smiled as she thought of her time alone at the cabin. As much as she dearly loved her parents and four younger brothers and sisters, she would enjoy her temporary isolation. Abel sighed in contentment at the thought of doing whatever, whenever, and not having to worry about dorm roommates or parents bugging her.

She changed the radio station as a string of

commercials came on, then finally gave up. Opening her sun visor, she grabbed a CD at random and slid it into the player then turned up the volume.

❧❧❧❧

The figure watched as a car approached the two cabins, distanced a mile apart, from the rarely used road. Its keen ears listened, trying to place the make. Once it was sure it wasn't the Wilkins' truck, the lithe body moved quickly through the trees, hiding behind massive trunks, and streamlining its slim figure behind thinner trees. The dark blue two-door, made its winding way up the road, slowing around the numerous turns. *A careful driver, not aggressive or impulsive. Must be a woman.*

Silently the figure neared the road, watching to see which way the sedan would turn–left to the Wilkins', or right to the Cohen's. When the car turned right, a sharp intake of breath could be heard, unsettling some nearby birds. Muffled steps followed as the shadow swept across the forest floor, rested a large calloused hand on a rough tree trunk, and closed its blue eyes. As the car pulled into the drive, a warm, familiar feeling stole over the crouched figure. The door to the sedan opened and the driver stepped out, her long blonde hair blowing in the breeze–a constant companion to the forest.

"She's back." The words were barely a whisper upon the wind. "Spinney."

❧❧❧❧

Abel was still humming the song she'd been

listening to as she rounded the corner to her parent's cabin. Upon seeing it again, a soft smile lined her lips. So many incredible memories. It saddened her to know her time here was coming to an end. As a junior in college, she knew as more and more demands were made on her time, she would have less to spend with her family.

Her parents bought the three-room cabin when Abel was four. Over the years, they added onto it as their family grew, creating the wood and glass beauty that stood before her now. It had six bedrooms for five kids and her parents, and provided a cozy environment for a fun-filled summer, or special holiday season. She looked around, noting the sun-splashed landscape. The lush forest around the cabin looked as it always did, trees as far as the eyes could see, with the lake and dock not twenty yards from the house.

Her smile faded as she scanned the dense forest to her left. She felt like she was being watched, and an odd, unsettling feeling came over her. Eyebrows drawn, she turned in a circle, searching. "Hello?" Her voice echoed over the lake, bouncing off the surrounding foothills. The squawk of far-off birds was her only reply. She decided to shrug it off and began to unpack three months worth of clothes, and a weeks worth of food–just enough to sustain her until her parents arrived.

Humming loudly and badly–knowing there wasn't a soul around to hear–she made her way up the dirt walk that led to the wrap-around porch. She dug out her keys holding the screen door open with her butt, and maneuvered around as she juggled bags and boxes while unlocking the heavy door.

"Yuck." She wrinkled her nose at the stale air as

she dropped her bags and disabled the alarm system before it sent dozens of police cars swarming the cabin.

≈≈≈≈

A squirrel scampered by as the dark figure moved yet closer, hiding behind a small thicket of trees near the cabin. Inside, she could see Abel unpacking a brown paper bag on the kitchen counter. The figure moved to the other window to see her better. She studied the face of the angel that she had dreamed of for years . . .

≈≈≈≈

Zac grabbed the cold metal handle of the boxcar and heaved herself up into its cavernous depths, looking around to make sure she was alone. Satisfied, she dropped her heavy knapsack and slid down the metal wall landing on her butt, her knees bent and her wrists dangling over them. She brushed her long, dark hair out of her eyes, angry that she had lost her comb running from the cops.

"Bastards." She ran her fingers through the tangled strands, bracing herself as the train groaned to life and began to move. She watched as the snow-swept scenery whooshed by faster and faster. She was forced to move further back in the car to avoid the blowing snow. Stretching her legs, she leaned her head back and closed her eyes with a sigh. A slow smile curved her lips as she invoked her favorite daydream.

Spinney ran through the trees, her long, beautiful hair like spun gold flying behind her. Squeezing her green eyes shut, she stopped, raised her arms to the sky, and spun like she did when she was five. Zac imagined what she would look like as a young woman. She wondered how tall Spinney was now. She was so tiny as a rowdy five-year-old.

Spinney stopped spinning. Her eyes shone. With a smile on her face, she walked over to the brunette and reached out her hand. Zac took it, entwining their fingers and smiling in return. Zac felt so safe with her friend, as if nothing or no one–the cold weather, life, or the Boogie Man–could ever hurt her again.

Sitting in the cold boxcar, Zac reveled in the bliss of the warm feelings her daydream sent through her. Somehow she felt the presence of her old friend, even though she hadn't been with her in so long. She could feel her, knowing she was out there somewhere, and she missed her. Her only friend.

"I had such a crappy day today, Spinney," Zac whispered into the empty boxcar, her voice quiet with fatigue. "Almost got thrown into the can again. Damn, sucks."

She looked out into the night, the star-filled sky mostly hidden by heavy, pregnant clouds, threatening to drop more snow on them. "More snow, Spinney," she whispered, her words coming out in puffs of air, as she huddled her long body in upon itself, wrapping long, gangly arms around her shins. "Cold."

Zac wondered if it was snowing wherever Spinney was. Was she warm and safe? She knew she was, and had the distinct feeling that she'd know if something were wrong. She'd feel it like she felt the cold snow blowing against her skin. As sleep overtook her, she wondered if Spinney was thinking about her, too. She smiled at the thought.

꧁꧂

Abel sat in her father's recliner with a plate of baby carrots and a blob of ranch dressing on the side. She put her feet up on the attached ottoman. Humming with delight in her relaxation, she grabbed a carrot, dragged it through the white goo until it was half covered, and smiled at the satisfying crunch it made between her teeth. She loved carrots. Her mom used to tell her she'd turn orange if she continued to eat as many as she did.

Grabbing the remote, she flipped on the TV and waded through the channels. Settling on ESPN, she continued to eat her carrots, her feet tapping together as she nearly bounced from her excitement: summer break, a whole week completely alone, and another 4.0 GPA to add to her files. Although she and Kyle broke up the previous semester, that wasn't exactly a storm cloud in her sunny day…just a detail. An eerie feeling washed over her. She felt as if she weren't alone.

꧁꧂

The figure moved around the large cabin. Hearing talking within, she listened to determine if it was Spinney. She hadn't seen anyone else go into the cabin, but she heard a man's voice. Moving around the stand of trees to look into another window, she bent down, balancing her weight with a hand on the rough bark of a tree and the hard ground beneath her feet.

Not a sound was made when she moved. Even a hummingbird that was feasting on a birdfeeder didn't move as it sucked down the sugary, red-colored water.

Standing again, with one blue eye peeking out from behind her hiding place, she saw Spinney sitting in a chair, her feet up and an empty plate on her lap. She smiled then threw her head back and laughed outright at what humored the young woman so much, spying a large, black rectangular thing with a cord running from it. She realized it was probably a TV. She had seen them a few times in store windows when she was traveling.

Her gaze moved back up to Spinney's, looking into those bright green eyes and wishing, hoping, needing to see them up close again. She wanted them to see her.

"Soon, Spinney," she whispered. "Soon."

Chapter Two

"Zac?" Abel asked as they walked through the forest hand in hand. It had been two weeks since the Cohen family arrived at their cabin and Abel had managed to get herself lost.

"Yeah, Spinney?" the older girl asked, looking around, her gaze keen as she watched their environment carefully, wanting to make sure they weren't seen.

"Will you meet my mommy today?" She gazed at her companion, hopefully. She asked the same question nearly every day, and got the same answer.

Zac looked down at her best friend of two whole weeks, and seeing her hope radiating, felt her heart drop. She knew her hide would be tanned good if she did, but oh how she wanted to make her only friend happy. She loved to see the small girl smile, and acted like a complete goof half the time just to ensure that response.

"Can we, huh?" Spinney insisted.

"No, Spinney. I can't," Zac said, her voice soft and filled with sorrow. She watched Spinney's slender shoulders droop and her head drop. "I'm sorry, Spinney. Please don't be mad, 'kay? I don't wanna get into trouble." Zac pleaded for understanding.

"Why? Will your mommy get mad?" Spinney asked, a perplexed look in her very expressive eyes.

"Um, yeah. Yeah, that's right." Zac lied, but since Spinney seemed to understand that possibility, she'd go with it.

"Oh, okay. Can we spin today?" Her green eyes lit up at the idea.

"Sure, come on!" Zac called out as she ran.

⚜⚜⚜⚜

Present Day

Deciding she would leave Spinney alone for a bit, the dark figure sat in her lean-to consisting of a tarp she found, and a large piece of canvas that she carried with her during her travels. The pieces of material were tied just outside a rock overhang that served as part of the shelter. She hoped it would keep her protected from the summer rains. At the same time, it allowed her to see through the darkness of night if the lights at the Cohen cabin went out.

She looked around at her meager belongings: a small stack of books, either "borrowed" from libraries or left over from her childhood. A small fire ring sat just outside the shelter; she wasn't too keen to see just how fireproof her few personal effects were. A bundled up bedroll was in the corner, dirty and grungy from years of use and very few washings. It was hard and flat, but at least it kept her off the ground, for the most part.

Looking out from the opening in the scant moonlight, she could barely make out the charred ruins of the cabin she grew up in. After her father died, she packed up everything she owned and made for the rails. When she returned to Wachiva Forest three months ago, it was burned to the ground. She had an idea who had done it, but left it be. She knew he'd be back soon enough, anyway.

"Bastard," she muttered, as she removed one of her three sweatshirts. She tucked it into a ball to lean back on so she could read, then clicked to life a small penlight she'd found left behind by campers.

As she opened a book about wildlife preservation by Judith Duncan she looked over at the blackened rubble again. Someday she would rebuild. As soon as she could get supplies. She may have to go back onto the rails for that. She called it a touch-n-go. If she saw something she liked, she'd jump from the slow-moving train, grab it, then run like the devil to get back on and out of there.

Yep. A touch-n-go would definitely be necessary.

She settled back onto the sweatshirt, opened the hardcover book, and began to read, glancing every so often toward Spinney's cabin.

❧❧❧❧

Abel stood, stretching her screaming back. She sat too long. Driving from college in Boston to her parents' house, then the six hour drive from her parents' to the cabin, topped off with sitting on her rump to watch TV, was not so smart. She rinsed her dish under the faucet then put it into the dishwasher. It was late and she was dead tired. She locked the cabin door and set the alarm, then stopped. The hair on the back of her neck prickled to life.

Drawing aside the curtains, she looked out into the night. Her father installed a light post near the drive, but it only illuminated about twenty-five yards around it, leaving everything else to the moonlight. Stands of trees surrounded the house on two sides, and at night they looked like giant soldiers standing guard over the cabin. She walked to the window over the sink in the kitchen, looking into the small but dense copse of trees nearby. Still nothing.

Abel could almost imagine a pair of eyes on her as she looked into the inky blackness. Though she could see nothing, she somehow knew that someone or something was out there. She wasn't one to believe in fairy tales or monsters, but this was ridiculous and she couldn't shake the feeling. She couldn't identify exactly what she felt, but it was eerie. With a shiver, she let the lacy curtains fall back into place and headed upstairs to her parents' bedroom. She didn't want to sleep in the attic in her own bed; tonight she needed the security of their familiar smell, as faint as it was. Now all she had to do was remind herself she wasn't six years old. She pulled back the covers, climbed onto the large bed, kicked her slippers off, and sank into the warmth and comfort. "I'm not six years old, I'm not six years old," she muttered, then shut the light, laughing at herself.

The figure moved through the dark once more, making sure all was well. She saw the lights on the second floor die out. Blackness filled the windows. She sighed, longing to wish Spinney a good night.

Lying on her back, Zac cradled her head in her palms as she looked up at the rock ceiling of her shelter, her belly full of fresh rabbit and wild berries.

She was glad it was summer time, as all the good fruit would be ripe. She smiled to herself as she thought of her day. She had been lucky in the hunt as well as lucky to see her friend again. Spinney had long since gone to bed, but she was still very much awake and alive in Zac's mind. She closed her eyes, conjuring up Abel's face behind dark lids. She would say sweet things to Zac, with her soft-looking mouth, just as she did as a child. Spinney would smile and be so happy to see her again. Zac couldn't wait. It had been so long, so very long. She had waited for fourteen years to say hello again. Maybe she could tomorrow? *Maybe not.* She'd have to see what Spinney was up to. She wanted to allow her some time alone first. Instead, she would ease her pounding heart with memories . . .

"Look at me, Zac! I'm spinning!" Spinney's voice was sucked up by the incredibly dense foliage that surrounded them–a tall, deep thicket with a solid canopy of tree tops, leaves and branches reaching out to embrace overhead–save for one lone hole that allowed sunlight to filter in, a spotlight for the spinning child.

"I see you!" Zac exclaimed, running around in the shadows, growling like the bear she had seen the week before. A grizzly, her father had called it. She brought up small hands, arching them into menacing claws and baring nearly unnaturally white teeth as she ran by Spinney, swiping a 'paw' at her, making the small child giggle.

"Do it again!" Spinney cried, cringing even as she laughed.

"Raaarrr!" Zac growled, swiping again, making the girl spin in a circle to keep up with her frantic gallop around her. "I'm a bear! Raaarrrr!"

She smiled, almost laughing again as she

remembered the look on Spinney's young face. *Oh, she was so much fun.* Within moments, however, her smile faded…

"Abel! Abel, where are you?" A woman's voice echoed throughout the forest. Spinney stopped in her tracks and tried to look out past the wall of trees around her.

"Uh, oh," she said. "I have to go, Zac. I'll see you tomorrow, 'kay?"

"'Kay." Zac hung her head. She'd miss her friend.

Abel hurried over to her and gave her a soft kiss on the cheek. With a wide grin, she said, "Bye!" gave her friend a small wave, then disappeared through the trees leaving Zac alone.

Always alone. Zac sat on a large rock, burying her face in her hands.

✦✦✦✦

Abel stirred, then flinched as bright light hit her closed lids. With a soft groan of protest, she rolled over and opened her eyes. Sunlight stretched through the room, long, greedy fingers touching everything in its path.

"Morning already?" she grumbled, not wanting to be up yet, but knowing that since she'd awakened chances of falling back to sleep were slim to none. Stretching her short, but powerful body with a squeak, she swung her legs off the high mattress and planted her bare feet solidly on the floor. As she stood, she strained her ears thinking she heard something. After a moment she heard it again. "Shit!" She ran through the door, flung her body around the balustrade, and barely made it to her cell phone downstairs before her voicemail picked up. "Hello?" she said, breathless.

"Honey? Are you okay?"

Abel rolled her eyes. "Yes, Mom. I just had to run to get my phone. When are you guys going to get the landline service hooked back up? I nearly lost a toe on the couch."

A soft chuckle floated through the line. "I know, honey. I'll talk to your dad about it again, okay? So how is everything? Cabin okay?"

"Yeah, it's great." Abel plopped down on the toe-stubbing couch in question, folding her legs under her body. "It looks great, nothing's amiss."

"Good, good. It looks like we're going to have to come up on Saturday instead of Friday," Sherry Cohen explained, disappointment evident in her soft-spoken voice.

"Oh," Abel said, halfway excited. *Another day alone. Woohoo!* "Why?"

"Well, turns out I have a meeting with the principal Friday afternoon about the new Spanish class I'm starting next year. Of course, it couldn't wait until later in the summer like everything else does." She clicked her tongue. "Man drives me nuts."

"Mom, hate to break it to you, but you're already nuts." She grinned at her own ribbing.

"Well, you come from that same tree, sweet pea." Sherry laughed. "Well, if everything's okay, I guess I'll go. We'll see you soon, honey, and I can't wait!"

"Okay. Oh, wait," Abel said, deciding to ask about the weird sensation she'd been having. "Mom, did anyone new move up here? Are the Wilkins still here?"

"Yeah, they're still there, and, no, not as far as I

know. Why?"

"Nothing." Abel chewed on her fingernail as she glanced out toward the window by the front door. "Well, okay. Since I got here yesterday, I've had the strangest feeling that I'm being watched. It's kind of creepy. I mean, it may very well just be a deer or something. Maybe I've disturbed its stash of food... but still . . ."

"Are you okay, honey?" Do you want me to call Jim for you?" she asked, referring to Jim Wilkins, a good friend of the family.

"Oh, no. If anything goes wrong or anything, I can always call him myself. I just wondered. I have no doubt I'm being a total idiot, just scaring myself. But," she shrugged a shoulder, still staring out the window and beauty beyond, "thought I'd ask."

"Okay. Well, if you need anything, Abel, you tell me. Okay? Do not hesitate to call. Anything. Got me?" Her mother's words were an order, but Abel knew she was only worried.

"Yes, ma'am," she promised. "I'll see you guys Saturday, then. I love you."

"I love you, too, sweetie."

She hung up the phone and looked around, trying to decide what to do with her day. She could go read by the dock, or go for a walk through the woods. To her, that sounded amazing!

She put on a pair of jeans and a T-shirt, laced her hiking boots, and was ready.

༄༄༄༄

Using the toe of her boot, Zac tried to bury the evidence of her morning release, not wanting any uninvited guests to come sniffing around. She stopped mid kick when she heard the snapping of a twig probably fifty yards to the north. Looking in that direction she quickly ducked behind a tree. She spotted a lone figure over the ridge, gently swinging a long stick. Instinctively, she knew it was Spinney.

Grinning she ducked to another tree, matching her quarry's pace, soundlessly following her through the forest. She wanted to make sure the young woman was okay, and didn't fall or find anything that could hurt her. Zac's heart pounded as she watched. She'd watch Spinney do anything, even stand stock still, and she'd be happy as a camper. Spinney was whistling, though the song was a mystery to Zac.

As she watched Spinney walk toward the natural spring that Zac often bathed in, she felt herself becoming antsy, afraid that the young blonde would stumble upon her home and find evidence of her existence. She couldn't be found–the Boogie Man would find her, then. With stealth developed from years of hiding and moving like a ghost, she followed Spinney to the cliffs that overlooked an abandoned old town.

"Wow," Spinney said, startling her stalker.

Zac hadn't heard a person's voice in nearly two years.

༄༅༄༅

Abel looked down at the old town, hearing about it from her father since she was a child. She really wanted to go exploring, but feared she'd lose her way back. She hadn't wandered through these woods in a few years, and didn't trust her instincts anymore.

Smiling up at the warm sun that kissed her face, she stopped, her body becoming very still, her smile frozen. There it was again. That feeling. She felt chilled. The sun's heat now felt like ice as her blood ran cold. Fear clutched her chest like a vise, leaving her short of breath. She scanned her surroundings. "Hello?" she called, her voice echoing throughout the deserted valley below.

She heard movement in the trees, something caught her eye and she snapped her head in that direction to see a red fox scamper out of his hiding place. "Shit!" She placed a hand on her pounding chest and closed her eyes, taking several deep breaths. "Damn fox." *Maybe that's what I felt.* Hearing or feeling nothing more, she opened her eyes and looked around one last time. The feeling was gone and she was alone.

※※※※

Sensing Spinney's discomfort, Zac shrank back into the trees, deciding to lay this one out. Spinney would be just fine watched from afar. Nothing would happen to her. Ever.

Zac watched the clouds moving overhead, knowing that storms would soon be coming. She could smell them in the air. She went to the far end of the lake where she wouldn't be seen, and kicked off her worn boots. The shoe strings were too thin to hold tight now, but they were better than nothing. She peeled off the three layers of socks she wore. Although the summer heat was coming, the nights were cold, and one of the first things she'd learned from her father was never let your feet get cold or wet. Besides the practical, it also helped make the oversized men's boots she'd found fit better.

Stripping down to smooth, white skin, she made her way into the water, mindful of rocks on the lake floor. Though the bottom of her feet were like leather, it still wasn't nice to pick lake crud out of the cracks of her skin or between her toes. She closed her eyes, moaning in delight as the cool water washed over her. Since her dip hadn't been planned, she didn't have her bar of lard soap, so she'd have to make due. For now, she'd just enjoy the feel. It was a bit cold yet to be swimming around naked, but it was certainly refreshing on her feet and lower legs.

Later, Zac roamed through the forest wearing the top sweatshirt layer of her many layers slung over her shoulders. She enjoyed the feel of the almost-warm, night breeze against her face. She sniffed the air, loving the smell of the wild honeysuckle that grew sporadically throughout the forest. The fragrant vine of pink flowers wrapped around the tree trunks. "Nice." She began to hum quietly to herself, then picked up the tune in words. "El coqui, el coqui a mi me encanta." She hummed a few lines before continuing. "Por las noches al ir a acostarme . . ." She smiled when recalling the memory.

Abel giggled, showing the gap from her missing teeth. "It's el noches, not nachos!" she told Zac as the two girls lay on the lush forest floor.

"Oh." Zac flushed, feeling stupid.

Abel laughed heartily, her voice like music in the air, but she quickly sobered noticing that her taller friend wasn't so amused.

"What does it mean again?" Zac asked, trying to find a way to stop blushing.

"Okay," Abel said, clearing her throat.

Zac knew Abel could tell she was getting frustrated.

"It means the little frog, the little frog, enchants me." Abel explained patiently. "The singing of the little frog is so pretty. When I'm going to lie down at night, it induces me to sleep, singing to me. Pretty, huh?"

Zac nodded.

"My mommy used to sing it to me."

≈≈≈≈

"Es tan lindo el cantar del coqui; Por las noches al ir a acostarme; Me adormece cantandome asi; Coqui, coqui, coqui, qui, qui, qui." Abel smiled at the comforting words her mother used to sing to her as a very small child.

She hummed the little tune as she, once again, stared up at the ceiling in her parents' room. She needed the extra added comfort of the old lullaby after the day's events. She felt nearly scared out of her mind. All day long, save for a brief reprieve after the fox darted past her and into the dense forest, she felt eyes on her. Even going to school in a big city like Boston, she had never felt so watched, so *stalked*.

She was truly scared now. She had considered calling her mom and talking to her until she fell asleep, but then rationalized that she was being childish. They'd be there soon enough, and she would just stay closer to the cabin. Maybe she'd get her dad's gun out tomorrow. Abel sighed. She hated guns. But, if it would make her feel safer, then so be it. Humming the lullaby once more, she finally drifted off to sleep.

Chapter Three

I"I've missed you, Zac," Abel said softly, green eyes smiling up at her friend as they walked through the forest, holding hands. Just like the good ol' days.

"I've missed you, too, Spinney." Zac could feel the warmth of their connected palms, arms lightly swinging back and forth. The sun was bright and warm, almost burning through her sweatshirt, making her shoulders hot.

"I wanted to come back and visit, but you weren't here." Spinney looked so sad as she said those precious words. "Where did you go?"

"Far, far away. I needed to leave," Zac explained, holding the smaller hand within hers a bit tighter.

"Oh." Abel glanced up at Zac's profile, her gaze holding until Zac looked down at her, the two sharing a smile.

They met in the forest. Spinney was roaming around and then spotted Zac, who had been watching her from behind a tree. Zac knew it was only Spinney here, so she wasn't afraid.

"Do your parents still think I'm not real?" Zac finally asked.

Abel smiled and nodded. "But I know you're real . . ."

Zac's eyes fluttered open, non-seeing for a moment, the cramped surroundings of her shelter slowly coming into focus, followed by reality. She wanted to cry. A dream, it had been another goddamn dream. Sitting up, she rubbed her face with calloused hands, trying to scrub away all the leftover sleepiness and sadness.

So many times she'd dreamt of meeting up with Spinney again, and now that she was so close, so very close, she had no courage. Spinney had been at the cabin for four days and Zac had yet to find the courage to step out of the shadows and back into Spinney's life. "Shit." She sighed, wondering what to do. For some odd reason she felt afraid, intimidated, and unsure. She knew that Spinney had a good life with good parents who loved and cared for her. After all this time, and the realization that comes with growing up, would Spinney still find her interesting? Would she still be interested in being her friend?

A paralyzing thought occurred to her. "Oh god," she whispered. Would Spinney think she was weird and scary, living all alone in the woods, living off the land like some animal? Would she see her as nothing more than a specter in the trees?

Shaking these thoughts from her mind she pulled herself up, ignoring the screaming of her back from too many years spent sleeping on the ground. She was only twenty-years-old but felt fifty half the time. Tugging on a sweatshirt to ward off the early morning chill, she headed off to find some place to relieve herself. She'd drunk too much water the night before, and felt like she'd burst.

≈≈≈≈

Abel woke deciding today was the last day she'd be afraid. Too many visions of *Friday the 13th* were running through her head. She was up, showered, and dressed, ready to enjoy a day reading by the lake. She had packed herself a nice brunch, all fitted neatly in a basket her mom had buried with the holiday decorations…of all places. Basket and book in hand, she was ready to go. *Not scared today, no way, no how.* She was determined to have a good day even if it killed her! *Okay, maybe not quite that far.*

Whistling as she made her way down to the green dock, she glanced around, looking for anything remotely suspicious before she grabbed the fold-up chair that rested near the side of the cabin. Hoisting it under her arm, she continued on her way. It was a good day. The sun was out, the air was warm, and her fingers itched to dig into the book she'd brought with her. She set the basket on the dock and opened the folding chair. She looked to see which direction the sun was shining and positioned the chair that way. She wanted to make sure she had the absolute best light for reading, without being blinded.

"Oh yeah," she drawled with a goofy grin, as she slid her sunglasses into place. "This is what I'm talkin' 'bout!" Plopping down in the plastic chair, she reached into the basket and grabbed the tube of sun block SPF 45. Her light features meant quick burn time. Squirting the fragrant, white cream onto her palm she applied it liberally to her arms and shoulders, bared for the first time that summer by her tank top. She smiled when she noticed the bubbles from a fish that had just surfaced to snag an insect. Humming contentedly as the cream disappeared into her skin, she closed her eyes and smeared some on her face.

Zac made her way down the line of trees leading to the lake. She saw the white speck down on the dock she knew was Spinney. The breeze blew around her legs, wrapping winter-dried leaves around her ankles, only to flutter away as she made her way through them.

She hid behind a tree when Spinney turned to rub her hand over her shoulder. She watched, wondering what the blonde was doing. She moved closer, and saw that Spinney was smoothing something white on her skin, and wondered if it was lotion. She had a tube of it once, a long time ago.

As she found her way closer to the dock, she rested her palm against the trunk of a tree feeling the rough bark dig into her palm and finger pads. She didn't care. She was in sight of Spinney. Oh, how she wanted to talk to her again.

༄༄༄༄

Abel tossed the sun block back into the basket, noting her weapon of choice when she did. With a confident smile, she grabbed her book, opened it up to the first page and settled in to read. She cursed softly as she smudged the lens of her sunglasses with the greasy suntan lotion as she adjusted them on her nose. As she scanned the page, she felt that strange feeling again. She looked up at the lake listening, but heard nothing.

༄༄༄༄

Zac gripped the tree even tighter, fighting the urge to jump out from behind it and say, "Spinney!

How are ya?" Instead, she stayed put, her heart pounding in her ears, indecision making her blood rush faster. This would be the perfect chance for her to say hello to her old friend again. It was the perfect chance for her to put her dreams and daydreams to rest, and exchange them for new, fresh memories. She closed her eyes, licked her dry lips, and took several deep breaths before opening them again.

ม.ม.!ร.!ร

Abel made quick progress through the opening sequences of the story. As she lifted her leg to cross the other she froze.

A voice floated on the soft breeze. "Hi, Spinney."

Abel leapt out of her chair, heart rising into her throat. She heard a distant splash as her paperback fell into the water from her startled escape. There before her, standing at the head of the dock, not ten feet away, stood the ghost that had been haunting her since her arrival.

Chapter Four

Abel followed her instincts and instruction from her father. She grabbed her keys from her pocket, never once taking her eyes off the strange girl who stood before her at the end of the dock. Placing three of the sharp points between her fingers to use as weapons, she held her arm out in front of her. In her fear, she forgot about the pistol in the basket.

"Who the hell are you?" she asked, briefly eyeing the dock around her. She was trapped, water on three sides and this crazy woman in front of her. Her long, disheveled dark hair fell around her shoulders, face, and down her back, giving her a wild appearance. Though the woman's posture was calm and focused, Abel felt extremely uncomfortable and unsettled by her presence. She took in the strange woman's extremely baggy and dirty black pants, cuffs puddling around over-sized boots. Her gaze drifted back up to the old, worn sweater that was thin in places, and finally up into blue eyes that were looking into hers.

"Who are you?" Abel asked again.

"You don't remember me?" Zac asked.

Abel was amazed and confused. "Should I?" She held the keys out in front of her, her eyes darting to the picnic basket remembering the gun.

"It's me, Zac." The woman pointed to herself, blue eyes wide, looking shocked. "Spinney?" she said, hope in her bright blue eyes.

"I...I don't know you," Abel exclaimed, her heart about to beat out of her chest as fear clasped it in a vice. Again she pondered her options: *Go for a swim? Try to run past the taller woman? Stay and grab the gun?* The strange woman who called herself Zac didn't seem dangerous, somehow. She stood there, shoulders slumped, hands buried in deep pockets. Was she hiding a weapon there? "Let me see your hands," she ordered, her voice shaky.

Zac looked confused, but slowly slid her hands from her pockets holding them aloft. Abel felt better seeing her hands were empty. "How do I know you? And why do you keep calling me Spinney? Who is that? Do you have me confused with someone else?" Abel lowered the keys, feeling she wouldn't need them, but freaked out nonetheless.

Zac shrugged her shoulders. "We used to play when we were kids." Her voice was quiet, barely audible.

"What?" Abel was stunned. "As kids? What are you talking about? Why don't I remember you?" She gave a humorless laugh. "I'm sorry, Zac, but I think you've got the wrong person."

Zac shrugged, but said nothing.

Abel stared at her then reached into her pocket for her ever-present cell phone. "You stay there." Abel glanced down at her iPhone to dial her parents' number.

Zac watched Abel dial then her eyes grew wide. "No cops! No Boogie Man!" she murmured, backing away.

After dialing, Abel looked up, gasping when she saw she was alone. She looked around frantically, trying to find the strange woman. She even looked toward the lake. Nothing.

"What the hell?" she breathed, feeling all the more frightened. "I'm going crazy." Her train of thought was interrupted by her mother's voice on the other end of the line. "Mom? Oh my god. I'm losing my mind!" She scoured the landscape as she spoke, desperately trying to find any sign of the woman who called herself Zac.

༄༅༄༅

Zac ran through the forest, her eyes burning as tears streamed down her cheeks. The sensation felt strange. She could only remember crying once before. She climbed the bluff that she used as a perch to watch over the Cohen cabin. Plopping down, she sniffled and swiped at her eyes, leaving dirt smudges along her cheeks. *Why doesn't she remember me? She was going to call the boogie men on me. Why, Spinney? Why?* Devastated, she covered her face as a sob broke free, startling a bull frog who was croaking nearby.

༄༅༄༅

"Wait, wait. Honey, slow down. What are you talking about? An intruder? In the house?" Sherry Cohen sounded concerned but confused by what Abel was saying.

"No! Well, not exactly. She just showed up out of nowhere. God, I was so scared," Abel exclaimed, sitting back in the chair but turning it so she faced land. She wasn't about to be snuck up on again. "I was reading, like I told you, and she was just . . . just . . . there!" She brought a trembling hand to her mouth, covering her lips as she looked out into the woods. "Like some sort of mountain woman or something. It was so strange."

"Honey, I want you to listen to me," Sherry said, her voice stern but caring. "You need to call the police. Who knows who this person is? She could be dangerous."

Abel thought back to Zac, and deep in her heart she didn't feel she was dangerous. Those eyes, so brilliantly blue, were seemingly filled with the innocence of a child. She looked genuinely hurt when Abel told her she didn't know who she was. That look haunted her.

"No," she said, surprised as the word fell from her mouth.

"What? No? Abel–"

"No. She's not dangerous." *What are you saying?*

"Wait, I thought you said you didn't know her?" Sherry's irritation was evident in her voice. "Abel, this is ridiculous. You call me frightened out of your mind only to frighten me out of mine, and now you're backpedaling? Honey, I love you, but–"

"Mom, did I have a playmate when I was a kid?"

"A playmate? What does that have to do with the price of eggs?"

Abel let out a heavy sigh, her gaze ever watchful. "She said something about us playing as kids. Did I play with anyone here? At the cabin?" Abel drew her eyebrows together a headache beginning to pound dimly in the back of her head.

"Well, let me think." Sherry was quiet for a moment. At length she said, "Well, when you were really young you had an imaginary friend you used to talk about."

"An imaginary friend?" She drew her brows further. Abel pushed up from the chair and began to pace the dock, her earlier fear forgotten at this intriguing tidbit.

"Oh, yes." Sherry chuckled. "Shoot, we teased you about that for a while. Finally, one day you just stopped talking about her."

"Did she have a name?" Abel asked, chewing her fingernail.

"Oh, gosh. I don't remember what that would have been, now. I don't recall hearing about her since you were maybe, oh, eight or nine. But you always used to talk about her bright blue eyes."

Abel felt her stomach drop and her hands get sweaty. She surreptitiously looked around, somehow thinking she was going to find those eyes watching her again. "Bright blue eyes?" She ran a hand through her hair before letting out a sigh. "Mom, did she have a name she used to call me? Like, a nickname?"

Sherry was quiet for a moment. "Oh, gosh. Hmm, let me think. It started with an S, I want to say."

"Spinney?"

"That's it!" Sherry laughed. "Spinney. I never understood where you got that."

Abel felt sick now. "Oh, god," she moaned, running her hand through her hair again. "Was her name Zac, Mom?" Her voice was barely a whisper.

"Possibly. I truly don't remember." Sherry paused for a moment. "Honey, what's this all about?"

Abel flopped back down into the chair, her fear beginning to recede. "Her name was Zac, she called me Spinney, and she had bright blue eyes," she said, almost in tears. "Am I losing my mind?" She popped up again, an arm over her stomach. "I feel like I saw a ghost."

※ ※ ※ ※

Zac watched a white and orange truck pull up to the cabin and a rugged-looking man disembark. She recognized him from the cabin about a mile down the lake. He knocked on the door. A moment later, Spinney answered and invited him inside. Earlier Zac had watched as Spinney talked on the phone while still sitting on the dock where she'd left her. Her heart was heavy and it hurt. She felt a knot still in her throat, even once her tears had dried up. She was waiting for the boogie men to come, but they didn't. Only the guy in the truck.

Who had Spinney called? she wondered. She had seemed excited and upset. Although Zac couldn't hear her words, she could see her body language and the occasional wild gesticulations as she spoke.

Now Spinney hurried out of the cabin accompanied by the man, carrying a bag in her hand. She tossed it into the back of the pickup, took hold of the door handle, then stopped and looked toward the woods. Zac's breath caught as it seemed those green eyes were staring right at her. She held her breath, waiting, watching to see what would happen. She knew there was no way Spinney could see her on the bluff, but still . . .

A few breathless moments passed, then the blonde opened the door, jumped in and with a muted drone, the truck drove away.

※ ※ ※ ※

Abel sat next to Jim Wilkins watching out the side window, her eyes peering into the dark thicket of woods. She no longer felt as if she were being watched. In some ways, Abel felt like a child. Her mother had talked her into staying with the Wilkins until her family arrived at the cabin. When Abel tried waving off the idea, Sherry let her know it was either call Jim Wilkins or the police. Ultimately, Abel had acquiesced.

She couldn't help but wonder who the hell this Zac person was, and what her imaginary friend had to do with things. An imaginary friend she had no memory of. Was this person a ghost? She looked so real! She looked as real as Abel herself. Was she someone she conjured up in her mind? The mind of a lonely child playing in the woods?

With a sigh, she concentrated on the road before them.

⁂

Abel stretched out on the twin bed opposite Marie Wilkins, Jim's twelve-year-old daughter, who slept peacefully while Abel stared at the ceiling. Her mind whirled over the events of the last few days. She was going to stay with the Wilkins' family until Saturday, when her parents would arrive. She persuaded Jim Wilkins not to grab his hunting dogs and search the woods. Abel didn't want Zac to be harmed, and if there was no Zac, she didn't want others to think she had lost her mind.

She lay in the small bed, in the cramped bedroom, and thought about the mysterious young woman who seemed so crushed, yet, she had no idea who she was. Even her mother remembered Abel talking about her as a child. Why didn't she remember?

She turned onto her side, staring at the wall, hands curled up under her chin. Was this woman a figment of her imagination still? Was she even real? Abel didn't believe in ghosts, but now she was beginning to wonder. Apparently, she was the only one who ever saw her. According to Jim's wife, Ava, no one had seen this dark-haired woman, or anyone strange at all.

Abel tried to think of how old the woman looked, probably not much older or younger than herself. She looked as though she had been in those woods forever. She was so dirty and weathered, obviously not someone who had spent her life in a warm cabin or house somewhere. What if Zac was a ghost? What if at some time she had been killed, or had gotten lost and died from exposure? What if she had fallen into the lake and drowned, destined to forever roam those woods?

Abel shivered, thinking her scenarios were ridiculous, but they disturbed her all the same. Why her? Had she totally made up this apparition in her mind as a child, and it was still there in her sub-consciousness? Had she been so lonely at the cabin that she'd conjured her up again?

"That's ridiculous," she muttered, rolling her eyes. "So who is she?"

She realized in the two days she'd been with the Wilkins' that she hadn't felt that... that... feeling. She knew she wasn't being watched anymore, and although that was calming, it was also slightly disconcerting.

Zac wandered through the woods looking out over the lake. The water was calm, the surrounding woods and foothills reflecting off its glassy surface. She picked up a small rock and threw it, breaking that perfect picture, turning the upside down world into ripples.

She was tired. Disappointment and hurt made a nasty bedmate.

Spinney had been gone for two days, and Zac missed her. Despite what happened on the dock, and the obvious fear that Zac had instilled in her friend, she still missed having her presence around. She hadn't been able to feel Spinney since she'd been whisked away in that orange and white truck. She felt empty again. Now, even Spinney's memory couldn't keep Zac company.

She turned away from the lake and walked more, knowing her little furry buddy with the big, bushy tail, was following her. He was scampering from tree to tree, wiggling his nose and cleaning his face with reddish brown paws at every limb. She looked up, seeing Teddy sitting up there, beady black eyes looking down at her.

"Hey, little fella," she said, waving to him, hearing a squeak in return. Zac chuckled and moved on, shoving her hands deep into the pockets of her pants.

The sun was hot today, but she dare not leave too many layers at home. She knew that she had to conserve her body heat and not allow herself to get too cold. When night came, her body heat would drop substantially. So, she plowed on with the pants, boots, and two sweatshirts, though she did give in to removing the top sweatshirt and tying it around her waist.

Just up ahead, she saw the edge of the cliff and stopped, not wanting to get too close. Just beyond was the ghost town, her dad called "Spectreville." It was haunted. An old lumber town back in the nineteenth century, it had been abandoned for seventy years or more. The place scared Zac. She heard noises from there all the time, and it's been said that when people venture inside, they never come back out again. She also knew that a few homeless stayed there from time to time, and not all of them were kindly old men. She'd found that out the hard way over the years. *All the more reason to stay away from there.*

Shivering in the warm May sun, she hurried away from the scene below her, and continued on through the woods. Maybe she'd start making maps again. That's what she used to do to keep herself busy. She would tear out a sheet of paper in one of her books and draw maps. She'd map out the entire area, including each little stump, large set of rocks, anything. Once she'd even sold one to a group of hikers that were lost.

Yeah. That's what she could do. That would keep her mind busy, and she wouldn't have to think about Spinney. "Oh, Spinney," she sighed into the unfeeling forest.

Chapter Five

Abel was following Marie back to the cabin with a stack of freshly cut wood in her arms. The pre-teen stacked it neatly next to the house and Abel followed suit, hissing as a small piece of wood snagged her finger.

"Damn," she said, picking at it. "I hate splinters."

"You okay?" Marie asked, looking up at Abel with adoring eyes.

"Yeah, I'm fine. Do you guys have tweezers?"

Marie nodded. "Uh huh. In the bathroom upstairs. In the cabinet over the sink."

"Okay. Thanks." Abel smiled and hurried inside. Marie drove her nuts. She was a nice kid, but she followed her everywhere she went, constantly asking questions. She was definitely more annoying than last summer. Abel hurried up the stairs, taking them two at a time. She scurried off to the bathroom and found what she was looking for. Sitting on the closed toilet lid, she began to concentrate on trying to pull the bugger out.

She grimaced as the sharp tips of the tweezers pulled at the skin of her fingertip. As she worked, her mind began to wander. She wanted so badly to just go home. The Wilkins' had been so nice, and she'd known them forever, but still, she wanted her own cabin with her own things.

She thought about leaving, but decided against

it. There was still the question of this Zac person. As she thought about it over the past few days, she began to wonder if that feeling of being watched was purely linked to Zac. Had it been her for the first few days Abel was at the cabin? Why? Why had she been stalking around the place? What did she mean to do? If they supposedly knew each other, why hadn't Zac simply come to the door like any other normal person?

"Ow!" Abel pulled the splinter out and looked at it, holding it up to the light that streamed in from the small window above the bathtub. Cleaning the tweezers off into the trashcan, she put them away and washed her hands, sure to wash the area thoroughly where the splinter had been.

What was she supposed to do with this person? With the situation? Should she head out into the forest once her folks got there and look for her? How long had Zac been there in the forest? Did she live in one of the neighboring cabins? That would make sense. There were a lot of families that lived in Wachiva Forest year round, or in the small, neighboring towns, but she had never seen her before. Though Zac seemed to know Abel, or thought she did. Mistaken identity?

Her mind spun to the conversation with her mother. Imaginary friend. Spinney. Bright blue eyes. Zac.

Abel cleaned her mess, studied her reflection in the mirror, and noted the slight wrinkle of concentration between her eyes. It had been a habit since childhood, and her mother used to warn her that she'd be wrinkled by thirty if she wasn't careful. She made a concerted effort to relax not only her face, but her mind as well. "This is just strange."

Zac peered around a tree, watching as the orange and white pickup truck pulled up in front of the cabin. She saw Spinney smile at the burly man behind the wheel, and nod as he said something to her. She grabbed her bag and opened the truck door.

"Bye, Jim!" She waved to the man then headed for the porch. She set the bag down then stopped.

Zac watched as Abel looked around. The moment the truck pulled out of the dirt yard, with her bag slung over her shoulder, she seemed to be looking for something, her green gaze focused and intense.

"Are you there?" she called out, her voice echoing off the trees and into the early afternoon. "Come out!"

Zac's fingers clawed nervously at the bark of the tree. She heard Abel's words, but felt like she was going to vomit. Unwilling to lose this chance, she took a deep breath and stepped out from her hiding place, twenty yards from where Spinney stood hands on hips.

Abel gasped in surprise at Zac's sudden appearance. "You scared me."

Zac stood, hands shoved into her pockets. "I'm sorry," she said, her voice soft. The truth was her heart was about to pound out of her chest.

"Were you watching me?"

Zac nodded. "Yes."

"Why? You scare me, you know," Abel said, her voice softening a bit as they stood mere yards apart.

Zac looked down at the ground, rocking on her heels a bit. "I'm sorry," she murmured.

"Are you real?" Abel asked quietly, seeming to drop her guard a bit as she dropped her bag to the dirt.

Zac's head raised, surprised blue eyes bored into Abel's cautious green ones. Zac nodded.

Abel continued to hold her gaze. "Just like Mom said," she murmured, not bothering to expound upon what she meant as she looked away. Finally, she met Zac's gaze again, hers a bit hard. "Why don't I remember you? Why does my mother say you were my imaginary friend?" Abel crossed her arms over her chest in a defensive position. "Why did my parents never meet you?"

"I didn't let you," Zac stated, as if it was the most obvious answer.

"Why?"

"Because they'd take me away."

Abel drew her blonde brows together in confusion. "Taken you away to where?"

Zac shrugged. "I don't know. Just … away."

"This is making no sense," Abel said, running a hand through her hair. "Let's try something else. Why do you watch me? *Do* you watch me?"

Zac nodded with a bright smile. She liked that the air was somewhat getting cleared, even if she didn't feel she was remotely on solid footing, yet. "Yes. I like watching you."

Abel shifted her weight slightly to her hip, her hands still resting there. "Do you have any idea how creepy that sounds … Zac? Why?"

"Because you're my friend. And to protect you."

"From who?" Abel asked softly. "I mean, the crazy thing," Abel said with a small laugh, "is that I feel you're telling me the truth as you see it. But, you have to admit, this is all pretty crazy." Again, she ran her hand through her hair then met Zac's gaze. "Who are you protecting me from?"

"The Boogie Man," Zac answered, her voice deepening just a bit.

Abel rubbed the back of her neck with a hand as she looked away. She sucked in her lower lip, as though trying to hold back some emotion. "Boogie Man?" Her voice held a certain amount of amusement.

At Zac's nod, Abel shook her head and let out a small laugh. She picked up her bag and walked toward the front porch. Zac's heart beat faster, she thought their reunion–as strange and uncomfortable as it was–was over. But, after dropping the bag on the porch, Abel walked to where the dirt met the beginnings of the wooded green, stopped and tucked her hands in the back pockets of her shorts.

"Oh," was all she said once she'd settled into a spot again. She studied Zac for a moment before saying, "I won't bite, you know." She gave a rueful laugh. "Ironic, considering I worried about that from you."

Zac ignored the last comment, but got the hint as she took a few steps forward, her hands still deeply buried in her pockets. She didn't want Spinney to see her hands trembling.

"Where do you live? Why are you here?"

"I live here," Zac said with pride, indicating the forest behind her. "I'm here because you are, Spinney."

"Why do you call me that?"

Zac noted Spinney sounded slightly agitated, as if she were hearing a joke that only Zac knew the punch line to. "Well, you like to spin." Her voice became somewhat wistful as she continued. "When you did, your hair would fan out around you, looking like spun gold." She smiled at the memory, one of her favorites. Spinney had such pretty hair. Still did. Though now it was even longer than the shoulder-length style of her childhood.

"I did like to spin," Abel whispered, then shook herself out of her reverie. "Tell me more. Something that would convince me you're not a loon, or some weird figment of my obviously hyper imagination. "Why did you run the other day?"

"You were going to call people and get me in trouble," Zac answered, feeling the sting again from the other day.

"Call people? What, like the cops?" At Zac's nod, Abel's head cocked to the side. "Should I? Are you in some kind of trouble?" She raised her eyebrows in challenge.

"No."

Abel studied her for so long, she made Zac nervous. "Show me where you live."

"No."

"How am I supposed to believe you, or know anything about you if I don't even know if you're real?"

"Touch me." Zac took a small step closer, only for Abel to take one backwards.

"Oh, no way! Not a chance in hell I'm getting that close to you." Abel stared at her like she was nuts.

Zac wasn't able to hide her hurt expression and looked down. She couldn't help but feel the same rejection she had her entire life, rejection from her father, her mother, and society at large. She shook those morose thoughts out of her mind and cleared her throat. "Then throw something at me. There are rocks down at your feet."

Oblivious to how she was making Zac feel, Abel shook her head. "No. Just show me where you live. If there's a slim chance that I'm going to trust you, this isn't the way to do it, by being obstinate." Abel pointed an accusing finger at her.

Zac nodded. Without a word, she turned around and headed off into the woods, like some sort of Bigfoot disappearing into the foliage.

Abel brought out her pocket knife, opening the blade and casually, discreetly, marking tree trunks as she went to mark her way home. Just in case.

Zac led the way, her heart heavy as she had to prove herself to her friend, confidante, and only person in the world she cared about. She felt an immense sadness consume her, taking over the absolute joy of being with her Spinney again. She knew Spinney didn't trust her, and she hated it.

※※※※

Abel was led through the dark forest, to places even the sun couldn't penetrate. She was amazed Zac knew the way, the path marked by small, subtle markers that Zac glanced at. The smallest group of leaves acted as the biggest highway sign, marking an exit as Zac took a sudden right. Abel followed. Fascinated, she asked, "How do you know where you're going?" her voice hushed in the dense trees, as her ever watchful eyes tried to take in everything.

"Lots of walks."

She headed toward a large cropping of rocks, turned the bend around them, then suddenly they were upon a campsite. Abel noticed the burned pile of rubble next to the rock overhang, where a small, thrown together lean-to was set up. Next to it was a fire ring, the rocks covered in soot on the inside. She took in the blue tarp that was tied to a tan canvas, both anchored to the ground to form a wall and entryway.

The unnatural blue stuck out in sharp contrast to the natural colors of everything else.

"This is where you live?" she asked, her voice a whisper.

Zac nodded.

"My god. How can anyone survive in this?"

Hurt by the comment, Zac dug her hands further into her pockets while kicking at some rocks at her feet. "I just do."

"What was that?" Abel pointed to the burnt ruins.

"That's where I used to live. When I was a kid. When I knew you. My dad and me lived there."

"Your father?" Abel looked stunned. "Where is he now?" She walked over and looked through the rubble, noting the semblance of certain things, including a dented, half melted teapot. "What happened?"

"I don't know. He died when I was thirteen, so I left here. When I came back a few months ago, I found it like this. Don't know when it happened. I plan to rebuild someday." She met Abel's green-eyed gaze. "I have my suspicions, though, as far as who burned it down."

"Do you own this land?" Abel asked quietly. She felt her fears begin to melt away as she saw the humble, yet proud dwellings of this young woman, who could easily have been one of her classmates back at BU. Even so, she remained cautious.

"No. That's why I stay out of trouble," Zac said, her voice somewhat defensive.

Abel seemed to recoil a bit from Zac's tone. At length she asked quietly, "Can I look inside?"

At Zac's somewhat hesitant nod, she walked over to the flap and knelt down to peer inside. It was small, maybe large enough for the tall girl to stretch out, but not much more than that. She had a rolled up bedroll at one end, with a small stack of books piled near it. An old, weather-beaten canteen hung on a natural ledge in the rock wall, and a small leather pouch sat on the ground under it, a nearly melted candle next to it.

Zac stood back and watched, hands fidgeting in their pocketed confines. She chewed on her lower lip and bounced nervously on the balls of her feet.

Abel backed out of the small space and stood, brushing her knees off. "Tell me something about myself then, Zac. Why should I believe you?" She wanted to understand this great mystery. "Tell me something other than I like to spin."

Zac looked up into the blue sky, thinking of what she could say to make Abel understand and believe. She looked at the blonde, and began to sing:

El coqui, el coqui a mi me encanta
Es tan lindo el cantar del coqui
Por las noches al ir a acostarme
Me adormece cantandome asi
Coqui, coqui, coqui, qui, qui, qui
Coqui, coqui, coqui, qui, qui, qui
Coqui, coqui, coqui, qui, qui, qui
Coqui, coqui, coqui, qui, qui, qui.

Abel listened as Zac sang, her voice quiet but pleasant.

Oh my god. "How did you know that?" she breathed.

Zac looked at her, confused, head slightly cocked to the side. "You taught it to me," she said, the smallest of smiles tugging at the corners of her mouth.

"When?" Abel was flabbergasted. She remembered when her mother used to sing that to her as a small child. She always planned to sing it to her own children someday.

"That summer. You used to sing it all the time." A large smile lit up Zac's face. "I told you I was afraid one night, so you taught it to me. You said the frog song would keep me safe."

"I don't believe this." Abel put a hand to her head, covering her eyes for a moment. "Did I ever see you again?"

"Not after that summer, no." Zac's voice became even softer, making it hard for Abel to hear. She looked into those bright blue eyes.

"Why?" Abel took a slight step forward, but quickly moved back to her original spot. "I saw you with your friend. She had dark hair and a blue bow in her hair," Zac said, looking down at her boots. "I didn't want to intrude, so I stayed away."

"Friend?" Abel thought for a moment, then brought her hand to her mouth, remembering that summer. She was six years old. Her parents made her bring a friend along for some reason, so she brought her friend Melanie with them that summer. "You saw us?"

Zac nodded, finally meeting Abel's green eyes. Zac suddenly looked toward the road.

Abel looked to see a car approaching. "My family's here." She turned to Zac. "Will you meet them?"

"No."

"Why not?"

"I can't." Zac took a step back, looking terrified.

"Okay, okay. I won't make you." Abel put her hands up as if to placate the woman. "But I have to go. Um…can you lead me?"

Zac nodded.

❧❧❧❧

The women were quiet as they walked toward the cabin. Zac was trying to reconcile the fact that someone had just been to her dwelling, while, she thought, her blonde counterpart was probably trying to reconcile that such a place existed at all.

Zac stopped, turning toward Abel. "Spinney, I've taken you halfway. Follow that line of trees and it'll lead you to the dock."

"You won't go any further?" When Zac shook her head, Abel nodded. "Okay. Thank you." She starting walking then stopped and looked over her shoulder. "Zac?"

"Yeah?"

"Please don't hide. It makes me uncomfortable."

Zac looked down at her shuffling boots and nodded. "Okay."

She watched as Abel followed the path that she pointed out to her, a sad sigh escaping her lips.

"Well, guess that's that." Zac turned and headed home.

❧❧❧❧

Abel ran to her family at near breakneck speed while they unloaded the car.

"Honey!" Her mother hurried over to her daughter and gave her a huge hug. "We were so worried." She brushed a soft kiss atop her daughter's head and looked at her.

"Oh, I'm fine." Abel brushed off her concern. "I just talked to her, actually." She glanced over her shoulder at the woods behind her. Abel's father, Adam joined them.

"Is she still here?" he asked, body stiffening slightly. "I'm not okay with some whacko scaring my baby girl."

"Yeah she's here, but she's not dangerous, Dad." Abel suddenly felt the need to defend Zac. "She's harmless, really."

"How do you know?" Sherry asked, slinging an arm around her husband's waist.

"I talked to her," Abel said simply, as if that should be answer enough. "She lives out there, and...", she looked pointedly at her father, "we're going to leave her alone." She eyed him, knowing full well the mighty father routine her dad would often try.

"Adam, go help the kids unload the car," Sherry said, sensing her husband's need to protest. Once he walked away, she turned to her daughter. "What's going on, Abel? I mean, you called us up, frightened out of your mind, and now you're protecting this girl." She looked at her with concern.

"I know, I know. It doesn't make any sense. She's still creepy, but this morning when Jim brought me back, I called out for her, and there she was!" She pointed to a nearby tree and snapped her fingers. "Poof! She just stepped out from behind that tree right there. I don't know how she does it." She ran a hand through her hair, realizing she was still a little weirded out by the situation, but no longer frightened.

Sherry studied Abel for a moment. "Honey, I had to almost grab onto your dad's leg to prevent him from loading the car and coming here right then and there. Honey, what is going on? Who is this person?" Sherry put an arm around her daughter's shoulders and led them toward the cabin.

Abel shook her head. "I don't know. She told me things, Mom. Things that she couldn't have known unless she really knew me." She glanced at her mother. "She knows the frog song," she said quietly.

Sherry looked at her daughter with a stunned expression. "How on earth could she know that?"

The two women headed into the kitchen where bags of groceries waited to be unpacked and put away. "Help me, Abel."

"She said I taught it to her, said that I told her to sing it to herself when she was afraid." Abel laughed, unsure about so much. "It's crazy. Oh, she also remembered the summer I brought Melanie Waynes. Remember that?" She looked at her mother, just an inch shorter than herself.

Sherry Cohen nodded with a smile. "Yes. Your father and I felt it would be best if you brought someone up to play with. We thought you were so bored you had to make up imaginary playmates." She shook her head with a small smile. "Is . . ." She stopped, as she put away several canned goods.

"What?" Abel put a carton of milk in the fridge then turned to her mother. She could see the older woman was troubled. "What is it?"

Sherry closed the cabinet door. Hand on hip, she turned to her daughter and sighed. "Is Zac real, honey, or is she still just something that's around when you're lonely or alone up here?"

Abel took a step back. "What! Are you asking if I'm crazy? Mother! I'm almost twenty years old. I think I can be alone without having to make up some damn imaginary person to keep me company. God, you make me sound like I'm really pathetic or something!"

"Oh, honey. Please don't be mad. I didn't mean to upset you. We're just trying to understand." She walked over to her and bundled her up in strong, motherly arms. She spoke as she stroked the long, blonde hair. "I've even thought that perhaps this girl was a ghost." She chuckled.

"Me, too." Abel laughed in turn. "Crazy, yes. So maybe I am. I don't know. She took me to where she lives," she explained while still enveloped in her mother's warmth.

"Really?"

"Yup. She just has this crappy lean-to under a group of rocks. I was so stunned."

"How can anyone live like that?" Sherry asked.

"I don't know. I wonder the same thing. How she doesn't freeze, I'll never know." She pulled away from her mother. Continuing to put groceries away, she said, "You know, the strange thing is, I think I can feel when she's around." She glanced out the window, wondering if she'd see Zac out there. She felt that feeling. Kind of like a constant hum.

"Really?" Sherry tossed a box of cereal on top of the fridge, and turned back to the bag that contained a large can of coffee.

"Yeah. Strange."

Chapter Six

Zac lay on her bedroll, the night sky making everything dark and beautiful. She loved the dark, the way it could hide her and keep her safe. She almost saw better in the dark, feeling her way through the woods and allowing her senses to take over for her. She smiled as she tucked her hands behind her head, remembering that afternoon. She still felt slightly uneasy about having her privacy so intruded upon, but let it slide, knowing it was for Spinney. She'd do anything for her, and if bringing her to her home helped Spinney remember her, or at least not be afraid, then it was worth it. Oh, how she wished her friend would remember her. The feeling of being around Spinney again was priceless. That one hour of time they had was worth all of it. The blonde of her hair, the green of her eyes...

Zac sighed, feeling happy and content. She knew that Spinney was okay, safe and happy, and that meant everything else would be okay. She watched from the bluff as Spinney joined her family, and was certainly surprised at how much that family had grown. And when she spotted the little one, her heart leapt into her throat.

The girl looked young, younger than Spinney when she'd met her, but had the same blonde hair and curious face. Zac had to smile when she saw her. She could read trouble all over that girl. It had been Spinney all over again, and nearly made Zac's heart weep for a time lost. A time when she had been trusted by Spinney, and had been her friend. And remembered.

Zac sighed. She'd watch from afar, to make sure the entire clan was happy, healthy and safe. No Boogie Man for them.

☙❧☙❧

Abel grabbed her brush from the dresser near the window. It felt good to be back in her family's cabin, in her attic room. She looked at the posters and pictures hanging on the walls. Some had been there for years, while others were only a year or two old—sports figures, movies she liked, actors and actresses, or just simple sayings. In the corner near the closet was a stack of crates, all filled with memories of the cabin from her family's years here. She was quite the nostalgic one, and loved to keep everything, though she refused to embrace the term 'pack rat' that her mother insisted on calling her.

Just fresh from her shower, she stood in the center of her room, slanted ceilings on either side also covered with posters. She wore her sleep wear, tired from a long week. A pair of silk boxers–covered with little Tweety Birds–and a tank top. She carefully ran the bristles of the brush through the wet, golden locks as she thought back to her day. She had finally convinced her parents to trust her. They, especially her dad, were determined to borrow Jim Wilkins' hounds and set them free in the woods. It was ridiculous. She couldn't do that to Zac, no matter what the situation was. She'd never allow Zac to be hurt, even though this whole thing was odd.

Abel closed her eyes, enjoying the comforting strokes of the brush. She thought back to what Zac referred to as the Boogie Man. *What the hell was that? The cops? Was Zac afraid of police?* She had no idea. She stopped brushing in mid-stroke. There was that feeling again. Abel set the brush on her bed and walked over to the window. She swept the sheer curtains aside and looked down. She wasn't surprised when she saw the figure standing below, half hidden by a tree. She smiled, knowing it was Zac, and raised a hand in greeting.

※※※※

Zac leaned against the tree, her head peeking out from behind the mighty oak. She saw the silhouette in the window on the third floor and knew it was Spinney. She looked up at the dark figure, wishing she could see those green eyes again. A soft smile spread across her face when she saw a hand lift in greeting, and she mirrored the action, her stomach rising in her throat as she was nervous...but happy. She watched as the figure slowly slipped away, the curtains floating back into place. Within a few moments, the light flickered off and all was silent and still.

Still smiling, Zac turned, making her way through the darkness to her home. She'd sleep well tonight.

※※※※

Abel smiled as she climbed into bed, knowing for certain now that it was indeed Zac that she felt, and knew that it was Zac that watched her. She also smiled because she realized she didn't mind anymore.

Chapter Seven

"That is so not fair!" Ben Cohen shouted, scattering a few frightened birds off their perches nearby.

"Don't be such a whiner." Jake grinned, smacking his older brother in the arm. The incensed fifteen-year-old looked down at the twelve-year-old brat.

"You suck, Jake." Ben ran over to the tree and began to climb, the Frisbee taunting him from a branch just out of his reach.

"You guys both suck." Abel grinned as she carried a plate of raw hamburger patties to her father, who was manning the grill.

"Shut up, Abel!" Ben yelled from the tree. Finally his fingertips grabbed the toy, and he hurled it at his younger brother, nearly beaning him in the head.

"Jerk," Jake grumbled.

"Here, dad." Abel noticed his dark blonde hair beginning to show a few streaks of gray. *Soon enough you'll look like grandpa*, she often teased.

"Thanks, sweets." He smiled taking the patties from her.

Abel wandered back into the cabin where Sherry and little Rachel were preparing a salad. The nine-year-old sat on the counter top, tearing apart lettuce as her mother chatted with her.

"Hey, you two. Dad's got the burgers going." Abel opened the fridge and grabbed herself a bottled water, then settled into a chair with a magazine The summer was nearly a week in, and the weather was improving exponentially. The boys had even gone swimming the day before.

"Okay, honey," Sherry said, continuing to slice a block of Cracker Barrel's Sharp Cheddar. "Bring those out to your dad, Rach." Sherry helped her down and handed her the plate of slices. "Abel, did you bring down the laundry?"

"Oh, crap. I forgot. Hang on."

Abel popped up, threw down the magazine, and ran upstairs. Grabbing the laundry, she noticed her youngest sister's hot pink shirt with the koala and smiled. The four year old was so cute, though utterly evil. She stopped. *Where is Becky, anyway?* "Hey, mom?" she called as she headed down the stairs, dropping the clothes in front of the washer and dryer, "have you seen Beck?" Abel stood, hands on hips, in the archway that led to the kitchen.

Sherry stopped what she was doing and thought for a moment. "Isn't she out playing with the boys?"

"I don't remember seeing her out there. I'll check." Abel headed outside, curious, though not quite panicked. The youngest was very prone to following her curiosity and finding trouble. Her mom often told her that Becky was a lot like she was at that age. Always wandering, following a bug, or even a wind-blown leaf.

"Hey, Jake. Go far!" Ben yelled out, trying to get his brother to land in the lake with a well thrown Frisbee.

"Hey, any of you guys seen Beck?" Receiving negative answers all around, Abel began to worry.

The small blonde child walked on looking around with green-gray eyes, large with growing apprehension and fear. As she walked through the woods, one tree began to look like the next in a maze of unending forest.

Worried now, she chewed her finger nails as tension filled her tiny body, her long golden hair becoming damp with sweat. She clutched her hand into a fist to keep herself under control. She didn't want to call for help because her mommy would be angry at her for wandering off.

Suddenly feeling eyes on her she stopped, imagining all sorts of monsters hiding in the shadows of the trees. Monsters who wanted to eat her up and never let her see her mommy or daddy again. Whimpering in fear, she looked around, small, white teeth still chewing painfully on her fingernails.

"Hello?" her small, high voice caused a bird to take flight from a nearby branch. Following its progress above the tree tops, she wished she could fly like that.

"Hi."

Whipping around, eyes the size of saucers, the little blonde immediately let out a sigh of relief when she saw an unassuming young woman standing before her. She had long, dark hair, and bright blue eyes.

"Who are you?" the little girl asked, knitting her brows.

"I'm Zac," the woman grinned, her bright blue eyes seeming to glow under the canopy of trees.

"You have pretty eyes, Zac."

"Thanks. What's your name?"

"Becky. Nice to meet you, Zac."

"Nice to meet you, Becky. I think you're lost." Zac squatted in front of the petite child.

"Yep. Can you help me?" Becky asked, hoping beyond hope that Zac knew where to go.

"Sure! Are you from that house with the green dock?" At Becky's nod, Zac smiled and stood, holding her hand out for the little girl. "Come on."

༄༅༄༅

Zac led the way through the trees, glancing down at her smaller companion who held her hand with small, sweaty fingers. This was Spinney in a smaller, slightly different form. She couldn't help but marvel at how much alike this little one and her sister were at similar ages. Obviously just as curious, too. Zac stayed away from the cabin for a few days, giving Spinney and her family some space so she wouldn't get into trouble, and hoping maybe Spinney would remember her again. It was hard staying away, especially since that night they'd shared the small wave through the window. She knew if she got any closer, Spinney would be able to feel her, just as she felt Spinney. She wanted to give her some freedom and space.

"Zac?" The small voice pulled her from her thoughts. She looked down to see Becky's gaze peering up at her with something akin to hero worship. "Do you live here?" The little blonde's high-pitched voice charmed Zac to no end.

Zac nodded. "Yep, sure do."

"I like you," Becky announced with a beaming smile as she looked into Zac's eyes. "You're tall for a girl."

Zac smiled, then froze. Off in the distance she

heard someone calling Becky's name.

"Uh, oh. They're looking for you, Becky." Zac hurried the girl through the forest, then knelt down and pointed. "You see that trail right there?" she asked, making sure the little girl was paying close attention. "Follow that, and it will take you to the lake, okay? From there you'll be able to see the cabin and can get home." She looked at the little blonde. "Do you understand?"

Becky nodded. "Gonna go home now." With a big, toothy grin, the little blonde let go of Zac's hand and ran off.

Zac watched to make sure she went the right way, then hurried back into the trees.

༺༻

"She's got to be around here, Mom. Hang on." Abel, nearly as frantic as her mother, hurried with the older woman toward the lake, praying they wouldn't find anything. They had no idea how long Becky had been gone, but they had been searching for the past twenty minutes, getting more and more frantic with each tick of the clock.

She was about to tell her mother to wait on land as she headed for the dock, not wanting her mother to see if there was anything to see. But before she could speak, she saw a flash out of the corner of her eye. "Becky!" she screamed. She ran toward the girl and scooped her up. Sherry at her heels.

"Where have you been!" Sherry demanded, as she took the girl from her daughter's arms and inspected her for herself.

"I was talking to Zac," Becky said, as if it was

the most natural thing in the world. Sherry and Abel looked at each other.

"You were doing what, honey?" Sherry asked.

"I got too far, and got lost, and Zac saved me!"

"Oh my god," Abel breathed, her hand on her chest.

"You found her?" Adam huffed, running from the woods where he and the boys had been searching.

"Yeah," Sherry said, still in awe. "Here, honey. Take her." She handed the smiling girl to her father, and turned to Abel. "Holy shit."

"I told you." Abel reached out and jabbed her mother in the shoulder with her finger. "I told you I wasn't nuts." She was almost giddy. Someone else had seen Zac! She wasn't a figment of her imagination.

"I'm stunned, honey. Truly, I am," Sherry said, her eyes wide. "I'm sorry we didn't believe you." She took her daughter into a hug.

"It's okay. I was little," Abel said against her mother's shoulder. As they hugged, she couldn't help but look out into the woods, wondering where Zac was. She didn't feel her.

"Well," Adam said, putting his youngest back on her feet. "Let's get dinner going. Enough excitement for one day."

※※※※

Zac's ears perked up as she heard her name being softly called. She stood from her bedroll and closed the book she was reading, setting it aside. There it was again. She stepped out of the lean-to, and headed down the path that led to the Cohen's cabin. About halfway there, she saw Spinney.

"Where are you?" Abel whispered, looking around.

"Right here." Zac stepped out from behind a tree, looking shyly at the blonde from beneath bangs, needing to be cut.

"Thank you," Abel said, a soft smile of appreciation on her face. "Becky is safe because of you." She took an unsure step toward her.

Zac shrugged. "No worries. I'm glad she's okay."

Abel smiled. "Yeah, she's okay. My mother was frantic. I think you saved her a heart attack today."

"Your mom really should watch better. That's almost two of her daughters who got lost."

Abel was about to get defensive when she saw the twinkle in Zac's blue eyes causing her to smile Looking down at her shoes she nodded. "Yes, well. What can I say? All the Cohen children are far too curious for their own good." She looked up into Zac's kind, relaxed expression. "You said that was how we met."

Zac nodded. "Yes. You were lost." Zac shoved her hands further into her pockets. She was feeling warm swallowed by huge, baggy pants and layered sweatshirts.

"Then thank you twice." Abel looked shy. "Was there somewhere I used to go? Like a . . ." She paused. "I had a dream last night. It was kind of dark, but there was almost like a…well…a spotlight where I used to spin." She frowned. "Am I crazy?"

A smile spread across Zac's face, and she shook her head. "You're not crazy, Spinney. We used to go there all the time." Hope filled her heart as she thought Spinney might be starting to remember. "Do you want to go there?"

"No." Abel shook her head, hugging herself slightly. "I should go," she said, her voice quiet. "Thanks again, Zac."

"You're welcome, Spinney."

It was only as Zac watched Spinney walk away from her that she allowed herself to feel her disappointment in Spinney's rejection of her offer. With a heavy sigh, she headed back home, her unfinished book waiting for her.

※※※※

Abel–filled to the gills after a dinner of freshly caught trout–headed upstairs, ready for bed. Once she stepped into the spacious room, however, she saw the stacked crates in the corner and remembered she had hoped to go through them tonight. Fatigue forgotten, she took the first and set it on the bed. Every couple of years she went through the boxes, sometimes just for a hoot, others to actually throw stuff out. Standing over the crate she found pinecones she'd painted with Rachel, and awards from family game night two years ago when she was the undefeated backgammon champ. She'd save them for sure.

As she continued to pick through, a thought occurred to her, and suddenly her hands began to scramble through the memories, looking for something, anything, that would take her back to a forgotten summer. Pictures, measurements of how much she'd grown that year, when her brothers and sisters were born, a party hat from her eleventh birthday, a report card from second grade, a little stick figure made of Popsicle sticks . . .

"Oh...", Abel's breath caught, her eyes riveted to

what lay beneath a score sheet from a family game of UNO.

With trembling fingers, she pulled it out from under the other items. She brought her hand to her mouth as she studied the drawing by the impatient, inexperienced hand of a five or six-year-old, on finger paint paper. Two little girls, one with long, blonde hair, the other with short dark hair were holding hands. The one with dark hair had immense blue eyes, just twin dots of cobalt among the near colorless picture, and was dressed in overalls. A single tree was drawn on either side of the girls, and above their heads, in child's scrawl, read *Zak and Spinee*.

Abel sank to the bed, never taking her eyes off the drawing. "God, she was there," she breathed, heart racing as she tried to think back, tried to remember, tried to see Zac as she had when she'd drawn the picture.

"Come on, Zac! Follow me!" The little blonde darted between trees, doing her best not to crash into one. Her mom would get angry for sure then. "Last one there's a chicken!"

"A chicken, huh?" The taller girl ran hard, but seemed to hold her long legs back, giving her friend a chance to win.

"Come on, come on!"

"I'm coming, Spinney!"

Zac's voice echoed in Abel's mind, and tears threatened to escape as it all came flooding back to her.

"Come on, Spinney! I'll help you climb the tree!"

"Zac, wait up! I can't run as fast as you!" Giggles followed the galloping girls through the forest, running at breakneck speeds . . .

"Be gentle, Spinney. Hummingbirds are very

fragile," Zac explained, helping to steady the young blonde's hand. Green eyes widened in wonder as they took in the brightly colored body of the tiny bird that perched in her palm. She nearly held her breath, afraid that it would flutter away.

"How pretty," she whispered . . .

"Oh my god. I know you, Zac," she whispered, her gaze straying to the window and the night beyond.

Chapter Eight

Zac sang to herself, kneeling down by the lake as she cleaned off her boots, which had gotten thoroughly gross after she'd managed to step into a nice pile of deer sh–.

"Zac!"

She stood to see a very excited blonde blur running toward her. Concerned for a moment, she dropped the boot to the ground, hobbling over to her with only one shoe.

"Zac!"

Spinney's smile was infectious, and Zac smiled, wondering what on earth was going on. Spinney stopped, taking several gulps of air before continuing. Her bright, alert green eyes looked directly into Zac's.

"I remember you," she said, her voice soft, belying the excitement from only moments before.

Zac looked at her for a moment, trying to compute what Spinney was telling her, then a slow smile began at the corners of her mouth and gently spread throughout her entire face, landing squarely in her eyes. "You do?" she whispered.

Spinney nodded. "Yes."

Zac felt a warmth spread so quickly through her body that she thought she might melt right there.

"Take me there, Zac. Where we used to spin."

The look in those beautiful eyes, so full of

mischief, nearly brought Zac to her knees. With a smile and simple nod, she grabbed her boot, forgetting about the mess inside the tread, shoved her foot inside and hurried out. She'd worry about tying the long laces later. With a quick look into Spinney's eyes, she took Spinney's soft hand and led them deep into the forest.

"It's good to have you back, Spinney." Zac smiled over her shoulder.

Her friend gave her the sweetest, most endearing look. "It's good to be back, Zac."

ʂʅʂʅ

The two friends headed deeper and deeper into the woods and the comforting silence. As Abel followed along–still being led by her hand–she remembered the quiet strength that was Zac that she depended on so much as a child, and had craved. That morning she awoke with a smile on her lips and the need to revisit their friendship from more than ten years before. She thought back to the summer of her fifth year and remembered waking up, her mother amazed that her eldest had actually gotten up on her own. The little blonde had trouble waking even then. She would get herself dressed and run to the kitchen, begging for permission to go outside and play with Zac.

She had to smile at the look of wonder on Zac's face, as the brunette looked back at her from time to time. The energy in the air was so wonderful and light, and Abel wasn't entirely sure if it was coming from her or Zac. *Perhaps both.*

"What do you do all day?" Abel asked casually, looking at the beauty around them. The immense trees and thick shrubbery and greenery compelled her still childish mind to run and play, hide and make forts. Just like that summer.

"I look at plants and try to find animals," Zac answered.

"Do you like plants?" Abel asked, taking in her taller companion with the same clothes and same dirt smudges from the day before on her face. Even so, she was amused at the random thought that, amazingly, she didn't stink. She'd seen homeless people come around campus, begging for money or food, and they had stunk to high heavens. But not Zac.

"Yep. Animals, too. I try to figure out what they are. I stol...um, borrowed...a book from the library that has all sorts of varieties and species. I try to match them up."

"Did you go to school?" Abel asked, intrigued. She carefully stepped over a fallen tree, Zac waiting patiently for her on the other side before taking her hand and continuing their journey.

"Nope."

"Never?" Abel was stunned.

"Never." Zac graced her with a stunning smile that seemed to hold pride.

"You can read?"

Zac nodded, her smile of pride still brightening her features. "Yes, I can read. My father taught me a few things, then I taught myself the rest. I can write, too."

"Wow," Abel murmured, truly impressed. She remained quiet for a bit as they continued on, further and further, deeper into Zac's domain. She realized she felt absolutely no fear. After the memories had tumbled all around her the night before, she felt that she knew this woman, that she trusted her, and that she was indeed, safe.

Finally Zac pushed back a low overhang of branches, and held them aside for Abel, who walked under Zac's arm, eyes wide.

"Oh, Zac," she breathed, taking in the small clearing that she remembered so well from childhood. It looked exactly the same, towering trees with entangled branches forming a dark room in the forest. It was chilly inside, and Abel looked up, smiling when she saw the hole made by the overhead branches. She knew that when the sun was overhead, the spotlight would turn on.

"I can't believe it hasn't changed." She walked inside, dropping Zac's hand. She turned in a small circle, marveling at how small it seemed now. She saw the large rock where Zac used to sit and watch her spin, and turned to see Zac standing behind her, a soft, gentle smile on her lips. "How hasn't it changed? You'd think with the change of growth, storms, time ..." She hugged herself in the chilly temperature, turning in a small circle again to take in as much as she possibly could.

"I don't know," Zac said, also looking around. "Guess this place just wants to stand still in time."

"It's still so beautiful." Abel's voice was wistful. She stopped looking around and focused her attention on Zac, who watched her with kind, patient eyes. "Why didn't I see you after that summer? Where have you been?" As she looked at Zac, she couldn't help but wonder how there was so much peace in their depth. Abel had been lucky enough to be surrounded by amazing parents and loving, close siblings, but Zac had nobody. She wondered how she could be that strong.

"I told you. I didn't want to disturb you and your friend," Zac explained softly. "I didn't want to hurt you, Spinney. You two looked like you were having such a good time. You would run through the trees yelling and screaming, then go swimming in the lake." She looked away, her eyes suddenly very sad. "I didn't want to interfere."

"Oh, Zac," Abel whispered, reaching out and laying a hand on Zac's arm. "We used to have fun, and we could have then, too. Mel was a nice girl and would have liked you." She smiled, and Zac matched it, though it seemed weak. Abel walked deeper into the small, natural cavern, and then with a look at her friend, she spread her arms and raised them to the tree tops, which she could now almost touch, and began to spin, round and round, her hair whipping out around her shoulders.

Zac watched, transfixed with delight.

༄༄༅༅

"So where were you today?" Sherry asked as Abel helped prepare dinner.

Abel shrugged. "With Zac." She glanced over at her mom to see green eyes, just like her own, looking at her.

"Zac-The mystery girl who saved my daughter-Zac?"

Abel nodded, licking some ranch dressing from the tip of her thumb while placing it on the table. "One and the same." She smiled at her mom. "I remember her, now." She grinned and walked over to her mother, tugging lightly on the sleeve of her shirt to encourage her to follow. "Come here." She hurried toward the stairs, mounting them two at a time, her mother panting behind her. "Check this out..." Abel hurried over to her dresser and grabbed the drawing. "I found this last night."

Sherry studied the picture, a slow smile crossing her lips. "Oh, how cute is this!" she exclaimed, seeing the little girl with the overalls and blue eyes and her daughter's depiction of herself. She read the scrawled names and gasped. "Honey." She looked at her daughter, who was grinning smugly.

"I remember her totally, mom." Her smile widened. "We used to have so much fun. Don't you remember how you'd have to keep calling for me to come home? She and I used to do everything together that summer."

"I want to meet her," Sherry said, arms crossing stubbornly over her chest.

"Oh, I don't know about that," Abel hedged, placing the drawing back onto the dresser for safe keeping.

"Why not?"

"I don't know if she'll do it. I think she's afraid of people. I'm like the only friend she's ever had," Abel said sadly, sitting on the edge of her bed.

Sherry followed suit. "God, how sad. What is she doing in that forest all alone? How old is she?"

"I'm not sure. I'd guess she's about my age, maybe twenty or so, and all I know is she used to live with her father in a cabin. The cabin is nothing more than a pile of burnt rubble, now." She sighed. "I'm not sure it was much more than a shack, anyway. I worry about her out there. Obviously she can take care of herself, but still. No one should have to be alone like that."

"Zac? Are you out here?" Abel knew it was a stupid question. She could feel her.

Sure enough, Zac stepped out from the thicket just ahead, a smile planted firmly on her lips. "Hi," she said, her tone somewhat shy, stepping toward Abel, digging her hands into the pockets of her pants. She looked down at what Abel was carrying.

Abel matched her smile as she held out her offering. "Here. I brought you breakfast." She handed the warm plate to her companion, and smiled when Zac looked at it as Jake would a new toy.

"What is it?" Zac looked at the package she held in her hand. "What is this?" She gently ran a fingertip over the smooth surface of the foil that covered the dish.

Abel didn't say anything for a moment, Zac's question running through her surprised brain again. "Are you kidding? It's foil. You don't know what foil is?" She looked incredulous as Zac shook her head. "Come here." She led Zac over to a fallen log and sat down. Abel set down the small jug of syrup she carried and reached over, gently untucking the foil from around the plate, revealing waffles, eggs and bacon. She was about to crumple the foil when Zac stopped her.

"No. Save it," she said, awe in her voice..

"Oh. Okay. I can bring you more, too, you know?" Abel smiled.

"More? You have more of it?" Zac looked so amazed that Abel couldn't help but rest her hand on Zac's arm.

"Yes. We have more. Now, do you know what this stuff is?" Abel was amazed. She thought everyone knew what foil was. She felt like she'd just stepped back into the seventeenth century, and would have to explain all the modern marvels to a peasant she found there.

"Eggs." Zac said with a grin.

"Good! Yes, eggs. I had no idea if you liked them, so I just fried them. This is bacon, and these are waffles." She smiled when Zac looked at her like she had three heads. "Here." She picked up the jug of syrup, and uncapped it. "Do you like syrup?"

Zac shrugged, dark eyebrows drawn in concentration. "I don't know. What is it?"

The total look of innocence and trust on her face melted Abel's heart. "Try it." Abel cut a small piece of waffle, poured a smidge of syrup on it, and handed Zac the fork.

Zac took it and sniffed the food before bringing it to her mouth. With her tongue she tasted the sweet, sticky substance, letting it roll around, then quickly stuck the entire thing in her mouth, closing her eyes.. "Mmmmm," she moaned.

Grabbing the small bottle from Abel, she poured the amber fluid over the entire plate, covering eggs, bacon and waffles.

"Oh, Zac, um ..."

Abel watched, her face registering her shock then disgust. But, she needn't have worried as Zac ate the entire thing and licked the plate. She grimaced as she watched the spectacle. "Guessing you liked that." She outright laughed as Zac gave her a child-like grin and a vigorous nod. "I'll bring you more syrup."

Zac nodded as she licked her lips, a contented

smile on her face.

Thoroughly amused, Abel handed her the jug of Minsen's Own Maple Syrup. "Keep this."

"Wow," Zac whispered, looking at the jug as though she'd just been given a diamond ring. "Thanks!"

"Will you ever meet any of my family, Zac?" Abel asked quietly, taking the plate Zac handed her. "I know we covered this when we were kids, and kind of now, but ..."

Abel watched as Zac thought for a moment as she picked at her pants.

"I don't know, Spinney," she finally said.

Abel wasn't able to hide her disappointment.

Zac sighed. "Who's the most important person to you?"

"My mom," Abel responded, her face expressionless.

"Bring her here," Zac said, her voice very quiet.

"Oh, Zac!" Abel stood and went to hug Zac, but stopped herself. "You stay." She pointed at Zac, her face stern.

Zac nodded, seemingly defeated.

The smile fell off Abel's face. "Are you sure, Zac? I don't want to do anything that will upset you or make you uncomfortable."

Zac looked into Abel's face and gave her a small smile. "Yeah. Go get her. I won't move."

༄༄༅༅

After Spinney had taken off, heading for home, Zac stayed where she sat. She glanced over at the lake through the trees, the sun reflecting off the shimmering water like millions of dancing stars upon its surface.

She felt her stomach begin to churn as the nerves of meeting Spinney's mother ate at her, threatening to give her super sweet breakfast an encore performance. With a sigh, she glanced down at her new prize down by her booted feet. She lifted the small plastic jug and began to read the label and ingredients as she waited.

※※※※

Abel flew through the woods, taking the path that Zac had pointed out for her. She was nearly skipping by the time she reached the cabin and her family, who were all settled around the picnic table playing Scrabble.

"Mom!" she called out as she crashed through the trees.

Sherry looked up, looking startled by her daughter's impassioned cry. "What?"

"Come on," she gasped, out of breath from running. "Zac will meet you." She grinned from ear to ear, stopping at her mother's chair and playfully tugging at her mom's sleeve. "Come on." She was so excited.

Sherry gave her letter tiles to Adam and hurried after her daughter. "How did you get her to do this?" she asked as they made their way through the woods.

"I asked her. She said to bring you." She grinned at her mom walking beside her. "I think I may have inadvertently bribed her with breakfast."

Sherry chuckled.

They quieted as they approached Zac, who still sat on the fallen log, feet firmly planted, forearms resting on spread thighs. She looked nervous as she eyed the newcomers.

Abel gave her a smile of encouragement. "Zac, this is my mom, Sherry. Mom, this is Zac." Abel felt elated that she was able to introduce them.

"Hello, Zac," Sherry said with a kind smile.

Abel glanced at her mother and could easily read what was going through her head as Sherry's gaze took in the state of Zac's clothes and person. She knew for a fact that the wheels in her mother's mind were already turning regarding how to get Zac into a shower and new clothes. Sherry Cohen was the perpetual maternal presence for everyone she met.

Zac gave Sherry a small smile. "Hi." Her voice was quiet and soft.

"So you do exist," Sherry said with a quiet chuckle.

Zac smiled as she lightly slapped her own cheek to prove she was real. "I do. Thank you for taking care of Spinney," she nearly whispered.

"Well, I love my daughter. Of course I'd take care of her." She smiled, her eyes twinkling.

Abel watched the exchange, curious at how Zac would handle it. She knew her mother was a sweetie, and would do her best to put the girl at ease. But still.

Sherry walked over to the log and indicated the seat her daughter had vacated not twenty minutes before. "Mind if I sit down?" When Zac scooted over a bit, she sat. "So, why are you out here all alone, Zac?" Sherry's voice was calm and caring.

"Oh...uh...well...uh, my father died."

"Of what?"

"Mom," Abel said quietly.

Sherry reached out and squeezed her daughter's hand.

Zac fidgeted nervously, her gaze everywhere but

on either of the women. "Um, I'm not real sure. He was just dead one day."

"And so you were alone?" At Zac's nod, Sherry continued. "So what did you do then?"

"I left." Zac seemed to shrink slightly under the questioning.

"How? Where did you go?"

Abel was torn. She didn't know whether to stop her mother's gentle barrage of questions or if she should remain silent. Truth being, she too wanted to know the answers to the questions. She kept a careful eye on Zac. If she got too uncomfortable, Abel would put a stop to it.

"Um, I ran to the train, hopped on, and just went. Wherever it was going, I went."

"Really? How wonderful for you to be able to travel." Sherry smiled at Abel, who looked nervously back at her, then turned back to Zac. "Did you stay in the east?"

"Um, no." Zac pushed to her feet, her eyes darting back and forth, looking as though she were about to bolt.

"Mom," Abel said again, taking a step toward her. She could see how jittery Zac was becoming under the scrutiny, regardless of how innocent it was.

"Hang on, honey," Sherry said absently, obviously completely unaware of what she was inadvertently doing to a very gun-shy Zac. "So, Zac, when did you come back to Wachiva?"

"A few months ago, um..." Zac took a step back, stepping over the fallen log, putting some distance between her and the older woman. "I need to go." She took another step.

Sherry looked surprised and turned to her

daughter. Abel gave her a hard look.

"Zac, I'll find you later, okay?" Abel said.

Zac nodded and hurried off through the trees.

"What did I do?" Sherry asked, glancing over her shoulder to see where Zac went.

"You pounded her with questions, Mom!" Abel exclaimed. "She's not used to people."

"Oh..." Sherry covered her mouth with her hand, once again glancing off into the trees where Zac had almost literally disappeared. "I'm so sorry." She turned sorrowful eyes to Abel before calling out, "I'm sorry, Zac!" Her voice echoed in the woods and a distant bird squawk the only response.

Abel sighed. Sitting on the log next to her mother, she noted Zac had forgotten her syrup in her haste to escape. "It's okay. I'll talk to her," she said, picking up Zac's foil and syrup. "Come on." She stood, waited for her mom to do the same, then put her arm around her mother's shoulders to ease the upset she knew she felt. As they walked back toward the cabin she voiced a thought she'd been having for the past few days. "I was wondering if maybe we could buy Zac some stuff." She looked at her mom with hopeful eyes, and was met with a smile.

"I was thinking the same thing. Let me talk to your dad."

※※※※

Zac ran a hand across her eyes as she made her way to the lean-to, needing to regroup and gather strength from familiarity. Spinney's mother seemed really nice, but all the questions! She had no idea what to do with them, or how to answer them. She had freaked, and now felt really stupid. Would Spinney be mad?

She crawled in and plopped down. Bringing her knees up to her chest, she wrapped her arms around her shins, and took several deep breaths to calm herself down. *You're okay, Zac. You're okay. She meant no harm. You're okay and will be okay.* People made her feel so claustrophobic. She had never been around a great number of them in her life, let alone at the same time, and Sherry Cohen had the presence of several at one time.

She sighed, resting her forehead against her knees. *Spinney is going to think you're such a wimp. So pathetic!* Then Zac stopped berating herself and listened. There it was again.

"Zac? Where are you?"

Feeling nervous, Zac uncurled herself and crawled out of her self-imposed prison. She hurried through the forest until she spotted Spinney, who was looking around, walking backwards.

"I'm here," Zac said quietly, standing by a tree, her hands in her pockets and her head hanging.

"Hey," Abel said with a smile. "Are you okay?"

Zac flinched slightly at Spinney's comforting hand resting on her arm. She nodded, still feeling like an idiot, even though Spinney didn't seem to be mad. "I'm sorry," Zac whispered, looking into beautiful eyes filled with compassion.

"No, I'm sorry, Zac. I should have warned you. My mom means well, but she just worries. She's a mom, you know?"

Zac nodded, although she didn't understand because she never had a mom who cared like that.

"She feels really bad. She didn't mean to scare

you away." She gave Zac's shoulder a small squeeze.

Oddly, Zac missed the touch that had just startled her, once it was gone. "I'm sure she didn't. I just ... I just freaked." She ran a shaky hand through her hair and gave Abel an even shakier smile.

"I know," Spinney said gently. She raised her other hand, which held the jug of syrup and folded piece of foil. "Come on. Let's put this stuff in your house, okay?"

Zac smiled and nodded.

Chapter Nine

"You're kidding," Adam looked at his wife as though she'd lost her mind. "You want to buy this girl clothes? As in taking the credit card and putting items on it for her?"

Sherry leaned over the bathroom vanity closer to the mirror as she spread cold cream on her face and began removing her makeup. Her husband sat on the end of their bed, watching her through the opened doorway of the bathroom. "Yes. That's exactly what I'm saying. Adam, this girl has nothing. It looks like she's been wearing the same clothes for God only knows how long, plus I don't know if she knows what the word shampoo means." She turned to look at him, looking more like Casper the friendly ghost than the woman he'd been married to for twenty-five years. "She needs us."

"But she's not our responsibility, hon." He pushed up from the bed and removed his T-shirt, tossing it into the hamper by the door.

"So? Are we not supposed to help her just because I didn't give birth to her?" Finished washing her face, Sherry padded into the bedroom rubbing lotion into her hands and arms. She drew down the comforter and fluffed the pillow before climbing in. Adam shoved his shorts down tanned legs so he was just wearing his skivvies before turning off the overhead light and climbing into bed.

"I don't know," he sighed, sliding down in the bed. After adjusting his head on the pillow several times before reaching for his wife, he pulled her into his arms so her head could rest comfortably on his bare chest. "We'll see."

Sherry smiled into Adam's warm neck, knowing that meant yes.

※※※※

Zac cut up the last of the rabbit and placed it on her homemade spit over the open flames of her fire. She closed her eyes and inhaled the smell of the meat. Her mouth begin to water in anticipation. It was late, but she woke from a short nap hungry and went out to hunt. Her quarry had been easy enough to find, and was to be her dinner.

A small slice sat on her only plate and she was chewing happily when she saw something out of the corner of her eye causing her to chew her bottom lip in contemplation. Decision made, she scurried on her hands and knees over to the lean-to and grabbed the plastic jug of syrup and hurried back to her place near the fire. Unscrewing the cap, she looked down at the meat, then at the container of syrup, and without a further thought, poured the thick, sweet goo onto her plate, watching as the small reservoir flowed toward the meat. Taking up her knife and fork again, she cut a bite-sized piece then carefully dipped a corner into the syrup and brought it to her mouth.

"Mmmm," Zac closed her eyes, savoring the flavor of her beloved rabbit mixed with her newly beloved syrup. *Good stuff.* "Syrup makes a good condiment," she muttered, pouring more onto her meat.

Munching happily, Zac leaned back against the log she used as a backrest and stretched her long legs, crossing them at the ankles, her plate resting on her thighs. She let out a contented sigh as she chewed, looking out into the darkness. She was happy. She was really, really happy. Spinney had spent half the day with her. Her little friend had been filled with joy as she was led through the woods, given a long-overdue reunion with Zac's much loved home.

Spinney had tried to get Zac to eat dinner with her and her family, but the idea had been met with a resounding and unflinching 'no.' Zac felt bad for putting Spinney off, but knew that it was a bad idea. She had nearly lost it when she'd met Spinney's mother a few days before. She knew she'd be overwhelmed meeting the entire clan. Besides, she couldn't take any more questions.

So, for the time being, she'd just enjoy the time she had with her old friend, and just live with being a social moron. She was afraid of people, not knowing what they could do or were capable of. Well, that wasn't true. She knew exactly what they were capable of. She learned that lesson the hard way many years ago, and it was, in fact, still a lesson in progress. Zac's dad used to tell her that a person never stopped learning, and when he did, he died. Maybe her father had finally stopped learning.

She tried and tried to figure out what had happened to Bud Lipton, but was no closer to figuring it out as she ate her dinner, than she had been the night she'd come back from a two-day hike to find him dead. He had been sitting in that disgusting armchair he loved so much. His hazel eyes open and staring into forever, never to blink again. At thirteen, Zac had already been tall for her age–just like her dad–and strong from endless days outdoors chopping wood, hiking, running from the law, whatever. Strong inside and out. But she had crumbled that day. The only person she knew, the only one she knew other than Spinney, that is, was dead.

Zac felt she had nothing left to stay for. So, one morning after she'd buried her father in the dense woods, she got up, gathered her belongings and headed out. She caught the first freight she came upon, climbed on, and didn't look back. She'd traveled all around the west, seeing different parts of the country, expanding her world to an amazing degree. Born in Rhode Island, she and Bud moved to the Wachiva Forest when Zac was two years old, and there she'd stayed.

During her travels, she did her best to stay away from the other rail riders. She had come into contact with some pretty nasty characters. Ironically, the only truly evil person she'd ever met had been at the cabin. Zac was twelve-years-old, and her father was off on a job, actually casing a job, leaving her alone. Hearing strange footsteps she knew weren't her father's, she left the tiny cabin to investigate, club in hand just like her father had taught her. The footsteps had gotten louder, the person having a very pronounced limp marking his every step. Zac had known that gait well. She shuddered at the memory. *Bastard. That damned bastard Boogie Man.*

If it hadn't been for her father's unexpected return, Zac often wondered where she'd be. Probably dead...surely damaged. She'd seen it in those dark, beady eyes. Purer evil she'd never seen. The Boogie

Man had intent that night. Intent she felt pressed demandingly against her lower back as he grabbed her. The Boogie Man, with his long shaggy graying hair that hung in greasy strands around his shoulders, was a homeless man who sometimes lived in the abandoned ghost town. His I.Q. was below the norm, but his strength was above average. Bud had taken him along on a couple jobs, giving him a small portion of what they managed to get. More than once the Boogie Man had shown interest in Zac, his midnight eyes always undressing her as a pink tongue glazed over his chapped lips.

Shivering, Zac turned back to the remainder of her rabbit, which was beginning to burn. She took it off the spit, and placed it on her plate.

She wished her father had killed him that night, but he hadn't. After a good whoopin', he had let the man go with the promise that if he ever returned, he wouldn't be so lucky.

Zac sighed, poured more syrup on her meat, and dug in.

⁂

"Zac? Where are you?" Abel headed into the woods near the lake, not wanting to go very far. She was hoping her friend would come out and not force her to turn back. "Zac!"

"I'm here." Zac stepped out from behind a tree about ten yards away.

Abel brought a hand to her chest. "You startle me every damn time you do that," she scolded, with a smile. A heavy bag swung at her side. "I brought you some stuff." She grinned triumphantly, excited to show Zac all the new things her mom bought for her.

"What?" Zac followed her friend toward the lake.

"I brought you some stuff," Abel said again. She turned in time to see Zac's eyes quickly avert from her behind. It took her by surprise, but she shook it off, thinking she must be mistaken. "Sit." She pointed to a log. Zac sat. Abel sat next to her and reached into the bag. "We'll start with this." She pulled out a folded pair of brand new jeans.

Zac's blue eyes lit up then quickly dulled. "Your jeans are very nice, Spinney." She licked her lips as she eyed the garments.

Abel looked at her with drawn eyebrows. "No, silly. They're for you." She grinned, standing and unfolding the denim and holding them up to her own waist. "Man, these are really long." She grinned, looking down at Zac. "We had to guess on size, but my mom's got a pretty good eye with that. I mean, with the boys growing like weeds, she has to keep up on sizes, you know?"

Zac nodded dumbly, watching.

"Okay, hold these." Abel handed the jeans to Zac then reached into the bag again. Hell, just the look of shock on Zac's face had been totally worth the dip into her savings account. She had insisted on footing the bill herself. She felt the smooth plastic of a bag and pulled it out. Six pairs of thick white socks were bundled up in a pack, and she handed it to Zac. "Again, we had to guess on sizes, but we should be close."

Next came a package of eight pairs of underwear. Abel looked a little sheepish as she handed them to Zac. "Um, hope you don't have a problem with French cut," she grinned.

Zac, looking stunned, took the garments and added them to her growing pile.

"Okay, now they're not fancy, but I figure they could serve dual purposes," Abel explained as she brought out a package of twelve white Hanes undershirts.

"Um, Spinney?" Zac said, finally finding her voice. "Why are you doing this?"

Abel met Zac's gaze. "Because you need this stuff. I hate the idea that you're all by yourself out here, Zac, and won't allow me to help you. So, I'm doing what I can. Okay?" She waited for Zac to process this information and smiled when she got a nod. "Okay, on with the goodies." She stopped, turning to look at her silent friend. "Speaking of, how are you doing on your syrup?" She grinned at the sheepish look on Zac's face. "I'll bring you more. Okay, do you know what this is?" She brought out a large bottle of Herbal Essence.

"It says shampoo."

"Have you ever used it?"

Zac shook her head. "I only have my bar of lye soap."

"Ah. Okay, well that's going to change." Abel looked at her friend, letting her eyes trail over the long, unkempt dark hair that she figured was probably beautiful when washed. It was long, too, and she wondered how Zac felt about that. Was it a hardship having all that hair when she was running through the woods? "When was the last time you had a haircut, Zac?"

Zac shrugged. "I don't know. A long time."

"Want one?" Abel cocked her head to the side as she studied her friend, watching for any signs that she was going too far, or that her help wasn't wanted.

"Okay." A small, quick smile graced her lips.

"Great!" Abel jumped up and reached into the bag again. Her hand came out with her fingers in the loop holes of a large, shiny pair of scissors.

Zac was off that log faster than Abel could blink, looking terrified.

"Zac? Are you okay?" She followed Zac's eyes to the scissors. "What is it?"

Zac's eyes were wide and glued to the scissors. Taking several deep breaths she reached down to her tattered sweatshirt and lifted it, revealing a muscular stomach and an ugly scar that ran the length of her side.

"Oh, Zac," Abel breathed, taking a step closer to look at it. "What happened to you?" She put a hand on Zac's forearm, looking up into those amazing eyes to try and show her that she cared.

"Someone I came across on the rails used to carry scissors," Zac said quietly, looking down. "I thought I was going to bleed to death that night."

"I'm not going to hurt you, sweetie."

After a long moment, Zac nodded. "I'm sorry," she said, still keeping a close eye on the scissors as she sat on the log again, letting her sweatshirt drop back into place.

Abel took a few quiet breaths, the ugly scar on Zac's body leaving her a bit shaken. She was discovering that there was so much behind the quiet, sweet young woman. "Okay, now that we've got that out of the way, I'll show you what else I have." She smiled, feeling terrible for scaring Zac. She had no idea that the tool would set her off. She was beginning to understand that she'd have to approach Zac carefully and with understanding. The truth of the matter was, Zac was essentially a child of the wild. She went on to show Zac the can of Skin So Soft and a package of Bic razors.

"Have you ever shaved before, Zac?"

For about the hundredth time that morning, Zac shook her head no. Creasing her brow she brought a hand up to her face. "I don't need to though, do I?"

Abel held her laughter in, not wanting to upset Zac by her amusement at such an innocent comment. "No." She smiled, her gaze wandering over Zac's features. "It looks nice and soft. I'm talking about other parts of your body. I'm going to teach you how. This will be for your legs and your underarms, okay?"

Zac looked at the two areas in question then looked at Abel as though she were nuts.

Abel chuckled. "Trust me."

She watched Zac mess with the fragrant pink shaving gel. That it began as pink goo and quickly turned to white lather seemed to amaze Zac, which charmed Abel to no end.

"How does it work?" Zac asked, again squirting the gel onto her palm and lifting the hand close to her eyes so she could watch the amazing metamorphosis.

"I don't know." Abel laughed. "Pretty cool, though, huh?"

Zac nodded absently as she brought the stuff to her nose. "Yum."

"Yeah, well, don't eat it. Come on." Abel led them to the water, bottles of shampoo and conditioner in hand. "It's time to wash your hair."

Zac swallowed, but nodded in agreement.. Together they splashed into the water until it reached their knees, Zac still fully dressed although she removed her boots. She knelt down, letting her long hair dip into the cool water.

Though the weather was still a bit cool for shorts, tank top and sandals, Abel had dressed for the event, hoping Zac would allow it. She knelt beside her friend in the cold water and worked the long, dark strands through gentle fingers. She massaged Zac's scalp as she worked the shampoo into a thick lather. She smiled when she heard a small moan come from Zac, who had her eyes closed, a smile on her lips.

"Feel good?" she asked, and smiled at the vigorous nod that was tossed her way. She rinsed the long strands, then decided to wash it again, then a third time, always giving it a thorough scrub, and the scalp a thorough massage. She enjoyed doing these things for Zac. She knew without a doubt that Zac would do anything for her, and wanted to be able to return the sentiment in some way. She was glad Zac trusted her to do these things. Abel applied conditioner, which she had to explain to an overly curious Zac. Once rinsed, she helped Zac to her feet, wrapped her hair in a towel and led her back to shore and to the fallen log.

"Okay. I brought you a brush in case you don't have one."

"I have one."

"Awesome. Well," she said, wiggling the red brush, "now you have two."

Zac tensed a bit when Abel moved behind her, brush in hand. Abel tenderly began to brush the long hair, admiring the way it shone in the late morning sunlight. It was truly beautiful. She would love to see the Zac beneath those horrible clothes and the layers of grime. She intended to do just that, starting with the hair.

"You know, when I was a kid, I used to love to brush my doll's hair. I'd do it for hours at a time,"

Abel said softly. "I used to brush your hair all the time that summer." Her voice softened even more. That was such a special time for her. Now she remembered it, and could recall every moment she and Zac had shared. She held them close to her heart, so glad they were able to make new memories.

Zac smiled. "Yes, I remember, Spinney. You'd sit there and do it for hours."

"You were so patient with me. Still are, I suppose. Guess I'm just doing an older version of dress up, huh?" She brushed the dark hair off the back of Zac's neck, seeing the tanned, smooth skin. "You had short hair then, though. When did you let it grow?"

"Well, my dad said I had to let it grow. I had been seen with short hair, and most thought I was a boy for a long time. Said I needed a new disguise."

"Disguise? For what?" Abel continued brushing Zac's hair. She knew that Zac would tell her anything she wanted to know, but always felt strange asking, somehow.

"He was a stealer," Zac said, her voice matter-of-fact, but quiet.

"A stealer? Like a robber? A burglar?" At Zac's nod, Abel said,"Oh. So this was where he would hide out?" Another nod. "Wow."

She stopped brushing and let that soak in for a few moments. Zac's hair shone like polished mahogany. Her heart hurt for this young woman who never had any semblance of a normal childhood. Abel understood that there was no such thing as a perfect childhood, or even perfect parents, but still. She deserved so much more than she got. Zac didn't deserve to live terrified of what she called the Boogie Man, or of people finding her and kicking her out of her home. Or even of wild animals attacking in the night.

Abel did everything in her power to get Zac to stay with her and her family in the cabin, but she'd hear nothing of it. She tried not to push, as she knew she was prone to do, but couldn't help it. She wanted a guarantee that her friend would be safe once they left, in just under two months.

"I'm going to cut now, okay?" Abel said softly, running her fingers through the beautiful dark strands that felt like silk. She smiled when she felt a small shiver pass through Zac, who nodded stiffly. "How much do you want cut off?"

"Well, longer hair keeps me warmer in the winter and at night, but how about here?" she brought her hand up to just below her shoulders.

Abel nodded her approval. "You really do have beautiful hair, Zac," she tied the dark hair in a ponytail where Zac indicated.

"Thank you." Zac smiled. "Never had a compliment before."

Abel snipped several times as Zac's hair was thick and one cut wasn't going to do it. "Yeah?" she said in response to Zac's admission. "Well, I think we're going to have to keep 'em coming, then." Finally the pony tail came off in her hands and she held it out for Zac to see. "You could donate this, you know? There are places that take hair like this and make it into wigs for kids who have cancer and lose their hair."

"Really?" Zac took the offered hair and ran it through her fingers..

"Yes, ma'am," Abel said as she began to even out the bottom of Zac's new do.

"Then maybe you should do that."

"Yeah? You want to donate it?" Abel quit cutting and looked at Zac over her shoulder. When Zac nodded, Abel smiled. "Then I'll do it."

She continued to snip, trying to even things out before she brushed out the smooth strands, glad to see the hair taking some shape. She also knew that Zac was just humoring her, and she loved her for it.

"Okay, lady. Check it out!" Abel produced a mirror from the bag everything had been in and watched expectantly as Zac looked at herself.

༄༅༄༅

Zac had seen her reflection in storefronts and in the lake on a calm day, but never so clearly. She even forgot about the haircut, and instead studied her face. She saw some lines around her eyes from years of being outside and squinting into the sun without benefit of sunglasses. She noted the pure color of her eyes, and had to admit they were kind of pretty. She made a funny face in the mirror, amused at her own silliness.

༄༅༄༅

Abel was growing nervous as her friend hadn't said a word. *I bet she hates it, and doesn't have the heart to tell me. When will you learn to stay out of other people's business, Abel?*

"I have really high cheekbones," Zac marveled.

Abel drew her eyebrows together. "Huh?" That certainly hadn't been what she'd expected to come out of Zac's mouth.

"I do. Look." Zac ran a finger over her cheek.

Abel looked at her in astonishment before realizing chances were slim to none that Zac ever had the chance to study herself. "Yes, you do. Do you have some Native American ancestry in there somewhere?" She began to play with Zac's new hair, running her fingers through it.

Zac closed her eyes at the sensations and shrugged. "I don't know." She looked over her shoulder at Spinney. "Would that be bad?"

Abel laughed and shook her head. "No! Of course not. Okay, now that we've gotten this taken care of, what say you get cleaned up so you can put on your new clothes?" Abel was excited to see her friend cleaned up and freshly dressed. At the suggestion, she could see the bubbling excitement on Zac's face, lying just under the surface. It was almost like Zac was trying to hide it, which surprised her considering Zac seemed so open about what she was feeling and thinking.

"Okay." Zac looked as if she may have been blushing.

Abel rested her hand on Zac's arm. "Zac, are you happy about the stuff I brought?"

Zac nodded.

"It's okay to be excited, you know. It's good to get excited about things."

"Yeah?" Blue eyes peered at her through dark bangs.

Zac's insecurity made Abel's heart hurt.

"Yeah." She gave Zac the most reassuring smile she could conjure and took Zac by the hand. "Now, I'm going to show you a new and exciting way to get clean." She gave her a mischievous smile. Grabbing the handle of the bag she'd brought, she stopped at the shore and reached in bringing out a few items.

"This, dear Zac, is called a loofah." She held up the peach-colored bathing scrubber. "And this is called body wash." She held up the white bottle of Caress Body Wash. "Here's how it works." She knelt down by the water's edge and dipped the loofah in making sure it was completely saturated.

Zac stood next to her looking fascinated. "What does it do?" She knelt down, reaching out a finger to touch the strange-looking sponge.

"It helps to clean you. And it feels really good against your skin." Abel ran the wet loofa over Zac's arm, making her shiver.

"Strange," she whispered.

"Yeah, it's kind of cool. Now, this stuff," she popped the top of the body wash and squirted some of the creamy liquid onto the sponge, "is soap. Here's how it works." She began to rub the web-like wings of the loofah together, causing the body wash to lather. Zac's eyes opened wide. "Then you rub it over your body." Abel mimicked the motion over her arms. "Understand?"

Zac nodded, never taking her eyes off the loofah. "I want to try!"

Abel was definitely glad she'd caught Zac's attention with her wares, but as she stood and looked around she was trying to figure out how this was going to work. She wanted to stay near in case Zac needed her, but wanted to give her privacy, too. "Hmm. Okay, bath time." She set the loofah on a rock and turned to Zac.

Without warning, Zac reached down and whipped off her sweatshirts in one try, the thick bundle of clothing falling to the sand at their feet.

"Oh, uh . . ." Abel stood there, stunned. She took in Zac's muscled stomach, shoulders, and arms. Firm breasts tipped with dark nipples that were growing hard before her eyes, were no more than a foot away from her. She had to admit, Zac was gorgeous. Her skin looked smooth and soft, satiny over the hard muscle beneath. She'd never been so close to a half-naked woman before, not even in gym class. It left her a bit unsettled. Zac's somewhat child-like, naïve nature almost made Abel forget that Zac was very much a woman. Now, literally faced with that fact, it made her see Zac in a new light. Under all the layers of oversized clothing, Zac just looked like one large blob with no curves, helping to add to the child-like image. Now, there was no denying it–Zac was all woman and very beautiful.

Finally, Abel shook herself out of her reverie, tearing her eyes away from Zac's body. "Um, Zac, what about modesty?" She grinned.

Completely unaware of Abel's thoughts or perusal of her body, Zac grinned. "Modesty?" She raised an eyebrow. "Out here?" She indicated the woods around them and the obvious lack of people as she leaned down to untie her boots. She took them off.

"Okay." Abel chuckled, knowing she was right. "Well, I'll let you get to it." She walked over to the log and sat down, her back to Zac. If Zac wasn't interested in privacy, Abel still was. She could hear Zac finish undressing then wade through the water.

॥॥॥॥॥

Zac looked at the loofah. She followed Spinney's instructions and ran the strange sponge over her body.

Her eyes fell closed at the sensations. "This feels really good," she called out to her friend, who still sat with her back to Zac. She started with a small gasp when she ran the loofah over her breasts. Sensation shot down into her lower belly.

༄༄༄༄

Abel sat with her legs apart, the bag on the dirt between her sandaled feet. She was ruffling around setting out her next task alongside her on the log. A long shadow stole her sun, and she looked up.

"What next?" Zac asked, water still dripping from her naked body.

"Oh, uh . . ." Abel blushed, looking away. If she didn't know better, she'd think Venus herself just stepped out of her shell and onto the banks of the Lake. "Well, first off you need to dry off." She grabbed the second towel out of the bag and stood, wrapping the soft terry cloth around Zac's broad shoulders. "Next, put something on." She walked over to the package of panties and ripped it open. She held it up. "Which color?"

"I like red."

"Red it is." Abel handed them to Zac.

Dutifully Zac pulled the cotton underwear up her legs and into place. She looked at Abel, waiting further instructions.

Abel noted Zac's naked torso again and mentally slapped herself for not thinking to get Zac a bra. Even a sports bra would have worked. Refocusing, she said, "Okay. I'm going to teach you how to shave." Abel picked up one of the disposable Bic razors and the can of Skin So Soft, and held them up for Zac to see.

"Razor. You take this protective cap off." She popped the plastic blade cover off and showed the razor part to inquisitive blue eyes. "Don't touch this," Abel warned.

Zac nodded. "Now what?"

"Now lift your arm for me."

Zac lifted her deeply tanned arm and took a step closer.

Able felt a slight blush at the extremely intimate act she was about to perform. She studied the dark thatch of hair under Zac's arm. Holding the razor between her teeth by the handle, she squirted some of the pink shaving gel into her palm and watched as it began to grow and fade to white.

"Wow," Zac breathed, eyes wide at the second show of the shaving cream.

Abel chuckled. "This may tickle." She spread the cream over the hair, doing her best to keep her opinions off her face. She handed Zac the razor. "Now. This is what you'll do." She took hold of her wrist, and showed her the motions.

Zac was a quick study, and in no time her underarm was smooth and smelled really good. She ran her fingertip across the silky smooth skin over and over, amazed.

Abel was amused. Do your other one, okay?"

Zac nodded then did as she was told. Abel watched Zac's almost child-like amazement at this new skill and the results it produced. She proudly showed off her freshly shorn armpits, rewarded with Abel's smile of approval. Next, Abel handed Zac the deodorant and explained its use.

"Okay. Last thing." Abel, feeling decidedly piggish and blushing, gazed at Zac's breasts, trying to gauge their size. She knew that running around the forest without any support could not feel so hot. "Zac, does it hurt when you're active?"

Zac raised a brow in question.

"I mean, like when you run? You know, your breasts." She pointed and Zac looked down at herself.

Finally understanding, she nodded. "Yes. Especially when I run," she said quietly.

"Okay. I'm going to guess you're a C, maybe a D," Abel said, mainly talking to herself as she looked at them again. She made a mental note to talk to her mom later. She grabbed the bag and took out one of the T-shirts. "Put this on." She watched as Zac tugged on the clean shirt, sniffing it first and inhaling the scent of new, clean clothes. "Now for the legs."

༄༅༅༄༅

After showing Zac how to shave her legs–and a couple bloody cuts later–Abel thought about their afternoon. Even though it was an odd activity–trying to teach Zac about things Abel had known her whole life–it was nice. She smiled as she packed things away. It felt good to help her, to be able to do things for her, and introduce her to new things. Abel couldn't get over the fact that Zac had never seen or heard of the most basic, simple, modern conveniences. *Foil, for God's sake! Truly endearing.*

"Spinney?"

Abel looked up and froze. A soft smile spread across her lips as she took in what stood before her. Zac's newly-cut hair shone in the sunlight, beautiful and clean. It framed an amazingly beautiful face with chiseled features and the most beautiful eyes Abel had ever seen. She had always thought Zac had the brightest blue eyes, but now with Zac cleaned up Abel could take in the woman behind the grunge.

Her gaze traveled from the face to the clean clothes that actually fit, showcasing Zac's long, lean body. She looked like a girl for the first time since Abel knew her. She noted the boots, which were way too big. She'd have to do something about that, but other than that, Zac looked fantastic.

Abel's eyes met the uncertain blue eyes again, and she smiled, reassuringly. "You look great, Zac." Her voice was low. "Really amazing."

Zac looked down at herself, nervous fingers rolling the hem of her bright white undershirt between long, strong fingers. She grinned at Abel. "Really? I'm afraid to move. I might get dirty again."

Abel laughed and reached out to straighten Zac's shirt before looking into her eyes. "Yes, really. If you'll let me, I want to take your other clothes home with me and wash them. Is that okay?" She ran a hand over Zac's shoulders, smoothing out the material of the shirt. "You definitely clean up nicely."

"Well, if my taking a bath makes you smile so much, I might just have to do it everyday!"

Chapter Ten

Zac was happy as a cucumber as she swung their joined hands back and forth, grateful Spinney hadn't pulled away when she'd reached for her hand just like when they were little. She was so happy, despite her earlier embarrassment.
She looked at Spinney who caught her eye and immediately began to giggle. "What?" Zac asked, her free hand thrown up in the air in exasperation. "I thought it looked nice."
"Zac, I didn't give you the can of shaving cream so you could make tree art." She grinned, biting her lip. "Though you're talented with it, I must say."
"It looked pretty." Zac smiled big, totally aware that it would get her out of trouble.
"You're so adorable," Spinney said with a grin, squeezing Zac's hand tighter and getting a squeeze in return.

※ ※ ※ ※

As they walked on, Abel couldn't get the picture out of her head from earlier that morning. She had decided to try and navigate her way through the forest to Zac's place, and along the way, had seen small signs that someone had been there. Then it became clear who. On a tree trunk just ahead of her had been the image of a squirrel in white cream. Shaving cream, to be exact. On the trunk next to it was a sun. Next to it a smiley face. All over the place, tree after tree, large rock after large rock. Never had the forest smelled so good.

She literally fell to the ground laughing, only to be helped up by two large, competent hands. Now as they walked, she felt close to Zac. They had been spending nearly every single minute together over the past five weeks, and she loved it, relished it and was glad to have her friend back. Whether she realized it or not, she had missed Zac's quiet strength. She had always felt completely safe as a five-year-old child, and still did as a nineteen-year-old woman.

"Zac?"

"Hmm?" Zac led them through patterns of trees and foliage, pointing out different kinds of plants to her companion, explaining their properties.

"Whatever happened to the overalls you always used to wear?" Abel asked, looking up at her taller friend. She smiled when the bright blue eyes met hers.

"I outgrew 'em."

"Want some more?" She remembered how much Zac had loved those. She would play with the clasp when she was bored or nervous, doing and undoing the shoulder part.

Zac grinned at her and nodded. "I doubt they'd fit anymore though." She winked, and Abel giggled, making Zac light up like a Christmas tree.

"They make them for adults, too, you nut."

"You're kidding?"

"Nope." Abel shook her head. "Annnnd..." She looked up at the person who was quickly becoming her best friend, her eyes twinkling. "I'll get you some if you meet my family." She raised her eyebrows in challenge. She wasn't above bribery to get Zac to give her family a chance.

"Oh, Spinney...I don't... I don't know." Zac looked away.

Abel stopped and grabbed Zac's arm. "Zac, listen. I know you haven't had much contact with other people, and I know your father scared you to death when it came to other people, but that's over now." She looked deep into those azure eyes. "No one's going to hurt you." Her voice was soft as she stroked Zac's arm.

"I wouldn't know what to do," Zac admitted, looking down at her boots, her shoulders falling.

"Honey, I know it's hard for you." Abel smiled and tried to look as reassuring as she could. "But you can't hide out here forever. I know how capable you are, and how special you are. I want to be able to share that. My dad asks about you constantly. I still don't think he believes you exist." She laughed.

Zac's smile was small. "Your mom can testify to that."

"Yeah, well, she misses you, too."

"Really?" Zac raised her eyebrows in surprise.

Abel nodded. "Yep. Just think," she said sweetly, trying to entice. "Your very own pair of grown up overalls..." She flashed smiling green eyes up at Zac, who was glaring at her.

"Oh, that's not fair," Zac growled.

"Life isn't fair. Please, please, please?" she begged, her bottom lip jutting out for emphasis.

Zac pursed her lips, studying Abel's face, making her sweat it out. "Oh, fine!"

"Yay!" Abel jumped in the air and clapped her hands together.

Zac smiled at the antics, but her nerves were

showing through like crazy.

Abel calmed herself, and took her friend in a hug. "Thank you, Zac. You have no idea what this means to me." Her voice was soft.

Zac closed her eyes as her body was swallowed up by Abel's enthusiastic hug and nodded.

Abel squeezed a bit tighter. It was their first hug, and she was enjoying it.

≈≈≈≈

"So, why exactly are we making a big deal out of this?" Adam asked, as he diced up veggies for a salad.

"Because it's important to Abel." Sherry tossed a piece of carrot into her mouth.

"No, get away from my veggies!" Adam swatted her hand and she giggled. "But still. This kid just seems weird to me. And what the hell kind of name is Zac for a girl, anyway?"

"I didn't name her, honey," Sherry said as she busied herself with opening a can of Pillsbury biscuits, and setting them evenly spaced on the cookie sheet. "But she's a nice girl. And Abel just adores her." She looked over at Adam who continued to cut vegetables. "I think you'll like her, honey. Besides, she saved both our girls, huh?"

With a sigh, he nodded. "I guess. I just don't get why we have to continue buying her clothes," he grumbled, nearly missing the tomato and slicing his finger instead.

"We're not. Abel has paid for most of it, and don't be such a Scrooge."

≈≈≈≈

"Okay, now remember, we can leave at any time, okay?" Abel held Zac's hand as she reminded her friend for the fifth time since they'd left Zac's lean-to. They were headed toward the Cohen cabin where the entire clan was waiting to meet the mysterious Zac. Becky was bouncing in her mother's arms, a huge grin on her cherubic features.

※※※※

"She comin'?" she asked, over and over again.
"Yes, honey. Zac's coming." Sherry looked to her family, the two boys looking bored out of their minds sitting at the picnic table outside the cabin. "You two behave yourselves," she scolded once again.
"Yeah, we know," the boys said in unison. Just then, Sherry heard footsteps, and turned toward the trees to see her daughter and her friend walk out, almost like Sasquatch in public view, so elusive was Zac. Abel was holding Zac's hand and was whispering something to her. Poor Zac looked like she was about to jump out of her skin.
"Zac!" Becky squealed, squirming in her mother's arms to get down.

※※※※

"Hey, kiddo." Zac smiled, yet fully aware of the five pairs of eyes trained on her. She gave Spinney's hand a final squeeze then released it.
"Welcome, Zac," Sherry said, putting the little blonde fireball down.
Becky ran to her new friend and was wrapped up

in strong arms and looking into those blue eyes again.

"Hi," the little girl said with a big, bright smile, which Zac returned.

"Hi. How are you? Are you minding your mom better now?" Zac asked.

Becky nodded, her little voice gravely serious. "I don't go far no more," she said, small fingers entwining themselves in Zac's new sweatshirt.

Zac smiled, warmed by the reception from the adorable little girl and the comfort of Spinney's hand on her back.

"Hello, Sherry," she said quietly. She felt okay around the older blonde, she seemed nice.

"Hi there," Sherry said with a welcoming smile. "It's so good to see you again. And you look wonderful!" She looked Zac over.

"Zac, this is my father, Adam," Spinney said, garnering Zac's attention.

Adam walked toward them, hand extended.

Zac looked at it, then remembered something she'd seen once. She grabbed it and squeezed, quickly pumping it up and down.

"Uh, hi, Zac," Adam said, his face registering the pain of Zac's exceedingly tight grip. "How are you?"

"Good," she said with a smile, though her voice was weak at best.

"Good, good," he said as he took his hand back, cradling it with his other.

Spinney was quite obviously hiding a grin. She cleared her throat and turned to her brothers who were standing by their father.

"This is Ben. The one you saw in diapers."

The blonde boy took a step forward, giving Zac the once over. "Hi," he said, avoiding the handshake.

"Hi, Ben. You've grown up," Zac greeted. He stood almost as tall as she was, and was already a handsome kid. He had the barest bit of peach fuzz forming over his upper lip and near his sideburns.

"Jake, say hi to Zac." Spinney put her hand on her youngest brother's shoulder.

"Hi," he said with a small wave.

"And finally, my sister, Rachel."

The small girl with strawberry blonde hair smiled up at Zac. "Hi, Zac. It's nice to meet you." The girl was pretty, but not as much as her sisters. She was shorter, but larger framed than Spinney.

"Um, nice to meet you." Zac swallowed hard. She felt like she was getting closed in.

"Zac, you gonna go swimmin' with us today?" Becky asked, her arms wrapping around one of Zac's legs.

Zac looked to Spinney, no idea what to do. "Oh, um, I'll watch."

"Yay!" Becky cheered, giving Zac's leg a squeeze.

"Beck, behave," Sherry warned. She turned a warm smile to their guest. "You sure do look pretty, Zac. All cleaned up with new clothes."

"Oh." Zac looked down at herself. "Um, thank you. For everything."

"You're welcome, honey. Any time," Sherry said, with a gentle smile.

"So, you do exist, eh?" Adam said with a light chuckle.

"Um," Zac muttered. Sweat began to gather between her breasts and down her spine. She felt hot and almost faint. "Yes, I do."

"Dad," Spinney hissed. "Be nice."

"What? I am being nice."

"Um." Zac wiped sweat from her brow.

"Are you okay, Zac?" Spinney asked, rubbing slow circles over Zac's back.

"I ... I need to go." Zac turned and disappeared into the trees.

Spinney hurried after her.

"Was it something I said?" Adam asked, the last words Zac heard before she took off.

୬୧୬୧

"Zac! Zac, wait up!" Abel ran after her fleeing friend. Zac slowed, allowing Abel to catch up. She turned Zac to face her, her hand on Zac's arm. "Are you okay?" she panted, the chase leaving her breathless.

Zac nodded, then looked off toward the lake. "I'm sorry, Spinney. I tried." She looked back at Abel, tears brimming in her eyes.

"Oh, Zac." Abel rubbed Zac's bicep. "Don't apologize. You did great. I'm sorry I dragged you to the cabin." She chewed her lower lip. "Maybe that wasn't so fair."

"No, it's okay. I know you've wanted me to meet your family for fourteen years, Spinney. I wasn't gonna let you down, again."

"Oh, Zac." Abel looked up at this woman who she realized was quickly becoming very important to her. "You could never disappoint me. Okay?" She studied those incredible blue eyes until she saw acceptance. With a smile, she grabbed Zac's hand and they began to walk, both silent as they absorbed their own thoughts.

୬୧୬୧

Zac almost felt the need to puff out her chest she was so happy with herself. She made Spinney happy and mustered the courage to meet her family, even if she didn't stay for the planned lunch. That was okay. She seriously doubted she would have been able to eat, anyway. The Cohen bunch seemed to be nice enough people, though in truth, she likely wouldn't recognize any of them up close again, she'd been so nervous.

"Zac?" Abel asked after about fifteen minutes of walking.

"Hmm?"

"Do you think you'd ever want to see a city? Or live in one?"

Zac thought about that for a moment. She had never even thought of a city, or living in one. While on the rails she had passed through some, seen some pretty darn big buildings, too. "I don't know, Spinney. I just don't know."

"Do you think you'll live here forever?"

Zac swung their clasped hands between them as they walked. "Maybe. Will you come visit me?" She grinned.

"Oh, gosh I don't know," Abel teased. "Maybe once in a great while." She grinned up at her friend. "You should stay in the cabin with us this summer," she offered lightly.

"Why?" Zac asked, truly perplexed. After all, she had her own home and was quite comfortable there.

"Why not?" Abel countered. "It's cooler in the day, warmer at night, and you can have all the syrup you want." She grinned

"Oh, that's not nice, Spinney." Zac wagged her finger and clicked her tongue. "You said I could have all the syrup I wanted, anyway." She raised a challenging eyebrow.

"Oh, damn. I did say that, didn't I? Hmm..." Abel chewed her lip. "Okay. I'll buy you a huge thing of foil?" She gave Zac a huge, toothy grin, which made her friend match it.

"I don't think that would be a good idea, Spinney," she said, all kidding out of her voice. "If I freak out during a simple lunch..." She kicked a rock, feeling disappointed in herself, and angry that she couldn't be like Spinney.

"Hey, it's okay. Just a suggestion. And totally selfish on my part," Abel said with a sheepish grin. "No worries, my friend. Ohh!" She let go of Zac's hand and ran toward the edge of the bluff. "I've seen this before on another walk." Zac stepped up behind her. "What is it?" Abel asked.

"It's an old, abandoned logging town." Zac's voice held a touch of fear. "My dad used to call it Spectreville."

"Spectreville? Why?"

"Because it's haunted."

"Haunted? Zac, there's no such thing as ghosts," Abel assured her.

"Sure there is. I hear them at night." Zac looked at her with frightened eyes.

From where they stood, wind chimes that were placed all over the town could be seen. Though most were broken or hanging limply, they were still able to make noise.

"Does it scare you during the day?"

Zac shook her head, her gaze locked on the old town below them. "Not as bad."

Abel tucked her bottom lip beneath her top teeth for a moment. "Well, if you feel okay about it, will you show me?" She looked up at her friend with pleading green eyes.

Zac met her gaze for a long moment then, with a smile, nodded and they found a way down.

≈≈≈≈

Abel listened intently as Zac weaved a tale of history.

"In 1830, this was a shanty town set up so loggers would have somewhere for their families to live." Zac led her through the quiet town, hushed from years of disuse. "And then it began to expand and actual buildings were built. By 1870, it was a full-out town."

Abel ran her hand over a wooden sign that had fallen and now leaned against the dilapidated building it had once been anchored to. "Pyre's Liquor," she read, much of the white paint peeled or gone.

"My great-grandfather worked at the mulching mill." Zac tried to rub the grime off the label of a glass bottle with her thumb. "He was killed."

"How?" Abel asked as she poked through a pile of random items, including a chair, kindling, and a man's leather shoe.

"The mulching machine went haywire one day," Zac explained, snapping her fingers. "Died just like that. They say he didn't even know what hit him."

"I'm sorry, Zac," Abel said quietly, walking over to her friend and studying the bottle Zac held.

Zac shrugged, tossing the unreadable bottle to the ground. "I never knew him. He was on my mom's side."

Zac was so matter of fact about it, Abel was surprised. Usually, her friend seemed to feel things on such a deep level, things that Abel wouldn't even notice. One time, for instance, Zac found a robin's egg on the ground, the crack in the shell making it evident that the little one within was already dead, or didn't stand a chance of survival. Zac had carefully picked up the egg and buried it, her blue eyes–similar to the shade of the shell–brimming with tears. So compassionate and kind. She knew how much Zac loved animals, and was always awed by how much she knew. She could easily see Zac as a forest ranger or botanist, something... anything, to do with the outdoors. If only ...

Zac led her friend through the town, explaining from time to time what some of the buildings were, and what their original purpose had been. She was about to take her into the old saloon when she stopped, Abel nearly running into her from behind. Curled up in the corner of the large, dusty room, was a form. He was covered in a tattered coat, head nearly totally buried. All that could be seen was a tuft of dark, greasy hair.

She quickly turned and moved Spinney back out into the dusty and weed-riddled street. "Um, let's move on, Spinney. This doesn't look so sound, huh?"

Abel nodded. "Who was that?"

Zac shrugged, glancing over her shoulder. "Dunno. Sometimes the homeless or teenagers come here to do whatever."

"Oh." Abel's eyebrows fell as she thought about that. "Not very safe." As they walked on, she remembered something. "Oh, Zac!" Abel stopped.

"Yeah?"

"I have something for you. Come on, before it gets dark."

With one final look at the ghost town, Zac hurried after Abel, who was jogging towards the way they'd come.

※.※.※.※

Abel sat Zac on the log while she ran back to the cabin to grab her surprise. Nearly out of breath, she ran back, panting, a painful stitch pulling at her side. "Here," she huffed, handing the large bag to her stunned friend. "Well, look!" Abel exclaimed, excited for Zac's reaction.

Zac set the bag on the ground between her feet and pulled out a folded garment. She stood, grabbed an end, and let it unfold down to her feet. It was a heavy, canvas pair of overalls. Her eyes were huge as she looked at Abel.

"What do you think?" Abel nervously chewed her fingernail.

"They're wonderful!" Zac put the garment up to her body and looked at her friend again. "How do you think they'll fit?"

"I think they'll look great on you. They should be nice and warm this winter, too. These are the same kind that farmers and folks who work outside wear." She crossed her arms over her chest and looked at Zac with accusatory eyes. "Since someone I know is so damn stubborn she'll stay in a virtual tent!" Abel could feel her hackles rising again, but knew it was born out of worry.

Zac smiled with infinite patience. "I know. Now let me peruse my gifts in peace."

"I'm sorry." Biting her lower lip to keep her mouth shut, Abel sat on the log.

"S'okay," Zac said then gave her a heart-melting smile. Carefully refolding the overalls she set them in Abel's lap. She reached into the bag a second time and brought out a large box with a flat lid on top. She looked at the picture on the side, and her face lit up. "No way," she breathed, and quickly tore the lid off.

"I tried to guess on a size. If they don't fit, please tell me and I'll exchange them." Abel said, watching intently, her body nearly bouncing on the log with excitement at Zac's obvious anticipation and delight.

Like a five year old who had received a coveted bicycle, Zac sat on the log next to Abel, and shoved off her boots. She quickly reached into the box with the Columbia boots logo on the side and grabbed one. She studied it, holding it up in awe.

"I've never had new ones before," she breathed, inhaling the smell of the new leather. Abel watched, amazed, and somewhat saddened. She relished in Zac's excitement and enthusiasm, but felt bad Zac had lost out on so many simple things in life. A new pair of boots for crying out loud! How many pairs of new shoes had Abel had in her nineteen years? Many, many pairs. Yet, here was Zac, twenty-years-old, who never had the pleasure... until today.

"Can I, um . . ." Zac chewed her lip, stealing glances at her friend.

"Yes. Put them on." Abel took the other out of the box and removed the tissue paper from within the toe then laced the long laces before handing the boot over.

Zac didn't hesitate. Shoving her socked foot into the new boot, she sighed. "Wow," she said, grinning like an idiot at her friend. "Thank you so much, Spinney," she whispered, and leaned over to give Abel a one-armed hug.

Abel gladly returned it and smiled. "You're very

welcome. But, there's more. You dig while I lace your other boot."

Zac nodded and dug further into the bag as Abel knelt in front of her, lacing the second boot. The boots were high, ending about four inches above Zac's ankles. She wanted to make sure that Zac had lots of support as she climbed around the woods. Plus, they'd be really warm for her. The guy at the store had promised that these boots were the absolute best for the conditions Abel had described to him.

Zac exclaimed over the pair of thick, heavy gloves she found, and the ski cap, and then the heavy winter coat. This stopped her cold. It was so beautiful– a light gray color, almost white, matching the gloves and hat, sure to camouflage her in the snow in the winter.

"This should keep you warm. It's lined with goose down," Abel explained, rubbing her fingers over the quilted inside.

"Wow," Zac breathed. "Put it on. Let's see." Abel watched with a critical eye as Zac tried on the coat. The sleeves were just slightly long for her, but not enough to make an exchange. "You look great. How does it feel?" She pushed up from the log and walked around her, tugging at various parts of the jacket, making sure Zac could move well in vital areas.

"It's warm." Zac grinned, moving her arms and rolling her shoulders. "I love it."

"Yay!" Abel clapped happily, and roamed around to the front of Zac. She made sure the zipper worked, and snapped the covering flap so Zac was all bundled up. When she felt okay that Zac would in fact be warm over the winter, she gushed, "There's more, there's more!"

At Zac's squeal of delight, Abel watched as she

pulled out not one, not two, but *four* Audubon Society books, the subjects covering North American birds, plants, animals and fish.

"Oh, Spinney," Zac breathed, caressing the slick covers of each of the small, heavy books in turn. She looked at Abel with wonder in her bright, blue eyes. "Thank you." She put them gently back in the bag, and Abel found herself nearly bowled over by Zac's enthusiastic hug.

"You're welcome," Abel whispered into her ear.

They parted and Zac looked up into the cloudy sky, raising her face and closing her eyes. She took in a deep breath. "You should go, Spinney," she said softly, opening her eyes and looking at Abel.

"What? Why?"

"There's a big storm coming."

Abel creased her brows and looked into the sky to figure out what Zac had seen. "How do you know? I mean, the sky is a little gray, but ..." She grinned over at Zac. "You secretly watch the Weather Channel in that home of yours?" Abel teased.

Zac grinned, shaking her head. "I can smell it. It'll be raining within ten minutes. I don't want you stuck in it." She began to pile everything into the bag Spinney had brought, getting it ready to go.

"You're serious?" Abel watched, hand on her hip.

Zac nodded. "Very."

"Zac, I'm a big girl. I think I can handle a little bit of rain." She drew her brows in irritation.

"Spinney, we always get at least one big rain storm each summer. This is it. Please listen to me. It's getting dark as it is. Please?"

Abel studied her friend, arms crossed over her

chest, her irritation melting into acceptance. She knew that Zac was only telling her this for her own good, and she trusted her. Finally, she nodded.

"Okay. Come with me? To the lake," she quickly added at Zac's panicked look.

"To the lake."

As they walked, hand in hand, Abel looked up at Zac. She studied her profile and the determined set of her jaw. She looked worried or concerned, but Abel figured it was just for her own welfare. Zac was like that, always worried about others before herself. She smiled, enjoying their time together. All the things she'd learned from and about Zac in a short time was amazing. But then, she reasoned, Zac was one of the most amazing people she'd ever known. She was as kind as she was beautiful, and her intellect astounded Abel all the time. How was it that, this child of the wild could possess so much self-awareness and intelligence? Every bit was self-taught, and Abel was impressed every time she laid eyes on Zac. It was all there in those stunningly blue eyes, Zac's soul laid out for all to see and experience.

Zac glanced over at her. "What? Why are you staring at me?"

Abel shook her head, a content smile on her face. "Do you really like what I got you?" Abel asked, glancing at the bag that swung lazily from Zac's fingers.

"Yes. Very much so." Zac smiled happily, the worry leaving her face for a moment.

"Yay! I'm so glad." Abel looked up when she felt a raindrop land squarely on the bridge of her nose.

Zac smiled. "Told ya."

"Yeah, yeah." They finally reached the shore and Abel turned to her friend. "Zac, are you going to be okay?"

"Yeah. Why wouldn't I be?" Her brows furrowed in confusion.

"Okay, okay, I'll leave it be. I just worry about you" she said, poking Zac in the chest, smiling. "I'll see you tomorrow."

"'Kay. Goodnight."

"Night!" Abel called out as she began to run toward the house, the rain coming down in earnest.

༄༄༄༄

"I'm worried, Mom." Abel sat on the window seat in the kitchen, curled up in her sweats with a cup of hot cocoa in her hands. She stared out into the raging rainstorm.

"I know, sweetie, but you can't help her if she doesn't want to be helped, you know?" Sherry continued rolling dough for the pie she was making. "Did you give her the stuff you bought?"

"Yeah. She loved it," Abel said, the thrill she had felt earlier no longer in her voice. "She was so excited. Especially over the boots." She chuckled, looking out into the darkened sky again. The rain was pouring down in sheets, saturating everything in its wake.

༄༄༄༄

Abel shot up, ripped out of sleep for some reason. Breathing heavy, her heart pounding, she looked around her large, third-floor bedroom. It was dark, only offset by the seemingly continuous bolts of lightning. The things in her room were given strange shadows and shapes, the gauzy curtains in the windows turning near white with each strike.

Throwing the covers aside, she hurried over to the window and looked out. The rain was still coming in torrents, causing leaves to rip from trees and mud droplets to pop up from the ground with its force. The wind was blowing, howling through the rafters under the shingles of the cabin, sounding lonely and desperate.

"Zac!" Abel gasped, jumping up and pulling on her sweats and tennis shoes.

Abel ran down the two flights of stairs. The house was quiet, everyone in bed. As she ran through the house, she grabbed a large garbage sack from under the kitchen sink, tucking it into her shirt, and heading out into the immense storm. She covered her head instinctively as a massive crash of thunder split the sky in two, rocking the forest and rattling Abel's bones with its power.

"God," she breathed as she hurried through the maze of trees, the way instinctual as she thought of her friend. She had the distinct feeling that Zac was in trouble, even though she knew what *she* was doing was also not safe.

Abel pushed wet bangs out of her eyes as she pushed through even wetter foliage. At the rock outcropping that usually housed her friend, she nearly screamed when she saw most of the tarp was gone.

"Zac!" she cried, trying to be heard over the freight-train volume of the wind. "Zac!" She hurried around the rocks and found her friend huddled, trying to push the ropes back into the ground that held her lean-to together.

Zac was soaked to the bone, her sweatshirt sticking to her like a second skin. Her long hair was twisted and plastered to her head. Zac leaned over, a body-shaking cough erupting from her. "Spinney?" she wheezed, still trying valiantly to get her house back together. "Go home!"

"No! Not until you come with me!" Abel hurried inside, gathering as many of Zac's belongings as she could, shoving them into the plastic garbage bag, including the new coat. Tied securely shut, she hurried back out into the storm. Zac fell into the mud, slipping as she tried to hold on to the last piece of canvas she had.

"Let's go, Zac! You can't save it. Come on!" She yanked on Zac's hand, only for it to be pulled away. "Dammit, Zac! Don't be so stubborn. You can die out here, now come on!"

She pulled one more time, this time getting her friend to her feet. She held on as best she could, the wet plastic nearly slipping from her grasp, but somehow she managed to keep hold of both her prizes. She could hear Zac coughing over the raging wind and rain as she hurried them through the forest to the warmth and safety of the cabin.

Abel nearly cried out in relief when she saw the cabin come into view. "Almost there, honey!" she yelled back to her captive as they ran across the open space and onto the front porch. As Abel pushed Zac through the door, she could see how miserable she looked. She had heavy, blue bags under her eyes, her skin pale and wet. Her lips were blue as her teeth chattered.

"Oh, Zac. Damn, why didn't you come home with me? Let's get you into a hot bath. Come on." She dropped Zac's stuff by the door, and helped remove her muddy boots. Removing her own shoes, Abel took

Zac by the hand and led her to the main bath on the first floor.

Looking very miserable and lost, Zac stood in the bathroom, her arms wrapped around herself and her teeth chattering so loudly Abel worried she'd chip one. Abel hurried over to the large bathtub and began to run a hot bath.

"Stay here. I'll be right back," she instructed, softly.

Cold herself, Abel hurried to the kitchen peeling off her socks as she went. They were muddy and wet and made her colder. She quickly put together the Mr. Coffee Hot Chocolate Maker, pouring in two cups of milk and two packets of Swiss Miss hot cocoa mix, then turned it on. She ran back to the bathroom, Zac standing exactly where she'd left her.

"Okay, lift your arms, honey."

Zac lifted her arms, her body trembling of its own accord from the bone-deep chill. Abel stretched on tiptoes to remove the saturated sweatshirt. She tossed it aside, removed another sweatshirt, then Zac's T-shirt. "Zac, honey, why didn't you wear your coat?" she asked, the growing pile of wet clothing making her angry. "It's water proof." She gazed up at Zac's face with disapproving eyes.

"I didn't want to ruin it," Zac managed, teeth still chattering.

"Oh, honey," Abel murmured, hugging Zac briefly. "I'd get you another one."

"I'm sorry, Spinney. I'll do better next time."

"Oh, Zac. I'm sorry, I'm just worried, okay?" Abel unbuttoned Zac's jeans and tugged at the wet denim until they were finally off. "Take your socks off and get into the water, okay?" With Zac's nod, Abel hurried into the kitchen and poured two mugs of steaming hot chocolate.

˙◈˙◈˙◈˙◈

As Spinney left the room, Zac turned to the tub, feeling extremely inadequate in the cabin. Standing in her soaked bra and panties, she couldn't remember being this cold in some time. In truth, she had actually been scared. The rain came down in torrents, rendering her shelter useless. When she went outside to try to secure her home, a mud slide started from the immense saturation of the ground. That was when things got worse.

Cold and covered with mud, Zac had done everything she could to save her home. She had been out in the storm for no more than fifteen minutes when Spinney found her. Sighing deeply, she was feeling sad and out of control. She tiptoed toward the tub, seeing and feeling the steam waft through the air. Even from three feet away she could feel it. Looking into the seemingly bottomless tub, she was amazed to see the water swirling and churning as it continued to flow out of the taps. Fascinated, she reached a hand out, her fingers pushed into the roaring spray as the water tumbled out of the faucet.

"Guess we should turn it off, huh?" Abel said softly from behind her. She set the mugs down on the side of the large tub and leaned across it, twisting the knobs to off. "Get in, Zac. It will warm you up," Abel encouraged.

Zac felt shy and vulnerable as she lifted a leg, hissing when the hot water met her foot. The irony was that out in the wild she had no issues with modesty, whatsoever. Right now, however, she wished she was clothed or that her nudity was hidden by the steamy water. She could feel Spinney's eyes on her, and that was adding to her nervousness.

"It won't seem so hot once you're in," Abel explained as she began to undress, her body trembling from her brief foray out in the storm. She stripped down then stepped into the hot water, too, moaning softly as it immediately began to warm her chilled skin.

Zac slowly lowered herself into the bath, taking Spinney's cue. The moment she was in, her eyes slid closed in pleasure as her ice-cold skin was surrounded by warmth.

"Feels nice, doesn't it," Abel said with a lusty groan as she, too, began to thaw. She watched her friend closely. Zac nodded, her eyes still closed.

"I know how to make it better. Open your eyes, Zac." Abel grabbed the two mugs of hot chocolate and handed one to Zac.

"What is it?" Zac asked, smelling the light brown creaminess that filled the mug. It smelled sweet.

"Hot chocolate. Do you like chocolate?" At Zac's enthusiastic nod, Abel chuckled. "You'll like this, then. But be careful, it's hot." Abel blew on the steaming liquid, watching over the rim of her cup to see Zac following her lead.

Zac looked down into the contents again before cautiously sticking the tip of her finger into the hot chocolate and tasting it with a quick swipe of her tongue. Her eyebrows rose and her eyes got big. "Ohhhhh, that's good," she exclaimed, a giant smile on her face. She took a sip and let out a contented sigh.

❧❧❧❧

Abel chuckled, and reached over to wipe a chocolate mustache off Zac's lip. "Hot cocoa is one of my favorite ways to warm up," she explained. "When we were kids, all four of us, before Beck was born, would go out and play in the snow for hours during winter break. My mom would have a whole line of mugs ready for us when we went in."

She glanced over at Zac, who sat no more than a foot away. She was sitting up enough that the water level hovered just beneath her breasts, which were nearly exposed as naked flesh under the saturated material of her bra. Her gaze was snagged by the hard, dark nipples that pushed against the fabric. Not the first time she'd ever seen Zac's breasts, but for some reason, looking at Zac sitting there with her slicked back wet hair, wet skin, and the tease of her breasts, Abel felt a sudden flush stain her cheeks. Looking at Zac now, it would be easy to think she was an average woman reclining in a hot bath. Perhaps she was a college student, or perhaps the waitress at the local diner. In those steam-filled moments, she looked like nothing more than a gorgeous woman who was as normal or average as anyone else.

Abel looked away, feeling shy and ashamed that she'd been studying what was visible of Zac's body. She wasn't even sure why she had, as that body not only belonged to a woman, but to Zac, of all people– her best friend! She was pulled from her thoughts when Zac nearly blew out her sip of cocoa through her nose as she began a string of intense sneezes.

"Oh, Zac," Abel whispered, setting her mug aside as she scooted closer to the miserable woman, reaching out and rubbing her back. "Damn it, Zac. Why don't you try and take care of yourself?" As she saw her friend's misery, she felt her own anger build. "What if I hadn't shown up, Zac? What then, huh?"

Zac accepted the large wad of bathroom tissue Abel handed her to wipe her nose.

Abel watched as several emotions seemed to take over Zac's features, none of which were good. She realized she insulted Zac's fiercely independent nature. "Zac?" she asked, gently touching her friend's shoulder. Usually, Zac would almost melt into it, revel in it, but now it seemed as if she were fighting not to flinch from it. Abel removed her hand, letting it fall back into the warm depths of water.

"I can handle myself," Zac finally said. She was looking away now, presenting Abel with the back of her head.

"Honey," Abel began gently, bringing her hand up again and running her fingers through Zac's hair. "I know how proud you are and I know what an incredible job you do surviving and using that wonderful mind of yours to come up with all sorts of ingenious ways to make it." She paused, relieved when Zac again seemed to melt back into her touch. Even still, she felt her emotions rising again. "You didn't even wear the jacket that I bought you." Abel could feel her own anger rising. "Why not? I know what you said, but Zac, that's what it's for! What happens if you get sick when I'm not here? What happens if you get caught up in another storm like that? And then there's no one there to save you or help you!" She was nearly yelling in frustration and worry by the time her tirade was over.

The look on Zac's face nearly made Abel cry.

"Don't you think I know what I'm doing?" There was so much pain in that simple question. "After my whole life spent out on my own, you don't think I can do it?" The look turned to one of frustration and hurt. She looked down, her long, dark, wet strands of hair providing a curtain to hide her profile.

Abel looked at her for a long moment before her heart sink. She realized what she had done. Though her intentions were pure, by questioning her friend's abilities, she had questioned everything about Zac. Her survival, her pride, all she had. She felt the sting behind her eyes as her heart swelled, ready to burst with shame and regret. "Zac?"

Zac didn't respond for a long moment, her jaw muscles working. Finally she raised her head and looked at Abel, repeating her earlier question. "Don't you think I know what I'm doing? How do you think I've survived all these summers, winters, and everything in between, Spinney?" Her voice was soft, slightly edged, but mostly filled with pain.

Abel nodded, Zac's soft words reaching in and grabbing her heart. She suddenly had a very new respect for Zac and realized she needed to stop trying to save her. Zac was doing just fine.

"You're right," Abel whispered, unable to keep the tears from her eyes anymore. One of them lazily slid down her cheek, but before it could fall from her chin, Zac caught it. "I'm sorry, Zac. So sorry."

"No, Spinney," Zac said gently, catching another tear. "I overreacted."

Abel could easily see Zac didn't feel that way but that she was simply trying to make her feel better. She gave her a loving smile and briefly cupped Zac's face with a warm hand. "No, Zac. No, I was wrong. You're absolutely right. I had no right to question you and I'm so sorry. Please forgive me?"

Zac nodded.

With a sigh of relief, Abel flung herself at her, taking her in a massive, crushing hug, their near-naked breasts pressed together. "Thank you."

❧❧❧❧

Water swept over the edge of the tub with the force of the hug, and Zac was nearly left breathless. She started at the shock sent through her body as Spinney's breasts pressed against her own, surprised by the strange sensation that shot to her lower belly. She pushed the unfamiliar reactions away as she closed her eyes, feeling her friend cry against her shoulder.

"Don't cry, Spinney," she soothed, rubbing Abel's back. "Please don't cry."

"I insulted you," Abel said, burying her face in Zac's neck. "I'm sorry."

"Shh. It's okay." Zac rested her head against Spinney's as she allowed herself to absorb the incredible feeling of their flesh touching. She'd never felt so much of a body against her before. It left her with confused feelings.

"No," Abel said, shaking her head. She sniffled and ran the back of her hand across her eyes and nose. "I shouldn't have interfered. I was just so worried about you, Zac. God, now that we found each other again, I could lose you." Fresh tears began to spring forth, Abel's efforts to wipe them away failing.

"I'm not going anywhere, Spinney. You're stuck with me as your 'wild child' friend." She grinned and Spinney laughed through her tears. Zac stroked Abel's long blonde hair, enjoying the texture between her fingers.

After several minutes, Abel got herself under control. She scooted away from Zac and gave her a shy smile as she reached for some more toilet paper, this time for her. "I'm sorry." She sniffled. "I got kind of carried away. I just got really scared tonight, Zac. It killed me knowing you were out in that."

Zac nodded in understanding. "It's okay. Thanks for caring."

Abel smiled and squeezed Zac's hand. They were both quiet for a moment.

Finally, Zac broke the silence. "What's your college like, Spinney?" Her voice was soft as she relaxed into the water once again and sipped her forgotten drink.

"Well, I don't know. I guess it's nice."

"Tell me about it?"

"Sure."

As Abel began to talk about her school, her classes and the people she knew, Zac found that she was feeling jealous of all these people. She wanted so badly to be more involved in Spinney's life, and not just every six months when she came back to the cabin. She knew there was no way to, but she still wished it.

"You should go to college, Zac. You're very smart. I bet you'd do well," Abel set her empty mug aside and added hot water to the cooling bath.

"Oh." Zac ducked her head, peering at her friend through her bangs. "I couldn't."

"Why not? I bet you'd kick ass," Abel said, grabbing Zac's empty mug and placing it on the side of the tub next to hers.

"I never went to school, Spinney. I don't have

a diploma. Everything I've learned was from reading, and even that I taught myself." She shrugged her broad shoulders. "I wouldn't know what to do." Zac sneezed and didn't stop.

"Oh, honey. I bet you caught a cold out there." She rubbed Zac's back as she continued to sneeze then cough. "Here," she said gently as she handed her more tissue to blow her nose. Zac looked miserable. "Let's get you into bed," Abel said gently as she stood, the water draining down her body as she grabbed a towel. Stepping out, she wrapped it around herself and tucked it in so it would stay, then held open a big, fluffy towel." Come here."

Zac stepped into Abel's embrace, allowing her to wrap the towel around her. She felt like shit, and just wanted to go home. Then she remembered there really wasn't a home to go to. This made her feel even crappier.

Chapter Eleven

After much arguing, Abel finally put Zac to bed. She took her to the third floor and into her own bed. She was worried as Zack's cough was getting worse, and she seemed to be running a fever. She was pale, and beginning to sweat heavily.

Once they'd arrived in her bedroom with towels still wrapped around them, she found Zac an oversized T-shirt of hers, as well as a pair of sweatpants. Though they were short on Zac, they fit her slim hips well enough. Dressed in another T-shirt and pair of shorts, Abel used her own body heat to try to keep Zac warm.

Initially it had been amusing watching Zac get used to a real mattress and real blankets. The look of amazement and comfort would have been extremely amusing if Abel hadn't been so concerned for her health. She lay with her friend, listening to her breathe. As she spooned Zac, she thought about the events of the day. They'd had such a wonderful time. Abel loved how knowledgeable Zac was about the forest, and even the state of Maine. She loved to listen to her stories and history lessons and what she knew about the animals and plants of the Wachiva Forest.

She sighed. She enjoyed having Zac so close, knowing that she was okay and safe. The thought of her friend trying to stay warm over the winter nearly drove her to distraction. She was beginning to learn just how stubborn Zac could be, but she was beginning to understand that Zac's pride was all she had and she would have to learn to respect that. Pulling Zac closer against her, she finally drifted off.

Chapter Twelve

*I*t was a day like any other, nothing special about it. Bud Lipton was out scouring God knew what, leaving his eleven-year-old daughter at the cabin to do whatever. Zac hummed softly to herself as she swept off the rickety old porch, the boards uneven and buckling in places, yet still solid. She looked out over the forest, a smile on her face. She would go bird watching later. Until then, she took the broom back inside, hanging it on the old, rusted nail she had found. Trying to decide between staying inside and reading, or going outside and exploring, she decided to go outside. Maybe bird watching would start early.

She grabbed the old pair of binoculars that were held together with a weathered piece of duct tape. They were Army green, swiped by her father from her grandfather's World War II gear. Continuing her humming, she hitched up her overalls and headed out. Grabbing the empty canteen from the nail on the outside wall–intent on filling it in the lake–the young girl stopped and listened. She craned her neck, hearing something. There it was again. Not too far in the distance she heard footsteps, though they were uneven footsteps, as if the owner were limping or dragging a foot. Finally, a man emerged from the trees. He looked haggard and dirty, but had small, alert, dark eyes. It took a moment before she recognized him. His long, graying hair gave him away as the man who worked with her father from time to time.

When he spotted Zac, he grinned, showing rotting, crooked teeth. "Hi there," he said, his voice slightly lispy from the teeth he was missing.

Zac said nothing, just watched as he approached. The hair on the back of her neck was beginning to stand up on end, and she was about to run when he moved faster.

"My dad isn't here!" she cried out as he grabbed her.

"Oh yeah?" he grinned down at her. "You're the pretty one, ain't ya?" he said, grabbing her by the left strap of her overalls as she tried to get away from him again.

The move caused her to fall to the ground. The binoculars and canteen flew across the forest floor, out of her reach. She scrambled to a sitting position, not wanting her back to be to this guy for a minute.

"Leave me alone!" she panted, trying to crab crawl away from him.

"Come 'ere, you," he growled, jumping on her and pinning her down. "Your dad owes me money, you little bitch."

She could feel the heavy weight of his body and smell his sour breath on her face. Trying not to gag Zac looked around her, finally seeing a rock. Grabbing it, she brought it down, whacking him on the left temple.

"You little bitch!" he spat, a hand flying up to the wound. There was blood on his fingertips.

With a determined growl, he pulled himself up and straddled her tugging at the clasps of her overalls. Unclipping them, he began to rip at the material, trying to get them down the young, writhing body. His superior size and strength helped keep her under his physical control as he tugged off the denim overalls, leaving a mewling Zac in her flannel shirt and underwear.

"Ohhhh," he breathed, looking down at his conquest. He grabbed the waistband of the panties with his dirty fingers, leaving smudges on creamy white thighs and yanked them off. "Just becoming a woman," he moaned, his penis hardening in the baggy pants he wore.

"No, no!" Zac cried, trying to do her best to push him off, but he was big and determined. "Help!"

"Shut the fuck up!" He used the back of one meaty hand and slapped her across the face, making Zac's teeth rattle in her head.

She watched in horror as he reached down to unzip his pants.

"Hey!" a loud voice boomed, and before Zac knew what was happening, the man had been yanked off her, leaving her exposed to the sunny day.

She curled up within herself and watched as Abel's father grabbed the man by the back of his coat and threw him. He landed with a loud crash against a water barrel. Baring his teeth he stood and charged Bud Lipton.

As the fight began to move her way, Zac grabbed her clothing and scrambled to her feet, pulling her pants on and holding them to her. Her legs were shaky, almost giving out on her. She watched as Bud pummeled the man, sending more of his rotten teeth sliding across the dirt, splatters of blood raining on the ground.

Unable to watch anymore, Zac turned and ran.

꙲꙲꙲꙲

"No! No! Daddy!" Zac shot up, sweat pouring

down her face, hair plastered to her head. She looked around with wide, disoriented eyes and her breathing was heavy and labored.

"Zac?" Abel sat up, her own eyes wide from her bedmate's abrupt awakening and scream. She looked over to see that Zac was sitting up in bed, clutching the covers to her chest, her eyes open and wild. "Hey, honey. Zac. Are you okay?" She tried to put a comforting hand on Zac's back, but was pushed away.

"No! Don't touch me!" Zac cried out, fear lining her face. She looked as though she were about to bolt.

"Hey, Zac. Honey, it's me. Spinney." Abel tried to use the most calming voice she could, realizing that Zac wasn't completely awake yet and hadn't escaped whatever was dogging her nocturnal steps. "It's me."

Zac stared at her with a stranger's eyes, then suddenly blinked. "Spinney?" she said in the thinnest of voices. "Is that you?" The relief was unmistakable.

"Yeah. It's me." She reached out her hand again and placed it gently on Zac's arm. "Are you okay? I think you had a nightmare." When her touch wasn't rejected this time, she moved it up to Zac's forehead. "Oh, Zac. You're burning up. Come here." She opened her arms, and immediately Zac fell into them, her body trembling from the residual fear. "It's okay. I've got you," she whispered into Zac's ear. "I've got you."

≈≈≈≈

Zac melted into Spinney's embrace, craving the calm that her friend could always instill within her. She lay with her head on Spinney's shoulder and her arm draped across a flat stomach. She cuddled in a bit closer, even as her eyes closed and peace stole over her.

❧❧❧❧

The morning dawned, but he wasn't feeling particularly refreshed. Dark, beady eyes opened and he let out a heaving cough. He'd gone to sleep in one of the rundown buildings of the ghost town, often a place of sanctuary for him during his travels. Today, however, he found his blanket caked with mud, as well as the floor of the old barber shop. Sitting up, he grunted as he shoved the earth-heavy blanket off his rail-thin body, his long, gray hair also caked in mud. He reached behind his head, using long slender fingers to grab what he could of his hair and pulled it over his shoulder grimacing as it plopped obscenely into the thick mud that pooled up to his waist.

"This sucks," he grumbled, bracing a hand against the wall as he pushed shakily to his feet on one leg, the other fairly useless.

Looking down at what used to be his belongings he cursed under his breath and began to strategize in his mind, deciding what he'd do to get new supplies and where he'd go. Remembering where he was – even though it had been many years – he thought that perhaps he knew where he could get what he needed, plus a bit more. With an empty grin, his teeth long rotted out of his mouth, he carefully limped his way through the mud and headed to the doorway of the old building and the rain-fueled mess beyond.

❧❧❧❧

Zac turned out to have a pretty bad flu. She was in and out of delirium for the next day until her fever finally broke around six p.m., and this after Ben had been forced to go find the Piñon Mushroom that Zac kept calling for.

To the surprise of everyone, the mushroom actually made Zac feel better. She ate it raw, and within a few hours, her temperature had gone down. Abel was always there, ready with a cool cloth and liquids, and plenty of Kleenex. By the third day, Zac was doing much better and was getting restless. She was ready to get out of the suffocating confines of the house. She woke, feeling more like herself than she had for two days. When she opened her eyes, she found herself lying on her side in Spinney's big, comfortable bed with its owner curled up behind her. Abel's arm was tossed over her waist. She could feel Abel's warmth along the entire backside of her body. As she lay there with a mostly clear head, she allowed herself to look around the large room. The truth was, she hadn't slept inside a building since she was thirteen, and had never spent any time in another person's house.

It was strange to be staring at Spinney's belongings, from crumpled clothing on the floor to posters on the wall, to a stack of books lying on a corner table. She would be far more intrigued and curious if she wasn't feeling so claustrophobic. She tried to figure out how to get up without waking her friend. She needed to get out of there. Being cooped up for more than two days was beginning to really get to her. She needed fresh air and to try to find the rest of her house. The rain stopped the morning after it started, but Zac figured that a good four inches of water had been dropped, more than enough to put her in a very bad mood.

Carefully, she grabbed Spinney's wrist and moved

her arm. She waited to make sure her friend didn't wake up. *So far so good.* Slowly, she scooted her body toward the side of the bed, inch by inch, until she nearly fell off. Once her bare feet hit the soft carpet, she headed to the bathroom. Zac had to admit that the use of a toilet was so much easier than digging a small hole to cover in the woods, but she was used to it. This time in the cabin would be a short treat; a treat that will end today.

Looking at herself in the mirror above Spinney's sink, she saw how horrible she looked. Though, frighteningly enough, she looked a ton better than she had just the day before. Her skin wasn't as pale, nor her eyes as washed out and red. Her hair lay haphazardly all over her head, the strands wild and unkempt. She knew Abel would be after her to take a bath. Maybe she could leave before that happened.

Relieving herself, she made sure she used the toilet paper as her friend had instructed. Not sure whether she should flush, not wanting to wake Spinney up, she finally decided that another lecture from the girl wasn't worth it. She winced at the loud WHOOSH!

Padding out of the bathroom in a clean pair of Adam's sweats and another of Spinney's T-shirts, she looked around the room, relieved that Spinney hadn't woken. She had to smile though, when she saw that, in her sleep, Spinney had grabbed Zac's pillow and was hugging it.

She noticed that the clothing she'd been wearing the night of the storm was washed and folded neatly on the dresser. With another quick glance at her friend, she quickly and quietly got dressed. She tried to imitate how her clothes had been folded with those she had taken off, the sweats and T-shirt left in place of her own clothing. Dressed, she glanced over again at the bed. She was loathe to leave without saying goodbye, but she was also loathe to wake Spinney up and let her down by refusing to stay, as she knew her friend would try to convince her to do.

Spinney looked so peaceful and beautiful. Her long, blonde hair spread over her pillow, her face relaxed as she soared in the world of dreams. She cuddled up a bit closer to the pillow Zac had deserted, smacking her lips softly in comfort and contentment. So lost in watching Spinney in her peaceful slumber, she missed the fact that sleepy lids slowly opened to reveal the green depths behind.

"Zac?" Abel said, her voice thick from sleep. She raised herself a bit, looking around until she spotted her friend, who stepped beside the bed.

"Hi," Zac said, a small smile and wave following her simple greeting.

"What's wrong? Are you okay?" Abel asked as she sat up, bringing a hand up to rub her eyes. "Why are you dressed?"

"I'm going home today."

Sleep forgotten, the green eyes popped open. "What? Zac, please stay. Just one more night," Abel pleaded. "You're not well."

"I have to, Spinney," Zac softly explained, sitting on the side of the bed.

"You're going stir crazy, aren't you?"

Zac nodded. "I need some space. I desperately need some air."

"I'm sorry," Spinney said, looking down as she picked at the sheet with nervous fingers. Zac reached over and rested her hand on Abel's calf. "It's not you, Spinney. I could spend all day with you." She smiled warmly. "I have!" They shared a smile. "It's not your family, either. It's–"

"Just who you are," Spinney finished for her, a nod of understanding punctuating her words.

"Yes. It's just who I am and the situation. The cabin . . ."

"You can't be cooped up," Spinney whispered, as though she was finally getting it. "Okay. Are you sure, Zac? If you're still sick . . ."

"I feel much better. Really. Trust me, okay?"

Abel stared into those stormy eyes, so indicative of what she was feeling, and nodded.

"I'll miss you."

Zac smiled. "Spinney, you'll see me every day. And for your birthday." She smiled big, knowing that she had something cooking for the blonde.

"Thanks, Zac." Spinney smiled. She watched as Zac pushed up from the bed and grabbed the plastic trash bag that held her belongings. "Zac?"

Zac faced her at the door. "Yeah?"

"I really hope you know just how much I respect you. How much I know you're capable of." She gave her a small smile. "Sometimes maybe I try and 'civilize' you too much," she added, using her fingers as quote marks, "when you're just fine as you are."

Zac met her gaze for a long moment then smiled. "Thanks, Spinney," she said softly. "That means so much to me."

∿∿∿∿

Zac made her way through the forest, the garbage bag slung over her shoulder. She ran into Sherry on the way out, and admitted it was nice to see so many people sad to see her go. She'd accepted a quick hug from Spinney's mom, then was on her way. Though she still had somewhat of a cough, she felt glorious. She looked up into the trees, bright green from the moisture of the storm, the birds out, seemingly welcoming her back.

She closed her eyes and inhaled the smell of fresh, damp soil. That was one of her favorite smells of all time. When she opened her eyes again, she spotted something blue. Peering through the dense trees, she smiled again.

"There's one." Hurrying over to the tarp that was entangled in a tree, she set her bag of belongings down and gently pried the tarp loose. Now if she could find the canvas, she'd be in business. Heading to the lake, she left the tarp and her bag there then headed back into the woods.

※※※※

"Was it something we did?" Sherry asked as she sipped her coffee. She watched her oldest daughter preparing a large breakfast, complete with eggs, bacon, waffles and lots and lots of syrup.

Abel shook her head. "No. Zac just can't stand to be cooped up. A true wild child, Mom. The raised by the wolves kind." She glanced at her mother, then turned back to the stove and her eggs.

"I just absolutely hate the idea of her out there all alone, Abel." Sherry's brows drew, a worry line forming between them.

Abel smiled as she continued her preparations. "I know and I feel the same way. But, alas, No matter how much pleading and prodding, she's stubborn.

So I figure the least I can do is make sure she's fed." Turning the gas range off, she loaded the eggs onto the near overflowing plate then wrapped the entire thing with foil.

※※※※

"Got'cha!" Zac exclaimed, carefully climbing down the big pine with a muddy, wind-torn canvas. It may be damaged goods now, but she got it! Jumping down the last five feet, she landed with a grunt, then ran toward the lake. The sooner she could get these babies washed off the better.

※※※※

After taking a side trip to the lake to rinse off his body and things–clothes and all–he made his way towards familiar territory. He first saw the burnt ruins of the cabin, which of course brought a smile of satisfaction of a job well done to his chapped lips. Upon further inspection, he saw a rock overhang, which made for great shelter. Taking a closer look, he noted a circle of arranged rocks, singed from campfires. He noted a canteen that still hung from a sharp, jutting rock in the overhang, and what was left of a ruined bedroom that was covered in mud, molding material and leaves that had been tossed inside from the storm.

A rotted smile curved on his grizzled features.

"You've been here, you little bitch," he whispered. Eyes closed, he raised his face to the heavens and inhaled the scents of the day.

※※※※

Abel sang quietly to herself as she did her best to avoid the bigger mud puddles. She was amazed at just how green and fresh it was out. The rain had done something, because she felt a new vigor as she headed toward Zac's home. She was pleased that she had the offering she did. She smiled, knowing her friend would love it.

༄༅༄༅

Zac knelt down, trying her damndest not to end up bathing with the tarp as she scrubbed at the caked mud. Nearly growling with frustration, she turned her fingers to the laces on the new boots to take them off, but stopped. Head slightly cocked to the side, she listened trying to figure out what it was that made her stop in the first place. Kind of like when you wake out of sleep, but you don't know why.

There it was again. Footsteps, but, but…she tried to get a clear picture in her mind. They were heavy steps, but not normal, a dragging sound, limping, maybe? And another set of footsteps, light and carefree.

"Zac?" she heard Spinney's sweet voice carry on the breeze. The heavy, foreign footsteps stopped, and so did Zac's heart. Suddenly they started again, but at a run. Well, as good of a run as someone with a twisted leg could manage.

"Boogie Man," Zac hissed, then something struck in her, something animalistic and wild. She took off at a dead run toward the woods, tarp forgotten and teeth bared. Her eyes narrowed with hate and fear. She could feel the blood pounding through her head, a steady beat of a drum in her body, pushing her forward, all else forgotten.

※ ※ ※ ※

He stopped, a slow smile spreading across his features when he heard soft singing, not twenty yards from him.

"Gotcha," he whispered. He dropped his things and brushed wet gray strands of hair out of his eyes as he headed in the direction of the singing.

※ ※ ※ ※

Abel smiled as she continued on, her song forgotten for a few steps. She was excited to see Zac's face when she rolled the foil back from Zac's favorite foods, including about two pounds of syrup soaking everything! Happily, she began to hum.

※ ※ ※ ※

Zac felt everything slow to a trickle. Her breathing echoed through her head, her nose burned with the early morning air, coursing through her nostrils, down into her lungs, and spreading from there. Booted feet crushed everything in their path as she desperately tried to make it in time.

※ ※ ※ ※

He quickly ducked behind a tree, beady eyes watching. A cute little blonde trolled across the forest floor, a foil-covered dish in her hands.

"Where are you heading, my sweet?" he whispered. Perhaps he'd have a meal in a few different ways. With a pink tongue running over his chapped lips, he put his years of learned stealth to work.

☙❦❧

Scampering through the forest, Zac spotted the clearing and saw Spinney breaking through the trees to the right, completely oblivious to the danger. To the left she saw him. He was looking directly at Spinney, lust in his dark, predatory eyes. As she watched, he reached into his hip pocket and brought out a switchblade, the sunlight glinting off the metal as it flicked into view.

With an inhuman cry, Zac launched herself at him, just moments before he reached Spinney, knocking them both to the ground and falling head over heels with each other until finally she had him pinned. He looked up at her eyes filled with fear.

☙❦❧

Abel was nearly knocked off her feet from shock at both the man that had been about to plow into her, and the sight of Zac doing her best impression of Superman as she bowled the man over, knocking them to the ground.

"Zac!" she called out, her mind spinning in confusion.

☙❦❧

Zac began to pound on him, punching his face

and slamming his head into the soppy ground with each strike. Abel's eyes were huge with shock and fear as she watched her friend attack. This was not her Zac, though. This was someone else entirely. She was fierce, scary, and truly powerful.

※※※※

Zac grabbed his head, not daring to give him the chance to touch Spinney, raised it, and slammed it against the ground unaware there was a rock half-hidden in the earth. Again and again she slammed it, her rage far too strong for her to see the blood on the rock when she lifted it for another slam. His eyes rolled back, then closed, blood rushing from the corner of his mouth.

"Zac!" was screamed from somewhere far away, in another place. But Zac was in another time. She was saving Spinney. She was saving herself.

"Zac! Stop!"

She froze, looking down at what she was doing, then felt the rage seep from her pores as she looked into the terrified, pale face of her friend. She slowly stood, her eyes never leaving Spinney, which was nearly her undoing.

"Zac!" Abel screamed, too late.

He groaned, but managed to get to his feet, switchblade in hand. "You're gonna pay, bitch!" he roared, flinging himself at an unsuspecting Zac.

Again, the pair ended up on the ground, this time with him on top. He was straddling her hips, both hands wrapped around the handle of the switchblade as he tried to thrust it down into Zac's chest. Zac's teeth were bared as she fought him, using all her strength to keep the knife at bay.

⁂

Abel watched, horrified. Shaking herself out of her shocked state, the foil-covered dish clattered to the ground as she took off in a blur, screaming for her father as she sprinted back to the cabin.

⁂

Running out of options, Zac desperately tried to get him off her, but he wasn't having it. His determination to kill was equal to her determination to live. Finally, with a fierce growl she popped her head up as hard as she could, cracking their foreheads together. Though she was left woozy and feeling like she could vomit, no doubt just giving herself a concussion, his neck snapped backward, his forehead smudged with Zac's blood.

The brief reprieve gave Zac enough leverage to push him off. It was then that she realized that upon impact, he'd dropped the knife in the mud. She lunged for it, but he managed to get his wherewithal back in time to throw himself at the knife first.

⁂

Adam did his best to keep up with his frantic daughter as she led him through a maze of trees and ankle-deep mud. "Wait!" he called out, losing his breath and his way. "Abel, I don't know these woods like you do."

"I can't!" Abel yelled over her shoulder, running

full steam ahead. "You've got to help Zac!"

※※※※

Zac looked on with wide, stunned eyes. She stumbled back into a pool of mud, unable to take her eyes off him. He stared, his deeply-tanned face growing pale, making the grizzled beard he now sported seem to leap from his features. Both their gazes slid down his thin body to the handle that jutted from his chest. He coughed a few times, blood dribbling over his lips and chin.

Zac was horrified and crab crawled back a few steps, unable to take her eyes off the dying man. He met her gaze again, his filled with pleading and fear. A moment later, he fell over to his side, his face half-buried in the mud, eyes still open and hands–stained with his own blood–clutching the switchblade.

It was only then that Zac was able to breathe, even as she heard quick footfalls charging through the forest, followed by heavy breathing as the newcomers got closer. Zac sat frozen, unable to move, unable to look at Spinney and her father as they stepped into the clearing.

※※※※

"Oh my god!" Abel screamed. Her father turned her away from the carnage, burying her face in his chest. "Don't look," he whispered, eyes pinned to the dead man. A moment later, his gaze moved to Zac, who seemed to be in deep shock as she curled her knees up to her chest and wrapped her arms around them, rocking slightly in a pool of mud. "Zac," he said gently, still holding Abel close. "We have to call the police, hon."

Zac looked up at him with panicked blue eyes. She pushed to her feet so quickly she nearly fell over backwards. "No," she growled, shaking her head violently. "No!" With that, she turned and ran, disappearing through the trees.

Abel pulled away from her father. "Zac!" She tried to run after her, but her father stopped her.

"No, honey, no. No!" He held her firm. "We have to get the police up here."

"She's terrified of the police," Abel said, her voice thick as the tears started to gather.

With one last look at the dead man, Adam gently turned Abel toward home.

Chapter Thirteen

Trying to see through her tears, Zac ran toward the lake, tripping a few times and skinning her hands on a broken tree branch, a few painful splinters now buried in the heels of her hands. She cried out in pain and surprise from the tumble, only to get back to her feet and continue on to the shore, ignoring the pain in her haste to get away. Dropping to her knees at the shore, Zac dipped her mud-covered hands in the cool water and splashed her face, washing the blood from her forehead.

Tears streaming down her face, she grabbed the plastic bag filled with her things and ran toward the bluff where she knew she wouldn't be seen. She couldn't stay here. Cops would be combing the woods at any time, just like her father said they would.

Out of breath from the events of the morning and her climb, she sat on the big rock she used to watch over things, and tried to think. She had to find somewhere to go, somewhere to lay low and hide. The bluff wouldn't keep her safe for long. Her father's voice echoed in her head: *Don't ever let 'em catch ya, Zac. The big bad boogie men will gobble you up!*

She tried to clear her head, but instead tears came in earnest. She would never forget the look on Spinney's face.

Abel hugged herself as she stood outside the cabin, her gaze everywhere and nowhere as her father spoke with the two policemen that had arrived ten minutes before. They were taking his statement and they'd need to talk to her, as well. She stood in the late morning sun feeling cold and numb inside. She couldn't get the dead man out of her mind, or the look on Zac's face. She'd never seen her face filled with so much hate. *Who was that man, and why did Zac attack him?*

❦❦❦❦

Finally pulling herself together, Zac grabbed her bag and headed deep into the woods. She remembered something she'd dug as a child. She used it as a fort and a place to hide when she played "Boogie Man and Zac."

She hurried across the mud-covered ground, praying the hole was still there. She didn't know how long she'd need it, but she needed to hide, and hide fast. They were coming, and she didn't want them to take her away.

Up ahead she saw the tiny rabbit bone she placed there nearly ten years before, marking the secret hiding spot. Dropping to the ground, she felt around until she found the edge of the plywood cover. Nearly whooping in victory, she tugged, grunting when it refused to budge. Not giving up, she bared her teeth and squeezed her eyes shut, until she finally managed to move it. She looked down into the hole. It was nearly exactly as she left it. Zac grabbed her bag and tossed it in, following quickly after. Standing up to her armpits, she grabbed the cover and tugged, nearly sealing off the hole, but leaving just enough space for air. She huddled in a corner, feeling as if she were in a grave.

※※※※

Abel sat on the couch, her baby sister curled in her lap. She was comforted by the continual motion of petting her blonde hair. The police had left hours before, scouring the woods for Zac. The medical examiner from Augusta removed the body.

The old man was Gerald Hivey. The last address on his fifteen-year-old license was Oklahoma. He was a wanted man with warrants in Oklahoma, Maine, and New Jersey for sexual assault on two teen-aged girls, attempted assault on a forty-three-year-old mom, and various counts of petty theft and larceny. Now, as she absorbed Beck's warmth and inadvertent comfort, she was beginning to wonder if Hivey hadn't done something to Zac at some point the way she'd attacked him—the viciousness of it. There was protecting yourself, then there was vengeance.

Abel glanced out the front window to the woods beyond resting her cheek against Becky's head, but wishing it were Zac's. "What happened to you, Zac?" she whispered, her heart in the woods with her friend.

※※※※

Zac started, her eyes opening to pitch black. She tried to focus, but it was impossible in the intense darkness. She listened hearing barking dogs and voices in the distance. The police were searching for her.

Please, please, Spinney! Know I would never hurt you. She closed her eyes again, and waited until morning.

༄༅༄༅

Abel, eyes red from a traumatizing day of crying and confusion, stood at the window in her room. There was no way in hell sleep was going to come tonight. She glanced over at her still-made bed picturing Zac lying there as she had been the night before, safe and sound. Now? Who knew. The police had combed the woods for hours, bringing out their K-9 Unit, and still found very little, the storm working in Zac's favor to dampen her scent. She had been thrilled but scared all the same. She knew Zac was out there somewhere, hiding, probably frightened out of her mind.

Abel knew in her heart that Zac had saved her life that morning, that Gerald had probably seen her as an easy conquest. She shivered at the thought. Wrapping her arms tighter around herself, she stared out into the woods. "Where are you, Zac?"

༄༅༄༅

It had been two and a half days and Zac was cramped, tired from not sleeping worth a damn in her hole, and hungry. All activity stopped the day before, early in the morning, and she hoped it was done for good. She did a lot of thinking while in her self-imposed prison. She scared Spinney beyond all reason, and knew her friend hated her. The trust that she had spent all summer building was wiped away in a few short moments. She saw it in Spinney's eyes.

Zac felt fresh tears and angrily swiped at them.

She was tired of crying and tired of hiding. She would just rebuild her home and stay away from the Cohen cabin. Maybe she'd even move her home further into the woods. That way the temptation to go to Spinney wouldn't be so strong. Eventually she would fade into Spinney's memory again, and then be forgotten all together. That would definitely be for the best.

❧❧❧❧

Things at the Cohen cabin were a bit quieter after the events of a few days before. Abel spent much of her time alone in her bedroom reading or sleeping. When she decided to join her family, her parents gave her a wide berth, though her mom sent her loving smiles from time to time, or gave her a random and quick one-armed hug before returning to whatever she was doing.

Abel appreciated the distance, but at the same time, she felt terribly lonely.

❧❧❧❧

Zac grunted as she shoved the board away, letting in the cleansing sunlight. She squinted against the brightness, having been in near total darkness for three days, and took a deep breath of air, letting it fill her lungs. Tossing her bag out, she climbed out, feeling weak and dehydrated. There was a natural spring nearby. She bent and gulped the water by the handful. Finally sated, she headed toward her house. When she got there, she nearly cried.

Everything was gone. Everything. The little things she'd made from the foil Spinney had given her, little birds and animals. The entire collection was to be given to her friend for her birthday. The canteen hooked on the rock ledge-gone. What Spinney had left behind the night of the storm, after shoving what she could in the bag-gone. All that remained were the remnants of the burned-out cabin, and the rocks themselves.

The police had confiscated it all, thinking it had been Gerald's hideout. She felt a strangled sob begin to form, but did her best to hold it in. She couldn't let this beat her. It just made her resolve stronger. Numbly walking down to the lake, she noticed her tarp and canvas were gone, too. She sat on a fallen log, placing the now sacred bag of all her worldly possessions between her feet on the ground, and cradled her head in her hands.

🌿🌿🍂🍂

As darkness fell, the family sat around the kitchen table eating. Adam engaged the boys in sports talk as Abel barely picked at her food. It was the end of day three, and still no Zac. She pushed her chicken around the plate, playing dodge ball with the rice. Suddenly she stopped the hair on the back of her neck prickling. She looked up, trying to see what she could through the kitchen window. She only saw the reflection of her family against the night beyond.

"What is it, honey?" Sherry asked, quietly.

"She's here," Abel whispered, pushing back from the table and standing.

"Where are you going?" Adam asked.

"I have to go talk to her," Abel said, dropping her napkin to the table and heading for the door.

"To her who? To that Zac person?" He shook his head. "No way in hell, Abel! She's trouble." He stood, but Sherry laid a hand on his arm, shaking her head.

Abel hurried outside, standing on the porch. She saw nothing-even once the motion detector lights that her father installed the day before flashed on-just trees throwing huge shadows. She felt her, knew she was there.

"Come out!" she called, keeping her eyes open for any movement. "Now!"

To her right, she saw a flash of movement, not surprised to see Zac standing there, her plastic trash bag in her hand. She was filthy and looked exhausted. Abel stepped off the porch and walked over to her, still feeling strange from the whole thing. She couldn't get that look on Zac's face out of her mind.

Zac said nothing.

Stopping within a foot of her friend, Abel let out a small sigh. She felt as tired as Zac looked. "Where were you?" she asked softly, hands shoved deep into the pockets of her shorts.

"Hiding. How are you?" Zac's voice was even quieter than usual. It was easy to see that she'd been crying. Her eyes were red rimmed and puffy.

"I'm fine," Abel said, shrugging her shoulders. "I guess."

Zac stared at her for a moment then took a deep breath. "I'm leaving."

Abel gasped, taking a step forward as her heart dropped in her chest. "What? When? Why?"

Zac looked away. "Now. As soon as we get done talking. I can't stay here."

"Where will you go?" Abel whispered, desperately wanting to beg her not to go, to stay with her, stay in the cabin, but the words wouldn't come.

Zac shrugged. "Back to the rails," she sighed, looking out into the night before briefly meeting Abel's gaze again.

"Oh." Abel looked down, not sure what to do. "Please, take care of yourself," she whispered, looking back up and staring into sad blue eyes.

Zac nodded. "Good luck in school." She sounded utterly defeated.

"Thanks." Abel blinked several times holding back tears. She opened her mouth as if she were going to say something, but snapped it shut again.

"Bye, Spinney." Zac gave her the tiniest of smiles.

"Bye," Abel whispered, feeling her throat constrict. She so desperately wanted to grab Zac in a bone-crushing hug, but something told her it wasn't a wise move. Instead she watched as Zac heaved the bag over her shoulder and walked back into the woods.

Chapter Fourteen

"Happy birthday to you!" the family sang poorly. Abel smiled, happy for the attention, but her smile was forced. Zac had been gone for two weeks and she felt every minute of it. It was almost as if when she arrived at the cabin at the beginning of the summer, she was a whole person, happy with her life, and content with her school and friends. After all, once she got back to Boston, she'd be moving into an apartment with her best friend, Jessica, and her friend Kendra. Cool family. What more could a girl ask for?

But now, going back to school in a week and a half, she felt empty somehow, like she was missing something. Since Zac left, she felt her absence acutely. She spent the last couple weeks wandering around the forest, finding her way to the rock overhang where she used to find Zac. All that greeted her was the long dead remnants of the old Lipton cabin and the fire ring of rocks Zac used. Abel would sit on the ground near the cold rocks and bury her head in her hands, letting her sorrow surface. She worried nonstop about her friend, wondering where she was, and what she was doing. She missed her terribly.

"I'm so sorry, Zac," she cried, staring up into the bright blue sky, so reminiscent of Zac's incredible eyes.

Now, sitting with her family surrounding her and a huge cake waiting for her, she felt sick. Why didn't she stop her? Why did she just let Zac ride the rails out of her life? Every time she heard the distant whistle of a lonely train, she thought of her. She was out there, all alone. But then, Zac had always been alone. What was the difference?

※※※※

The large plastic bag landed squarely in the center of the box car. Zac's pale hand grabbed the cold, iron handle on the outside of the car, and she heaved her long frame inside. She closed her eyes as she rested her weary head against the metal wall. The rhythmic chugging of the moving train, and the constant motion, worked like a glass of warm milk before bed. She tried to relax enough to sleep, but she was tense and hungry. She had managed to steal a couple of apples in Bangor from an outside market, and then made off for the rails. Now, six days into her travels, she was back in the swing of things.

Zac picked a train headed south, not wanting to get caught in the harsh winter of the north if possible. She didn't have a shelter any longer to keep her out of the weather. At that thought, she sighed, running a hand through her hair. For about the fiftieth time that week, tears began to sting already red eyes. She rubbed them to no avail. All that did was make them hurt more.

"Crap." She wiped profusely at them, using the hem of her T-shirt. Calming herself, she tried to relax, letting her mind wander again. She thought about her trips before, when she'd wandered around aimlessly for four years. She'd seen most of the country, and felt just about every type of climate known to man - the

Florida humidity, the heat of the south, the temperate climes of the mountain states, and the heat of the west. She'd been everywhere, saw a lot, and was determined to see more. Four years the first time, maybe more this time. Hell, maybe she'd never go back at all.

"Are you ready to go, honey? Everything snagged from upstairs?" Sherry put her arm around her daughter's shoulders as they walked to Abel's car.

Abel nodded her head. "Yes, I've got everything." They reached the blue Jetta, which was loaded with her bags of clothes and birthday gifts. "I just need to do something real quick then I'm outta here." The two shared a smile and a tight hug.

Abel was leaving a week earlier than the rest of the family. She, Jess and Kendra were going to be moving into their new apartment over the next week, the last week before school started again. Sherry kissed her daughter on the temple then went back inside the cabin. Abel turned toward the woods. As she walked, she remembered when she'd first gotten to the cabin that summer. How afraid she'd been, staying with the Wilkins' for a few days until her parents' arrival. She chuckled now, realizing just how ridiculous that had been. Now as she headed toward Zac's rock overhang–which she'd always see as Zac's home–she was amazed at how quiet things were. That hum she felt whenever Zac was around was gone, completely silenced, and the silence was deafening. She knew that Zac was far away. She felt it in her bones. Far away, and getting even farther.

With a heavy sigh, she found the overhang left exactly how she'd last seen it after the excitement of Hivey's death. She lay down her offering, a simple bouquet of wild flowers she picked and a white envelope bearing Zac's name, which she weighted down with a large rock.

She smiled as she remembered the wonderful, gentle girl who bore the letter's namesake. "Goodbye, Zac," she whispered, then turned to leave.

Chapter Fifteen

Abel hugged her best friend, Jessica, tightly, happy to see her after the entire summer. They had plans to travel together over the summer, but at the last minute Abel decided to go to the cabin instead.

"I missed you, girl!" Jess exclaimed, holding her friend by the shoulders and grinning.

Abel smiled at the dark-skinned woman. "Me, too, Jess. How was your summer?"

The two girls met at Jess's family's house, and would go to the apartment from there.

"It was great. I did some great relaxing, some lovin'. Mmm, mm." The girl grinned.

Abel smacked her arm as they headed out of the bi-level house. "You're such a pig." Abel laughed as they climbed into her car and headed to the apartment. Abel was happy to be back in the busy city of her school with the crazy drivers and hordes of people, all in complete opposition to the quiet peace of the forest. She sighed, deciding to not dwell on it today and get back into her life.

The apartment was small but would work for the three friends. The third, Kendra, would be back from London the following weekend. Abel and Jessica walked through the place, taking in the fancy molding around the ceiling, and the fireplace. She scurried down the hall to the biggest room that she and Jess would be sharing. There was enough room for both their beds and some of their meager belongings left over from the dorm. The room was just a bit larger than their shared dorm room had been.

"This place is great!" Jessica called from the kitchen.

Abel joined her there and looked around. It was tiny, but that was okay; it wasn't as if any of them really cooked. As the girls met in the center of the room for a hug, they both giggled at their good fortune.

"Dude, I can't believe we have our own place!" Jess exclaimed, holding her friend's hands.

"I know. It's surreal." Abel looked around at the white kitchen. The gold fridge was the only touch of color in the room. She noted the back door that led to the dumpsters and more parking, the nice thing about being on the first floor.

"Well, let's get started, blondie." Jess put her arm around her friend's shoulders and tugged her toward the front door of the living room.

※ ※ ※ ※

After Kendra's return the girls worked hard. With the help of Kendra's dad and his truck they managed to get things in place. The three pulled together their resources–both monetary and hand-me-downs from family–and managed to furnish the place. It may not have been pretty or match but it was more than adequate. The trio, tired and smelly, stood in the middle of the living room surrounded by hastily placed furniture and boxes.

"Shall we?" Abel asked, fingering a nearby box marked "kitchen."

Jess and Kendra sighed but nodded.

"Let's do it."

※ ※ ※ ※

Abel was glad when classes got underway. She was finally finished with all her prerequisites. Now it was time to focus primarily on psychology, her chosen field. She hoped to eventually teach at a college, and perhaps work with kids.

With an hour and a half until her next class she wandered around campus. She found a bench with a good view. She loved the look of the old campus, the architecture of the buildings. Her father always looked forward to coming to campus. As an architect himself, he fell in love with the buildings each and every time he saw them.

She smiled as she enjoyed the early autumn air. It was still nice, even if a bit too windy for her taste. She smiled up at the blue sky, fluffy white clouds lazily floating around. An airplane flew overhead, and she watched its progress until it was out of sight. Things had gotten back to normal, and she was glad of it.

※ ※ ※ ※

Zac heaved the bag up higher onto her shoulders as she walked along the tracks, trying to find the first train out of town. She wasn't in any hurry; after all, it was a beautiful day. She found herself in Boston the previous night, the city bright and alive with excitement and humanity as the train slowly made its way to a halt. She jumped off, noting a sign up ahead indicating she was about to exit the Boston Train Yard.

She felt her hand tighten on the plastic bag she carried. Though torn in places, it still held her most sacred belongings. It held her heart, her comfort, and her memories. She had been traveling for the better part of two months, and had been doing pretty well. As Zac zigzagged her way through the rail ties, she allowed herself to think of Spinney for the first time in awhile. During the course of finding her way through New York, Illinois, Iowa, into Colorado and Oklahoma, she realized a few things: Spinney would always be a part of her, but she was not the little girl that Zac once knew. She was a woman with her own mind, fears, and emotions. Zac had frightened her terribly, a fact that she would never forgive herself for. From their final meeting at the cabin, Zac could tell that Spinney was no longer as comfortable with her as she'd been before the incident, and probably never would be again.

She had given herself some time to grieve, then cut out any thoughts of Maine. Including Spinney. She had been pretty darn successful at that, too, until now. Being in her friend's college town, she felt that connection again. She stopped. Closing her eyes to breathe in the air and to feel, she swore she could almost feel Spinney. She knew she was out there somewhere, out in the city of Boston. "Hi, Spinney," she whispered, a smile touching her lips.

Zac promised herself she wouldn't go back to the forest ever again. She would leave Spinney and her family alone, never to bother or scare them again. It would also be easier on her heart. She had seen a lot in her short life, and had endured. That was nature, some good, some bad. You had to take it all in stride and realize that in the scheme of things, everyone was a wild animal in the kingdom ruled by the highest creatures It was give and take. But some things were just too painful to take, so she chose to give, instead. She'd give Spinney her love from afar.

※ ※ ※ ※

Abel moved around on the stone bench trying to get comfortable. She grabbed a textbook from her backpack, deciding since she was waiting for class she may as well be productive. Getting some reading out of the way would help free her night up. Opening it to the right chapter, she began to read. Tucking a long strand of hair behind her ear as she turned the page, she stopped and looked up. She had the strangest feeling flow through her. It was like a cry for help, a strangled moan inside her head.

"What the hell?" She looked around to figure out where it was coming from. Seeing nothing but fellow students meandering around campus, she concentrated again. The hair on the back of her neck stood on end, and she realized that she wasn't hearing the noise at all. She was feeling it.

※ ※ ※ ※

Zac continued on her way, hearing someone walking along the tracks behind her. She paid no mind and continued to move on.

"Hey!" a voice called out.

Zac felt herself begin to go into panic mode. *Leave me alone. Leave me alone . . .*

"Hey, I'm talking to you!"

Zac chanced a glance over her shoulder and saw

one of the track inspectors making his way down the tracks. He didn't look happy.

"Can't you read, you stupid transient? No trespassing!"

Up ahead the brunette heard the whistle of an oncoming train. She began to run, moving off the tracks, looking for a clear spot to hop the freight.

"Get back here! No one is allowed in here, kid! Come here!"

She could hear the inspector running behind her so she increased her speed, putting her legs into it. She knew that she could be arrested for trespassing, or worse with these guys.

Crap, crap, crap!

The train came into view and she breathed a sigh of relief. The guy was closing in. She just needed to get on. These guys could be rough. She had run-ins with them before. This one looked no better. Raise a fist, ask questions later. She ran down the tracks as the train whooshed by, blowing her coat out from her body. Holding on with dear life to the bag, she reached out to get purchase on the handle of the open box car. She felt the cold, hard metal against her skin as she caught it and was about to heave herself into the car when she felt herself reeling backwards toward the ground, a strong hand taking hold of the coat tails. Maybe going back to the forest wouldn't be so bad, was her last thought before she was forced to let go.

༄༅༄༅

Abel visibly shivered for just a moment. She winced. She knew something was wrong. She had no idea what was going on, but felt very... strange.

Shaking her head to clear it, she slammed her text closed. "What the hell was going on?" Again looking around, she saw nothing and no one. "Zac?" she whispered, looking desperately around the buildings, any place where someone could hide. Nothing. She felt her stomach sink with disappointment.

She buried her face in her hands for a moment then shook herself out of her crazy notions. It was nothing. It was nothing, and Zac was nowhere near her. Deciding she needed some coffee, she packed her backpack again and headed toward the cafeteria.

≈≈≈≈

Abel was still bothered by the events of that afternoon as she and Jessica roamed the aisles of Nelson's Local Grocers. She pushed the cart absently as Jess prattled on about her day and the new guy she met.

Abel was focused on Zac and what she had felt that day. She knew in her heart that it had been related to her friend. That somehow Zac was hurt. "Jess, I'm going to grab the trash bags," she muttered, needing some space.

"Oh, okay," Jess said, eyebrows drawn in confusion. She shrugged her shoulders and kept going. A few moments later, Jess turned down the aisle where the trash bags and food storage baggies were stocked. "Hey, chickie, I got your Cap'n Crunch," she called out, pushing the cart toward Abel. When she reached her, Abel stood with her back to her, shoulders shaking slightly. Jess stopped the cart and placed a hand on the petite blonde's shoulder. "You okay?"

Abel turned around, her arms wrapped around

a box of foil. "Foil!" she exclaimed, her red-rimmed eyes brimming with tears.

Jessica looked absolutely baffled. "Hon, are you pregnant?"

Later that night, Abel lay in bed staring up at the ceiling. She wasn't sure whether to laugh or cry. She knew that Jess already thought she was crazy. Was she? She hadn't told her about Zac totally. She had no idea where to start, plus in some ways she wanted to keep Zac to herself. Even so, she could see the questions in Jess' dark eyes. Abel had broken up with her last boyfriend the previous semester just before summer began. She got the feeling that Jess was thinking Zac was some tryst she had over the summer. Understandable, for sure, but she still wasn't ready to share Zac with anyone else, even her best friend.

She was worried about her; she couldn't feel her anymore, and felt the loss profoundly. She wondered if maybe Zac had gone back to Maine. She had the feeling that her friend wasn't close, but couldn't be sure. Coming to a decision, she glanced at the bedside clock and saw that it was only three in the afternoon. Jumping up, she grabbed a backpack from the closet she shared with Jessica, and began to shove clothes in it.

"Hey, girl. What's up?" Jess asked, coming in to get her clothes for work.

"I've got to see if she's okay," Abel said, as she continued to stuff clothing into the bag.

"Who?"

"Zac!" Abel grabbed her wallet and a baseball cap.

"Wait." Jess raised her hands in supplication. "She? Honey, who is this Zac person? Who is this *she*?

What's going on?" She placed a hand on Abel's arm, forcing her to sit on her bed. "Talk to me."

Abel sighed, looking at her friend, who looked so worried. She decided to be honest with Jess. "You know my family's cabin in Maine?"

Jess nodded.

"Well, when I was five years old, I met a girl named Zac who lived in the woods with her father. She was a year older, and that was the last time I had ever seen her. Until this last summer."

"Okay," Jess drawled, obviously not getting it. "So, why not call her?"

"I can't! She ran away, and hopped the rails, and I don't know where she went. She may have been in the area. At least that's how it felt. She felt close, you know?" Abel looked at her friend with expectant eyes, expecting her to understand.

"Felt?" Jess looked at her like she'd lost her mind.

"Yes. Felt. So," Abel stood, grabbing her bag again, "I'm going to drive out there for the weekend and see if she's okay."

"Out there? What, to your folks' cabin?"

Abel nodded.

"Okay, so you have this crazy friend who lived in the woods and ran away to go ride trains?"

"Yes, but she's not crazy." Abel turned to the mirror and began to brush her long hair.

"No, but you are. Honey, it's going to be dark soon, and the weather sucks out. By the time you get there, it will be ridiculously late."

Abel glanced out the window noting the skies were already overcast and knew that snow was predicted for the weekend. Chances were good that not much, if any, would fall, though. "Damn," she muttered. "It is late to head out. Okay, fine. Tomorrow morning." She headed out of the bedroom, leaving a very bewildered friend looking after her.

༺༻

The windshield wipers did their very best, but even they were beginning to falter under the weight of the immense snowstorm that was raging across the east coast. The further Abel's little blue car went, the harder it snowed.

"Where the hell did this come from?" she muttered, squinting through the small bit of progress that the wipers were making. The snow was beginning to stick to the road, making it more and more icy. "Shit," she grunted between gritted teeth as she began to slide. She gripped the wheel and tried to remember what her father had told her. Let up on the gas and gently tap the breaks until it slows. Her heart slammed into her chest as she barely missed slamming the car into a snowdrift. Finally the sedan came to a stop, positioned nearly sideways on the road, and Abel rested her forehead against the steering wheel.

"Okay, this is not worth getting myself killed for." Taking several deep breaths, Abel put the car in gear and slowly, carefully, turned it around. She'd have to visit the cabin another time.

Blowing out a breath of relief, she continued on. Glancing in her rearview mirror, Abel saw that a car behind her met the fate that she nearly did. An SUV slammed into the side of the snow bank. She stopped and pulled out her cell phone. Managing to get through to the police, she decided she shouldn't wait around. The weather was getting worse.

※※※※

The household was busy as the girls readied themselves for the party that Jessica was holding to celebrate the end of the fall semester. At first news of this, Abel decided to go to the library, but changed her mind. She was in need of a little fun.

She tugged on her favorite jeans with the hole in the right knee and looked in the mirror. She looked good. Her hair was brushed to a shine and her thin, yellow sweater fit well. She examined her body, hard from years in track and gymnastics. Running a hand down her front, she smiled at the feel of her flat stomach under her palm. She was proud of her abs. Next, she scanned her profile, looking over her shoulder at her butt. Though she'd only broken up with her ex a matter of months ago, it had been a really bad relationship and had been a while since she'd had any sort of real romance in her life. She was lonely, and knew that Will would be at the party. He had been flirting with her since freshman year, so why not? He was cute and seemed nice.

As she looked over her body again, she realized that it was in dire need of some attention. A sexy little grin in place, she ran her hands through her hair and headed out into the living room.

※※※※

The music was pumping through the house filled with laughter and talking. Jessica and Abel had been sure to lock their bedroom door. They had no interest in any couples messing around on their beds.

The beer flowed freely, and so did the dancing. Abel and Jess were just glad that Kendra and a few of their guests were old enough to provide the alcohol. Abel, arms lazily wrapped around Will's neck, swayed with him to Pink. She looked up into his face, his blue eyes looking back at her. They chatted as he continued to caress her back. She'd had a few beers and was feeling no pain.

"So, Will," she purred. "How's school? You start medical school next year, right?"

He nodded. "Sure do. You gonna miss me?" He grinned, white teeth glinting in the light.

"Oh, I don't know," she teased, "maybe, maybe not." She could feel the shot of tequila racing through her body and clouding her brain. She felt a little unsteady and most definitely horny. She was playing with fire with Will and she knew it, but she didn't care.

"Oh, playing coy are you?" he asked with a sexy little grin of his own, his hand slowly rubbing circles on her back, getting lower with each pass. Finally his fingers reached the very top of her ass.

Green eyes widened slightly, and then fell to half-mast. "I think you nearly touched my ass, Will," she teased.

He pulled her closer and fully cupped her behind.

This surprised her. "Okay," she said with amusement in her voice. She reached around and removed his hand. "Down, boy." She may want to have some fun, but it would be on her terms. As it always was. No guy got his way with her without her leading the way. Most of the guys didn't even realize they held absolutely no control until it was too late and she had broken it off.

"Oops," he quipped, no remorse in his voice.

"Hey, girl!" Jessica slurred as she walked by with her own man, Jerome. The darker girl smiled, though it was sloppy and vodka-induced. Jerome looked like a happy camper, though. Abel had always thought him handsome with his smooth, brown skin, and dark eyes. He always seemed to have a smile on his face, and she knew that Jess loved his big hands and what they could do.

"Hi, sweetie." Abel broke away from Will and gave her friend a hug, both girls hanging onto each other, their balance compromised. The men grinned knowingly at each other.

"Okay, gotta go now," Jess said, pulling away. She leaned in and whispered, "Got me some business to attend to." She winked, and grabbed Jerome again. They wobbled out of the room together. Abel gave her a playful swat on her behind as they passed.

"Lucky guy," Will said, taking Abel in his arms again.

She put her hands on his chest starting to push him away, but changed her mind. She grinned up at him, fire dancing in her eyes. She grabbed him by the front of his shirt and led him over to the kitchen. Once there, she pulled him to her and laid one on him. He responded immediately, his hands going right to her ass, pulling her into him.

Abel kissed Will, enjoying the attention and physical contact. He was actually a fairly decent kisser, considering most guys sucked at it. She didn't think she'd have to wipe her chin this time. That was a plus, wasn't it? It was about as much as she could hope for. She just hoped that he was better in bed than her ex had been. That boy needed some serious training. She was lucky if he found the right spot half the time.

As they continued to kiss, she could feel Will's excitement. This excited her as well, but only to a certain degree. She wished that she could find a guy who was content with a good make-out session. Why was it always necessary for sex to follow? But, knowing she had to play the game to get what she wanted, she continued to run her fingers through his short brown hair.

After long moments, she broke the kiss and gave him a smoldering look. Without a word, she grabbed his hand and led him through the apartment, trying to avoid the other partygoers. Abel took a deep breath as she felt that feeling of arousal spread through her, laying a blanket of warmth over her. She pulled her key out of her pocket, and unlocked the bedroom door she shared with Jess. She was glad her friend had left to go to Jerome's place.

Will followed her in and closed the door behind him. Once they were all alone in the dark room, he pulled his shirt off. Abel marveled at his strength and power as his muscles flexed with the motion. She spread her fingers out over his chest, feeling the course hair that met her palms. The next thing she knew, she was taken in a kiss again. This kiss was not just filled with flirtation and possibility, but with actual intent. She felt large hands caress her ass, then pull her into his bulging need.

"I've got something, baby," he whispered into her mouth, reaching around to his back pocket. He pulled his wallet out as he stepped away from her and began to unbutton his jeans. She turned to the room, lit only by moonlight, and made sure the bed was clear. Luckily she had actually made it that morning. She didn't want this guy to think she was a total slob.

She began to tug at the tightly tucked bedding. She felt him come up behind her, pushing himself into her backside, as he tossed a packaged condom on the bed.

"You are so hot, Abel," he said into her neck, as he nuzzled her long hair aside.

She closed her eyes, appreciating the feel of his hands snaking around to cover her cotton-clad breasts. Abel began to moan when suddenly a feeling began to gnaw at her stomach. She faltered for just a moment then her eyes slid closed as she closed her mind to the man behind touching her, and just focused on the sensations themselves. It hit her again.

Guilt.

Her eyes snapped open as her body stiffened. She was in her dark bedroom with a gorgeous guy behind her, fondling her, and admittedly, it felt wonderful.

Will paused. "Hey, baby, you okay?"

"Yeah. I think so," Abel said quietly, trying to remember what made her stop. Her pickled brain was fuzzy.

Will leaned down, beginning to kiss her neck again.

Abel allowed herself to be kissed, but the feeling kept nagging at her. Talk about a buzzkill. And, talk about confusing. "Wait, Will, stop." She pushed away from him, taking a step back. She closed her eyes, shaking her head to clear it. When she opened them again and looked up at him, she could see the confusion and slight anger in his face. She felt horrible. "God, Will, I'm sorry," she said softly. She knew he'd be in some pain, and wished she could help him. He stood there, jeans open, erection clearly visible, and an unopened condom laying on the bed, but she had no desire to jerk the guy off just so he wouldn't have the infamous blue ball syndrome. "I can't do this."

"What the hell? Why not?" he asked, his anger apparently winning over his confusion.

"I just can't. Okay? I'm sorry." Her voice was slightly more forceful now, and she took another step back from him. "I feel like such a shit," she whispered to no one in particular.

"You bitch!" he shouted, reaching down and buttoning his fly. "Man, a fucking tease!" Abel said nothing, as she knew she deserved his anger. As realization dawned on what she'd done, she was relieved he was going to be a gentleman–albeit an angry one–about it. She could have gotten herself into trouble. She watched as he grabbed his shirt from the floor and tugged it back on. She hugged herself.

He snatched the condom and shoved it into his pocket as he walked over to the closed bedroom door. He glanced back at her and spat out, "Bitch," then was gone, the door slammed shut behind him.

Abel buried her face in her hands then ran them through her hair. "Shit." She flopped down onto the mattress. "What the hell is wrong with me?"

That never happened before. She had not slept with many guys, but she had never stopped it, either. She knew what she wanted, and went after it. So what the hell had happened? What did she have to feel guilty about?

Chapter Sixteen

As with summer break, winter break would be the same, in that Abel would make it to the family cabin in Maine a week earlier than everyone else, due to her mother's and sibling's school schedule. She had been left shaken by the events of the night before, and wanted time to think it over, so was glad for the respite.

Zac popped into her mind. She had been absent from her thoughts for a few days, which was a nice reprieve, though Abel missed her. Zac's memory became a sort of companion for Abel. She understood now what Zac meant when she'd said that Abel had been her traveling companion while she'd ridden the rails as a young girl. Abel felt the same way. As she drove on, she did her best to change the subject in her mind. She thought back to her bags and holiday packages in the trunk, which she loaded that morning. She hoped she packed enough for the harsh Maine winter.

Reaching down, eyes still firmly set on the road, she grabbed her iPod which was already connected to her car's stereo system, and began to channel surf through the more than one thousand songs. She came across an oldie but goodie, The Pretender's *I'll Stand By You*.

She hummed along with the song, but suddenly the lyrics began to penetrate her brain, and then her heart. She was stunned, as thoughts of Zac began to flood her mind. Her eyes begin to fill with tears as it hit her square in the heart at just how deeply she missed Zac. The part in the song that affected her the most was when she sang about feeling alone when night falls, you won't be on your own. Abel wiped her tears. "You'll never be alone, Zac," she whispered. "I promise."

≈≈≈≈

Abel pulled up to the cabin, not looking forward to leaving the warmth of her car. Shutting the engine down, she tapped her fingers on the steering wheel for a moment, turning her head to look out into the amazing snow-covered landscape. Every year she came for Christmas and was always blown away by the immense beauty. This year was no different. Finally gathering the courage to face the harsh cold, she unbuckled her seatbelt and opened the car door. She would unload the car then start a fire and curl up with a good book.

"Fuck, it's cold!" Abel growled as she tugged the ends of her coat closer together. Grabbing her keys from the ignition she searched through them with gloved fingers until she found the trunk key. She sucked in a breath, the air chilling her lungs and making her cough. She looked up when she felt a snowflake land on her lashes. *More snow.* She'd have to hurry to get the car unloaded. Thinking of possibly just taking in what she'd need for the night, she unlocked the trunk. Watching it slowly rise, she paused and looked out over the white landscape. Truly breathtaking. Of course she couldn't help but wonder if she was truly alone. She studied the trees watching the snow, which was steadily getting stronger, fall onto the branches. "Zac?" she called, but, her voice seemed to be swallowed by the silence of the landscape. Nothing. Just the falling snow. "Zac?" she called out again, louder this time. She could have been the last person on earth for the stillness. Not even an animal responded to her cries. Disappointed and feeling sad, she turned back to the car. Maybe tomorrow she'd go explore Zac's old haunt. For now it was getting late, and was far too cold.

≈≈≈≈

Abel was tired as she plopped the last of her bags onto her bed. One entire bag was filled with things she'd bought for Zac, both Christmas gifts and the things she'd picked up for her around Boston. She knew it was likely a silly venture to do so, but she couldn't help it. Everywhere she went she saw something Zac would like or something she wanted to see her experience for the first time.

She moved to the window and looked down, quickly finding the thicket that was just away from the house where Zac used to hide most often. She peered through the naked branches of the trees, hoping beyond hope that she'd see some kind of movement there. Again, nothing. Sighing deeply, she decided to unpack now so she wouldn't have to worry about it later. She wanted to chill for the rest of the night.

After twenty minutes of unpacking and getting organized, Abel made her way downstairs and headed outside for some firewood. Luckily her father thought ahead and paid Jim Wilkins to bring wood starting in early November. As always, the wood was stacked neatly next to the house, covered by a tarp. Abel folded back the heavy blue material and began to pile the small logs into her arms. She turned to look over her shoulder, swearing she had heard something. Scanning the quickly-darkening forest, she saw nothing. Feeling a slight shiver run up her spine, she hurried inside with enough wood to get her through the night.

The night was cold and beautiful and Abel was again looking forward to her time alone. Her family would arrive once public school was finished, closer to Christmas. She had just over a week. Things felt different this time around as she sat curled up on the couch, a warm fire popping in the stone fireplace. She watched the dancing flames, her novel forgotten in her lap. As she sat there enjoying her night, she allowed herself to think about the events toward the end of the summer. She had suffered from nightmares for weeks after the incident with Zac and Gerald Hivey. They heard nothing more after giving their statements, and no doubt they never found Zac to question her. How had that day affected Zac? Was she traumatized as well?

"How could she not be?" Abel whispered, shaking her head. Suddenly, in her mind's eye she saw the sheer ferocity in Zac's face from that day, something Abel had never seen nor even considered possible from her laid-back, sweet-natured friend. "Nothing you confess can make me love you less," she sang softly, another of the Pretenders' song lyrics popping out. She smiled at that, grasping her cup of hot cocoa in both hands as she glanced to the large picture window, now a mirror reflecting Abel's own fire-lit image.

"Well," she said with a tired sigh, setting her

book and mug aside before she pushed to her feet. "I will see you again, Zac." She glanced toward the window before heading to the fireplace to put the flames out before going to bed.

≈≈≈≈

She moved swiftly through the darkness, not making a sound across the hard-packed snow. A skill, developed for hunting.

The lights of the cabin were dim, limited to one room, and the tell-tale smoke wafting up from the chimney told of the source. Large, gloved hands reached down, gathering snow.

≈≈≈≈

Humming softly to herself, Abel puttered around the kitchen. She was dressed in flannel pants, a sweatshirt, and slippers. The scenery around the cabin was beautiful, and she was warm and cozy, with a nice fire ablaze in the other room. Coffee started, she headed toward the fireplace to see how much wood she'd need. She preferred to gather it at the beginning of the day and then relax inside. As she neared the hearth, she glanced out the front door and noticed something. Stepping closer, she peered out the small, square panes in the door and saw a snowman. He was sitting on the cabin's porch and was about eighteen inches tall. Two thin sticks stuck out the sides of the triple layered body with a small stick for his nose, but what caught her attention the most were the two bright blue buttons that were used as eyes. Setting off the masterpiece was the small stones placed in an upward semi-circle to depict a smile.

She gasped, hands coming to her mouth. Knocked out of her shocked stupor, her fingers trembled as she fumbled with the locks. She tugged the door open, the fresh morning air hitting her in the face. The day was sunny but cold with more snow predicted.

She almost ran out onto the porch to kneel down to look at the little guy. She reached out a hand, looking at the snow creature with reverence. The snow was cold and wet against her fingertips as she traced the roundness of the head. Her gaze traveled down to the button eyes, cementing who made it.

"Zac!" she yelled, bounding off the porch, looking frantically into the woods for any sort of sign or movement. Nothing. Abel's heart was pounding as she took a few steps further, her slippered-feet disappearing into the deep snow. "Zac!" she yelled again, her voice echoing back to her. She was almost frantic when something caught her eye. Deep within the forest, about fifty yards from the cabin, a dark figure stepped out from behind a tree.

"Zac!" She ran through the snow pushing her legs up high to clear more ground. Her arms were like pistons through the air as she flew toward the figure walking toward her. As Abel got closer, she could see Zac's features clearly. "Zac!" she called out again, pushing her body harder through the snow until she reached her, throwing herself into waiting arms. Abel panted into her neck, the cold air and exertion nearly her undoing.

The momentum of her body had nearly knocked Zac backward into the snow, but somehow they managed to stay upright as they clung to each other. Abel could feel her smile about to break her face in two, but she didn't care. She closed her eyes and dug her fingers into the material of Zac's coat, clutching at what she could for the moment, the cold forgotten.

"Oh, Zac," she breathed into her neck, the warm air displacing the small hairs, making Zac shiver. Abel was held tightly. "I thought about you all semester," she exclaimed, rambling stupidly as she kept her tight hold. "I saw you everywhere I went. And now my best friend thinks I'm crazy or pregnant because of foil!"

Zac said nothing, just continued to hold her.

"And," Abel continued, "I missed you so much! I can't believe you're here!" She pulled away just enough to look into Zac's cold-flushed face. "I called for you," she whispered, her words white puffs of cold air. "Why didn't you answer?" She gripped the open ends of Zac's coat, tugging at it to emphasize her words.

Zac took a moment to answer, seemingly as affected by their reunion as Abel. Finally she said softly, "I didn't want to bother you anymore, Spinney. I don't want to scare you again."

Abel looked up into the most sincere eyes she had ever seen. "Oh, Zac." Abel grabbed her for another hug. "You can't scare me, honey. I'm not angry with you, not frightened of you." She reached up to cup Zac's cold cheeks. "You saved my life."

It took a moment to sink in, but finally Zac smiled, and Abel's heart melted. With an audible click, her world was righted again. That is, until she began to shiver violently.

Zac looked her over. "Oh, Spinney. You're going to freeze." A small wrinkle formed between Zac's eyes and she nodded toward the cabin.

Without a word, Abel began to retrace her steps.

Now that the adrenaline died down somewhat, her body was revolting against the harsh temperatures, which she was not dressed for. Abel's lips were trembling and blue once they reached the porch. She turned to Zac who waited at the bottom of the stairs. She knew not to push her friend. "Zac . . ." She shivered, her words coming out in a staccato rhythm. "I d...don't w...w...want...t...t...to lose you...a...again."

※ ※ ※ ※

Zac looked at her knowing there was no way she could deny herself of Spinney's presence again. With a deep breath, she made a decision. "Then let's go in," she said, taking the steps two at a time so she was standing next to Spinney in two giant strides. Her green eyes widened and sparkled. "Come on, before you freeze to death."

Without another word of encouragement, Abel reached behind her and grabbed the doorknob with trembling fingers, unable to control her movements.

Zac smiled in understanding. "Here." She placed her larger, gloved hand over Spinney's, turned the knob, and the two hurried inside. Zac stood near the door, not sure what to do. She looked around, hands clasped behind her back.

Spinney kicked off her snow-encrusted slippers and hurried over to the fire. Zac glanced over at her thawing friend, their gazes meeting. Spinney's smile was wide and welcoming.

"I can't believe you're here, Zac," Spinney said quietly, her voice filled with awe. Zac smiled, but said nothing. "Come on. Let's get you warmed up and showered."

"Showered?" Zac voice was uncertain.

Spinney smiled and grabbed her hand. "Yes, showered. First, get out of this stuff." She bent down and unlaced the snow-encrusted boots, helping her friend out of them then pushed Zac's coat off her shoulders. "You're wearing the coat I gave you," Spinney said, her beautiful smile flashing, yet again. Come on." She led Zac up the stairs to the second-floor bathroom where the largest shower was.

"Okay, my friend. This is a shower," Spinney explained, pulling the glass wall open.

Zac looked curiously inside then looked to Spinney for further explanation.

"You're gonna love this." Abel turned on the water, using her hand to gauge the temperature.

"Strip," she instructed over her shoulder.

Zac quickly complied, letting the garments fall at her feet. She stood naked in the middle of the bathroom, well-muscled from a difficult life, yet a bit thin. Spinney turned from testing the water temperature and froze as her gaze washed over Zac's body. She swallowed then looked away, a slight flush rising up her cheeks. "Um," she stuttered. "Come here and let me show you something. This is kinda like taking a bath in the lake, but under the waterfall."

"Oh, wow," Zac breathed, looking around the stall before stepping inside. At first, she stayed away from the warm spray.

"Okay," Spinney said, leaning slightly into the stall, her voice loud enough to be heard over the spray. "Those two purple bottles are shampoo and conditioner." She pointed. "Soap right there."

Zac nodded.

"Okay, sweetie!" Spinney smiled. "I'll leave you

to it. Take as long as you want, and I'll leave some towels on the counter for you, okay?"

Zac nodded and stepped fully under the spray as Spinney slid the shower door closed.

Zac groaned loud and long at the feel of the warm water beating down on her skin. She heard Spinney chuckle while leaving fresh towels and gathering Zac's discarded clothing and watched as Spinney glanced over her shoulder at her friend then left the room, closing the door softly behind her.

༄༄༅༅

Once Zac was alone, she ran her hands through her hair, letting the water slick it back from her face. She grimaced at the oily texture. Once, while traveling down in the Ozarks, she found a waterfall. It was summer, so the cold water was more than welcome. That was one of her favorite things about traveling in those parts, and now to have a waterfall inside, but with hot water! She was amazed and overjoyed.

Thanks to Spinney's generosity that summer, she understood how to use shampoo, conditioner, and of course, soap. She'd had her own lumps of homemade lye soap for years, so this Irish Spring stuff was pretty awesome! Sighing at the feeling of clean skin and hair for the first time since early winter, she thought about where she was, and just for a moment berated herself.

After the brutal violence in the fight with the rail inspector–a fight she'd nearly lost–she had decided to go home. She was tired of running and tired of having to look over her shoulder. In short, she was tired. She knew in the Wachiva Forest she would be safe. So, home bound she'd been. Arriving back in October, she worked quickly to fashion some kind of shelter. She managed to make something that would last, and be much sturdier than the canvas over the summer. Blushing slightly at the memory of where she'd gotten the materials, she was proud of her home. She'd do whatever was necessary to keep it. But first, it was time to make Spinney happy again.

❧❧❧❧

 Abel stood with her hands resting on the closed lid of the washing machine, the gentle vibration moving up her arms. She could hear the shower running, which took her back to what had her slightly unsettled. Zac was beautiful. There wasn't a person on the planet who would deny that. She had a natural beauty that was unlike anything Abel had seen in movies or magazines, let alone real life. So what?
 She thought about Will and the moments they'd spent together in her bedroom back at her shared apartment a couple nights ago. She thought about how good it had felt to be touched, to be wanted, then she thought about how much guilt she'd felt as his touch had wandered over her body. Now, she realized she'd felt like she was kissing the wrong person.
 "That's absurd," she muttered, pushing away from the machine. "Totally, absurd."
 Maybe she'd call Will once she got back to school.

❧❧❧❧

 Zac reluctantly turned off the water. She looked down at herself as she wrapped in the towel Spinney left for her. Her newest scar caught her eye. She raised her arm and looked at the puckered flesh there. The scar extended up from her wrist about four inches. She was lucky she hadn't bled to death after that one. Bastard rail inspector and his bastard screwdriver. Running her fingers over the scar absently, she looked around the bathroom, still hot and steamy from the long shower. What was she supposed to wear? Spinney had taken her clothes with her for some reason. She could go downstairs wrapped in the towel but was she supposed to walk around like that? She always just put the same clothes on after bathing.

She looked down at herself again. The towel was around her shoulders and barely covered her. Most of her front was exposed from the navel down. "Hmm," she muttered, looking around the room for some sort of covering. She saw a door behind the door that led out into the hallway. Opening it, she found more towels and wrapped one around her waist.

Padding along the cold, wood floor, she headed downstairs. She inhaled and her stomach began to growl. It was hard to find decent game in the snow. Nibbling on the same rabbit for nearly two weeks wasn't even remotely enough for her tall frame. She'd been essentially snacking rather than eating meals, just to save on supplies.

She reached the kitchen and heard soft humming, smiling when she saw Spinney shaking her hips to some tune on the iPod. She was moving around the small room with a fun little dance move, her head bobbing lightly. Spinney had changed clothes, and was now in a warm pair of sweats, sweatshirt, and thick wool socks. Zac watched from the doorway, amused.

"Shit! Zac!" Spinney gasped, nearly jumping out

of her skin when she turned to see her friend watching her. "God, you scared me." She put her hand to her chest.

"Sorry," Zac smirked.

Spinney glared good-naturedly then her gaze traveled over Zac's towel-clad body. "Shit! I'm sorry." She grabbed Zac's hand and hurried into her parents' bedroom, Zac holding desperately onto her towels so they wouldn't be left in their wake.

Seeming to realize this, Spinney turned to her. Here," she said, moving behind Zac. "Let me show you an easier way to do this." Spinney reached around her and grabbed the ends of the towel draped over Zac's shoulders. "Lift your arms." When Zac complied, Spinney wrapped the towel around Zac's torso, the edge running just over her breasts. Spinney moved around Zac again, ducking beneath an arm that was still raised. "You can put your arms down, sweetie," she said with a small smile. "Take hold of the end here," she instructed, wiggling the edge of the towel that overlapped the rest of the material, "and tuck it in." Spinney watched as Zac did as she was told. "There! See how much better that is?"

Zac looked down at herself then met Spinney's gaze with a grin. "It covers a lot more."

Spinney chuckled as she turned to her father's side of the dresser and searched through drawers until she found her father's sweats. "Here, these will fit you better than mine or Mom's." Spinney tossed a pair onto the bed. "Use the drawstring to tighten them." She grabbed a sweatshirt from the closet along with a pair of socks.

Zac pulled the clothing on, her eyes sliding closed at the feel of the warm, dry material that was instantly warm.

"Better?" Spinney asked, finally turning back around.

"Much. Thank you."

Spinney grabbed one of the discarded towels and walked around Zac again, using the thick terry cloth to squeeze the excess water out of Zac's long, wet hair. "You've got the most gorgeous hair, Zac," she said softly, gently and lovingly, working to absorb as much of the loose water as she could.

Zac smiled, her eyes closed at the pleasure of Spinney's gentle tugs on her hair. "You said that last summer, too."

"I'll say it again. You've got gorgeous hair, Zac." They both laughed. "I know you said the long hair keeps you warmer in the winter, but would you let me trim it a bit for you? I still have those nice, shiny scissors here."

"If it feels this good, you do whatever you want," Zac murmured, nearly lolled to sleep by the sensations on her scalp, especially once Spinney went from squeezing the water out to using her fingers for a gentle scalp massage. Zac groaned low in her throat.

"I think you like that," Spinney said softly from behind her.

Zac could only nod, in far too much pleasure to verbally respond. Suddenly, Spinney's hands were gone. She felt the loss immediately. She turned to see if something was wrong, only to see Spinney turn away and head towards the doorway.

"Um," Spinney said from the doorway, glancing at Zac over her shoulder. "In the bathroom where you showered, there should be some brand new toothbrushes and toothpaste in the drawer. You're welcome to it, if you like. When you're done up here, come to the kitchen." She flashed a quick and bright smile. "I've got a surprise for you." Spinney grinned, her green eyes twinkling.

Zac watched her go, then brought a palm to her mouth, blowing some breath on it. She winced at the smell, then headed to the bathroom.

Several minutes later, Zac padded down the stairs and into the kitchen. The smile that came to her lips was immediate when she saw Spinney standing at the stove. The smells that filled the kitchen were incredible, and Zac felt her mouth begin to water. Stepping up behind Spinney, she watched over the shorter woman's shoulder as Spinney expertly flipped pancakes in a pan. "Pancakes!"

Spinney smiled with a nod. "Yes, and they're almost ready so sit." She placed her newest batch of pancakes on a plate. "These have chocolate chips in them." She grinned over her shoulder. "And . . ." She brought out a brand new bottle of Aunt Jemima syrup. Zac's eyes instantly lit up. Spinney grinned then brought out a new can of Reddi Whip.

Zac made her way to the large dining table and looked at the two sets of plates, with folded napkins and forks on top. There was also a glass at each spot. She glanced back toward the kitchen, not entirely sure what to do or where she should sit. She'd never sat at a table to eat in her entire life. During those few days the previous summer when she was sick, Spinney always served her in bed, the little bit she was able to keep down, that is.

※※※※

Abel realized everything had gotten quiet. She

turned from her place at the stove to see Zac standing at the dining room table, looking uncomfortable and uncertain. She turned off the stove and wiped her hands on a towel before walking over to her. She had intended to help get her situated, but instead, looking into Zac's face, a face she'd missed so desperately, she took her into a warm embrace, which Zac immediately responded to.

Resting her head on Zac's shoulder, Abel basked in the warmth that surrounded her. She smiled when Zac ran her fingers through her hair, then rested her cheek against the top of her head. "I missed you so much," she whispered into the hug.

Zac tightened her hold. "We're together now, Spinney," she whispered.

Abel nodded as she let out a heavy sigh of contentment. She could have stayed there all day, but the extremely loud sound that radiated from Zac's stomach sent her into a fit of giggles.

"Okay, you," she said, pulling out of the hug. "Let's get you fed." She pulled out a chair and patted the seat.

When Zac sat, Abel served her, Zac watching with hunger-filled eyes. Abel was sad. She wondered just how long it had been since she'd had anything substantial to eat.

Abel sat, too. "Okay, I know you have a sweet tooth to kill a horse, so I've got a cavity-making breakfast for you. Here's how this works. This is whipped cream. Try it." Holding up the can of Reddi Whip she squirted some on Zac's finger.

Zac studied it with drawn eyebrows. "This looks like the stuff I shave with," she said, looking to Abel for an explanation.

Abel grinned and shook her head. "But it doesn't taste like it."

Zac smelled the creamy treat before sticking out a tentative tongue. She drew her eyebrows again for a moment as she rolled it around in her mouth, then closed her eyes.

Abel grinned, heading back to get them some milk and juice to drink. Returning, she sat again, giggling at the mountain of whipped cream that topped the stack of flap jacks. After setting down their drinking glasses, she sat, chin resting in her palm, and watched in amazement as Zac shoveled the food in. She wasn't sure Zac was even tasting the food. There was not a chance in hell this girl was going to starve over the winter. She'd buy her an entire store of food to keep in the snow for after she left, if need be.

※ ※ ※ ※

Zac savored the tastes that assaulted her mouth and tongue. She closed her eyes at every bite, quickly taking another, enjoying it as if it were her first. During the three seconds between bites, she realized that Spinney was no longer eating, but instead watching her. She was far too involved in her meal to stop and ask why. "This is so amazing to be able to eat without fighting the bugs," she managed between bites.

Finally the plate before her was empty and she began to scan the kitchen for more. A few seconds later, Zac looked down to find Spinney's uneaten pancakes sitting in front of her. Zac sent her a grateful gaze, then the ritual began again.

"Where did you go?" Spinney finally asked, picking at the replacement pancakes she'd gotten herself after sacrificing her breakfast to Zac's ravenous appetite.

Zac glanced up from her breakfast after downing the cold glass of milk.

Spinney, snickering at the mustache it left, reached over and wiped it off with her thumb.

Zac sat back in her chair resting her hands on her flat tummy that seemed like it should've been the size of a nine month pregnant woman, with as much food as she inhaled. "A little of everywhere," she said quietly. "I went down south for a bit and headed over toward Illinois and Indiana." She looked up shyly. "Went through Boston, too."

Spinney's eyes opened wide as she sat forward in her chair, pushing her nearly-finished breakfast away. "When?"

Zac shrugged. "About late summer…September."

Spinney stared at her for a moment. "September?" At Zac's nod, Spinney's gaze bored into hers "Zac, did something happen to you there?"

Zac nodded.

"What?" Spinney breathed, her eyes wide.

"I was pulled from a train." Zac raised her arm, sliding the thick sleeve up to her elbow, exposing the angry scar.

"Oh…" Spinney sucked in a breath as she rose from her seat and hurried over to Zac, kneeling next to her chair. She took hold of her arm and gazed down at the mark marring the perfect flesh. "Oh, honey," she whispered, looking into her blue eyes, her own filled with tears.

Zac looked with concern into her friend's face. She brought up a hand and caught the single tear that slipped free. "Why are you crying?" she asked, her voice soft.

"You got hurt," Spinney answered, gently touching the scar. "How did you get cut so badly?" Looking back at the mark, she rubbed her thumb over the skin, rough and puffy from scar tissue. "This probably needed stitches, Zac."

"When I fell, I landed on a jagged tie," Zac watched the gentle movement of Spinney's thumb on her arm. "And, the guy had a screwdriver that made the cut worse when we were fighting." She hadn't intended her words to make her friend more upset, but that's exactly what they'd done. Spinney was silently crying, now. "Please don't cry, Spinney."

Spinney looked up and met her gaze. She gave her a brave smile and a nod, even as another tear slid lazily down her cheek. "Okay."

Getting to her feet, Spinney grabbed a napkin from the table and wiped her eyes and nose. She took several deep breaths before tossing the napkin back to the table. Once again looking at her friend, she smiled. "I have a surprise for you," she said for the second time in their time together. She turned and hurried up the stairs, leaving Zac to watch after her.

※ ※ ※ ※

Abel ran up the two flights of stairs to her room. She looked around for the duffel bag she crammed full of gifts for Zac, on the crazy chance she'd see her. Once spotted, she grabbed it and turned to head back, only to stop, realizing just how ridiculous it had been to buy all this stuff, and bring it with her. Hell, she carried it in the trunk of her car for months, just on the chance she'd see her friend. "I'm crazy," she said, shaking her head. "Absolutely crazy." The smile on her face utterly belied her words as she headed out of the room.

Abel pounded down the stairs and set her bag on the floor in front of the fireplace. Zac watched from where she sat at the table. She waved her over. "Come here."

Zac joined her, plopping down in front of Abel, the bag between them.

Abel eyed her friend as she slowly unzipped the bag. "Now you stay still, and I'll give you this stuff one at a time, okay?"

Zac nodded.

Abel felt like a child playing Santa on Christmas morning as she rose to her knees and reached inside the large bag. "Okay, first we start with this. Close your eyes."

Once Zac's eyes were closed, Abel ripped open the package and brought out one of the eight units inside. She held the item aloft before telling Zac it was okay to look. "This," Abel explained, "is biodegradable toilet paper." She handed the roll to Zac. "See, when you use it and throw it out in the forest, it will break down really fast."

Zac took the roll, bringing it up to her face to study and smell it. "I've heard of biodegradable before," she murmured, looking at the toiletry in awe.

Abel smiled, handing over the remaining package of rolls. "Awesome." She watched as Zac set it aside, looking at her expectantly. "Next . . ." Abel gave her a devilish look. "Close your eyes."

Zac closed her eyes.. At Abel's okay, she opened her eyes. It was a black knit cap. She turned it over in her hands, smiling at the little squirrel that was sewn into it. She grinned up at Spinney. "It's my little squirrel."

"Yes, ma'am, sure is." Abel grinned, happy to see the sparkle in Zac's eyes. Without further ado, Zac placed the cap on her head, tugging it down to just shy of the top of her eyes. Abel laughed, then turned back to her bag.

She pulled out the small box, making sure it was right side up. She placed it in Zac's open palm. "Okay. I'm not sure if you even need this, but figure better safe than sorry."

Zac looked at the small box then looked at Abel with confused eyes.

"Open it," Abel encouraged.

Tugging off the lid with calloused fingers Zac peered into the shallow box and pulled out a small, silver compass. She looked at Abel for an explanation.

"It's a compass, Zac. I doubt you need it. I'm sure you can just look at the moss growing on the side of a tree or something." She grinned. "But . . . here." She crawled over to where her friend sat, and showed her the merits of the instrument. She showed her how it would clip onto her belt loop.

"So I can tell which direction I'm facing no matter where I am?" Zac asked, turning the small dial this way and that, amazed at how the pointer stayed in the same place. "Wow, can I go try it?" she asked with childish glee.

Abel laughed. "Tell you what, why don't we finish up here, then we can go outside. Okay?" Zac nodded amiably, her eyes automatically going back to the compass. Abel moved back to her bag. She grabbed the thickly folded, hooded sweatshirt, and tossed it at her friend, who caught it easily.

Zac unfolded the hoodie and held it up. It was

red with pockets in front, and on the back. The words Boston University were proudly displayed in black lettering.

"That's from my school," Abel said, her voice shy.

Zac hugged the hoodie to her, rubbing her cheek against its thick softness. "I love it," she whispered.

Abel grinned huge. She had been worried Zac might think she was trying to push something on her. Her smile turned to a look of shock when, yet again, Zac was stripping. She whipped off Abel's father's sweatshirt, leaving her topless for a moment before she tugged on the hoodie in its place. Abel shook her head and laughed inside at the flush that, yet again, stained her cheeks.

She cleared her throat, getting back into the moment. "And finally," she reached into the bag, grunting slightly at the weight of a large text book. It was a used copy of a very expensive textbook from the campus bookstore.

Zac's eyes widened at the sight. "Zoology," she read from the big black letters spelled across the picture, which portrayed a montage of insects and animals.

"This is an older edition text book for the class. I hope you like it," Abel explained, watching Zac's reaction closely.

Zac took the heavy text, fingertips lovingly caressing the smooth cover. She looked up at Abel with expectant eyes, compass forgotten. "Can I read?" she asked quietly. Abel smiled warmly and nodded.

"Honey, you can do whatever you want." She knew that as soon as her friend got her hands on the book, she would lose her.

Chapter Seventeen

After finally winning a full-out battle over where Zac would sleep, the two sat peacefully in Spinney's large bed. Spinney was dressed in her flannel pajamas soft to the touch and very comfortable and warm. Zac sat next to her dressed in a pair of Spinney's father's running shorts and the Boston U. hoodie, which she refused to take off. The two sat shoulder to shoulder in the large bed, the only light in the room that of the moonlight shining in through the window.

Zac glanced over at her. "I still don't understand why you want me here." She felt as if she was pushing Spinney right out of her own bed.

"Because there is not a chance in hell that I was going to let you sleep on the floor in the middle of December in Maine, Zac!" Spinney said, sounding exasperated. She looked at her with fierce green eyes. "If you don't want to sleep here, that's one thing. But if it's because of some sense of honor or something, not gonna happen. Got me?" She poked Zac in the shoulder. With Zac's reluctant nod, the subject was dropped. "Good. Now come here. I need warmth."

Spinney had shown Zac one of the great modern marvels in keeping warm–the electric blanket. Zac was immediately stunned and amazed at how it worked, and how warm it made the bed. The two slid down in the sheets, Spinney instantly curling up next to Zac.

She rested her head on Zac's shoulder and rested her hand on Zac's flat stomach. Zac was baffled as Spinney wiggled in a bit closer, making cute little humming sounds.

"What's the matter with you?" Zac laughed, utterly charmed.

"I'm just happy," Spinney said. She patted Zac's stomach. "I got my Zac back."

Zac's smile was huge and she held Spinney a bit tighter.

"Zac," Spinney said softly in the darkness. "Would you tell me more about what happened with the scar on your arm?"

"Well," Zac said with a sigh, her fingers absently running through the silky strands of Spinney's hair, unbeknownst to her, the sensations she was causing were slowly making green eyes droop. "I had jumped off the boxcar the night before in Boston. So, I was wandering around the tracks, trying to spot when the next train would show. I was on government property, though. They're not real fond of us." She chuckled lightly, though there was little humor in it. "So a rail inspector came along. See, these are rough guys who hate hoppers-"

"Hoppers?"

"Yeah. Rail hoppers. Those of us who ride the rails. Anyway, they can't stand us. He came after me so I grabbed the train that was passing, but he pulled me right off."

"What did you do?" Spinney lifted her head to look into the faraway gaze of her friend.

"I had to pummel him," Zac said, turning her face away from the heat of Spinney's gaze.

"You beat him up?" Spinney asked gently,

brushing a few strands of dark hair away from Zac's face.

"Yes." Zac seemed ashamed of her actions.

Spinney lifted herself onto an elbow. A tear fell slowly down Zac's cheek. "Zac, why are you crying?" She brought her hand up to catch the wetness on her fingertip.

Zac's pained blue eyes met hers. "I don't want to scare or disappoint you again, Spinney," Zac whispered. "I don't want you to think I'm just a brutal monster that always turns to violence."

"Oh, Zac." Spinney pulled her in for a hug. "I'm not either, and I could never think of you as anything other than the beautiful soul that you are. You did what you had to do. I know that now. I never doubt your actions."

Zac closed her eyes and allowed herself to be enveloped in Spinney. "Really?" she whispered, her voice filled with hope.

Spinney pulled back from the hug. "Yes, ma'am. I trust you implicitly, Zac. Always will." A gentle smile spilled across her lips and she caressed Zac's soft cheek.

Zac studied her for a moment, then believing what she heard and saw, snuggled into Spinney, her face buried in her neck as Spinney leaned over her. They held for a long moment before finally Spinney pulled away, giving her a warm smile before settling back on Zac's shoulder.

"So, when did you come back here?" she asked softly, her hand tucking into one of the pockets on Zac's hoodie, making Zac smile.

"It was mid-October."

"You've been here since October?" Spinney

asked, surprise in her voice.

Zac nodded. "Yes. After my fun with the rail inspector, I decided I wanted to come home," she said simply. What she didn't say was that she'd come home to be closer to where she'd last seen Spinney. She had made the promise to leave the smaller woman alone, but still needed to feel that familiarity, needed to know that she would be near at some point. She made her feel safe and warm.

"Well, I for one am glad." They were silent for a moment before Spinney spoke again. "Zac?"

"Hmm?" Zac responded absently, her fingers still playing in golden hair. She squirmed a bit when Spinney playfully tickled her belly through her hoodie pocket.

"I have a really strange question for you," Spinney said, though her voice sounded a bit hesitant.

"Ask away, Spinney."

"Well, I guess, um, basically, well..." She swallowed. "Zac, do you feel me?"

Zac took mental note of all her body parts that were touching Spinney. "Yes. I feel you against my shoulder. And against . . ."

"No," Spinny broke off in soft laughter. "I mean feel me. Like when we're not together?" Spinney lifted her head again, looking down into Zac's smiling face.

Zac studied her, her mind working on the question. She felt Spinney all the time. Even when she was on the rails she had a vague feeling of her, like she was out there somewhere. Finally, she nodded.

"What is it?" Spinney asked, lifting her head once more and holding it up on her palm. The confusion was very apparent in her voice.

Zac shrugged. "I don't know. I've always felt

it with you, Spinney," she said quietly. "It's just a connection." She shrugged, as if it were a natural thing.

"A connection?" Spinney repeated, the look on her face as though she were tasting the word and idea. Her gaze returned to Zac's. "But how?"

"I don't know." Zac turned onto her side to look at her friend. She had no way of explaining what she had always taken for truth. "It's like you call out to me somehow, Spinney. Like, no matter where you're at, I can hear you."

"Exactly! A hum," Spinney said, her voice low and serious.

"Yes. A hum." Zac liked the analogy. "I hear it now. When I left last summer, it quieted, but didn't die."

Spinney smiled. "I'm glad you hear it, too." She gave Zac a quick, but tight hug and a light kiss on the cheek. "Let's get some sleep."

☙❧

Zac lay in the dark, listening to the soft breathing of her friend sleeping next to her. She woke not long ago, the howling wind outside the window rattling the glass in its pane. She stared out into the black night, knowing it was snowing again.

She gazed at the beamed ceiling above and thought back to the day. It had been an amazing one. She was stunned to find herself inside the Cohen cabin, again. She thought she'd be the luckiest woman in the world if she managed to steal a glance of Spinney outside at some point. Hearing the storm rage out in the frigid night, she was grateful.

She hid behind numerous trees as she watched

Spinney come home and unload her car. She wanted to help her, but stayed back, even when Spinney called out to her. That had been hard to resist. She wanted so badly to jump out from behind the tree, not ten yards away, where she'd been hiding. If Spinney went further into the forest, she would have seen footprints everywhere.

She thought of the gifts that had been bestowed upon her that day. She knew that Spinney had a job back in Boston, but hated the thought of her spending her hard-earned money on her. There was just no purpose for that. All the same, Zac loved what she bought. Her eyes flickered over to the chair where her zoology book sat, just begging to be read.

Zac glanced at her sleeping Spinney, and carefully, quietly, eased out of bed. She reached over to the chair and snagged the book. It was heavy, and she bit her bottom lip as she tried to grip it with one hand long enough to make it back to the bed. Mission accomplished.

Settling in, she smiled at the slight creaking sound of the spine as she opened the cover. She loved the clean smell of the smooth pages and colorful illustrations and photographs, along with detailed text. Her eyes widened in wonder and awe. Living so much of her life without the advantage of electric light, her eyes were well adjusted to the dim lighting conditions of the bedroom. Even so, it was still a challenge to read the text, even if the pictures were easy to make out. She was absolutely fascinated by what she saw and read. Things she had never known or even thought to know. Her brain felt as though it were swelling from the wealth of knowledge she was absorbing from just the first few chapters.

※ ※ ※ ※

Abel shifted in her sleep, turning over onto her side. Her brows drew as something dragged her from sleep. She felt a strange weight next to her head. Reaching her hand out behind her, she felt a knee. She glanced over her shoulder and saw Zac sitting up in bed, the covers pulled around her waist and the large textbook in her lap. She was bending over it, trying to read in the faint light.

"Zac?" she said, her voice thick with sleep. The darker head turned toward her, Zac's face completely hidden in shadow. "What are you doing? Why aren't you asleep?"

"I wanted to read."

Abel chuckled and patted the pillow next to her. "Come here, you nut. You can read tomorrow." She glanced at the bedside alarm clock, "It's past three in the morning."

Zac closed the book, put it on the bedside table, then slid back down into the warm bed.

"Spinney?" she whispered after a moment.

"Hmm?"

"Can I take the book with me when I go?"

"Of course, Zac. It's yours," Abel murmured, already falling back asleep.

"Good," Zac whispered, getting comfortable. "I like it a lot."

※ ※ ※ ※

"Okay, my friend," Abel said, an authoritative tone in her voice. "I've seen that you put syrup on just about everything that will stand still, so today I'm going to show you a little something different for lunch." Abel held up a plastic jar. "This is peanut butter. And this," she held up the plastic bear, "is honey. They go on bread, and it's quite yummy."

Zac sat perched on the counter, watching as she lightly drummed her socked heels against the cabinet below.

"Have you ever heard of peanut butter and honey?" Abel asked, a quirked brow highlighting her question. At the shake of Zac's head, she sighed, sad her friend had missed out on such pleasures. "Okay. Well, then you'll get to discover it all together." She slapped a liberal amount of the creamy stuff on the split-top wheat bread, then squeezed honey all over it in a fancy pattern. Sticking the two pieces of bread together, she put it on a plate, and presented it to her friend. "Try it."

Zac took the plate and looked at the offering on it. She grabbed the top slice and lifted the corner, peering between and taking a sniff. Liking what she smelled, she took a bite.

Abel watched, utterly amused. She watched Zac's face carefully as she chewed the bite, her expression full of concentration as she tasted the new flavors on her tongue. The explosion of sweetness would assuredly please the sweet tooth she discovered her friend had. Good thing she could keep her supplied with a toothbrush and toothpaste.

Zac's eyes widened, as a smile formed on the tanned face. "Good!" she exclaimed, happily digging into the rest of her lunch.

Abel chuckled. "I'm so glad. Today, my dear Zac, we will be making chocolate chip cookies," she declared, looking at her friend, a huge smile forming on her lips. Zac looked confused, a bit of peanut butter smeared on her chin. Abel chuckled again and reached over to rub it away with her thumb. "Have you ever had cookies?"

"Just those you gave me last summer."

"Ah. No, those were Oreos. These are chocolate chip. What you had in your pancakes the other morning." Abel set about gathering the ingredients as Zac finished her sandwich. "Okay." She grabbed a recipe from her mother's recipe file. "Jumbo chocolate chip cookies coming up." With a wicked grin, she told Zac what needed to be done.

Zac quickly finished her sandwich then hopped down from the counter, hurrying to do what she was told, grabbing the flour canister from the counter, the milk from the fridge, along with two eggs, and the five pound bag of sugar.

All the ingredients around her at the counter now, Abel cracked the required amount of eggs into the bowl. "Um, we need one cup of sugar," Abel said absently as she read over the recipe. She heard Zac opening the bag of sugar. "Zac, the measuring cup..."

Abel's words trailed off in fascinated horror as she watched Zac aim the bag over the bowl, sugar gathering at the edge of the flap before beginning to spill out. A large flood of white covered the unbeaten egg yolks, the level rising in the bowl.

"I think we'll be having really sweet cookies," Abel said numbly.

꙳꙳꙳꙳

Abel's fingers flew across the touch screen of

her phone, responding to a text from her mother: *Yes, she's still here and it's going amazing! Oh, you may want to pick up some more sugar when you guys come.*

❦❦❦❦

"Since you won't do this yourself," Spinney growled playfully, buttoning and zipping Zac's coat for her.

Zac grinned, secretly loving the attention and care her Spinney gave her.

"Will you show me?" Spinney asked. She handed her a pair of thick, warm gloves. "Put these on."

Zac pulled them on. "Yes. I'll show you," she said quietly, wiggling her fingers to make sure they were snug in the warmth. "Come on."

Zac was getting super restless in the cabin after two full days and nights. Undoubtedly Spinney could see it. Earlier that morning she asked Zac if she wanted to go out into the snow and play. Zac, of course, had been thrilled at the prospect. The two women finished bundling up then Spinney opened the front door. The snow had stopped early that morning, and the accumulation was magnificent. The world outside the Cohen cabin was marvelous with all its white intensity. The quiet that ran through the area was palpable. No usual sounds of small, woodland creatures. Once in a while, the sound of snow falling from the tops of branches or the roof was all that was to be heard.

"It's so beautiful," Spinney breathed, taking it all in from the porch.

Zac nodded with a huge, proud grin. "Yes." She always felt as though the wild was truly her home, her living room, her kitchen, and bathroom. As she looked out over the exquisite beauty before them, she felt proud to share it with her Spinney.

"I almost don't want to mar it," Spinney said softly. Looking at the virgin snow, not even animal tracks could be seen. "You know, when I was a kid, when snow was perfect like this, I used to think it was the white cream in Oreos."

"Come on!" Zac's excitement was barely contained as she jumped off the porch into the soft, giving snow. Spinney followed suit.

Zac let out an excited whoop before she fell backwards in the deep snow, her arms and legs flailing wildly, almost as though she were doing the backstroke. Spinney watched her antics and laughed.

"Yeah, you definitely had a pretty severe case of cabin fever."

Zac stopped her movements and looked up at Spinney, who made her way through the deep snow over to her. "I don't have a fever."

Spinney grinned as she shook her head. She reached a hand down and helped Zac to her feet. "It's just an expression, you goof. Come on. Let's go for a walk."

Once on her feet, Zac shook herself off like a dog, covering Spinney with the snow that flew from her hair and clothing.

"Zac!"

Zac grinned. "Oops."

As they wove their way through the winter wonderland, Spinney broke the silence. "Are you in the same place?" she asked, using a small branch from a tree that Zac grabbed for her as a walking stick.

"Yep," Zac called out from just a few feet ahead. Usually the two would've walked hand in hand, but

Zac was beside herself to be out in the open air and couldn't keep still, let alone maintain a slow walking pace. She was glad that Spinney seemed to understand. Then Zac remembered. Grimacing inwardly, she knew that her tenacious little buddy would spot it right away. Still, she continued to lead them to her place.

Eventually they made it to Zac's new shelter. Spinney's eyes widened as she checked out the new and improved version of what Zac had had the previous summer. Most of the debris from the burnt cabin was buried beneath the blanket of snow, and all that was left was the rock overhang and the solid side that Zac had built. It was built out of planks of wood with drywall sheets beneath it. It seemed to be anchored close enough to the rock as to nearly seal out any wind, rain or snow. An entrance had been cut out of the drywall that was about three feet high and two feet wide. Some sort of material was attached on the inside that formed a curtain.

As she got closer, her brows knit. Wilkins Co. was stamped into the wood. She looked over her shoulder at a very sheepish Zac. "Zac?" she asked, running her thumb over the stamp. Amusement sparkled in her beautiful eyes.

Zac couldn't meet Spinney's eyes. "Huh?" she finally said, shoving her hands deeper into the pockets of her jacket, kicking at some snow. She looked up when she felt a gentle touch to her arm.

"It's a great place," Spinney said with a broad smile. "To be honest, I'm pretty impressed with your ingenuity."

Zac smiled. "Thanks."

"Can I go in?"

"Of course!" Zac grinned and nodded, quite

proud of herself and even more so at Spinney's words of praise.

Spinney dropped to her knees and brushed the heavy curtain aside and crawled inside. It was a bit more spacious than the one Zac had before. There wasn't much in way of belongings and personal effects. Zac had lost a lot the previous summer, so only a small pile of books was tucked neatly in the corner. Her clothing, folded neatly as Spinney had shown her, was in a black plastic milk crate she'd found. Her bedroll was rolled up and tucked onto a natural ledge in the rock face that worked as a perfect, natural shelf. Further back in, away from the wood, was a circle of medium-sized rocks, their blackened surfaces indicative of the ring's purpose, which was to keep Zac warm and cook her food.

Zac waited anxiously to see what her Spinney had to say about her new digs. It didn't take long, as Spinney crawled out after a few moments of survey. Zac helped her to her feet, Spinney brushing the snow off her knees.

"Okay," she said, her words white puffs. "I'm essentially satisfied that you have a decent place to stay, though I still worry about you."

"Eh," Zac said, waving off her worry.

She shouldn't have, as suddenly Spinney's eyes narrowed and a mischievous glint filled them. Before Zac knew what was coming, she was nailed right on her neck by a snowball.

Stunned, she brought up a hand, and when she pulled it away her glove was covered in white. She turned curious eyes to her friend, who was grinning wickedly.

"What the . . ." SPLAT! "Pah!"

Zac reached up, wiping the snow from her left cheek, and then got the hint. She hurried back around the overhang, and grabbed her own fistful of snow. Packing it, she looked around for a little fiery blonde, and aimed, hitting her target squarely in the back as Spinney was running for the shelter of nearby trees. She giggled and dropped to her knees once more, gathering as much of the powdery stuff as she could.

"Bombs away!" she heard as a slew of well-shaped snowballs bombarded her, many splattering against the tree she was near, though many others managed to hit their intended target. She laughed and cried out as she tried to cover herself. She heard her friend laugh as well.

"You're next, Spinney!" she called back with a grin as she stood, her arsenal in her arms. She grabbed one at a time, aiming quickly, and throwing. Spinney tried to cover her face, but was laughing entirely too hard, and ended up falling on her butt, the snow nearly rising to her shoulders as she sat laughing on the ground.

"You okay?" Zac asked, concerned. Spinney was laughing too hard to reply, so she simply nodded. Convinced her friend was okay, Zac kept up the barrage.

"Ugh!" Spinney cried, falling further back into the snow, giving up trying to protect herself.

Zac dropped the rest of her snowballs, made her way over, and plopped down next to her, grinning like an idiot. "You okay?" she asked, extending a hand to help Spinney sit up.

"Yeah," Spinney said, still laughing, her cheeks rosy from the cold. She ran a hand through her snow-encrusted hair, then drew it all together, bringing it over her shoulder and out of the way. "That was fun." She grinned.

"Yeah, it was."

"Okay, I need to stand up. My butt's frozen."

≈≈≈≈

They stood, wiping the snow from their clothing. Abel looked at her friend as they made their way back toward the cabin. Zac took her hand. Though their time out had been enjoyable, it was still cold, and they were wet. She studied Zac's profile, the calmness that seemed to emanate from her was so very soothing for Abel's soul. She felt as though she would forever be protected and watched by this magnificent woman. A soft smile curved along her lips. She felt a satisfaction, a happiness, a wholeness, that she never could have expected to find. When she was with Zac, everything was okay and beautiful again. Though her winter break had basically just started, she already dreaded having to go back. The thought of leaving Zac in the harsh Maine winter made her feel sick.

With a sigh that blew out in a white puff of air, she turned to her friend as they walked.

"So, I imagine you know that Gerald Hivey died on the scene," she said casually, though her voice was soft.

"Who?" Zac turned furrowed brows on her friend.

"The guy last summer."

Zac's jaw clenched briefly before she nodded. "Oh, the Boogie Man."

Abel nodded. "Yeah, the Boogie Man. He was not a good person, Zac. He had a whole bunch of warrants out for his arrest for some pretty brutal things." She turned her attention back to the path they were taking, carefully retracing their earlier steps so as not to lose a boot in the deep snow. "Rape, burglaries, all kind of stuff." She shivered, remembering the look of the filthy man lying dead on the ground.

"He's evil," Zac whispered.

"Yes, he is. *Was*." She looked up, studying the hardness of Zac's face, that same look from last summer, just without the intent. She shivered again, this time not for fear of Zac, but somehow knowing that something had given birth to that look. "Zac?" she said quietly, seeing the muscles in the brunette's jaw working.

"Hmm?"

"How did you know?" Abel asked, stopping their progress, her hand resting lightly on Zac's arm. "How did you know I'd need you that day? You knew how dangerous he was. How?"

Zac's eyes wouldn't meet Abel's. She looked around the forest, and for a moment Abel wasn't sure if she was going to answer. Finally, Zac met her gaze and held it.

"I'd seen him before," she said, her voice barely above a whisper. "He hurt me once."

"What!" Abel grasped her friend's arm tighter, almost digging her fingernails into the thick padding of the jacket.

"It was a long time ago, Spinney. I recognized his limp. He would have hurt you." Tears brimmed in the bright blue of Zac's eyes, and Abel felt them tug at her heart.

"Oh, Zac," she whispered, reaching up to collect one that managed to spill over onto Zac's cold cheek.

"Honey, you saved me. It's okay. I'm fine." She smiled.

"You don't hate me?" Zac whispered, so much pain in her eyes. "I never meant to scare you, Spinney."

"I know you didn't. And, no. I could never hate you. Okay? Ever, ever!" Abel's smile grew as she saw a small light begin to shine in Zac's eyes.

Zac nodded.

Abel pulled her into a massive hug. "You're my friend, Zac, and you always will be." Abel smiled as she rested her head against Zac's shoulder. "My hero."

Chapter Eighteen

Zac rested the large zoology text on the arm of the couch, her eyes swiftly following her finger over the slick page. Her other hand rested lightly on Spinney's shoulder as Spinney read a novel, her blonde head resting in Zac's lap.

She looked up from her book, smiling down at her friend then looking around the cabin. Spinney had shown her what decorating a Christmas tree was like. They had used tons and tons of shiny tinsel, balls, ornaments and little things that the Cohen children made in school over the years. She watched as the colorful lights over the mantel chased each other in an endless game of tag. Christmas music played softly in the background, and the large, seven foot fake spruce stood proud in the corner, lighting up Zac's heart as well as the room. She'd seen Christmas trees in store windows before, but never in person and certainly had never decorated one. It had been fun, both women teasing each other and almost ending up in a tinsel fight. It had been a glorious day.

A deep sigh of contentment and happiness escaped her. Never had she felt such peace.

Glancing at the digital clock on the DVD player, she gently nudged her friend. "Spinney. It's time."

Spinney looked up at her, then at the clock, and eased into a sitting position. Stretching her arms above her head, she stood, reaching for Zac's hand.

Zac had no idea just what exactly Chanukah was, except what Spinney told her. She knew the word meant dedication and commemorated the rededication of the Holy Temple in Jerusalem after the Jews' victory over the Hellenist Syrians in 165 B.C. After the victory, the Jews wanted to light the menorah, and found only enough oil that had not been defiled in the war to light it for one day. Miraculously, the oil lasted for eight.

As the light was fading outside, Zac watched as Spinney brought out the beautiful, silver menorah and placed it on the table in front of the large picture window.

"Come here, Zac." Spinney reached for her friend. Zac took her hand, and watched as Spinney placed a candle in the first slot, and lit another that she held in her hand.

As she used the one candle to light the other already placed, Spinney began to sing, softly, her voice pure and melodic.

"Baruch atah adonai eloheinu melech ha'olam asher kid'shanu b'mitzvotav v'tzivanu l'hadlik neir shel Chanukah." The low singing chant was quickly followed by another, "Baruch atah adonai eloheinu melech ha'olam shecheyanu v'kiy'manu v'higyanu lazman hazeh."

Abel placed the candle in the taller, central holder of the menorah, and turned to Zac with a loving smile. "Happy Chanukah, Zac."

Zac smiled and echoed the words.

※※※※

As the days went on, Spinney and Zac forged a closeness that neither had thought possible. Even Zac was shocked and pleasantly surprised by how much deeper their friendship had gotten. The small blonde had been everything to her for so long. What she felt for her Spinney filled her entire heart.

The rest of Spinney's family would arrive the next day, and she was sad. She liked Spinney's mother, and certainly liked Becky, but she loved having Spinney all to herself, not having to share her with anyone. And, in all honesty, she wasn't looking forward to going out and freezing at night–a strange thought and concept for her, as she'd long held the belief that living inside a house with a "real" bed was not for her. But, sleeping beside Spinney every night in the warmth and comfort … well, she was beginning to see a few advantages. *Maybe.*

Every night, she and Spinney cuddled in the bed on the third floor, watching as the snow fell, knowing they were safe and warm. Spinney had asked Zac repeatedly to stay for the winter in the cabin, but Zac declined. Despite the cold, she did miss her freedom, and the outdoors. Just the smell alone made her smile. It was confusing at times, the way she saw both pros and cons in her dual situation. She did that now, standing at the window in Spinney's third-floor bedroom.

"What are you grinning at, hmm?" Spinney asked. She put a hand on Zac's back, leaning into her as she looked over Zac's shoulder. "It's so beautiful out there," she whispered.

Zac nodded.

"I'm really going to miss you, Zac."

Zac look at her over her shoulder. "I'll miss you too, Spinney." She reached back and urged Spinney to stand beside her, putting an arm around the slim shoulders of her friend. "A whole bunch."

Spinney smiled up at her. "Come on," she urged, issuing a final pat to Zac's strong back, and Spinney turned away, heading toward the warm, inviting bed.

≈≈≈≈

Abel watched her friend, still standing at the window. She knew Zac was restless after a week of virtual captivity with her in the cabin. More than that, she sensed something else within her friend, a sort of sadness. Since she'd come back to the cabin and met up with Zac again, something was a little different about her. Something had changed since last summer, and she wished she could put a finger on it. It was almost as if she had grown slightly more quiet, if that was possible. More mature, perhaps?

Something had happened to Zac after the attack last summer. Some sort of deep down, elemental change had taken place. Abel knew her friend had been terrified of losing her friendship, although she tried valiantly to assure her that wasn't the case. They had grown so close over the last week or so, closer than Abel had ever known was possible with another person. Even she and Jess weren't that close. She felt Zac on a deeper level, a soul level. She felt her in her bones, and wanted to do everything she could to make her happy, and to assure her safety and comfort. She already had a small pile of Christmas gifts under the tree for her friend, and she knew her mother was bringing more for her. The cool thing about Abel's family was, her father was Jewish, her mother Catholic. Somehow they made it work, and they had compromised in teaching their children the merits of both worlds. The kids loved it because they got twice the gifts between Christmas and Chanukah.

Finally Zac turned away from the window, and hurried across the cold floor, hopping onto the bed, bouncing with a huge grin. Abel watched her childish enthusiasm and couldn't help but grin herself.

"You're gonna break the bed!" she laughed. Finally Zac fell onto the soft mattress, winded. "Come on. Warm me up, woman!"

Zac hastily kicked until she got the blankets out from under her, and wiggled around until she was comfortable, automatically opening her arms wide for Abel to cuddle into. Abel grinned like an idiot. She loved this part of the day, and dreaded when she'd have the big bed alone again. Zac's warmth and quiet protection were so comforting to her. They laid there in silence for all of four minutes when Zac sighed.

"I can't sleep," she declared, about to sit up again when Abel pressed her hand down on her flat stomach.

"Can't sleep? Zac, it's been like five minutes!" Abel lightly slapped at the flat stomach below her hand again. She had managed to put a little weight on her friend over the week they'd been together. She had loaded her up with protein, whipped cream, and chocolate chip cookies that were almost shockingly sweet. She still shivered at that first initial taste, which didn't seem to phase Zac in the least.

Zac sighed.

"Okay, okay. Want to sing?" Abel asked, raising her head just enough to look into Zac's face. She knew this was the magic suggestion, as Zac loved the special song she'd taught her when they were kids, and saw the excitement flush Zac's features.

"Okay!"

Abel grinned, and began singing the frog song. Zac quickly joined in, their voices, low and high, mingling and filling the quiet space of the dark bedroom. Soon, within about ten minutes, Zac's voice began to falter then fade, then it disappeared altogether. Abel smiled and laid a gentle kiss on her friend's cheek.

"Night, Zac," she whispered, and closed her eyes.

Chapter Nineteen

Zac sat in her lean-to, proud of her accomplishment of making something more sturdy, and amazingly warmer. The fire ring that sat in the small space lit up the place, throwing strange shadows on the walls. She checked the spit over the fire, making sure the hot dogs Spinney gave her were done. She had never eaten these, made by some guy named Oscar Meyer.

She eyed the package that read hot dog buns. They looked like long rolls, which Spinney said they basically were. So, hot dogs, hot dog buns and a bottle of ketchup, which Zac had had before, were all ready. Her mouth watered at the smell of this new food. She was so tired of rabbit, even if Spinney had said she had no idea what hot dogs were actually made of.

A small smile played across her face when she thought of her small friend. It had been wonderful to spend so much time with her. She glanced over to the corner to see the large zoology book waiting to be read. She would have hours to dedicate to that tonight. She had gotten to read some at the cabin, but she wanted to focus most of her time on Spinney.

Spinney.

Zac smiled broadly as she removed the hot dogs from the fire, placing them on a plate. Preparing the 'dawgs' the way Spinney had instructed her, Zac got her dinner ready. She couldn't get the smile to leave her face. She was happier in that moment than she figured she'd ever been. She had a new home, new book, her Spinney, and Oscar Meyer.

❦

"Okay, close your eyes," Abel said softly, guiding her friend by the hand toward the bouncing bundle.

"Where are we going, Spinney?" Zac asked quietly as they headed from her place through the trees. She could tell they were headed toward the Cohen cabin.

"Shh. Just trust me." Abel pulled her eager friend behind her, a grin covering her face. Abel let go of the larger hand and bent down, picking up the whining, whimpering body. "Open."

Zac's blue eyes opened, then opened wider." A puppy!" she exclaimed, white teeth shining in the sunny day.

Abel grinned, nodding." This is Peanut," She held the eight-week-old golden retriever up for Zac's inspection.

"Peanut." Zac reached a tentative hand out, looking into Abel's eyes for approval and finding it. She touched the soft, velvety head and ears. Zac felt her heart lost to the little guy. Big brown eyes looked up at her, a pink tongue fighting valiantly to find any purchase on her face. She giggled as she moved her head from side to side, trying to avoid being kissed in the mouth by the anxious little guy.

Abel watched, as if completely and utterly charmed by her friend and the newest member of the Cohen family. "Take him." She handed the wiggly bundle to Zac, who was more than happy to take him.

She was muttering nonsense to the slobbering beast, the puppy squirming and whimpering, trying to get even closer to his new friend. Abel led them over to the porch stairs and sat down, followed by Zac. As she watched her friend wrestle with the pup, a grin from ear to ear on her face, she it reached out and gently pushed the thick, dark hair back over Zac's shoulders. Zac's blue eyes met hers and made Abel smile. Zac smiled back then turned her attention back to the dog.

"Zac?" Abel watched with amusement as Peanut grabbed onto one of Zac's long fingers, little teeth, sharp as needles, gnawing.

"Hmm?" Zac said absently, playing with the pup with infinite patience, only wincing slightly when the dog got too rough.

"Have you ever thought of living in a city? Or even a small town?" Abel leaned back, resting her weight on her hands on the shoveled porch behind her.

Zac stopped playing for a moment, though Peanut continued to chew on her. "I don't know, Spinney. I guess I haven't given it much thought." She turned back to the dog, which grabbed hold of the pull-string hanging from her Boston U. hoodie. She gently nudged him away from it, grabbing the golden bundle into her arms and kissing his head. She giggled as once again she tried to dodge little puppy kisses.

"Do you think you could ever do it?" Abel asked gently before she bit her bottom lip. "Well..." Zac absently petted the puppy. "I don't know. I sometimes think it would be interesting. You know, to see what's out there?" She smiled wistfully. "I read about so many things, hear airplanes flying overhead..." She gazed up into the blue sky. The snow had ended, for now.

Abel felt her heart stop at Zac's softly spoken words. She was desperately trying not to get her hopes up. "I could show you." Her voice was barely above a whisper. She wanted so badly to take Zac back to Boston with her, show her all that the world had to offer someone as bright and beautiful and kind as her friend.

Zac looked at Abel, who looked back at her with uncertainty in her eyes and a shy smile on her face. She smiled in turn. She reached a hand out and, with the barest of touches with the back of her fingers against the softness of Abel's cheek, said, "If I ever went, Spinney, there's no one else I'd want to show me."

With Zac's soft words and the loving look in her eyes, Abel was unable to look away. She reached up and wrapped her fingers around Zac's hand, cradling it in both of her own. "Anytime, Zac," she whispered. "Anytime."

≈≈≈≈

"Oh, mom! It's beautiful!" Abel clapped her hands together happily as she stared at the large box. "She'll love it."

"Really? You think so?" Sherry asked, eyeing her daughter, who was nodding vigorously. "You don't think she'll be offended?"

"No. Dad let you get this?" Abel fingered the smooth cardboard box.

Sherry grinned. "It was his idea."

"You're kidding!"

Sherry chuckled. "Nope. Believe it or not, he's concerned and protective of Zac." Sherry busied herself getting the wrapping paper and tape, handing her daughter the scissors. "The moment he found out what really happened last summer, that was it. He changed his entire perception of her."

"Well, well," Abel said with a small chuckle. "Mr. Negative finally sees her merits and not just her flaws, huh?" Both women laughed as Adam was known for not easily trusting or allowing people to get close to him or his family.

The two women sat on the floor in the middle of Sherry and Adam's bedroom, surrounded by rolls of wrapping paper and gifts to wrap. "Will she like the rest of the things we got her?" Sherry asked, wrapping a few small packages.

"I think so. She's so grateful for anything she's given." Abel's face beamed, her eyes dancing as she thought of her friend's innocent excitement in everything new she encountered. As she lovingly wrapped a gift for Zac she could feel her mother's eyes on her. She turned and met her gaze. "What?"

Sherry shook her head as if to say, "Nothing," though her lips were curled into a knowing smile. She turned back to her task. "Honey, is Zac coming for Christmas dinner?" Sherry casually folded the shiny paper over, creasing along its edge then folding it over the box that contained a new pair of jeans for Ben.

"I don't know." Abel sighed, taping the edges of the wrapping paper together and moving the box around so the open ends faced her. "I'm trying." She grinned at her mother. "I've been slowly working on her. I think I've worn her down."

"What? Do you have to manipulate the poor girl?" Sherry asked with wide eyes. She took the paper off the sticky part of the bow and stuck it on her wrapped gift, writing Ben's name on the top in clear, neat strokes. She set it aside, grabbing the new tool set for Adam.

"Kind of," Abel hedged. "She's stubborn, Mom."

"Ah. So you've met your match, huh?"

"Yeah, yeah. Yuck it up."

※※※※

Zac looked to the rock ceiling as she lay on her bedroll. She chewed on her lip for inspiration. She had re-read Abel's note that she found waiting for her at the overhang when she'd returned to the woods. She nearly memorized it.

Zac,

I'm not entirely certain how things fell apart as badly as they did this summer. Just when I found you, you are lost to me again. I'm very sad and wish I could turn back the clock and do things differently.

Please know that I know the truth of that man who was going to attack me. The police came and we found out who he was. Where did you go when they were here? How did you escape? I was so worried. Still am. And I miss you!

Please be safe and take care of yourself. I think about you all the time, and wish, oh how I wish, that things were different. I won't forget you again, Zac. I promise. My savior.

Love always,
Your Spinney

Zac smiled, plucking the note from where it lay on her chest and carefully refolding it. She didn't want it anymore torn than it already was. She kept it in her pocket at all times so when Spinney wasn't with her, she'd know her friend was still there.

With a sigh, she sat up and turned back to the paper before her, pen poised over its blank surface. Chewing on her lip, she once again tried to find inspiration. She had no money to buy gifts, but wanted Spinney to know that she cared.

Bringing the tip of the pen down, she began to write:

Spinney,

She chewed harder on her lip, cursing silently when she tasted a bit of blood.

"Ow..." She brought a finger up, seeing the pin prick amount of blood. Sucking on the tiny wound, she gazed at the decorated wall of her home. She had taken a pen and had marked the backside of the drywall with marks of her making, making the home more personable.

She saw where she had written the word SPINNEY in large, dark letters. Grinning like a fool, she turned back to the task at hand. Zac began to write again but stopped and listened. *Footsteps.* She closed her eyes to concentrate, trying to figure out who it was. It was getting dark, and she had left Spinney with her family that day.

"Zac?" came the soft voice, which immediately made her smile.

She quickly rolled the paper up, and stuffed it under her bedroll, then crawled to the entrance of her home.

"Here, Spinney," she called out softly, and heard the footsteps hurry over. A blonde head appeared through the cloth covering over the entrance. She smiled at her friend.

"Hi." Spinney pushed through the curtain then turned back around to make sure it was pulled snug behind her. She looked around as she settled next to Zac. "It's warm in here," she said, surprise in her voice as her gaze settled on the small fire that danced merrily in the ring of rocks.

"Yes, it's nice and comfy now." Zac smiled. "What are you doing out, Spinney? It's cold and dark." She moved over, giving her friend the choice spot near the fire, as she could see Spinney shivering.

"I missed you," Spinney said simply, getting comfortable in the warmth of the fire. She reached into the pockets of her coat and brought out three large apples. Zac's favorite fruit.

Zac's eyes lit up as she grabbed one of the offered pieces of fruit and happily bit into it.

Spinney watched, amusement in her eyes as she turned the stem on hers, naming a letter with each turn, just as she had done since she was a child. Zac chewed happily as she watched the familiar game, her eyes twinkling at this wonderfully unexpected surprise.

"...j...k...l...." SNAP! Spinney held the brown stem in her hand, looking at it. "L. Hmm," she drew her brows together.

"So, whatever letter you end up with is who you'll marry?" Zac asked with a grin, knowing the game was silly, but liking it anyway.

Spinney nodded with a smile. "Yep. But I don't know anyone with a name beginning with L, so, oh well." She grinned, dropping the stem into the fire, and bit into her apple. "So what are you doing?" she asked, wiping juice from her chin.

"Nothing," Zac said, though couldn't lie worth a damn. Her eyes darted all around.

"Zaaaac," Spinney drawled.

"Yessss?" Zac drawled right back, making them both grin.

"What are you up to?"

Biting her lower lip, Zac finally met her friend's gaze. "I can't tell you," she said softly, giving Spinney a pleading look. "Yet."

"Okay, okay. I'll get you next time, Gadget!" Spinney pointed a sticky finger at her friend, who looked utterly baffled.

"Gadget?"

"Never mind." Spinney grinned, looking happy and content as she chewed on her latest bite of apple. She set the third apple down on the stone shelf for Zac for later. "So, what do you wanna do tomorrow?"

"Tomorrow?" She drew her dark brows together. "Tomorrow is Christmas." Zac eyed her as she continued to eat her treat.

"Uh, huh." Spinney grinned over at her friend.

Zac took it in and realized what Spinney was getting at. With a heavy sigh, her resolve crumbled. She took the last bite of her apple, tossing the core into the fire and nodded. "Okay, Spinney. I'll spend it with you. And your family."

Squealing with delight, Spinney launched herself at Zac, who fell backward under the force of the hug. Zac returned the hug despite the rock digging into her back. Spinney pulled out of the hug, resting her weight on her forearms as she lifted herself slightly. "Oops," she grinned, looking down into Zac's amused face. "Guess I got a little excited."

"It's okay," Zac said, resting her hands on Spinney's lower back. Truth be told, she wasn't entirely minding the position…save for the rock, that is.

☙☙❧❧

Abel felt Zac's hands on her lower back, and suddenly a wave of heat shot uncomfortably through her. She moved off her friend and reclaimed her place by the fire. She grabbed Zac's hand and pulled her back into a sitting position. She sent her a sheepish smile of apology, suddenly feeling a bit shy. Shaking herself out of it, she gave Zac a genuine smile of affection and gratitude. "Sit closer to me, Zac." She moved over a bit and patted the ground next to her. She waited until Zac joined her, their shoulders touching, then rested her head on Zac's shoulder. "Thank you," she said softly. "You have no idea what this means to me."

Zac nodded, resting her cheek against Abel's head. "You're welcome."

They were quiet for a long moment. She realized as they sat together in Zac's cave-like structure, she really liked being with Zac in her own territory. It was so cozy and warm. For the briefest of moments, she could imagine living there with Zac. Startled by the thought, she shook it free.

Looking around, Abel noticed the drawings. "Zac? What are these?" She reached out and ran a finger lightly over the drawings on the drywall. The artwork reminded her of those found in caves and dwellings, though slightly more sophisticated in their construction. Her smile broadened when she saw her name written in big, bold letters.

"My art," she said with a proud smile. "Different

things go there that are important or that I'm happy about." She watched as Abel traced the lines of her name, as well as some of the faces she'd drawn. They were funny, expressive faces, characters Zac made up years ago. She explained in patient detail who each character was, and what they represented, and the story behind their conception.

Abel grinned at her. "You're talented, Zac," she said, looking at her friend in wonder. "You just... you never cease to amaze me." She looked back to the artwork.

Zac rubbed the back of her neck "Oh. Um, well, thank you, Spinney." Zac looked shyly at Abel.

"You're so cute." Abel grinned, gently nudging Zac's shoulder with her own. "Can I add something?"

"Yes!" She dug out the marker from her belongings. "Here."

Abel took the proffered Sharpie and gave Zac a soft smile, which was returned. Without thought, she reached up with her other hand and gently stroked Zac's cheek. She felt her heart swell with affection for this special woman who had come to mean so much to her. "Thank you," she said softly, knowing Zac would take that as a thank you for the marker, but it was so much more than that. So very much more.

With maker in hand, she turned away from their connection and faced the wall looking for an empty spot. Once found, she concentrated on what she planned to fill it with. Stroking the pen with her thumb, she chewed on her lower lip. She could feel Zac's expectant presence behind her and turned to look back over her shoulder.

"You, missy, can't watch," she said, waggling the marker at her friend. Zac looked into the twinkling green eyes, and grinned, nodding. She turned her back, grabbing the zoology book.

"What'cha reading about?" Abel asked, turning back to the wall.

"The mating habits of otters," Zac murmured, already lost in her studies.

Abel smiled and shook her head as she stared at the blank spot of wall in front of her and continued to chew on her lower lip, thinking. She smiled. If she could draw it once, she could most definitely draw it again. Taking the cap off the marker, she began. She didn't have the colors this time, but that was okay. In her older, more experienced hand, she could create details that would make color unnecessary.

"Can I look yet?" Zac asked, impatience and excitement in her voice.

"Hang on," Abel said absently, putting the final touches on her masterpiece. "Okay. You can look."

Zac set the book down and turned around, excitement buzzing in her eyes. When she saw what Abel had drawn, she smiled, slow and wide.

Standing on the wall were two stick figures, holding hands. One was much taller with dark hair, the other small and no color in her hair. They were smiling, and the taller one wore overalls. Above their heads was written: Zac and Spinney, Friends Forever.

She smiled at that, looking at her friend, and nodded. "Yes."

Chapter Twenty

"People! Lazy people!" Abel growled when she grabbed the near empty tea jug from the fridge. She wanted everything to be perfect for when Zac arrived. Scurrying over to the counter, she grabbed the Mr. Coffee Iced Tea Maker and the box of Lipton tea bags from the cabinet. There was a small knock on the front door and Abel growled again.

Abel got the iced tea pitcher ready and steeping. All the food was set out and ready to go, the table set and all her siblings accounted for. The iced tea was to be one of the main options to drink, but more than likely Ben had come along last night and finished it off, too lazy to make more.

"Damn him," she growled as she pushed the on button. "Okay. Just about re–" She stopped, nearly running headlong into Zac. She looked up into amused eyes. "Hi!"

"Hi," Zac said, softly.

Abel immediately wrapped Zac into an immense hug, so relieved she'd come. In truth she didn't doubt her, as it seemed her friend had more integrity than anyone she knew, but she still was worried she'd freak out at the last minute. "You smell good," Abel said, inhaling the smells that wafted around her as she buried her face in Zac's neck. Very natural, spicy.

"Oh." Zac pulled away from the hug, grinning down at her friend. "I bathed this morning."

"What? Zac, it's freezing out there!" Abel exclaimed, pointing to the window and the falling snow.

Zac shrugged with a grin. "It had to be done." Her smile slid from her lips as she walked past Abel, brows drawn when she saw the box on the counter. "It's me," she said, turning to her friend, holding up the box to show her.

"Huh?" Abel walked over to Zac, looking at the box, then at her friend, utterly confused. "What's you?"

"This." Zac pointed a finger at the word. "Lipton," grinning from ear to ear.

Finally catching on, Abel grinned, too. "Lipton, huh? I guess you had told me that. Zac Lipton." She tasted the name on her lips, and smiled. Then she chuckled, looking down at her feet. She remembered her game from the night before with the apple stem. "Gee, Zac. Guess we're meant to be together forever, huh?" She nudged Zac's arm with her shoulder. "The apple stem last night?"

"Oh." Zac smiled, and put the box down. "You landed on L."

"Sure did." She hugged her friend again. Hands still resting on Zac's shoulders, she smiled up at her. "Merry Christmas, Zac." At Zac's bright smile she took her hand. "Come on."

☙ ☙ ❧ ❧

The family was already seated, two empty chairs remaining side by side. Flanking them was Becky, who looked up at Zac like a goddess, and Jake.

"Zac. Nice to see you," Adam said from the head

of the table. He smiled at her. She returned it with a weak, unsure smile.

"Um, you, too, Mr. Cohen," she said, almost imperceptibly.

"Sit," Spinney said softly, motioning toward the seat next to Becky, who was nearly bouncing out of her booster seat.

Zac sat, smiling at the small girl, then looked around the table. Sherry sat across from Spinney's father, and across from her was Ben, next to him, Rachel. She smiled at each in turn, noting that Ben seemed to be staring. He had eyes much like his sister's, though not as bright or friendly.

"Hi," he said, his eyes traveling over her face and down over her sweatshirt-clad chest.

"Hi," she said quietly, not sure what to make of him.

"Ben," Spinney hissed. "Don't be a pig."

He glared at her, but shifted his eyes elsewhere.

Sherry chuckled at the situation. "He's a bit smitten with you, Zac," she stage whispered to a confused Zac. who simply smiled.

"Mom!" Ben growled.

Spinney and Sherry shared a grin before Sherry offered up a prayer to keep her family safe over the year, and the food was dished out.

Zac was excited, the smells of the new foods nearly driving her to drool. She listened as Spinney explained what all the dishes were, and was more than willing to try everything–several times. She felt eyes on her and turned to see Spinney watching her, as well as the entire Cohen family, some members with forks halfway to their mouths. Feeling nervous, she leaned over towards Spinney. "Am I doing something wrong?" she whispered.

Spinney smiled and shook her head. "No. We're all just so glad to see you with such a good appetite." She snagged the last roll from the covered bread basket and set it on the edge of Zac's plate. "Eat up, there's plenty. Plus, I'm sending you home with leftovers."

Zac didn't have to be asked twice, and continued her dinner. She smiled her thanks when Spinney grabbed the roll and split it in half, smearing on ample butter before replacing the roll on the edge of her plate. The two exchanged a look and smile, no words necessary as Spinney nodded then turned back to her own dinner.

Zac felt eyes on her again and turned to see Spinney's mom watching the two, her chin resting in her palm. Like Ben before, she wore an expression that Zac couldn't quite read. She'd been around people so rarely, she hadn't fully developed great people-reading skills, and it had gotten her into trouble more than once.

※※※※※

Zac began to feel a little more at ease with the Cohens, though only if Spinney was at her side. She pondered why it was that Ben kept staring at her. He made her uncomfortable, so she kept an eye on him. Dinner had been eaten and dishes loaded into the sink and stacked on countertops to be dealt with later. For now, everyone gathered in the living room.

"Okay, gang. Presents!" Adam exclaimed, his eyes shining brightly. He hurried over to the Christmas tree that the two young women had decorated, the lights blinking and chasing each other. Beck and

Rachel squealed as they raced to sit on the floor next to it, followed by the rest of the Cohen family and Zac.

"Sit with me?" Spinney patted the spot on the love seat next to her. She looked up at Zac with big, beseeching eyes.

Zac grinned, and plopped down. Like there was a chance she'd say no!

Becky and Rachel insisted on playing Santa, and were given the honorary red hats to go along with the role. Rachel helped Becky read the names on the labels, and they both passed the gifts around.

Zac watched in fascination as the family talked with each other, laughing, and playfully smacking each other. She felt a lump in the pit of her stomach, the wistfulness making itself known, and not for the first time.

"You okay?" Spinney asked softly, her green eyes full of understanding.

Zac nodded with a forced smile.

"Do you need to leave?"

"No," Zac hastily replied. She wasn't going to leave her friend alone this day. "I'm just watching."

"Okay," the blonde said softly, taking Zac's hand for a squeeze, then turning her attention back to the festivities.

The mountains of gifts were quickly disappearing, leaving behind piles of discarded wrapping paper, bows, and hordes of giggles and squeals of excitement. Zac watched, smiling and chuckling now and then, especially when her Spinney opened her gifts, her green eyes sparkling and dancing, and she showed Zac every single thing she received.

Finally everyone had opened their gifts, Adam crawling around on the floor to collect the trash, dragging a growing black trash bag behind him. Spinney looked to her mother, and after seeing Sherry's nod, hurried out of the room. Left sitting alone on the couch, Zac felt a moment of panic, looking around to see all eyes on her. Ben smiled, and she weakly smiled back, relief flowing through her when she heard Spinney's footsteps return to the room.

"Merry Christmas, Zac!" she boomed, with Rachel's help, setting down a myriad of gifts at her shocked friend's feet. The Cohen's watched eagerly for Zac's reaction. *No pressure.*

Zac looked around at all the anxious faces, then at Spinney, who was kneeling in front of her with a grin from ear to ear. "I, I don't know what to say," she said quietly, so only Spinney would hear her. She suddenly felt so unsure.

"You don't have to say anything," Spinney said, placing her hand on Zac's knee for support. "Just open your gifts." Her smiling reassurance gave Zac the confidence she needed.

As she tore into the gifts, she couldn't keep the dopey grin from her face. She had never felt so warm or accepted as she did with the Cohen family in that moment. She had never felt so loved. Spinney explained what each and every thing was that Zac unwrapped. Zac didn't have the heart to squash her friend's excitement, considering she could read the descriptions on the packaging or figure it out from the picture on the side of the boxes. She "oohed" and "ahhhed", enjoying the smile that graced Spinney's lips.

Zac was truly touched by the thoughtfulness of Spinney and her family. She looked on in awe at the nice, comfortable and warm sleeping bag that Spinney had bought all by herself. It was waterproof, and lined with down, whatever that meant. She was also given a thick, heavy-duty foam mattress, large enough to fit a twin-sized bed. She was anxious to put the solar-powered heater to use, given to her by all of Spinney's brothers and sisters. The cookware, Igloo cooler, and finally the big box, which turned out to be a nice three-person tent, were from Adam and Sherry.

Spinney's dad went on to tell Zac about all the virtues of this particular tent, and told her that after much discussion, he and his wife wanted Zac to stay in the tent on their property. He said that way she would have no fear of being shooed away by forest rangers for staying on the government's land, and she could look after the cabin for them.

Zac almost felt overwhelmed by the generosity and caring from Spinney's family. It was quite evident Spinney didn't fall far from the apple tree.

"And last but not least," Sherry said, sitting next to Zac on the couch. She handed her a simple key. "This is to our cabin, Zac. Should you need to come in, for any reason, you can. Okay?" Sherry's green eyes, so much like her daughter's, regarded her with warmth and friendship.

Zac nodded, taking the shiny key from her fingers.

"Any reason, Zac. You need a shower, you need to watch TV, whatever," Spinney said softly, placing her hand on her friend's knee.

Zac met her gaze, and smiled with a short nod. "Okay." She wanted to cry with the trust that was being bestowed upon her. At what cost? And for what reason? She didn't understand it, but didn't feel right not accepting it.

Zac noted with excitement the stack of her new toys by the door. The tent, still in its box, which Spinney promised to help her set up, the large cooler, which Sherry promised to fill with enough food to keep Zac fed throughout the winter, and the key that rested in her pocket. Adam had promised to show her how the alarm system to the cabin worked, and how to disengage it.

So many promises, her heart felt light and happy.

"Hey."

She started, turning to see Spinney's brother, Ben, leaning against the doorframe to the kitchen. "Oh. Hi," she said, feeling a bit nervous. She surreptitiously looked around for Spinney.

"Did you enjoy your Christmas?" he asked, his voice light, eyes sparkling with amusement.

"Yes. It was nice." Zac tried to smile, but it didn't work so well. Her nerves were growing, her heart racing as she tried to fight the urge to run, or at the very least, search for Spinney.

"How much do you know about Christmas tradition?" Ben asked, pushing off the doorframe with his shoulder, his hands tucked into the pockets of his jeans. He flicked his gaze up.

Zac's eyes followed where he indicated, and she saw a simple little bunch of leaves and berries attached to the wood of the overhead doorframe. She met Ben's gaze with confusion. "It's called mistletoe," he explained.

"Mistletoe," she repeated, tilting her head to take in the small plant. "What is it for?" She reached up to touch it, but her hand was caught. Her startled gaze met Ben's, his grin widening.

"Not for touching," he said, releasing her hand after holding it a few moments longer than necessary. "It's said that if you're caught underneath the mistletoe, you have to kiss the person standing there with you." He raised a challenging brow. "Have you ever kissed a guy before, Zac?"

"No." She slowly shook her head from side to side, not sure what to make of this, or of Ben.

"Uh oh! Who's standing under the mistletoe?" Sherry beamed, entering the entryway with her arms full of leftovers she planned to stow in Zac's cooler.

≈≈≈≈

Abel bounded down the stairs, her bladder eternally grateful after being full for so long after the meal. She heard laughter and looked toward the kitchen. There she saw her mother and Rachel watching as a nervous-looking Zac and Ben stood in the doorway. Under the mistletoe.

Her steps slowed as she neared, watching.

"Come on, Benny. Kiss her!" Sherry encouraged, grinning.

Ben looked at Zac and leaned in. Zac turned her head at the last second, Ben's lips catching her cheek.

Abel felt her blood go cold when she saw her brother kiss her friend, even on the cheek. She was surprised that Zac had allowed that! And that little rat of a brother… and, why on earth was their mother encouraging this?

She moved past the kitchen to the front door, picking up the cooler, loaded a few moments before with the leftover food. "Come on, Zac. You wanted to get this stuff to your place," she called out, her voice sounding slightly more harsh than she had intended.

She heard Zac hurry over to her. She was agitated and irritated, and had no idea why. She nearly dropped the cooler as she picked it up and cursed softly under her breath as she gathered a roll of paper towels that had been included atop the foil-covered dishes.

"You okay, Spinney?" Zac asked, suddenly next to her.

"Fine," Abel bit out. She balanced the cooler on her thigh as she opened the front door. Zac watched in confusion. She looked back over her shoulder to see that Sherry was watching, too.

Abel and Zac walked through the forest to Zac's place in silence. Zac's arms loaded up with her goods. When they finally pushed through the trees that opened to Zac's overhang, Abel turned to her friend. "Are you okay?" she asked, setting the heavy cooler down at the entrance of Zac's home.

"I'm fine. Why?"

"Well..." Abel kicked at some snow with the toe of her boot, wondering if she was being stupid or overreacting, but it had made her angry when she'd seen Ben kiss Zac. How could he take advantage of her like that? She growled at the memory. "Did my brother make you uncomfortable?"

She watched as Zac sank to her knees and crawled through the curtain, tucking it up once inside so they could load everything in. She appeared in the open entrance and looked up at Abel. "A little," she finally muttered.

Abel let out a sigh and grunted as she slid the cooler over to Zac, who quickly took hold and pulled it inside. "I'm sorry, Zac. That was really stupid of him." She squatted down in front of the entrance, watching as Zac maneuvered the heavy cooler to where she wanted it. When she was ready for more, Abel handed them to her. "Very stupid."

"Why?" Zac grunted as she tugged at her bedroll, rolling it up to replace with her new bedding.

"Because," Abel stammered, as she crawled inside. "You don't know him that well, and he was taking advantage of you and your lack of knowledge of that kind of thing," she said softly. She looked up and met Zac's kind gaze. "And you don't even know what mistletoe is, or what the tradition is. Or even really know him well enough to do something like that–"

"Spinney?" Zac cut in, looking at her babbling friend.

"Huh?"

"It's okay." She smiled gently.

"It is?" Abel looked at her for a moment, trying to process the events. Why was she so up in arms? It was innocent, and she was putting way too much into it. Wasn't she?

"Yes." She moved over to squat in front of Abel. "Spinney, you're right, I don't know him really, but I don't think Ben meant anything by it. Did he?" She cocked her head to the side. "I mean, right? He wasn't trying to do anything…bad…was he?"

Realizing what Zac was asking, and knowing it wasn't the case, Abel quickly shook her head. "I don't think so. I think he was just trying to be cute." Abel smiled, though it didn't fully reach her eyes. She knew her brother was interested in Zac, but would never do anything to hurt her, but still…

"Spinney?"

Abel was pulled from her thoughts by Zac's soft voice. She met her gaze, so close to her own in the confines of the small space.

"I didn't want to kiss him."

"No?" Abel asked, suddenly feeling relieved.

Zac shook her head.

"Oh. Good."

Chapter Twenty-one

Abel lay in her bed, hands tucked behind her head as she listened to Paramore's *Only Exception* with headphones from her iPod. She stared up at the ceiling. It had been a good Christmas, and she was so happy that Zac had joined in the fun. It didn't take long for her mind to turn back to the vision of Ben and Zac standing under the mistletoe. She felt the burn start again, and was clueless to figure out just why it was there. Ben was a boy. Zac was a girl, and a beautiful one at that. The kid had every right to have a crush on her. Zac didn't feel the same way, luckily, but still. What if she did? What if Zac and Ben got together, or what if Zac met someone? Maybe on the rails somewhere? Where would that leave Abel?

She felt completely selfish in her thinking, but Zac had needed her for so long, and she wanted so badly to be the one there for her. To teach her new things, and be the one that brought that sparkle of awe and wonder into those incredible blue eyes. She wanted to be Zac's Spinney.

"What is wrong with me?" she whispered into the darkness.

She knew she had no right to be jealous. In truth, there really wasn't anything to be jealous about. But, the truth of the matter was, she'd never even given it a thought that perhaps someday Zac wouldn't be there, wouldn't be waiting for her to return. Her Spinney.

Her Zac. Sighing in frustration and feeling quite childish, she closed her eyes and tried to focus on the music. The particular song she was listening to wasn't helping. She sighed again.

"I seriously need to get my shit together," she murmured then closed her eyes, losing herself to the music.

❧❧❦❦

Abel glanced out the window, looking out at the red dome tent she and her father had helped Zac put together two days before. She held her phone to her ear. "You'll be here in how long? Five? Okay. I'll get her." She pocketed her phone then ran outside, noting her siblings engaged in a fierce snowball fight. She bypassed them and called out Zac's name.

The zippered flap of the tent opened and Zac poked her head out. "You rang?"

Abel chuckled, knowing full well Zac didn't even fully appreciate where those words came from, as she knew Zac had never seen The Addams Family. "I just love having you like ten yards away instead of God only knows where," she said with a grin, as she made her way across the ten yards or so to where Zac stood.

Zac glanced over at her new palace, which had room for everything she owned plus much, much more. "I love that the bugs can't come in. What's up?"

"I love how you're picking up on the lingo," she chuckled, then grabbed Zac's hand and led her to the cabin. "And, nothing much." Abel grinned up at her, but kept them going at their steady pace. "You stay here." Abel sat her down on the top stair of the porch. They both watched as Adam's black SUV pulled into the snow-covered driveway. "Close your eyes, Zac," Abel said before jetting off across the yard to the SUV, which had just barely come to a stop.

"Hey, Zac!" Rachel called out from her snowball fight with Jake.

"Hi!" Zac called out, waving before closing her eyes.

Taking careful steps to not jostle the bundle she'd grabbed from the backseat, Abel made her way over to where her friend sat, hands in lap and eyes tightly closed.

"Okay," she said softly, placing the box on the step between Zac's booted feet. "Open your eyes, Zac."

Zac opened them to see the box, the flaps haphazardly closed. Peeling one of them back, she smiled massively. "Oh," she breathed, opening the rest of the flaps, the tiny whimpers rent the air. "Another one." She looked into Abel's expectant eyes, then back at the box. Reaching in, she felt the soft velvety fur, and found the small, fat body. "So cute," she whispered, looking at the little yellow lab puppy she was holding in her hands. "How old is he?" She looked into the droopy brown eyes, the little guy looking as though he'd been sleeping.

"I think a couple of months old," Abel said, her voice soft and reverent as she looked at the puppy who was coming around. He turned and looked up into Zac's face.

"Hi, baby," she cooed, running her hand through the soft fur on his back. "How are you, fella?"

Abel watched her friend with the gift that her father had rushed to town to get. She was awed and inspired by how gentle Zac was, how much caring and nurturing poured from her.

"What's his name, Zac?" she asked, petting the pup's ears.

Zac glanced at her. "I don't know. What is it?" she asked, grinning as the pup reached out until his cold, wet nose was nearly resting against hers.

"He's yours, Zac. You name him."

Zac looked over at Abel as she sat on the stoop beside her. Her eyebrows flew up. "Mine? But how?"

Abel looked up, smiling at her family who gathered on the porch behind them. "He's a gift from all of us," she said, indicating everyone. "This little guy here will be your company, and you can protect him." Abel winked making Zac grin.

She looked behind her, seeing the people she hadn't even realized were there. "All of you?" she asked, her voice barely above a whisper.

Sherry nodded with a soft smile from where she stood, leaning against her husband. "I hope you like him, honey." She placed a hand on Zac's upper back.

"Wow." Zac turned back to her new little friend. "It's just so much," she whispered, awe in her voice. She grabbed the puppy beneath his front arms and lifted him high so she was looking up into his sweet face. "What am I gonna name you, huh?" She grinned when a pink tongue came out to lick the tip of her nose. She wrinkled her brow as she studied him.

Abel watched her friend, utterly warmed by Zac's reaction to this gift, who just happened to be Peanut's brother.

After a long study of the little guy, Zac declared, "I'll call you Aureate, Aure for short." When the family looked at her like she'd lost her mind, she explained. "It means golden." She gave Spinney a sheepish grin.

"It's a good name." Abel smiled. The two shared

a look, both communicating what words could never say.

※※※※

Zac watched with sadness as her friend loaded up her blue car, ready to head back to school. She stuffed her hands deep into her pockets, chewing on her lower lip. She felt such sadness wash over her, it was startling and nearly suffocating and she suddenly felt she wanted to cry. She could see that Spinney was fighting back her own emotions.

Spinney put the last of her bags into the small car and turned to Zac. She gave her a smile, though it was incredibly weak and watery. "Well," she said, letting out a heavy sigh, which came out in a white puff. "I guess I should go."

Zac nodded. Aure at her side, his too-big feet disappearing under the blanket of snow. Even he seemed to sense this was a sad moment as he stood quiet and still. Zac swallowed hard. "I'm gonna miss you, Spinney," she said, her head hung so Spinney couldn't see her pain-filled eyes behind the curtain of dark hair.

Spinney brushed away Zac's hair, tucking it behind a red-tipped ear. "Me, too, Zac," she said softly then opened her arms, which instantly were filled.

Zac closed her eyes, inhaling the scent of her friend and the feel of her warmth and comfort. *Not going to cry, not going to cry. Okay, not going to let Spinney see me cry.* She held on, holding her friend close and tight. When they parted, she looked into those green eyes to see that they were filled with tears. She brought a hand up and just barely caught the first tear as it began to fall. "Don't cry, Spinney," she said, her voice a bit rough from her own threatening emotions.

"I'm trying not to." Spinney said with a smile, still holding on to Zac's shoulders. "I'll see you this summer, okay?"

"Okay," Zac said, her voice a mere whisper now, knowing that Spinney's departure from her life was imminent. "Be careful."

"I will. You, too. And you stay put!" She jabbed a finger into Zac's chest. "I don't want to have to worry about you anymore than I already do." She smiled, straightening Zac's coat. "You know, I thought of something the other night. You and me, as different as A to Z." She smiled at her little joke. "But, like two bookends, we seem to cram all those differences between and they don't matter."

Zac smiled, not fully understanding the reference, but she got the ideology behind the words. She pulled Spinney in for one last hug, then let her go and reached into her coat. She pulled out a carefully folded piece of paper, and handed it to her. Spinney took it, then smiled up at Zac.

"Merry Christmas, Spinney," Zac said quietly.

"Merry Christmas," she whispered back. Spinney said her goodbyes to Aure then climbed into her car.

Zac stood sentinel with her dog, a hand raised in goodbye as she watched her Spinney drive out of her life, yet again.

≈≈≈≈≈

Zac made her rounds around the forest, noting the way the snow had melted in parts. Some vegetation could be seen, though still not much. She checked around the area where she used to live. The lean-to was still there, and she kept it up, making any repairs that needed to be made. Once the Cohens returned that summer, she'd move back into it.

She had to admit that she enjoyed living so close to the cabin. She felt like she was doing them a service, and loved the feeling. In truth she hadn't had to run off anything more offensive than a fox or two, but still she felt important. For the first time, she had a job that wasn't just surviving.

Aure ran up ahead, his tail wagging like crazy. Zac smiled at her dog. They'd been together for two-and-a-half months and, next to Spinney herself, he was the best gift Spinney could have given her. Zac whistled between her fingers, the sound echoing through the woods. "Don't go too far!" she called out, and heard a small woof in response. Yep. She and the pup got along famously.

Zac thought about her time back here in Maine since last October. She was glad to be home. And when she'd been able to spend so much of her time with her friend, it had made it all worth it. The events of the previous summer seemed like another lifetime ago. She felt safe in that Spinney would not leave her again. Well, leave their friendship, that is. Nor would the little blonde forget about her. She knew she had a firm place in her Spinney's heart.

Spinney had been gone for sixty-three days. Zac had been left with a ton of food and a huge bag of Puppy Chow for Aure. She was used to spending her days hunting, fixing her shelter, or trying to wash her clothes. Now, everything had been done for her so she wasn't always entirely sure what to do with herself.

Of course she did plenty of reading, and the flashlight she'd been left—with plenty of batteries—allowed her to read well into the night. In the tent, her and Aure had the solar-powered heater, so didn't need a fire, which certainly made things safer. So, at night she and her puppy cuddled on the extremely comfortable foam mattress, Zac in the unbelievably warm sleeping bag and Aure at her feet. Zac read for hours on end while Aure snored softly.

The truth of the matter was, she missed Spinney so much it hurt, and she even missed Spinney's family, especially her mom. Sherry was exactly what she'd want for a mother if hers hadn't died so early on in Zac's life. They all treated her with such kindness and respect. It was strange. Even Spinney's father. As they had put up the tent together, he joked with her and made her laugh.

She smiled at the memory, climbing onto the snow-covered bluff she used as a look-out point. She wished so badly that she were climbing up there to watch for Spinney. *Summer time.* As she looked around at the snow covering her world, it seemed like years away.

Zac sat down on a log, rested her chin in her palms and sighed.

≈≈≈≈

The weather in Boston was much better. Dirty piles of snow were plowed against the curbs. Other than that, the streets were clear and the skies were blue. Abel and Jessica walked along the street they lived on, Abel glancing over into the park across the street. A few winter-bare trees littered the area, which housed a couple people walking their dogs. She smiled as she watched one particularly active dog nearly run his owner ragged.

"Cute, huh?" Jess said, a smile in her voice.

Abel nodded. "Yeah. That dog's got some serious energy." She stuffed her hands into her pockets, looking back to the buildings that lined the other side of the street.

"So we're talking about maybe Cancun this time. Can you swing it?" Jessica asked, glancing over at her friend. "Not too horribly expensive, yet really fun." She grinned, her white teeth stark against the beautiful mahogany of her skin. "Lots of cute guys!"

Abel looked over at her friend, and chewed on her bottom lip. Spring break was in a month, and the roommates were trying to decide where to go. "I'm not sure," she said, butterflies filling her stomach.

She was nervous to tell her friend what she had been thinking of doing instead. Ever since she had left the cabin in January, she couldn't get Zac out of her head. She missed her so badly it hurt sometimes. Lying in her bed at night, or even while in the back of the store stocking canned goods at her job at a local grocery store, she'd remember her friend's smile. She could see it now as she and Jess walked down the street. It would light up Zac's entire face. Hell, it lit up the entire area. Those beautiful, straight pearly whites. It irritated Abel as she had had to endure braces. And then there's Zac with the most perfect teeth she had ever seen. Just one more little perfection God threw into the mix. Her friend was unusually beautiful and what made her even more so was the fact that she had absolutely no clue.

She smiled, feeling herself fill with warmth at

the thought of those bright blue eyes.

"Dude, you look like a dork."

Abel was snapped out of her reverie and looked at Jessica. "What?"

"What's up with that smile? You look constipated or something."

SMACK!

"Ow! Jesus!" Jess held her arm protectively, moving slightly away from her friend. "What's up with you?"

"Nothing!" Abel barked, embarrassed to be caught daydreaming. "Cancun, huh?"

"Yeah. But that was like five minutes worth of conversation ago. Where were you?"

"I was just thinking."

"About what?" Jess grabbed her key from her pocket and inserted it into the lock on the front door of their building.

"Nothing. So who's all wanting to go?" Abel hurried inside as Jessica held open the door for her.

"Not sure. I think the count's up to seven." The girls headed down the hall until they reached the door to their apartment.

"Wow. I'm not sure if I'll be able to afford it or not." Abel bit her bottom lip, knowing she was lying to her friend. She hated it.

"Really?" Key in lock, Jess stopped and glanced at her friend. "I thought you said your folks were going to be able to help you out."

Abel shrugged noncommittally. "I'm not sure."

Jess opened the door and the two entered, Abel closing and locking the door behind them. She headed straight to their bedroom and changed for work. She would have to give this more thought. As she opened the drawer to get her work shirt out, she noticed the neatly folded piece of paper on the dresser. Dropping the shirt on the bed, she unfolded it, a smile brushing her lips as she took in the carefully written words and beautifully drawn pictures. The best Christmas gift she'd ever been given.

The paper was bordered by an outdoor scene, trees, deer and wolves. Abel ran a finger over the art before her gaze scanned the words:

Spinney-

I'm not sure what to say in this, but will do the best I can. First, I want to thank you for making my life good again. You make my days bright and make me smile endlessly.

I'm no poet by any stretch, but you make my heart want to sing like a bard, shouting through story and lore at the top of my lungs just what you mean to me.

I'm no dancer, but my feet itch to glide across the earth in a ritual of comfort and joy every time I see your car round the bend.

I may not be the smartest girl in the world, but I know that what I have is precious and worth so much more than gold.

I am able to see you every day in the forest. I look up into the sky and see your hair in the golden sun, like spun silk shining down to warm my skin.

I see your eyes in the green brilliance of the new birth of leaves and grass.

I see your smile in the lake as it sparkles in the sun like diamonds.

I am indeed a rich woman.

Thank you, Spinney. Thank you for being my

friend.

> Merry Christmas.
> Zac

Abel read the words that had so touched her heart and sighed, pressing the paper to her chest.

"What a sweetie." She sighed again.

༄༅༄༅

Abel glanced out the driver's side window, smiling as a car passed her with the occupants cheering and the horn honking, signs of SPRING BREAK pressed against the windows. As she drove, she thought back to the week before when Jessica had all but cornered her in their bedroom as Abel had been reading on her Nook, loaded with questions.

"Soooo," she began. "What's going on?"

"With?" Abel asked, setting the reading device down on her stomach, eyes boring into Jess.

"With the trip. Abel, we've been talking about this for three years." Jessica leaned forward on the bed, forearms resting on her thighs. "Level with me, blondie."

She tapped her fingers on the steering wheel along with the music she was listening to. Her other roommate, Kendra had been extremely disappointed that Abel had decided against the trip to Cancun with their circle of friends. Abel knew she'd hear it from her best friend.

Finally, Abel let out a breath and began to speak. "Zac-"

"Ah, right. The Paul Bunyan of the north." Jess sat back on the mattress.

Abel glared at her, not liking how Jess was speaking of Zac. "Yes, my friend from our cabin in Maine. I just... I just get worried, okay?" Abel threw her hands up in exasperation.

"So give him a call and invite him to drive up here for a weekend or so." Jess shrugged. "Why should that get your undies in a twist?"

In truth, Abel had no idea why she didn't clear up Jessica's misunderstanding in thinking that Zac was male. She just... didn't, though she'd told her previously Zac was female. Jess hadn't pushed much beyond that, likely knowing how stubborn her friend could be, and that Abel would only tell her what and when she wanted to.

So, as her friends packed bikinis and flip flops, she packed long johns and sweatpants.

※ ※ ※ ※

Zac ran ahead, trying to beat the little mongrel that was close at her heels. She was laughing, her breaths coming out in small, white puffs as the early spring air filled the forest.

"Come on, you loser!" she called out, grinning and pushing even harder, her booted feet pounding the earth. She could hear the heavy breathing of her dog as he began to eclipse her. "Crap!" she growled. "Oh no you don't." Giving it all she had, she pushed even harder, throwing her head back, long hair flying back from her head in an ebony wave. She saw the finish line coming up. If she could just make it to between those two rocks.

"Woohoo!" she crowed, scaring some birds out of their spring nests. She slowed and tried to catch her breath. Aure ran in circles around her, whimpering as his five month old self was still full of energy. "What do you want, you mutt?" Zac gasped, resting her hand on a tree trunk for stability as she allowed her lungs to fill with air. The golden dog whined until Zac gave in and gave him some love. He turned his head and licked the palm that had just been resting on his fur.

Zac was about to kneel down for their daily wrestle when she stopped. Ears perked, she hurried up to the bluff and climbed on a large rock, exhaustion from their race forgotten and Aure nipping at her heels. She scanned the area, the sunglasses she had received for Christmas firmly in place. A huge grin spread across her face, and she jumped down.

"Come on, Aure!" she yelled, running as fast as her legs could carry her toward the Cohen cabin and her tent. The blue car would be there in less than five minutes, and she wanted to be there to greet her Spinney, regardless of how confused she was why her friend was there so early.

She saw the car disappear around the bend, only to reappear even closer. She could see Spinney's face clearly through the windshield, and was excited when she smiled and waved. She waved back, holding Aure back from wanting to catch this large, moving thing. The car came to a stop, and as soon as she had the engine cut off, Spinney unbuckled herself and threw open the door and ran to her friend. She was caught up in a huge hug, strong arms holding her tight.

"What are you doing here, Spinney?" Zac asked, but did not dare relinquish her hold on her Spinney.

"I came to see you," Spinney murmured into the intense hug. "It's spring break. I get a week break from school every March," she explained. She smiled up into sparkling blue eyes. "Surprised?"

"Yes! Definitely." Zac looked down at the whining pup who sat at her feet. "Spinney, Aure says hi." She grinned at her friend.

Spinney knelt down, looking at the yellow lab. "You have grown, little man." She grinned, petting the velvety ears. "He's so cute, Zac." She smiled up at her taller friend, then turned her eyes back to the big, brown ones closer to her eye level. The puppy was more than happy to share his wet kisses with his new friend. Spinney giggled while trying to dodge the smooches. "How's he doing with the Puppy Chow we left?" she asked, narrowly dodging a big wet one.

Zac watched, happy beyond all measure to have her Spinney back with her. And early, too! "He's doing okay. Be out soon. He likes Oscar's hot dogs, though," Zac said with a grin, mighty proud of herself for finding this little gem out.

Spinney laughed, standing and swiping at her dust-covered knees. She gave Zac another one-armed squeeze before walking to the trunk of her car. "Come on, my friend. Help me unload the car."

Fifteen minutes later Aure lay on the floor in front of the quiet fireplace, chewing his new bone, and the women were situated on the couch, watching him.

"These are good, Spinney," Zac said, her mouth near capacity with the Spaghetti-O's.

"I love these things," Spinney said, reaching over and fingering a little o that was hanging from Zac's lip. She grinned, popping the stray noodle into her own mouth.

"How long are you staying?" Zac asked, then sipped from her Coke, which she also found quite tasty.

"You get me for one whole week." Spinney

grinned, spoonful of Spaghetti O's halfway to her mouth. "You excited?"

Zac nodded vigorously. "Very. And did you know that the muskrat can stay submerged under water for fifteen minutes at a time?"

"Good. As you should be," Spinney said, even as she cocked her head at the random bit of knowledge. "Uh, no, Zac. I can't say I knew that." She grinned as she reached out to poke Zac in the side.

Zac squirmed, glaring. "Hey."

Suddenly, an evil look swept through Spinney's eyes. She put her lunch on the coffee table then reached for her friend's bowl.

Zac looked at her, eyes wide with surprise and curiosity. "What are you doing? I was eating that!" The words were no sooner out of her mouth when ten fingers began to attack her sides unmercifully. "Ugh!" she exclaimed, reeling back against the arm of the couch, trying to avoid her attacker, to no avail.

Spinney was laughing wildly. Aure jumped up and began to bark at the ruckus from the couch. He watched as the two women played, his ears flopping with each body-shaking bark.

"No fair! No fair!" Zac yelled, finally falling to the floor in her attempt to get away from the seeking fingers. Tears were running down her cheeks from laughing so hard.

"What do ya mean, no fair?" Spinney laughed, following her friend to the floor, straddling her taller frame, fingers digging into Zac's ribs and stomach.

"You... cheated... squirt!" Zac gasped between laughter.

Spinney stopped for a second. "Squirt?" Her voice was filled with incredulity. Zac grinned, nice and big. "Grr." Spinney began her attack again.

This time Zac fought back, her own fingers finding all her friend's ticklish spots.

༄༅༄༅

After more than an hour of the tickle fight, Zac lay on the floor, exhausted, her body wrapped around that of Abel, who rested her head on Zac's outstretched arm, snug as a bug in a rug. She was running her fingers through the sleeping Aure's fur who was curled up against her stomach. Zac reached her arm over Abel's waist and ran her hand down the length of her dog's side. Little puppy sighs escaped, making them both smile.

"He's so cute," Abel said, her voice quiet. For a moment, just a very strange moment, she felt like Aure was a baby watched over by two very proud parents. It was slightly unsettling, yet comforting, somehow.

"Yes he is," Zac said quietly in Abel's ear. She cuddled in a bit tighter against Abel's back. "He's a good boy."

"He seems to really love you." Abel caught Zac's hand in hers, and held it, resting on Aure's side.

"I love him. He keeps me company," Zac said, bringing their twined fingers up and studying them, Abel's shorter than her own, but strong and capable.

"You have big hands," Abel said, also noting their fingers. "Strong." Able ran a fingertip over some scars that ran along the back of Zac's hand. "Soft," she whispered, tracing the faint, white lines with a nail. "What are these from?"

Zac shrugged. "Who knows? Different stupid

things, I guess. Cuts, scrapes." She focused on a very faint scar right in the center of the top of Abel's left hand. "What's this from?" She ran a fingertip over it. "You have the softest skin ever."

Abel smiled at the compliment. "Well," she chuckled at the memory. "One time when I was like five, my mom was ironing real quick before work and dropping me off at school. I was standing there at the ironing board, barely able to see over the thing, and put my hand down. She was in a hurry, and didn't notice, zoom!" She moved her hand through the air. "Ran right over it. Burned me." She raised her hand, looking at the slightly raised skin, now only about the size of a BB. At one time it had been the size of a nickel.

"Ouch."

"Yeah. It hurt. I remember that pretty well." She smiled. "My mother got so mad at me."

"Why?" Zac took Abel's hand in hers again, bringing the scar to her eyes for a closer inspection.

"Because it made us late. She felt bad later, but at the time she was just concerned with getting us out the door on time."

Zac gently wrapped her fingers around her hand, bringing it to her lips and lightly kissing the sixteen-year-old scar. "All better." She smiled down at Abel, who was already smiling up at her. "I like your mom."

"Good. She likes you." Abel took her hand back, surprised at the slight heaving in her stomach at the light brushing of lips against her skin. She looked at the scar, and for the strangest second, it did feel better, even though it hadn't hurt in years. Shaking her head to clear it, she concentrated on where their conversation was going.

"I didn't think your dad liked me," Zac said

shyly, tracing a natural part in Aure's fur, the pup sighing contentedly in his sleep and flopping over to his back, his front paws bent at the wrist joint. "But now, I think he does, doesn't he?"

"Of course he does," Abel said softly, watching with rapt attention as the long fingers of her friend began to rub Aure's pink tummy. "I don't know if he was quite sure what to make of you." She grinned. "But I assure you he likes you. Believe me, he's a cheapskate. If he didn't like you, he never would have let mom spend all that money on you for Christmas."

"That was very nice of them," Zac said quietly, her voice almost wistful. "I really wish I had known my mom."

Abel twisted in the brunette's arms until she was resting on her back, looking up into the beautiful face of her friend. "Do you remember anything about her?" she asked gently, taking Zac's hand into her own, resting them both on her stomach.

Zac shook her head. "Not much. I remember she had the prettiest eyes."

"Were they like yours?" Abel asked, looking into the blue depths. "Because I have to tell you, Zac. I think you have the most beautiful eyes I've ever seen."

"Thank you, Spinney. Yes, I think they were like mine. My father had brown eyes I think." She thought for a moment, then nodded. "Yeah. But oh, they'd get so dark when he was mad." She shook her head at the memory. "He did that a lot."

"Got mad?"

Zac nodded.

"At you?"

"At whatever." Zac flopped over to her back, her free hand clasped behind her head, as she stared at the beamed ceiling. "I used to go hide in this hole out in the woods. I'd dug it years before to play in."

"Did he ever hurt you?" Abel asked, her voice quiet. She so rarely got her friend to talk about her past or her family that she would do everything in her power to encourage her.

Zac shrugged. "I just kept my distance."

Abel watched her friend, seeing the play of emotions in her expressive eyes, and could see that Zac was starting to retreat within herself. She decided to get off the subject of Zac's father, hoping it would keep her talking. "What about your mom? Tell me more." Abel was glad when she saw a small, soft smile play at the edges of Zac's lips.

"She was pretty. Very kind. She used to be so nice to the animals around our house. We didn't live far from here. But there were other houses. She would feed the animals, or leave food out for them."

"I guess you inherited that, huh?"

Zac turned to look at Abel, looking deeply into her eyes. She smiled and nodded. "Guess so."

"You could be my very own Dr. Doolittle."

"Who?"

"It's a movie. He's a veterinarian who talks to animals and can understand what they say back to him."

Zac looked at her friend like she was nuts. "Is he crazy?"

Abel laughed. "No, you goof. It's just a story. A movie, but it started out as stories and I think a television series. I don't know. That's just what you remind me of." Abel shrugged.

"So, I remind you of some crazy vet who thinks he can talk to animals?" Zac raised a brow, and received a poke in her side for the trouble. She grabbed Abel's finger, wincing. "Still sore from you ten minutes ago, woman."

Abel grinned and allowed Zac to hold onto her finger. She turned to her side and raised herself so her head rested in an upturned palm. "So what do you wanna do this week other than stay with me?"

Zac looked up at her friend. "Oh, that's not fair! That thing you're doing with your eyelashes, no fair!"

Abel grinned, still fluttering her eyelashes. "What?" She bent her head down, batting the lashes against Zac's cheek, breaking into laughter as Zac pushed her away.

"Feels like a bug on my cheek!" Zac said, bringing a hand up and touching the spot on her face. Eventually, she joined Abel's laughter. "You're not being very nice to me today." She sent Abel a fake pout before grinning. "I don't know. What do you want to do this week? And..." She leaned up on her elbows, almost nose to nose with her friend. "Yes, I will stay with you."

"Yay!" Abel launched herself at Zac, pushing her back to the floor and giving her a massive hug.

Zac wrapped her arms around the feisty blonde, who stayed where she was, her head resting on Zac's upper chest, her body almost entirely covering Zac's. They stayed like that for a long moment, both turning their heads to watch the fire.

Abel slowly became aware of just how close their bodies were pressed together. She could feel Zac's breasts pressed against her own. She could hear Zac's heart beat, a solid, comforting sound. She could feel Zac's fingers as they trailed through her hair and down her back. Even through the thickness of her college sweatshirt, she could feel her warmth seep into her. Suddenly, it was too much.

"I gotta pee," Abel claimed as she jumped up, extricating herself from Zac. She hurried up the stairs, a barking Aure at her heels. She grinned as she heard her friend call the dog back. Once behind the closed door, Abel took a deep breath.

She could still feel Zac with her, almost as if she were standing beside her. The buzz was so strong it was almost disconcerting. She closed her eyes, absorbing the feeling. Even when she'd been back at school, she had been able to feel her somehow. It was so strange, and she knew that Jessica would be trying to figure it out from Abel's vague explanation of her friend and why she had to get to her.

"Good luck, Jess," Abel muttered, unable to figure it out herself.

༄༅༄༅

"Okay," Abel said, plopping down on the floor of her room, Zac sitting across from her. She reached into her bag and brought out one of two very heavy "coffee table" books. "This first one," she grunted as she managed to get it in Zac's lap, "is all about the last century. Things that have happened in America's history from 1900 to 1999."

Zac watched with rapt attention as the silver book waited to be perused.

"We Interrupt This Broadcast," she read, and looked up at Abel with confusion. "Broadcast?"

"Yeah. You know, like a radio? Or even television. See, when something huge happens, disasters, that kind of thing, there's usually a special report of some kind telling you about it." Abel leaned over and opened the cover of the large text. "This is a really cool book, even if it's about ten years old. See, it comes with these two CDs." She tapped their little envelope just inside the cover. "You can listen to the actual broadcasts as you read what happened."

Zac smiled, looking at her friend as she grinned from ear to ear. "Like the news?" she asked. At Abel's nod, she turned her gaze back to the book. "Okay. How does it work?"

"Well, hang on." Abel grabbed the second book. "This one is on modern inventions. You know, things that have come about within the last hundred years or so. Cell phones," she brought her own from where it sat on the floor next to her. "Computers, different cars, telephones, all of it." She gave Zac a sweet smile, and reached over to brush some strands of hair behind the taller woman's ear. "I figure it's about time we get you into the twenty-first century." She was about to turn toward her desk when she heard Zac's voice.

"Spinney? Did you know that muskrats make their houses out of bulrushes, weeds and packed mud?" Abel took in the wide, excited eyes and the flushed features of excited knowledge, learned and now shared. "And," she continued, "they have a separate sleeping thingy for each member of the family. Pretty cool, huh?"

Abel smiled, completely and utterly charmed. "That's very cool, Zac. You've been reading from your zoology book again, haven't you?" Zac nodded, looking slightly shy, but still excited. Abel felt a wave of affection rush through her. She crawled over to where Zac sat and leaned over Zac's lap to wrap her arms around Zac's shoulders in a massive hug. "Good."

❧❧❧❧

She sat at her desk, laptop open and booting as she ruffled through her psych papers. She had a paper due, and decided to do some work. Glancing over her shoulder, she saw Zac laid out on her bed on her stomach, legs bent at the knees and ankles crossed. Her calves were swinging slowly back and forth.

Abel's gaze scanned up the long frame to see the yellow and black headphones on Zac's ears and the *Broadcast* book open in front of her. She could see from her vantage point that the 1937 Hindenburg disaster was the topic of point. She smiled, wondering what was going through that brilliant mind of hers as she learned about things other than animals and plants and the sleeping habits of the muskrat.

Suddenly, Zac pushed up on her elbows, looking at nothing in particular as she pressed her fingers against the headphones to hear even better. From her short distance away, Abel could just barely make out what was happening, and it appeared it was the emotional reporter who was describing the horrific events of the huge craft's crash. She could hear the words in her mind, her great-grandfather always talking about it, as he'd witnessed it.

"It's a terrific crash... it's smoke, and it's in flames now... and the frame is crashing to the ground... oh the humanity!"

❧❧❧❧

Zac could feel the sting behind her eyes as her own emotions rose with the young radio reporter's.

She quickly turned the page to see "Pearl Harbor Under Attack." No clue what Pearl Harbor was, she began to read as the voice in her ear explained what happened on December 7, 1941.

Tears began to fall slowly down her cheeks as she listened to the tin-voiced reporter tell the country of the Japanese attack on the Hawaiian base.

❦ ❦ ❦ ❦

Abel, who had turned back to her laptop and her paper, heard the soft sound of a sniffle, and looked over her shoulder. She saw tears flowing down Zac's face. She dropped the pages she'd been fingering through on the desk and pushed back from it, hurrying over to the bed.

She noted what Zac was learning about, now. "Sweetie, oh, Zac." She sat down next to her and put her hand on her back. "What's wrong?" Bright blue eyes looked up at her, made electric by the upset.

"We were attacked," she cried, lower lip trembling. "And then the thing blew up, and the reporter guy was so upset. And then we attacked on D-Day, then President Roosevelt died." She was crying now.

"Oh, honey." Abel reached over to the CD player and hit the STOP button then took her friend into her arms and let her sob. These were world events she knew Zac had never heard of, so it was almost as if it was happening for the first time for her. She was furious with Bud Lipton for stunting his daughter so much. "Do you want to stop?" she asked, reaching over to the bedside table and snagging a tissue. She used gentle touches to wipe Zac's tears away.

"No!" Zac looked at her with big eyes. "No, I want to know."

"Okay." Abel brushed back ebony hair from her face. She grabbed a second tissue and handed it to her friend. "Here."

Zac took the tissue and wiped at her eyes as fresh tears fell. With one last shared look, Abel headed back to her computer, keeping a careful eye on her friend.

After Abel turned the CD back on, Zac slowly turned the pages, eyes wide. Her face was a mass of expression. Sometimes she smiled and outright laughed, and then sadness would overtake her beautiful face again.

Abel turned to her computer screen, computer glasses firmly on her nose, reading over what she had already written when she squeaked in surprise. Suddenly a picture of a very dead student was before her.

"Look, Spinney," Zac said, pointing. "Is Kent State a good school?" she asked.

Abel looked at the picture of the massacre from 1970. "Oh, uh, I don't know, Zac. I've never been there."

Zac scanned the page again, such compassion filling her blue eyes. "Sad," she said softly.

Abel put her hand on Zac's forearm.

"Yes, it is. It's part of our history. From what I understand, the Vietnam War was a time of conflict in America. Lots of young people hated it. And died."

"Why?" Zac plopped down on the floor next to Abel's chair, still flipping through the pages, headphones resting on the bed.

Abel turned her chair to face her. She rested her forearms along her slightly spread thighs. "I'm not sure. I think mainly because they felt the Vietnam War was primarily political for the United States, and we had no right to interfere in the Vietnamese conflict. Especially once our boys over there started dying. It was kind of a loss of innocence for the country, I think." Abel stared just over Zac's bent head, lost in thought. "My Uncle Eddie was killed by a sniper in the war," she said softly.

"I'm sorry, Spinney."

"Nah. I didn't know him. He died before I was born, but I know it affected my dad a lot. They were pretty close, I think."

"Wow." Zac leaned back against the side of Abel's chair, closing her eyes when fingers begin to run through her hair. She released a soft sigh.

Abel turned back to her paper, fingers continuing to absently run through the long, dark strands.

Chapter Twenty-two

Abel woke suddenly, not sure why. She opened her eyes and looked around the moon-soaked room. A branch was scraping lightly against the window.

Taking inventory of her body, she felt the warmth along her back and thighs, knowing that it was Zac's body pressed to hers. She gently ran a fingertip over the larger hand that was draped over her side. Sighing deeply, she snuggled her body further back into Zac's, absorbing its warmth and softness. Zac sighed in her sleep and wrapped her arm fully around the blonde's waist. Abel noted that Aure slept the soundless sleep of puppies at the foot of the bed on her side, Zac's legs too long for the pup to have any room.

Abel stared out the window, a soft smile caressing her lips. The moon was bright overhead, and for a moment she had the urge to run outside and dance in its radiance. Deciding against it, she turned her thoughts to her friend instead. Lying with Zac in her bed made her realize just how much she had missed her. She missed Zac's touch, her voice, her laughter and the soft trust in her startling blue eyes. She missed the innocence that radiated through Zac and made Abel's heart melt. So much Zac had missed out on, yet she seemed remarkably well adjusted despite, or even perhaps because of it.

She loved Zac's purity and her playful streak that

showed itself in the woods earlier that day when Zac raced with Abel, only to tackle her to the ground. She remembered the feeling that coursed through her body when Zac was on top of her, her wrists pinned above her head on the ground, the unexpected urgency that had filled her and had settled down south, seeing Zac's flushed face above her own, those blue eyes blazing with the excitement of their play, and the way Zac's breath had caressed her face as they had stared at each other.

"God," Abel whispered, not sure what to do with these feelings that were beginning to wash over her. She wasn't entirely sure what these feelings were. They just... were. She knew she loved Zac dearly, and Zac was the best, dearest friend she ever had. But what was nagging at her? Why did it hurt so bad to think of leaving her to go back to school in a few days?

The hoot of an unseen owl answered her silent questions and made Abel sigh again. She felt no more enlightened.

꙳꙳꙳꙳

"No, no. Like this. Hold it straight out from your body, Spinney. Yeah. Rigid like that. There's no thrust involved, just patient swaying. There you go. Just like that."

"I got it! I got it! Look at it go!"

Zac laughed, pleased to see the large trout flinging itself at the end of Spinney's line. "Reel it in, Spinney!" she called out, walking up behind her, placing her hands on womanly hips to keep Spinney grounded. The fish was large, and certainly struggling. Aure stood on the bank of the lake barking his little golden head off.

"Oh, that was sweet!" Spinney squealed, bringing the dangling fish to the shore.

Zac quickly cut the line, and set the fish in the cooler that the Cohens had given her for Christmas. "You did real good, Spinney," she said, proud of her new fishing protégé. "Now, watch the master at work." She gave Spinney a nice, big toothy grin and baited her dad's old pole.

Spinney watched, grossed out as Zac impaled the squirming worm. "That is so nasty," she muttered.

"Eh, you get used to it." Line baited, Zac made a fantastic cast, her hook making a small plop in the still water.

"Nice," Spinney said, stepping up beside Zac and placing her hand at the small of her back. She watched, both of them breathless as they waited for the tell-tale sign of bubbles. Aure watched, muscles taut, a low growl erupting from his throat.

"Shh, Aure," Zac whispered, waiting for that perfect moment. The pup whined quietly, but obeyed. "Here it comes," she mumbled, slowly reeling in the line. "Come to Mamma."

The fish, large and lively, whipped out of the water, body flailing as droplets of water sprayed across the surface of the lake.

"Go you!" Spinney clapped wildly as she watched her friend reel in the fish, putting it with the much smaller one she had caught in the cooler. Zac turned to her, eyes shining. "I am impressed," Spinney said, a hand on her hip as she grinned up at Zac.

"As you should be. I'm the queen of fish." Zac matched Spinney's pose, daring the squirt to challenge her claim.

"Hey, who am I to question that one?" Abel smirked, making Zac frown.

"What? Aren't you impressed?"

"I already told you I was."

Zac eyed her, seeing the grin that was ready to peek out at any moment. "Uh, huh. Just for that your next lesson will be in cleaning said fish." She grinned, pulling her knife out of her boot, and handing it to Abel handle first.

※ ※ ※ ※

The two lay on the floor, having moved the coffee table out of the way. They'd created a little nest for themselves, using a thick old quilt to lie on, as well as gathering the cushions and throw pillows from the couches. Abel had gotten terribly sunburned while fishing, and now didn't want to move. With aloe vera slathered on her face and arms, she re-adjusted her head, which lay on Zac's shoulder, her arm draped across her stomach.

"I like that," Zac said, pointing to the Dodge Ram truck commercial on the television screen.

"I could most definitely handle one of those," Abel agreed. "I could totally see you behind the wheel of one of those bad boys. Look at it plowing over those hills and through the mud. That's so you."

"Are you saying I like to plow through mud and get dirty?" Zac asked, her fingers lazily running over the back of Abel's hand.

"Yes, I am."

"Gee, thanks."

"Anytime." She lifted her head and grinned down at Zac. "I mean, I know you can be a dirty girl." She froze. *Was I just flirting with her?*

"Well hey, you try and live out in the forest and see how clean you stay!" Zac exclaimed with a smile.

Relieved Zac hadn't caught the double entendre, Abel pulled herself into a sitting position. "I think I'm going to take a nice, cool shower," she said, running her hands through her hair. Her arms were sore from their long hours of fishing and her sunburned skin could use a bit of cooling off.

"Can we take a bath?" Zac asked, looking up into her friend's face.

For a moment, Abel felt butterflies in her stomach at the innocent suggestion. She pushed them away, knowing she was being ridiculous. She smiled. "Sure."

❧❧❦❦

Ten minutes later they sat in the huge tub, Jacuzzi jets on full power. Spinney sat with her head back, eyes closed and arms resting out along the back of the tub. Zac studied her. She watched the way the water rolled around Spinney's shoulders, and she could just barely see the tops of her bra-clad breasts. She was riveted by the soft-looking flesh. Spinney wore a black bra, so she couldn't see much of the skin through the wet garment, so she gazed upon the creamy flesh of her cleavage.

Her gaze moved from that to the graceful column of Spinney's throat, which was fully exposed with the position of her head resting back against the tub. She noted the delicate structure of her shoulders and collarbones, a bit shadowed from the angle of the light sconces which eased the bathroom into a buttery light. She noted the muscle beneath the pale skin of Spinney's shoulders and red skin of her arms, as Spinney had stripped down to a T-shirt at the lake. Spinney had called it a farmer's tan, for some reason. Her gaze scanned one of her arms, watching as her fingers–which dipped into the water–were gently moved to and fro from the force of the jets. She was fascinated by Spinney's hands. They were smaller than hers, but strong and beautiful with well cared for nails, unlike her own, which were bitten and jagged.

Her eyes rose to find she was staring straight into a curious gaze. The green of Spinney's eyes were almost luminescent in contrast to her sunburned face.

🌿🌿🌿🌿

Abel's eyes scanned the smooth skin and strong shoulders that led to a long, graceful neck. She took in Zac's face–uninhibited by hair , as it was slicked back–the angular features, straight, proud nose and full lips, which she realized were mesmerizing.

"What?" she asked, feeling eternally stupid, and like a cad.

"I asked if you wanted to do that thing you mentioned," Zac repeated.

Still feeling the rush of heat through her body from Zac's intense gaze painting her skin, Abel shook herself out of it. "Oh. Um, right."

Abel re-adjusted her position, spreading her legs and inviting Zac to turn around and back up to sit between them. She felt Zac's body scoot closer, water swishing around them from the movement. Abel was presented with the smooth expanse of her friend's back, and she brought her hands up and ran them down the warm skin hindered only by the bra straps. "Beautiful," she said, nearly a reverent whisper.

She began to massage the skin and muscle of Zac's shoulders, feeling them relax under her fingertips. The skin was smooth and silky from the water and Zac's natural softness. She heard Zac moan as she pinched the muscle that connected her neck to her shoulders, her head dropping.

"Like that?" Abel asked quietly. She smiled at the grunt she got. Her eyes dropped to the vertebrae in Zac's spine, then took in a few scars that littered the otherwise flawless skin. She brushed the long, wet strands of dark hair over one of Zac's shoulders so she could have better access. Zac gasped slightly as the thick, wet rope of hair dropped over one of her breasts.

≈≈≈≈

When the wet hair flopped across one of Zac's very hard nipples, she felt the sensation shoot like lightning straight through her body and land between her legs. It almost took her breath away.

"You're so tense, Zac," Spinney said, her voice a whisper in Zac's ear. Zac gasped slightly from the sensation it caused. She could not speak, but instead nodded. "We'll change that."

Doubtful, Zac thought. She felt her body becoming more and more keyed up with every touch. *What the hell is happening to me?* Her heart was pounding so hard, she worried Spinney could hear it.

≈≈≈≈

For Abel's part, she was enjoying the feel of Zac's skin immensely. She thought Zac was the most beautiful woman she had ever seen, and the fact that she was allowing such openness with her amazed her. If she put her mind to it, Zac could have any person she wanted. She wondered just what Zac did want.

"Zac?"

"Hmm?" She nearly purred in response.

"Do you want to date?" she asked softly, digging her fingers into a particularly sensitive spot and Zac winced. "Oh, sorry, sweetie."

"Date?" Zac asked.

"Yeah. You know, find some cute guy and go on a date with him. Have you ever had sex?" Abel cocked her head slightly to the side, studying the woman who sat between her legs. She felt Zac's hand wrap itself around the underside of her calf, the thumb lightly brushing over the water-soft skin. She smiled at the closeness she felt. In truth, she had to push out of her mind just what an intimate setting and situation they were in.

"No," Zac said quietly. "I've never thought about it. Dating, that is."

Abel smiled. "And sex?"

Zac shrugged. "Who'd want to do that with me?" She moaned again as the magic hands roamed down to massage on either side of her spine.

Abel smirked. "Probably just about anyone. You're gorgeous." She continued down Zac's back, her eyes lingering on the bra strap. She considered unsnapping it, knowing it would be easier to massage that way, but felt strange about it. She abandoned the idea; things already felt… strange.

"Oh." Zac laughed nervously. "Thank you. I think

you're gorgeous, too, Spinney." She looked shyly over her shoulder, a small smile playing across her lips.

"Aww, you're so sweet."

Abel snaked her arms through Zac's, clasping her hands just under Zac's breasts. She pulled her friend back against her, reveling in the closeness.

≈!≈!≈!≈!

Zac was surprised by the move, but went with it. She closed her eyes, sighing at the contact. Spinney's skin was so warm and soft. Unbelievably soft. She felt Spinney's hands lock under her breasts, and felt a brand new wave of heat wash over her. It almost made her feel light-headed.

"Would you ever have sex?" Spinney asked, resting her chin on Zac's shoulder.

Zac shrugged. "I don't know. It would depend on the situation and who it was. Besides," she said shyly. "I wouldn't have a clue what to do, anyway." She felt Spinney smile against her cheek.

"Have you ever kissed anyone?"

"No. Have you? Or, have you had sex, Spinney?" Zac was nearly holding her breath, not sure she wanted the answer. She had this strange feeling of an almost territorial nature with her petite friend. The thought of anyone touching her made her feel angry... and... jealous?

≈!≈!≈!≈!

Abel wasn't entirely surprised by the question, but she was surprised by the guilt she felt in answering it honestly. "Yes," she said softly. She was sexually responsible and certainly not promiscuous, but still... she felt almost... ashamed.

"Do you enjoy it?" Zac asked, her voice a bit guarded.

"I guess. It can be nice."

"Do you date? Do you have a boyfriend, Spinney?"

Abel was surprised by the timbre of Zac's voice. She almost sounded as though she were about to cry. Brows drawn, she answered, simply. "No." She wondered, however, if she had had a boyfriend if she would have told the truth.

☙☙☙☙

Zac smiled, feeling better as she snuggled in closer to Spinney's chest. It was usually her friend who snuggled into her, so she enjoyed this turnabout. She could feel the softness of Spinney's breasts against her back, the nipples grazing the bare skin. She felt a flush start from her toes and move steadily up to her scalp. She sighed contentedly.

Chapter Twenty-three

Zac led Spinney through the woods, hand in hand, enjoying the last day before she headed back to school.

"It's so peaceful up here," Spinney said, inhaling the coming spring.

"Yes, it is."

They walked on in silence, Aure running up ahead as he chased after a squirrel, not a chance of catching it.

Spinney broke the comfortable silence. "Do you have enough food? What about dog food?"

Zac smiled, squeezing Spinney's hand then entwining their fingers. "We're fine, Spinney. Honest. We won't starve."

"I know, I know. I don't mean to act like your mother." She smiled. "I am so going to miss you, Zac." She stopped and faced her. "A lot."

"I'll miss you, too." Zac looked down into the beautiful face of her friend. "So pretty," she whispered, lightly tracing the fine features.

"Thank you," Spinney said, closing her eyes as the soft fingertip grazed over her skin.

Zac traced her eyebrows, the slope of her nose, and forehead, a feather light touch across her bottom lip, just a butterfly touch. She sighed. "I hate when you leave."

Spinney met Zac's troubled gaze. "I know."

Spinney cupped Zac's face in her hands. "I hate it, too. I wish so badly I could just pack you in my luggage and take you back with me." She smiled, but it was sad. She sighed. "This is really going to hurt."

Zac smiled, trying to break the painful tension that was forming between them. "Wouldn't that make a funny picture?" she said softly, closing her eyes and leaning into the touch. "But I understand."

That night as they lay in bed, Abel could not sleep. She rested on her side facing Zac, and stared at the calm, relaxed face in sleep. She studied the way all of Zac's features worked together to form a beautiful picture. *So wonderful. So amazingly sweet.* Abel felt honored to know this woman and even more so to be cared for so deeply by her. *Come with me, Zac!* She so badly wanted to scream out those words and shake her friend until her eyes rolled, but she knew it wasn't an option.

She studied Zac's face, committing every line, every curve and every hair to memory. She would leave the following morning, and it would be more than two months before she'd see the perfection that was Zac again. Her gaze settled on full lips, ever so slightly parted with Zac's deep, even breaths. Abel leaned forward, her lips not an inch away from Zac's. She stopped herself and raised her chin, leaving a soft kiss to Zac's forehead before she turned to her other side and scooted back into the warmth of Zac's body.

Abel packed the last of her bags into her Jetta. She turned to Zac, hands buried in her back pockets. Zac and Aure waited patiently for their goodbyes.

Abel sighed. "I'll miss you." She felt large paws on her thigh and looked down to see a very excited puppy vying for her attention. "You, too, little one." She bent down and hugged the dog, allowing a few licks to her cheek. "I'll see you, little Aure. Though you probably won't be so little by then, huh?" Grinning, she stood again.

"I'll miss you, too, Spinney," Zac said, her eyes so sad it nearly broke Abel's heart.

"Come here." Abel pulled Zac in for a lingering hug, sighing with a strange mixture of contentment in the warmth, yet sadness as it'll be the last hug for months. The warmth of Zac, the smell of her, the comfort.... it was nearly too much for her fragile emotions.

"Please be careful," Zac said into Abel's hair.

Abel nodded, eyes closed as she rested her head against Zac's shoulder. "I will. You too, okay?" Abel pulled away, her eyes swimming. She smiled through her unshed tears. Hesitating for the slightest of moments, she leaned up and placed a soft kiss on Zac's lips. The contact lasted no more than a few moments, but she knew both would file it away in their hearts to get them through the next few months.

"Bye."

Abel pulled out of the dirt drive, glancing back in her rearview mirror. She saw Zac standing there, Aure at her feet. Zac placed two fingers on her lips, looking amazed. Abel smiled then turned back to the road, the first of many tears falling.

Chapter Twenty-four

Sighing again, Abel turned to her side. She fluffed her pillow, kicked the blanket off and turned to her stomach. Regardless, her eyes popped open. With a quiet growl, she turned onto her back again and stared up at the ceiling that held an orangish glow from the lights across the street in the park. She glanced at the clock, groaning when she saw it was only 1:17 a.m. She'd officially been in bed for two hours and seventeen minutes.

Trying again, she rolled to her right side, her back to the rest of the room and Jessica who slept soundly across the way. Trying valiantly to reach an itch that was right in the middle of her back, Abel gave up. With a heavy sigh of frustration, she sat up and became a contortionist as she reached for that damn elusive spot. Her hands plopped down onto her bare legs, hands rubbing over the smooth skin. She glanced over at her roommate and again, then looked at the clock once more, only four minutes passed.

"This sucks," she muttered. It had been three days since she'd been back in Boston. It was also the third night in a row that she could not sleep. She flopped back against the pillows again, thinking. *Okay, why can't I sleep? Let's analyze this.*

What was going on? School had been in session for a couple days, so nothing critical there. She was neither stressed, nor worrying about anything. Things were good at home, her job, and at the apartment. Something was missing at night. Like she'd forgotten to do something. Abel ran her tongue over her teeth, feeling the smooth cleanness. Check. She could still feel the tingle from her face cleanser. Check. She'd gone to the bathroom. Check. Homework was done. Check. Paper done. Check. Thought of Zac today. Double check.

Abel sat up in bed again, running a hand through her hair. "That's it," she whispered. She missed her friend. She missed Zac holding her in bed and cuddling with her. She missed the smell of her skin, natural and warm from the sun. She hugged herself, eyes closed as memories of the sensations coursed through her, of Zac's warm body wrapped around her, strong arms protecting her from the night, the comfort and satisfaction of Zac's breathing as she fell into a peaceful sleep. No demons ever found Abel when she was in Zac's arms.

Perhaps it was just having someone else there. She glanced again at her roommate and thought about climbing into bed with her. Jess would be warm, too. She was breathing nice and even, that comforting white noise. Chewing on her bottom lip, she contemplated this move. She had, after all, gotten used to having Zac with her every night, so it was natural to feel antsy. Right?

For a week? A single friggin' week is making you feel like you're lonely and separated?

"Shit," she hissed, sitting up again. She looked at Jessica. "Jess," she said, her voice quiet, but hopefully loud enough to wake her friend. She needed to talk. "Jessica!" she said louder.

"Hmm?" her roommate mumbled, face still half-buried in her pillow.

"I need to talk."

"Then write to Dear Abby," Jess grumbled and turned over, her back to Abel.

"About Zac and spring break." Abel grinned when dark brown eyes were suddenly peeking at her over a shoulder. "Come on, Jess. I need to talk about this."

"You need to talk about this at," her friend glanced at the clock, "one-thirty in the morning?"

"Sorry. Can't sleep." Abel scooted back so she was sitting against the wall, knees drawn to her chest.

"You can't sleep, so no one can, is that it?" Jess grumbled, copying Abel's position.

"Come on, Jessica. I've had midnight talks with you before."

"Alright, alright." Jess rubbed her eyes. "Talk."

"I miss her," Abel said, her words muffled by the blanket as she rested her chin on her knees.

"You woke me up to tell me that you miss your friend that you saw three days ago?" Jessica looked incredulous. She paused and drew her brows together. "Wait, I thought you wanted to talk about Zac."

"I do."

"So, who's 'her'?"

"Zac."

"Zac is a chick named after a dude?" Jessica stared at her. "I'm confused."

"Yes, Zac is female, you just assumed she was a dude, and it's more than that, Jess." Abel's voice was quiet. She noticed it had taken on an entirely different quality than her friend had ever heard before.

Jessica stared at her for a moment, seemingly more awake. "What's going on between you two,

Abel?" she asked softly. "You've been antsy as shit since you got back."

"I don't know," Abel said from behind her hands. She let them drop onto the mattress on either side of her as she rested her head against the wall, eyes half-hooded as she thought of this very question. It had been plaguing her whether she wanted to admit it or not. "We had such a good time." She smiled, remembering. "She's so much fun. And so very sweet. And gorgeous! Oh my god." She got off the bed, dressed in her nightly T-shirt, flannel shorts and socks, and snagged her phone off the dresser before hurrying over to Jess' bed. Sitting beside her friend she searched through her photo gallery until she found what she was looking for. It was a picture of Zac and Aure playing in the cabin. Zac looked young, healthy, and carefree.

Jessica took the phone in her hands. "This her?"

Abel nodded. "Yeah. I managed to snap it when she didn't know." She grinned.

Jessica took the phone greedily. "Wow," she murmured. "She's really pretty." She looked at the picture for several moments before she handed it back.

"Yes. She is very pretty," Abel said, looking at the picture, which brought an instant smile to her lips. She set it aside.

"So what's going on between you two, girl?" Jessica asked again. She leaned against the wall next to her bed again and studied her long-time friend.

Abel sighed, bringing her knees up to her chest and wrapping her arms around them. She shook her head. "I don't really know." She knew she must sound as miserable as she felt.

"Why don't you start by telling me about your

week," Jess suggested.

"Okay." Abel sighed and sat back against the wall next to Jess. "Well, she was there waiting for me with her dog, Aure." She smiled at the memory. "First time she's ever done that." She looked into Jess's face, nearly unseen from the shadows of the room. "Let me start at the beginning."

As Abel told her story, starting from the day she met Zac fifteen years ago, Jess listened intently, never interrupting unless she wanted to clarify a point.

Once Abel finished, Jessica studied her, finger tapping her chin.

"What?" the blonde asked, feeling slightly uncomfortable from the scrutiny.

"Dude, you've got a crush."

"What? I do not!"

"Yes, ma'am. You've got a crush. I have never seen you so excited and enthusiastic about one single person in our entire friendship."

"A crush?" Abel looked skeptically at her friend, though somehow she didn't feel it was right to argue. She was confused.

"Yes. If I say the name Zac, you light up." Jessica grinned. "Zac. Zac. Zac Lipton."

"Stop!" Abel smacked the darker girl, the smile still firmly in place.

"I rest my case." Jessica smiled triumphantly. "Okay. Now that we've got that settled, why don't you tell me why you woke me up at this ridiculous hour on a school night."

"I couldn't sleep." Abel pouted.

"You woke me up 'cause you can't sleep? I'm not so sure how I feel about that."

Abel groaned, burying her face in her hands.

"I miss her, Jess." She glanced over in the general direction of her friend, whom she could see a bit better as her eyes adjusted to the darkness. "She makes me feel so safe and comfortable. Content, I guess."

"So why can't you sleep? I can understand missing her during the day. So what's the deal now?"

"Well, um, she um… she sleeps with me in the cabin." Abel's eyes widened at the look on Jessica's face. "Not that kind!"

"Ow, ow!" Jessica giggled as she was barraged by a pillow beating.

"She is the greatest cuddler." Abel tossed the pillow aside, only for it to be snatched up by Jess so she could hug it to herself.

"Really? Even better than Davis?"

"Much better." Abel grimaced at the thought of her high school ex. "I think that was the only thing he did well."

"Honey, I still say that Davis is gay. I will say that till the day I die."

"Yeah, yeah. And I will say until the day I die that he is simply eccentric."

"Uh, huh."

Abel rolled her eyes. "Anyway. She's wonderful in the cuddle department. She has these warm, strong arms," she whispered as she wrapped her arms around herself and sighed at the memory. "She holds me so tight. God, it's just amazing."

"Man, you're gone."

Abel let her arms drop and let out a sigh. "I don't get it, Jess. I just so don't get it. She's a, well…a she!"

"So?"

Abel looked at her with shocked eyes. "What do you mean, 'so'? She's a woman. I'm a woman. This doesn't make any sense!"

"Abel, honey, what does it matter? She seems to really make you feel good. Right? And she's gorgeous, sweet, amazingly stuck on you, so why not?"

"God, I'm not programmed like that, Jess." Abel felt tears sting behind her lids as her confusion morphed into intense emotion.

"Sweetie," Jess laid her hand on Abel's knee. "Even I've kissed a chick."

Before Abel could absorb that little tidbit, Jess continued.

"How do you feel about Zac? Like, what's the first thing that comes to mind?"

Abel stared at her for a moment, about to probe her friend's brain on that bit of information she had never heard about, but decided that it was pushing two in the morning, and she better stay on track for both their sakes. "I really care about her. I crave her presence. God, it's the weirdest thing, Jess. It's like, when spring break came along and I thought about the trip with you guys to Cancun, I wanted to go. I really, really did. But, then I thought about the fact that I won't be able to see Zac until summer, and it tore me up. I wanted to see her so bad. I *needed* to see her."

"Girl, what's going on with you, huh? What's in your head? What do you want from this chick?"

"I don't know." She chewed on her bottom lip, a silent war in her brain for what she was about to confess. Finally, she glanced over at her friend. "Jess, I kissed her when I left." Abel fell against Jess's shoulder. An arm automatically went around her.

"Tell me about it," Jessica said quietly as she stroked the soft blonde hair.

"The night before I left, we were in bed and I was looking at her. God, she's the most beautiful person I have ever seen. And not just physically. Jess, she saved my life!"

"I know, sweetie. Was it a...romantic kiss?"

"No, just a peck before I left." Abel sighed. "She's amazing. Never in my life have I met anyone like her. Never. I'd be a fool not to have her in my life."

"Then keep her there. But, the question is: do you want her there as your friend or... something more?" Jess asked, carefully.

"Definitely. I want her with me. I want so badly to bring her here to Boston. Introduce her to things she's never seen or thought about. Things she's never even dreamed of. Things that only I can share with her..."

"Such as?"

"Please don't, Jess," Abel said quietly. "Don't debase it like that."

"Okay, I'm sorry. Have you asked her if she'd come to Boston?"

"In so many words. I promised her I'd never take her away from her safety zone. I can't ask that of her, Jessica. She'd never survive outside the forest or rails. Zac is special. Very unique. She's like nothing you've ever seen, and sometimes I think this world you and I live in isn't good enough for her."

☙❧

Zac sat in her tent, away from the warm rain. She sat cross-legged, her biology book in her lap with her bottom lip tucked into her mouth. "Breasts," she muttered, flipping to the index in back of the large text. She traced her finger down the page until she came to the body part in question. "Page 319."

Swiftly turning the pages, she found a colored drawing of the female body, replete with all private parts. She looked at the breasts of the drawing, the nipples erect to show what happens during certain stimuli. She saw the word written in bold print and began to read. "... can become hard during sexual arousal or when temperatures drop to colder levels." She looked down at her own breasts, clad in her thin T-shirt. She had yet to put her bra on, so saw her nipples standing at attention. She was not cold.

Flipping back to the index, she looked up the terms *aroused, sexuality, stimulated* and finally, *sex*. Turning to the indicated pages, Zac read all she could on the subject. She absorbed the information like a sponge. Spinney had been gone for nearly two months, and the most interesting things had begun to happen to Zac's body. Ever since that kiss before Spinney left for school, Zac had noticed the strangest feelings coursing through her body, always ending with her being most uncomfortable in her pants. The first time she thought she had perhaps peed her pants without knowing, or her monthly had caught up with her.

Nope. None of the above.

The previous night she had dreamt of her and Spinney in the Jacuzzi at the cabin again, but this time Spinney did not have her bra on. Zac had been able to stare openly at the beautiful flesh per her friend's request. Never seeing breasts in real life before, other than her own and the first time in the tub with Spinney, she decided to do a bit of research.

The first thing was to look up the strange discharge in her pants. She had come up with several possibilities but figured that, either her bladder was beginning to lose control, she had a sexually transmitted disease, she had a yeast infection, or she was sexually aroused. She was betting on the latter two, although she was not experiencing the burning discomfort said to accompany a yeast infection.

As she read up on the breast nipples and their sensitivity to sexual stimulation, she was absolutely intrigued. When Spinney had been at the cabin over winter break, and especially over spring break, Zac had noticed the oddest changes in her own body. Like, when Spinney would touch her she felt it all the way through her. The way she craved touching Spinney, craved being near her, and wanted to cry at the mere thought of being away from her–which she did once Spinney left. Never in her life had Zac had a problem with being alone. She had been alone for her entire life. But now... she sighed. She missed Spinney more than she cared to admit. She missed seeing those most amazing green eyes looking at her with so much love and acceptance.

Zac closed her eyes, slammed the book shut, and hugged it to her chest. She could still picture her dream. In the tub Spinney's blonde hair was wet and slicked away from her face, and she took off her bra. She had looked into Zac's eyes the entire time as she reached behind her to unsnap it. Zac had been too stunned to ask what she was doing, and she didn't want her to stop, anyway. She had absolutely no idea what she was supposed to do or what exactly she was hoping for, but the dream had caused a ton of that discharge stuff and had left her pulsing at what felt like the center of her being. She had woken with a groan, not wanting to be in her tent. And certainly not alone.

"Oh, Spinney," she breathed. "What are you doing to me?"

☙☙❧❧

Abel was quiet after her enlightening middle-of-the-night talk with Jess. It had been two weeks since and she had been in a state of total self-analysis. She had no idea what was going on within her, but her dream the night before had been quite telling. Never in her life had she had such a dream about a girl before. Hell, she didn't really remember having them about guys, either. She was very much a visual person with a reality-based nature. Rarely did the abstractness of dreams do anything for her. But this time, she sighed, leaning against the wall in the back cooler of the store where she worked, the dream images had assaulted her again.

She and another woman, who she had the distinct impression had been Zac, had been swimming in a lake, perhaps the lake up at the cabin. They were in bathing suits, but she could not keep her eyes off the body of her swimming companion, who conveniently kept getting out to get a drink of her bottled water. Abel's gaze would follow her form every time, taking in the beautiful curves and smooth skin.

Once 'Zac' returned she swam over to Abel, taking the smaller woman in her arms and nuzzling her neck with her lips and nose. Abel could feel the hardness of nipples against her skin as she had arched her head back, eyes closed as she reveled in the sensations. Unimaginable sensations.

"Shit," she groaned, feeling the warmth of arousal wash through her body again.

Jessica had been good by not bringing it up again, but making it more than apparent that if Abel needed to talk she was more than willing to listen. Abel knew that Jess would be a wonderful person to talk to about this, not judging her at all. She needed that kind of support for something she didn't understand.

Again, she recalled the feeling of lips moving slowly up her neck, under her jaw and finally to her mouth. The kiss was magnificent, sending tremors through Abel's body. Her body had been so responsive during sleep that she wasn't sure whether she had actually climaxed or not. In truth, she wouldn't be surprised if she had.

She needed to talk to Jessica. Finishing up with her day, she quickly hurried home.

Jessica sat at the kitchen table, her laptop and books spread out around her. Kendra was still at work, so it was the perfect time to talk.

"Hey girl," Jessica said when Abel came through the door. "What's up? Oh!" She was startled when Abel grabbed her hand and led her toward their bedroom.

"Sit."

"What's going on, girl?" Jess sat back against the wall and stretched long legs out to cross at the ankle as they dangled over the side of the bed.

"I am so..." Abel thought for a moment as she tugged a tank top over her head and tugged it down. Blowing disheveled bangs out of her eyes, she plopped down on her own bed. "Confused, I guess, though somehow that doesn't seem right."

Jessica waited patiently for her friend to figure out what it was she was trying to say.

"I had a dream last night, Jess. A sex dream."

"Okay. Thanks for sharing," Jessica drawled,

dark brows drawing.

"No, stop it. About Zac!" Abel's eyes were wide and bright. She felt like she was about to cry. "And I enjoyed it!"

"Ohhhh," Jessica took a deep breath. "How do you feel?"

"I have no idea. I mean, I thought about this thing all day. I mean, I love her dearly, you know that. And she is gorgeous, but how on earth can I be having sex dreams about her, Jess? Is it maybe that I haven't had sex in so long and am desperate? Or because I do find her so beautiful? Both?"

"Or that you're falling for her," she muttered almost to herself. She sat up and studied her friend. "Honey, you could have had sex long before now. You stopped that, remember?" Jessica raised an eyebrow in challenge.

Abel thought for a minute, then remembered the party at the apartment. That guy. Though she'd been pretty drunk, they'd gotten to the condom part, she knew that for sure. The guy had been ready and raring to go. But she had stopped him. Why?

"Right," she sighed, running her hand down the length of her ponytail in a nervous motion. "I remember." She thought about it for a moment, and then it hit her. "Oh, my God." She covered her mouth with her hand.

"What?"

"It was Zac." Sighing, she brought her legs up onto the bed. "I stopped him, Jessica, because it felt wrong. I was thinking of Zac." A tear managed to slip out of her eye. She was so confused, yet so clear at the same time. It was overwhelming.

"Ah, girl," Jess whispered. Getting up from her

bed she went to her friend and sat next to her on her own bed. "It's okay, Abel. It's all going to be okay. Hon, maybe you're like bisexual or something. Or maybe it's just Zac. I mean, you guys have been through some serious shit together. See what I'm saying? Maybe you two just have a really special connection."

"We do," Abel said, feeling relieved for a moment, a very brief moment. "God. I'm attracted to her."

"That's pretty obvious, sweetie," Jess said gently with a kind smile.

"Fuck. What do I do?" Her eyes bored into Jess.

"I don't know. What do you want to do?"

"Well, according to my dream, I want to kiss her and see her in a seriously revealing bathing suit," Abel said, managing a small smile through her upset.

Jessica nodded, her hand rubbing comforting circles over Abel's back. "Okay. But more importantly, do you want to pursue it? I mean, keep some things in mind, Abel. This chick has a real affinity for the woods, and not for people. She'd be there, you'd be here, and with you graduating next year who knows where you'll be. I doubt you'll have time to go to the cabin with your family much, you know?"

"Yeah." Abel nodded, her head falling into her hands.

"How do you think she feels?" Jessica asked as she ran her fingers through the silky blonde strands of Abel's ponytail.

"I don't know. Over spring break I asked her if she had ever had sex or dated or anything. This poor woman is so sheltered from the world. She has never kissed anyone, never had sex, nor really the opportunity I don't think. She's so innocent, Jessica.

It's absolutely amazing. She is like a child in so many ways, yet so wise and sensitive to others." She told her all about Zac's reaction to hearing and reading about the events of the last century.

"She cried?" Jessica asked in amazement. Abel nodded. "Wow. What a sweetheart."

"She is. I wish so badly there was a way for you to meet her. She's truly the most wonderful human being I've ever met. I want to bring her here."

"Then do it."

"I can't. I told you that." Abel sighed heavily. "That's all she knows. She'd be eaten alive here," she said, her voice sad as she glanced through the window, at the park with all its trees across the street. It reminded her in so many ways of Zac and her woodland wonderland.

"Sounds like the only one wanting to do any eating is you," Jess said with a wicked grin.

Abel pulled away and smacked Jessica.

"Jess! God, you're so gross!"

"I'm kidding, I'm kidding!" Jessica exclaimed, holding her hands up in surrender. "No, but seriously. Don't you think if she had you, she'd be okay? It seems you both have the same effect on each other."

"Hmm," Abel settled against her headboard. "I wish."

༺༻

Zac roamed the forest, summer temperatures firmly entrenched in the green growth that surrounded her and Aure. It was beautiful, and she wanted to be able to share it with Spinney.

She looked down at her golden buddy, stunned

by how much he'd grown. He was now a big boy at almost eight months old. Zac smiled, knowing that Spinney would be pleased at what a good job she'd done with the dog. He already knew tricks, and never left her side.

She glanced up into the sky, knowing from the direction of the sun that it was probably near one in the afternoon. Sighing, she headed toward the lake. Today she was going to take a swim. It was the first day nice enough for it. Aure loved the water, too, which was so neat. He'd follow her in, splashing around while she bathed, then he'd run to shore, shaking his coat free of the water droplets, making his fur stand on end in all directions.

Peeling her clothes off, she looked down at her breasts, still totally intrigued by the mounds of flesh. They were so soft and responsive. So many things had run through her mind over the past few months. She seemed to be terribly drawn to Spinney's body, and loved to learn about it, loved to touch it. She could not wait until her Spinney arrived for the summer and she could see her up close and personal again.

Happily, she ran out into the slightly chilly waters of lake Wachiva, yelling her contentment out into the still, late spring air.

❧❧❧❧

"You ready to go, girl?" Jessica asked, resting her hand on Abel's lower back and looking over Abel's shoulder at the suitcase she was about to snap shut.

"Yep. You?"

"Sure am."

"Going home?" Abel put the case with its twin

next to her bed.

"Yeah. Mom's birthday and all that. Soooo, off I go. And you, missy," she playfully punched Abel in the arm, "off to the cabin, huh?"

Abel took a deep breath and nodded. "Yes. I'm pretty excited, too. My folks will be there in about a week, so I'm gonna chill." She grinned.

"With Zac?" Jess asked with a winked.

"Stop it." Abel laughed as she hugged her friend. "I'll miss you. See you next semester, huh?"

"Yes, ma'am. If you need to talk this summer, you know where I'm at. Okay?" Jessica held Abel by the shoulders, looking deeply into her eyes.

Abel nodded. "Okay."

"I gotta go. See you."

Left alone, Abel sat on her bed, looking around the room and running her sweaty palms over the thighs of her shorts. She was very excited indeed to see Zac, but was nervous as all get out. She'd had no more dreams since the one two months ago, but still. That one dream stayed with her, and all the feelings and emotions tied to it.

She had no plans for the summer other than to be with Zac.

Chapter Twenty-five

The blue Jetta made its way around the largest of the dozens of blind curves as it wound its way into Wachiva Forest. A golden lab ran at full speed, followed by his master, desperate to get to the driver.

Abel pulled into the driveway of her family cabin, and she was surprised and a bit concerned when she didn't see Zac. All for naught, as once she opened the car door she was nearly bowled over by her.

"Spinney!"

Abel closed her eyes as she was enfolded into powerful, tan arms. She rested her head against Zac's shoulder, wrapping her own arms around her friend's waist. They hugged so tightly that not even a single breath could make its way between their pressed bodies. Despite Aure whimpering and pawing at their legs, they held onto each other, the hug lasting more than five minutes, neither wanting to let go.

Finally, Abel looked up into Zac's face, brushing a hand against a tanned cheek as though to make sure Zac was really there. "I missed you so much," she said. "Thought about you every day."

The twinkle in Zac's eyes made Abel smile. Abel forced herself to look away from the blue eyes she'd been craving to see for far too long, and give her attention to a whimpering Aure. "Hey, baby. My god, he's gotten so big!"

Like a growing child proud of his achievement, Aure began to chase his tail, whipping himself into a frenzy of excitement. Laughing, Abel knelt down and endured his kisses, which he tried to turn into French ones, and which were narrowly avoided.

Finally Abel stood. "Come on, gorgeous. Let's grab my stuff and go inside."

Together they unloaded the small car and carried everything inside, all the way up the two flights of stairs to Abel's bedroom. Once everything was unloaded, Abel sent a quick text to her parents to let them know she'd made it okay, and then turned to Zac. "I really, really missed you," she gushed, allowing herself to be caught up in a massive hug again.

She worried that it would be awkward coming here and seeing the star of her erotic dream, but she felt fine, and in fact closer to Zac than before. She felt an even stronger connection to the beautiful woman and didn't want to lose that. She did have to admit, however that, even as Zac was dressed in khaki cargo pants and a T-shirt, it wasn't hard to imagine her in the incredibly revealing bikini she'd been wearing in the dream.

ॐॐ☙☙

Zac's eyes were closed as she once again held her Spinney. Over the spring she'd studied what she could about human sexuality and the female form. She wanted to understand just what it was about Spinney that made her tremble with anticipation of seeing her again, as well as what made her own body tick. And boy, did Spinney make her body tick!

She sank into her Spinney's arms, eyes closed

at the feel of the warm body against her. Her friend's breasts against her caused a shiver to race through her, especially as they only had two thin layers of cotton between them. She inhaled Spinney's scent, wanting to be able to memorize every single thing about her friend for when she left after the summer.

At length, Spinney gave Zac a squeeze then pulled back from her. She looked into Zac's eyes and smiled, receiving one in return, then placed a soft kiss on Zac's even softer lips.

Zac closed her eyes at the contact, however brief, letting it filter through all her senses, a smile tugging at the corners of her mouth.

༄༅༄༅

Abel watched the transformation come over Zac's face, and wondered just what she thought of the kisses, this one and the one months before. She looked as though she really enjoyed them, but did she truly understand them? In some ways, Abel felt as though she were taking advantage of Zac's innocence. If her friend actually knew what lay behind those kisses, would she still be smiling so goofily?

She didn't know. She wished there was some way to find out, but alas, there was none. Hell, Abel could barely understand it herself. She knew without a doubt that she was attracted to Zac, but had no idea why or when it had begun. Never in her life had she thought of another woman like that, or thought past them being physically pleasing to the eye. She found them attractive, but was never attracted *to* them.

Instead of stepping into a think tank, she took Zac's hand. "Come on you. I'm hungry."

Zac sat on the floor, channel surfing, while Spinney made a telephone call to her mother begging her to bring more syrup when they arrived in a week. Aure snoozed next to her. Grabbing a pillow from the couch, she stuck it under her head and watched as some guy on the History Channel talked about the rise of Adolph Hitler. She was transfixed, seeing the images of history flash on the screen in black and white video, the dictator's harsh voice barking out words of encouragement to his comrades in German.

Phone call finished, Spinney plopped down next to her. "What'cha watching?" Zac was happy as a clam, sandwiched between her dog and her Spinney. "Something about Hitler."

Spinney grimaced. "Evil, evil man." She lay down, resting her head on Zac's stomach, wrapping an arm over her waist. She smiled when she felt fingers begin to play through her hair.

"How's your mom?" Zac asked, gaze still focused on the TV program.

"She's good. Trying to get the kids in her classes to actually pay attention. See, the year's almost out, so they couldn't care less about Spanish."

"Then they're foolish. If I had the chance, I'd relish every moment of class."

Spinney raised her head, looking into the blue eyes that watched the images on the TV. "Really? You'd like to go to school?" She began to tangle her fingers into the material of Zac's shirt, twisting and untwisting.

Zac met her gaze. "Well, I love to learn, Spinney,"

she said, taking hold of the smaller hand when fingers began to twist her skin, too. "Careful there, woman."

"Sorry." Spinney grinned. "So, if you could go to school, would you?"

Zac thought about it for a moment, staring up at the ceiling, her hand absently running through Aure's fur. "I guess so. Especially if there was a library. I've only been to one once, but it was amazing." Her eyes lit up. "So many books. It just felt like a smart place, you know? I felt smart when I was there."

"You are smart, Zac. You're brilliant, in fact. The most naturally smart person I've ever met. You ought to see the one at my school. Books as far as you can see. Our library there is huge. You'd love it, Zac. And there are so many different types of classes there. You could learn about anything. You could study plants or animals. You could even study forestry and become a forest ranger," Spinney said, her eyes lit up with excitement.

Zac studied her eyes and ran her hand through the fine hairs near Spinney's temple. "You're so sweet," she said, her voice quiet. She watched as Spinney closed her eyes, absorbing the touch. She sighed, the corners of her mouth turning up slightly in contentment. Zac was so charmed by her. She felt her heart expand and heart rate increase. She wanted so much for Spinney to kiss her again, but had no idea how to go about asking.

She didn't have to.

꙳꙳꙳꙳

Abel opened her eyes, noting the gentle look in Zac's, and felt drawn to them. Drawn to the woman herself. She held her weight on her elbow and moved up so she was level with her.

"Hi," Zac said quietly.

"Hi," Abel responded.

Abel looked down into Zac's face, eyes searching it—for what, she didn't know. She was beautiful, able to take her breath away with just one look with those amazing blue eyes. She sensed Zac was nervous. She could see the pulse point in her throat beating a bit faster, no doubt like her own. She searched Zac's eyes again, making sure Zac wanted this, too. Seeing only affection and to her surprise, desire, she closed her eyes and leaned down, brushing her lips against the softness that was Zac.

A small sigh escaped her as she felt one of Zac's hands entwine itself in her hair, holding her steady. Her lips rested against Zac's, their breathing soft and mingling.

≈≈≈≈

Zac felt her heart stop then begin to tick that much harder. She could smell Spinney's own special scent. This was the scent she wished there was some way to keep once Spinney was gone. She had wanted to ask her friend if she could keep her pillow after spring break, but had lost her nerve, as she didn't want Spinney to think her childish or simple.

But now, her nostrils were filled with it. She inhaled it like a drug, memorizing it for when Spinney left her again. She wanted to be able to bring it up again and again, lighting a smile on her face every time.

She reveled in the warmth that spread throughout

her body, not just from her friend's body heat, but the heat that her own body was generating. She felt like she could fly, but was bound to earth by the partial weight her Spinney was putting on her left side. Her fingers wound through the golden locks, so beautiful, so soft.

❧❧❧❧

Abel's lips lingered upon Zac's for a long moment before she pulled back just enough to break contact only to move in again for one final lingering kiss before finally pulling away. She was nearly breathless, though they were simple kisses. She felt weak kneed and was glad she was not standing. Looking into Zac's amazed eyes, she saw her own feelings reflected back at her. There was no need for words; anything Zac felt was plainly written across that beautiful, angular face. Abel smiled and Zac smiled back, her fingers still running lazily through blonde hair.

Finally Zac's soft words broke the silence. "I'm really glad you're here, Spinney."

"Me, too," Abel whispered, her eyes drifting back to the full lips that remained slightly parted. "Let's go to bed."

Zac nodded. The two got to their feet and Zac took Aure out to relieve himself once more as Abel began to turn out the lights throughout the cabin before heading upstairs. She knew Zac could find her way easily without them. She was always amazed how Zac seemed to be able to see in the dark.

Once upstairs, she grabbed shorts and a T-shirt, closed the bathroom door, flipped on the light, and stared at her reflection in the mirror over the sink.

Her heart was still racing and she had no idea how to stop it. In the grand scheme of things, the kisses had been so small and inconsequential, but even so, there was something about it that made it one of the most intimate things she'd ever shared with another person. The feelings behind it made it so profound.

She could still feel Zac's lips, so soft. Softer than anything she'd ever felt before. Images of kissing boyfriends popped into her mind, and she could not help comparing them. This, of course, was crazy. Giving Zac a couple sweet, soft, wonderfully innocent kisses had nothing to do with the harried, sloppy ones she'd gotten from the guys. *Totally different. Nothing alike, no siree, Bob.*

"Shit," she muttered, leaning against the sink, head hanging. "Yes, they do."

"Did you say something?" Zac called from the bedroom.

"No, I'll be out in a few," she called back, finally changing her clothes. She heard Zac talking to Aure, the pup whining and barking as they played.

Abel smiled. Downstairs, just for a moment, she almost had that same strange feeling she'd had over spring break. The feeling that she, Zac, and the dog were a family, living in domestic bliss.

What the hell is wrong with you? This is Zac! She's a she! We can't do this. It could never be. You know that, Abel. You're her Spinney, the strange city girl who encroaches upon her wild life in the forest every few months. She has no interest in you in any way other than her Spinney, the little girl who befriended her years ago.

She knew this to be true, but she also knew that there was more to it than that. Jessica saw it, and deep down, she did, too. She was so drawn to the beautiful brunette. She could not lie to herself anymore. It had been difficult back in Boston, but not totally impossible. After all, Zac had been a very long drive away. But now... she was on the other side of the door.

Brushing her teeth and combing her hair, Abel opened the door. Zac was changed and sitting cross-legged on the floor petting a zapped Aure. Zac glanced up at her and smiled.

"Hey, beautiful," Abel said.

Zac blushed and looked down. "Hi."

"Aww. What are you so shy about?" She walked over to her and knelt down, running a hand down Aure's golden back.

"I don't know. I guess I'm just not used to being talked to like that. You know, called sweet names like that." Zac looked shyly over at her.

"Want me to stop?"

"No!" Abel grinned at Zac's enthusiasm. Zac looked abashed all over again. "I mean, no. It's okay. I don't mind."

"Well good. It's true, you know." Abel cocked her head to the side and ran a hand through the dark strands of Zac's hair. "You are the most beautiful woman I have ever seen. Personally, I think on the entire planet."

"Oh. Well, uh, I don't know about that." Zac snuck a shy glance at her. "I think you're biased."

"Maybe. But I still think it." She stood, grabbing Zac's hand and pulling her to her feet. "Come on. Do your stuff so we can snuggle. I've waited two whole months for this!"

Zac's eyes blinked open several times before truly awakening. She stared at the golden hair before her eyes, Spinney's back against her front, her arm laced protectively over Spinney's waist.

She could feel the even breathing of her friend and it soothed her. The light was barely coming through the wispy curtains, but Zac always had a hard time sleeping that first night inside the cabin. It was partly getting used to being indoors, and part excitement. She was with her Spinney! She carefully, slowly disentangled her arm from Spinney's possessive hand, trailing her fingers along the soft skin, taking in the texture. She noted the soft blonde hairs that covered her flesh, glinting gold in the newborn sun. She ran her fingers over her forearm, feeling the curve and hardness of her elbow covered in slightly rougher skin, then trailed up to the bicep, sneaking in under the loose material of Spinney's shirt sleeve.

Spinney stirred, a small sigh escaping her lips as she snuggled even closer into Zac. Zac smiled, dragging her nails softly over the skin and muscle of Spinney's bicep. She heard another sigh, but Spinney seemed to be fully asleep. Zac could feel the contraction of the muscle under her hand and traced her fingertips down over the triceps. Her fingers worked their way further up the sleeve until she felt the roundness of a shoulder, then the sudden sharp contrast of her defined collarbone.

≈≈≈≈

Abel felt soft, almost tickling touches on her skin. Trying to concentrate on them, she kept her eyes closed and her breathing even. She could feel Zac's breath on the side of her neck as she continued to touch her. Pretending to still be asleep, she leaned back even further into the warm body behind her, wanting to give Zac as much access as possible.

※ ※ ※ ※

Zac stilled as Spinney moved, leaning even further back into her arms. Sure that her friend was still asleep she continued her gentle exploration. Her fingers left the defined collarbone and continued on. A few scant inches of smooth skin later, her fingers felt the soft swell of Spinney's right breast, and she nearly choked. She quickly moved her hand away, trailing back up to more familiar ground. The softness of Spinney's sun-kissed shoulder found her fingertips dancing again, her heart pounding.

Zac loved the feel of Spinney's skin, so unbelievably soft and wonderful. She loved the smell of her hair, her clothing, everything. She loved the color of her hair, the color of her eyes. *So green.* She wished Spinney would open them now. She leaned over a bit, taking in Spinney's profile. Her eyes were closed, her dark blonde lashes lying on her cheeks, face relaxed and peaceful, her lips slightly parted.

Zac's eyes concentrated on those lips. She brought her hand out of the sleeve, and tentatively touched Abel's lips with her index finger. Tracing the gentle curve and fullness, she smiled as the corner of one side twitched slightly from the touch. She ran her fingertip over the fullness of the bottom lip and received a kiss on it. Surprised, she looked to see, a soft smile on her lips. Spinney was awake.

She was making no move to get away from Zac, so she continued. She ran her fingers back across the lips, receiving another kiss, which sent shivers down her spine. The fingers continued on their path past the mouth, tracing the lines of Spinney's jawbone up and over her ear, tickling the inside and making its owner giggle. Zac then traced Spinney's brow bone, eyebrows, then her feather light lashes so soft, like butterfly wings. Abel grabbed Zac's hand and brought it to her mouth, kissing the palm. "I like you touching me, Zac," she said, her voice soft.

"I like touching you," Zac whispered, pressing her body even closer to Abel's, lining up their bodies to fit perfectly together. Abel's extremely shapely behind tucked nicely into Zac's crotch. She sighed in contentment as Abel pulled Zac's arm around her smaller body, so Abel was completely wrapped in her.

❧❧❧❧

Abel smiled, loving the feeling of Zac's body so protectively around hers. She also loved the feeling of Zac's hands on her. For just a second, Zac's fingers had come dangerously close to her breast, and in that second, Abel had wanted it there more than anything. She had held her breath, waiting for it, though somewhere deep inside she knew it would not happen. She figured Zac was probably scared out of her mind when she realized where her hand was.

Abel was beginning to believe there was no more holding back. She needed to connect with Zac in a way that very few had ever connected with her. She had connected with Zac in every way save one. She felt her body responding to everything Zac did, and there was nothing she could do about it. She stayed on her side with her back to Zac because she knew if she turned around, she'd do something that neither of them were ready for, yet. Hell, she still had no idea how Zac felt, or if she felt anything. Yes, she said she liked to touch her, but was that because she never had anyone to touch? Other than Aure, that is. She just didn't know. They'd been affectionate with each other since day one, so it was hard to tell.

God, she wanted . . . something. Abel was no stranger to desire or arousal, but this was approaching frightening proportions. She had no idea how to handle this. How the hell does one react to wanting a woman's hands on your body for the first time? The worry of what this could mean and the possible repercussions plagued her.

❧❧❧❧

The sun was beating down, unusually warm for a late May afternoon, the rays kissing Abel's face. The water was clear and calm, bubbles heard every once in a while as fish came up to lunch on the insects on the surface. Aure ran around, chasing the creatures of the forest to his heart's content, while Zac and Abel sat on the bank of the river. Abel sat with her back to Zac's front with Zac's arms wrapped around her Spinney. Abel sighed, leaning her head back against Zac's shoulder. She wrapped her arms over Zac's, eyes half closed as she looked out over the lake. "It's so beautiful out here," she said, her voice quiet and serene. "No wonder you love it so much."

"Yeah, it is beautiful. Personally, I think it's got to be the most beautiful place on earth," Zac replied, her voice just as quiet. Her cheek rested against Abel's head.

"Hmm," Abel looked down at the arms around her waist, bare from the tank top Zac wore. "You are so tan already. It's not fair." She ran her hands over the smooth skin.

"Well, I live mostly outdoors every day of the year," Zac murmured into Abel's ear.

"Do you use lotion when I'm not looking or something? You have got the softest skin of anyone I've ever touched. Smooth," Abel said, luxuriating in the feel of her fingers running up and down Zac's forearms. She had to admit, touching Zac was vastly different than touching a man. She had never been crazy about how hairy they were. She never was able to relate when her female friends talked about how sexy and masculine a hairy chest and facial stubble was.

"Well, I do what I can. There's this plant that you can pick, and when you squeeze the root, this gooey stuff comes out and keeps me soft."

"Really?" Abel asked, pulling away from Zac enough to turn and look at her.

Zac grinned. "No. I'm just naturally that way, I guess."

"Tease," Abel growled. She smiled as she playfully smacked Zac's arm. "You are the most beautiful woman I've ever seen," she said, her voice soft as a whisper.

Zac looked at her, stunned.

Abel laughed. "I'm sorry, I know I keep saying that, but I can't help it. Every time I look at you..." she shook her head in wonder.

"Thank you. Funny, I was just thinking the same about you."

Without a thought, Abel found her eyes closing and her body leaning forward. She reached a hand up, entwining her fingers through the thick, dark strands of Zac's hair. She swallowed a moment before she felt her lips meet the other woman's. She knew she couldn't pull away. Not this time. She tilted her head slightly, taking it slow. She knew Zac had never done anything like this and didn't want to scare or overwhelm her.

As Abel turned further in the circle of Zac's legs and arms, she raised up on her knees so she'd have better access and leverage. They both knew this kiss was going to be very, very different. She caressed Zac's lips with her own, and Zac followed.

༄༅༄༅

Zac was enjoying this kiss a whole ton more than the others, which was amazing. She had enjoyed them a ton in their own right. She brought her hands around, resting them on Spinney's waist. She loved the feel of Spinney's hands in her hair; it was making a little fire begin to flare in her belly, and she was afraid that even the antacids Spinney had once given her wouldn't be able to put out these flames.

She started when she felt the softness of Spinney's tongue against her bottom lip, then the lip sucked into the warm cavity of her mouth. A lightning bolt of arousal crashed over her, landing with a thud in her underwear.

"Open for me," Spinney whispered against Zac's lips. When her request was met, she tilted her head slightly deepening the kiss. She wrapped her arms around Zac's neck, burying her fingers into the short hairs at the nape and bringing their upper bodies closer. She was almost in Zac's lap, who certainly didn't mind.

Quite the contrary. Zac brought her hands up to mimic Abel's movements, her hands going directly to the silky blonde locks. Abel could feel the softness of Zac's firm breasts against hers, and this brought a sigh to her lips. Zac returned the soft noise in response. Abel moved her head slowly with every stroke of her tongue, savoring all the tastes and sensations. The kiss, which had begun sloppily with Zac's inexperience, was quickly turning into one of the most sensual things she'd ever experienced.

☙☙❧❧

Zac could feel her heart racing in record time, sending blood pounding through her head, the only sound she could hear. Even Aure's barking not ten yards away from them had disappeared. It was only Spinney and that kiss. She was melting right there on the shore that day in late May.

Chapter Twenty-six

Wrapped up in a blanket just outside the lean-to, Zac and Abel watched the sun go down. The brilliance of the oranges and yellows turned swiftly to pink and red, and finally faded to blue. The fingers of the sunset spread over the sky as the comforting blanket of night arose.

"So beautiful," Abel whispered, feeling that any louder volume would be a violation of perfection. She felt Zac nod behind her, the two sitting in much the same position as they had at the lake earlier. "Do you watch these very often?" she asked, turning her head back so she could see the face of the woman holding her.

"Yes. Every chance I get. Me and Aure will go down by the lake and watch the colors over the water. Truly amazing."

"You can't see this kind of thing in the city. I mean, there are sunsets, obviously, but you can't watch it in such purity. There are buildings to cover it and lights to wash it out."

"Then why be there?"

"Hmm." Abel didn't answer. Zac saw things so simply, and because she could not argue with her logic, she chose to remain silent.

It had been a truly amazing day. After their first kiss by the lake, Abel had broken it and wrapped Zac up in a massive hug. She'd needed to feel her close, even though they had just shared one of the most beautiful kisses of her life. She tried to dig deep to think about how she felt about that. It had felt so right that she could not deny it. Really there was nothing for her to deny. Even still, what did it mean for her? For Zac? Zac's experience with the erotic was nil and Abel did not want to take that innocence from her. Yet, she was drawn. She wanted to be the one to show Zac all that the world had to offer. And that meant the more worldly aspects of physical affection, too. She felt such a strong need to show Zac what passion and love was like. These were things that the world had thus far kept out of reach for the beautiful woman.

After the giant hug, she pulled away and suggested they get some lunch. As they prepared the food together, Zac was full of life. Abel had seen more light in those eyes in that moment than she had in all the time they'd known each other. Zac had also stopped their food preparations often to steal more hugs and kisses. Eventually, Abel stopped making their peanut butter and jelly sandwiches and just grabbed her and laid one on her. Zac nearly stumbled backward from the full impact of it, but had most certainly responded.

Zac was a very quick learner.

"Spinney?" Zac's soft voice pulled Abel out of her thoughts.

"Yeah?" She smiled as she felt Zac tucking the blanket more securely around her shoulders before wrapping her arms around her again, beneath the blanket's comforting warmth.

"What is your cabin like?" Zac asked, her voice was soft in Abel's ear, breath warm.

"My cabin?" Confused, Abel frowned before it hit her. "Oh! You mean my apartment?"

"What's an apartment?"

"Well, you have a large building and it's been separated into various, smaller cabins. Like in ours, we have a two bedroom. So, you have the two bedrooms, a bathroom and kitchen, then a living room. You know, like a communal place for us all?" She felt the nod.

"How many are there of you?"

"Three. But Kendra will be moving out at the end of the year. She's a year older than Jess and me. She graduates, and has a job lined up in California somewhere."

"What does your room look like?" Zac asked, tightening her hold a bit more.

"Well, Jessica and I share one. So, we both have our beds, which are tiny, against opposite walls. But you walk in, and the floor is hardwood. Like in the cabin. My bed is off to the left, and hers is to the right. There is a window smack dab in the middle of the wall that the headboards of our beds are against. Under that window we both have our own nightstand. You know, alarm clocks, reading lamps, that kind of thing. On the wall that the door is on is the closet. We share it, but most of our stuff is in these bags that I call body bags, that we keep under our beds. You know, more room that way."

"What color is the covering on your bed?" Zac rested her chin on Abel's shoulder, closing her eyes so she could picture it.

"Right now it's a dark red, like a maroon color. I change it from time to time. Get tired of the same ol' thing, you know? We both have a dresser at the end of our beds, too. Between the two of us, we could clothe a small village." She smiled at Zac's chuckle. "Our room is pretty simple, really. Nothing striking. We have some old posters hanging that used to be in our dorm room last year. You know, an Albert Einstein poster and some stuff on beer. Typical college stuff."

"Do you like living with Kendra and Jessica?"

"Oh, yeah. Jess and I have been roomies for the past three years and she's great. Kendra was a new addition this year, but she's great, too. We all get along. I'll be sad to see her go."

Zac was quiet for a moment before her soft voice broke the comfortable silence. "Do you like living in the big city like that? Boston is huge, with millions of people. Don't you feel lost?"

"Sometimes. But then at times it's nice. You can go somewhere and no one knows you. You can go to think, do homework, people watch, whatever. No worries about being bothered. That is, unless you're being hit on." She wrinkled her nose. "Guys just don't know when to leave a girl alone."

"Hit on? They hit you?" She felt Zac grow tense and put a steadying hand on her arm.

"It's just a phrase, honey," Abel explained gently, glancing back up into Zac's face, which she couldn't see very well anymore. "It means they find you attractive, and so give you attention. You know, make their intentions clear about their interest."

"Oh." Zac calmed. "Then I bet you get hit on all the time."

"Aww. Aren't you a sweetie." She turned in the circle of Zac's arms until she was facing her. She stared into those blue eyes, the brilliance of the color now mainly gone with the sun set. "Zac?" she said softly.

"Yes?" Zac responded, looking back into Abel's eyes.

"Can we talk for a minute?"

"Sure. What's wrong?"

"Well, I'm not so sure anything is wrong. Well, I hope not, anyway." Abel chewed on her bottom lip as she looked into the increasingly darker form that was Zac's face. "Um, you know how things have gone today? You know, the amazing cuddling, and... other stuff..."

"You mean the kissing?" Zac asked..

Abel smiled. "Yes. The kissing. How do you feel about it?" She could see, even in the faint light of summer's late evening, the whiteness of Zac's spreading smile.

Zac sighed, sounding happy and content. "I don't understand why it's happening, but I like it. A lot."

"Really?" Abel wanted to know that Zac understood just what it meant. "What is it to you, Zac?"

"What do you mean?" Zac's smile faltered. "Is it bad?"

"No! God no." Abel played with a few strands of Zac's midnight hair. "It's just that I want you to understand what's going on. At least with me." She gave her a sheepish look, then looked at the neckline of Zac's tank top, which she began to play with after releasing the silky strands of hair. "Zac, I am, well. I'm a little confused. You see, all my life I've been interested in boys. You know, wanting to date them, kiss them, that kind of thing. Then suddenly you come into my life and turn it upside down."

"I'm sorry, Spinney. I'm not trying to make things difficult."

Abel could feel Zac trying to pull away from her. "No!" she blurted, a bit louder than intended.

She could tell she startled Zac with her vehement response. She smiled softly, sending calming energy. "Oh, honey. No, that's not it. You've made things so much better." She reached out and touched the side of Zac's face, which was quickly disappearing as the sun took its final bow. "I'm about to sound like some cheesy Hallmark commercial, so bear with me." Abel took a deep breath, gently caressing the soft skin under her fingertips.

"It's okay, Spinney. I love to hear anything you have to say," Zac nearly whispered. For her encouraging words, she got a small kiss.

Abel smiled. "Thank you. You have made my life better, Zac. In so many ways. I look at things so different now." She paused, looking at the encroaching night around them. "It's like I see my surroundings with new eyes. Hell, I see them at all. I never used to think about it before. It was just there, and would always be there. You've changed that in me. You've changed me."

"Is that good?" Zac asked, rubbing gentle circles on Abel's back.

"Very." Abel smiled, running her thumb along Zac's jaw. "Very, very good. But the confusing part is how I feel about you."

"Why is that confusing?"

"Because as I said, I've always felt this way about guys. Not girls." She studied Zac's eyes. Although she couldn't see them very well anymore, she could still feel their intense power. "Honey, I've never so much as kissed a girl before. These feelings inside me kind of scare me. I really love what we do. I love to touch you, have you touch me," Abel's words trailed off as she leaned in and lightly kissed those irresistible lips.

Zac sighed into the kiss, leaning back against the tree behind her and taking Abel with her. Abel got herself more comfortable, once again almost sitting in Zac's lap. Zac trailed her hands up Abel's back. Abel sighed, loving the feel of Zac's fingers running through her hair and the feel of her lips. She brought her hands up to either side of Zac's face, holding her closer as the kiss deepened.

She could kiss Zac all day. Even though this was basically the third 'real' kiss for Zac, she kissed like a pro. Following all of Abel's leads, she held her own. Abel sighed again, feeling the kiss to her very core.

How on earth does Zac affect me so deeply, she had to wonder. Never has anyone–female or male–touched her so deeply nor made her body react and respond so much. After many moments, Abel broke the kiss, remembering that she had not finished what she had to say. Pulling back, she rested her forehead against Zac's. "Wait," She closed her eyes, taking several deep breaths. She wanted to get her racing heart under control before she continued. "God, I can't resist you," she breathed.

Zac waited patiently for the conversation to continue.

Getting her moorings back, Abel asked, "Zac, why do you think I kiss you?"

"Oh, uh… Well, the book said that oftentimes a kiss using the tongue is the prelude to sex. Foreplay, I think they called it."

Abel nearly choked on her own tongue. "What book have you been reading?"

"It's in my biology book," Zac said simply.

Abel grinned. "You've been reading about sex?" At Zac's affirmative, she asked, "Since when?"

"The past few months. I started having the strangest feelings and then I dreamed about you. You showed me your breasts." Zac trailed off. She looked down at the fidgeting hands in her lap.

Abel sat there, staring. She was trying to get her brain to compute what she had just been told. After a moment, she said, "You dreamed about me? My breasts? What?"

"It was nothing," Zac muttered.

"No. Wait. Don't clam up on me." Abel grinned, liking the fact that the beautiful brunette had dreamt of her, and her breasts no less! She felt renewed heat spread through her body. "Tell me about it."

Zac studied her for a long moment before elaborating. "Well, in the dream we were in the Jacuzzi and you took your bra off," Zac said with a grin.

"I did, did I?" Abel asked, brow raised. She felt fire rush through her and brought a hand up, finger tugging playfully at the neckline of Zac's tank top. At Zac's nod she chuckled. "You want that?"

"Oh, uh, I'm not sure," Zac stuttered, uneasiness in her voice. "It was a wonderful dream, though." She grinned.

"Well, then I guess I should be honest and tell you my dream," Abel said, feeling highly aroused, but highly nervous, too. "You see, according to my psyche, you and I went swimming in the lake. You were in this itty bitty bikini." She chuckled when she saw the grimace on Zac's face. "Calm down. I didn't say you had to wear one. Anyway, so we were swimming and having a good time. I could not keep my eyes off of you." She ran her finger along one of Zac's collarbones. "We kissed."

"Really? Did you feel the wetness between your

legs, too?" Zac asked, her voice hopeful. Her brows fell when Abel let out a bark of laughter. "What did I say?"

"Oh, Zac," Abel said softly, her fingers caressing Zac's face. "My Zac." Abel raised slightly to her knees and wrapped her arms around Zac's head, bringing it to rest against her chest. She felt overwhelmed with emotion and affection. "Yes. I felt it, too." *Hell, I feel it now!*

"Oh good. I wanted to make sure there wasn't anything wrong." Zac breathed a sigh of relief against Abel's cotton-clad chest.

"No, nothing wrong. It's very natural."

"It's called arousal… the book said that, too."

※※※※

"Zac?" Abel called to her friend, who was watching TV with Aure. She opened the cabinets, looking for… something. Nothing sounded good and she was feeling frustrated.

"Yes?" was murmured in her ear a moment later.

Abel smiled when she felt the warmth of Zac's body press against her back, her arms slide around her waist, and hands clasp over her stomach.

"What do you want for dinner?" Abel asked, one hand covering both of Zac's at her lower stomach, the other reaching up into the cabinet. "I can't find anything that sounds good." She fingered a can of Spaghetti-O's, and changed her mind. With a small growl, she leaned back into Zac's warmth. "Any ideas?"

"Well, how about I go catch us some fish?" Zac suggested.

"Zac, it's," Abel glanced at the clock on the microwave, "nearly eight-thirty at night. Into night fishing are you?"

"Hey, I've done it before and most certainly can do it again."

Abel chuckled, pushing the Spaghetti-O's aside to see what was behind it. "You know, the scary thing is I have no doubt that you'll pull it off. You go girl." Abel smiled at the soft kiss that was planted on the top of her head, then felt the coldness hit her back as Zac hurried out the door.

As the door closed, Abel's cell phone rang. "Hey, Mom. How goes it?" She began to rummage again, this time for veggies that would go well with the fish.

❧❧❧❧

Zac stood at the bank of the lake shimmering with the reflection of the large moon overhead, helping to light her way. She'd left Aure in the cabin with Spinney, as she knew the pup wasn't trained well enough to stay put and be quiet. Night fishing required more attention than fishing during the day. With expert efficiency, she impaled a night crawler on her hook and sent a fine cast hurling through the air to plop into the deep, cool waters. As she stood on the shore, waiting patiently, her mind wandered over the amazingly wonderful change of events with her Spinney over the past couple days, even just a matter of moments before, in the cabin when she'd hugged her friend from behind. The knowledge that Spinney enjoyed her touch as much as she enjoyed touching her or being touched by her was amazing, and the way Spinney had leaned back into her body... her eyes fell closed as she thought back to the warmth against her, the softness. It had been pure willpower to keep her hands from wandering further up from Spinney's stomach during that hug. Definitely before the dream, but especially after her dream, she was obsessed with Spinney's breasts.

She didn't tell Spinney that during the dream she reached out and touched the softness of her flesh, her thumb rubbing over a very stiff nipple. Zac woke not long after, her own breasts heaving, and her inner thighs slick with her nocturnal need. Though she had a basic biological understanding of all the moving parts from her reading, she couldn't possibly read to understand her personal need or the emotions behind it. That, she feared, would all have to come from actual experience, not academia.

❧❧❦❦

Abel chatted with her mom for the next half-hour or so, filling her in on how her semester ended, as well as some of the things she and Zac had done, of course leaving out certain details. That was one aspect of things she wasn't ready to share.

"I think it's fair for Ben to get his own room now," she was saying when she heard Zac's heavy steps jog up the stairs then her footfalls on the porch. She glanced towards the front door watching Zac saunter in with her fishing pole slung proudly over her shoulder and a string of fish dangling from the line in her hand. Abel grinned. Tonight they'd be eating well in the neighborhood! "Be right there, Zac," she said before returning to her conversation.

❧❧❦❦

Leaning her pole against the wall, Zac headed into the kitchen, laying the line of fish down on the table. She hurried up behind Spinney and reached up under her shirt to place very cold hands on Spinney's very warm stomach.

※※※※

"Ack!" Abel cried out, nearly dropping her phone as she tried to get away from Zac's icy hands. "Get those things off me!" she laughed, the icy fingers beginning to dig into her sides. "Mom, hang on," she barely managed to say before tossing the phone to the couch and turning to face her tormentor, leaving the line open.

Abel barely got Zac's hands out from under her shirt when she returned the attack.

"Oh, you are so dead!" Zac growled as she was tickled right back, fingers digging into her sides, ribs, whatever they could get purchase on. She tried to bat the persistent hands away, backing up toward the fridge in the process, lost in a fit of giggles.

"Mom, I'll call you back!" Abel yelled toward the phone on the counter. Far too involved in the war to hurry over and disconnect the line, Abel dug in with even more relish and purpose. She loved to hear Zac laugh and was thoroughly enjoying tickling her.

※※※※

Zac felt her back crash against the smooth coolness of the fridge and knew she was pinned. The feisty little blonde kept coming, her fingers now burrowing under the material of her T-shirt, cold fingers against the warm skin. Aure was barking his little head off, excited by the play of the humans. That is, until he got a whiff of the fish still lying on the table.

※ ※ ※ ※

Tears streamed from Zac's eyes as she gasped for breath, laughing too hard. Abel was laughing just as hard, watching her friend struggle against her, the veins straining in her neck. Her eyes were squeezed shut and her face flushed from the exertion.

She was beautiful.

Abel found her fingers slowing and then stilling, resting upon the warm skin of Zac's sides. She felt the insatiable urge to kiss Zac. So she did.

※ ※ ※ ※

Zac was startled by the total change in activity, but did not complain. She responded to Spinney's kiss, bringing her hands up to play in the thick, blonde strands, pulling her friend even closer. She was pinned between Spinney's body and the cold fridge. She soaked up the warm softness of Spinney, feeling every curve pressed against her, including of course, her breasts.

Spinney deepened the kiss, sighing softly as each of their tongues caressed the other. She pressed their hips tighter together, both moaning at the sensations it caused.

A small whimper escaped Zac's throat. Her body was buzzing and wanted something that she could not comprehend, but knew she had to have. She needed it, and only Spinney could provide it.

※※※※

Abel heard the whimper and melted. She felt a wave of desire course through her and matched the whimper with one of her own. Her body had never been so ready, though she really had no idea what she'd want Zac to do with it were she given the chance. She had no idea how this worked, so kept her thoughts on the kiss instead.

As Abel's hands remained under Zac's shirt, she felt a warm hand slip up the back of her own shirt, fingertips caressing the skin of her back. This prompted Abel's fingers to go on the move, the tips brushing the rounded undersides of Zac's breasts. She was about to move her mouth to Zac's inviting neck when suddenly she was pushed away.

"Aure! No!" Zac yelled, hurrying over to the dog who was about to yank the second of the four fish off the table by the line. She grabbed the fish, wrestling it out of the dog's mouth.

Abel joined Zac, helping her to get their dinner away from the dog and the floor. Her heart was still racing. She ran a shaky hand through her hair.

※※※※

Sherry cradled the handset as she sat at the kitchen table, contemplating what she'd just heard. Sure, it seemed like innocent play between her daughter and her dear friend, but something was niggling at her. From what she could hear, it brought back the early days when she and Adam were dating, and would look for any excuse or reason to touch. That was the fun stage, time for flirting, and cutsie words, and touches.

She rubbed her chin as her thoughts continued. There was a special connection between the two, nobody could deny that. As much as she wanted to just drop it there and move on, that little voice in the back of her mind continued to whisper, though what it was saying at this point was unclear.

Chapter Twenty-seven

Abel's family had arrived two weeks before. With yet another stolen moment, Abel and Zac were camped out in Zac's lean-to. With such a warm night upon them, they decided to take advantage of it. Besides, Abel wanted to be close to Zac and see the way she lived. What better way than to experience it first hand?

They lay on top of the sleeping bag, which lay on top of the foam mattress, their sides facing each other, sharing kisses and touches.

Abel ran her fingers over Zac's forearm. "Soft," she said, watching the path her fingers took. She followed Zac's arm until she saw their cotton-clad breasts were nearly touching. She'd seen Zac's eyes on her many, many times during the three weeks she'd been at the cabin. Those eyes seemed to burn blue fire through her every time she turned around. "Zac?" she said softly, her nails trailing down Zac's arm until she reached her hand, which she took in her own.

"Hmm?" Zac seemed to be lost in a haze inside the little cocoon of a lean-to.

"Do you like kissing me?" Abel asked, feeling somewhat like a one-trick pony, as kissing and touching Zac seemed to be about the only thing on her brain ever since that first time at the lake.

"Yes," Zac sighed, happily, contentment in her response and desire in her eyes.

Abel brought Zac's larger hand to her breast,

squeezing lightly on the hand she covered. "What do you think about touching me?"

Zac gasped at the contact. She didn't speak for a moment. Another gasp escaped when Abel squeezed her hand once again. "Yes."

"How does it make you feel?" Abel asked, her words somewhat breathy. She could feel her nipple hardening against Zac's palm, even through her T-shirt and bra. The heat was incredible.

"Well," Zac swallowed hard. Her gaze was locked on the hand that cupped Abel's breast, even after Abel's hand fell away. "It makes me feel very warm. Like somebody just started a raging fire six inches away from me. Like, it's inside me," she whispered, sparing a glance to Abel's hooded gaze. "I feel aroused, too."

You have no idea ... Abel was struggling to keep her control. Perhaps this hadn't been such a good idea. Of its own accord her back arched slightly pressing her breast even further into Zac's touch. She rested a hand on Zac's hip, fingers digging slightly into the material of her shorts.

"You make me feel things that I don't know what to do with." Zac's words were breathy. Her hand slipped off Abel's breast as she rolled over to her back, looking up at the stone ceiling. "It scares me, Spinney," she whispered.

Those quiet words snapped Abel out of her sexual daze and brought her rudely back to the present. She leaned up on her elbow and used two fingers on Zac's jaw to get her to look at her. She could see shame in her eyes. "Oh, sweetie," she whispered, caressing the soft skin of her cheek. "I'm so sorry. I didn't mean to scare you."

Though Zac continued to face Abel, her eyes

fell. "I don't know what I'm doing, Spinney. I'm sorry I disappointed you."

Abel felt her heart swell with love. "Zac," she whispered, lowering herself to her back and reaching for Zac. "Come here." Hesitantly, Zac moved into her arms, Abel holding her for a change. Abel rested her head against Zac's as she stroked her arm. "Maybe enough for one day, huh?" she suggested. She could almost feel the relief flowing from Zac. She placed a kiss to the top of her head. "You've never disappointed me Zac, and you never will. Let's get some sleep."

☙☙❧❧

Sherry watched the girls, amazed at how much time they spent together. Abel always spent a lot of time with Zac during the breaks since they'd reunited, but before, it was with the family. This summer they were off on their own doing their own thing. She didn't understand it. They even would spend the night in Zac's little lean-to out in the middle of the forest.

She didn't mind that her daughter and Zac had gotten so close; she thought the world of Zac. But this was Abel's last summer before she graduated from college, and probably one of the last times she'd be able to go to Maine with her family. Now, she stood out on the front porch of the cabin and watched as her daughter and Zac played Frisbee with Zac's adorable dog, Aure and their family dog–Aure's brother– Peanut. The two Golden Retrievers were barking with tails wagging wildly as the toy was thrown into the water, the pups splashing around, trying to beat each other to it.

Sherry's gaze turned from the frolicking dogs

to the two young women on the shore. They were standing close to each other, Abel animated as she was telling Zac something, which made the beautiful young woman throw her head back and laugh.

"Abel, honey," she called out. "Can you come here for a moment?"

Abel said one more thing to Zac before jogging up from the lake to the bottom of the stairs. "Yeah, Mom? What's up?"

"Well, first you need to grab some sun block. You're going to look like a lobster here before too long," Sherry said, reaching a hand up and indicating Abel's bare shoulders, which were already becoming pink.

Abel looked down at her shoulders. "Oops." She snagged the bottle of sunscreen that someone had left on the porch rail and squirted some into her palm. She glanced at her mother as she rubbed it into her skin. "You called me up here to lecture me on the virtues of skin care?"

"No." Sherry grinned. "I called you up here because I miss my daughter."

Abel's brows drew. "What? You miss your daughter? Mom, I'm right here."

Sherry sighed and placed her hands on her hips. "Honey, we've been at the cabin for three weeks now, and I feel like I've barely seen you. You're always off with Zac." She held up a forestalling hand. "Now, hold on a sec. You know I like Zac, but honey, it's not real likely we're going to see much of you after this summer. You'll be going off to grad school, and that program requires you to go all the way through the year, including summers."

Abel looked away and ran a hand through her

hair.

Sherry studied her easily able to tell her oldest was not happy. She stepped down until she was on Abel's level and put a hand on her arm. "I just ... I just wish you'd spend some time with us, Abel. We miss you," she finished softly.

Abel sighed and glanced back towards the shore where Zac had squatted down and was petting the dogs, her gaze meeting Abel's. Abel turned back to her mom. "I know, but Mom–"

"No buts. You can bring Zac into the cabin with you. There's no reason for the two of you to spend every free minute you get at her little lean-to thing. She stays there when we're gone. Let her enjoy the comforts of the cabin while she can."

"She doesn't want to, Mom. It's hot, and she likes it out in the open air..." Abel looked away again.

Sherry steeled herself. "You will be at dinner tonight, Abel. Zac's welcome, too. But either way, I want you there. And, I want you in the cabin tonight." With that Sherry turned and headed back up the stairs to the cabin.

※※※※

Abel was pissed! She made her way back to Zac, who stood as she approached.

"What's the matter?"

"My mother says I don't spend enough time with them," Abel growled.

"She doesn't like the time we spend together, does she?"

"No, I don't think that's it," Abel said with a sigh.

She glanced out over the lake where the two puppies still frolicked. Peanut saw Abel had returned so splashed back to shore to greet her, the Frisbee in his mouth. Abel smiled down at him and then sent the plastic disc zooming through the air again, both dogs splashing after it.

She let out a heavy sigh before turning back to Zac. "She said because I won't be back next summer that I should spend all my time here either with them, or with them and you."

Zac was quiet for a long time. She looked down as she played with the toe of her shoe in the rocky sand, her hands stuffed into the pockets of her shorts. Finally, she looked up and met Abel's gaze. "You won't be back next summer?" she asked softly. She looked as though she were about to cry.

"I graduate next spring, Zac. After that, I'm going to graduate school."

"But, what about here? What about our time together? I mean, won't I see you anymore?"

There was so much pain in Zac's extremely expressive eyes, it broke Abel's heart. She reached out and took Zac's hand. "Yes, you'll see me again. I promise you that. No matter what I have to do, you will see me. Okay?" Zac hung her head and nodded at Abel's soft words. "Come here."

Zac went most willingly into Abel's open arms. Abel held her to her, stroking her hair and leaving a soft kiss on the side of her neck. "I'm not leaving you, Zac. I promise," she whispered.

※※※※

Sherry stepped out of the cabin again, looking for

Abel. She shielded her eyes from the intense afternoon sun, and found the two young women where she'd found them minutes before, at the shore with the dogs. She watched them as they were hugging. Abel pulled out of the hug and gave Zac a quick kiss on the lips, to Sherry's shock. It hadn't been much more than a peck, but still... clearing her throat, she cleared her expression and walked over to them, calling out to her daughter in order not to startle them.

Abel turned to her, quickly dropping her hands from where they rested on Zac's shoulders.

"Abel, honey, we're going to need some more propane for the barbecue tonight. Care to run into town and grab some?" She looked from one to the other. "You can take Zac with you," she said brightly.

She watched as the two young women shared a glance, then a small nod.

"Okay, we'll go."

❧❧❧❧

Spinney kept a close eye on Zac as she drove down the road that led away from the cabin. Zac was tense, sitting in her seat, seatbelt clasped across her chest, though she kept tugging at it. She was trying to get used to the feeling of such restraint.

Zac felt strange, very strange. Even so, it felt good to be with her Spinney and do the things that she did in the regular world, away from the cabin. She looked around the blue Jetta, taking in all the gadgets, listening as Spinney explained what they all were and what they were used for. She nodded at the explanations, though she only understood some of them.

She did, however understand air conditioning. On the hot June day, she rather liked that gadget. The cool air blew out of the 'vents,' and hit Zac smack in the face. She closed her eyes and reveled in the feel, letting the air soothe her heated skin. She even leaned forward in her seat so her face was no further than two inches away from the refreshing air. It didn't take long before it felt like her nose was about to freeze off.

She leaned back in her seat and caught Spinney's amused grin. "That's cold."

She shifted in the small seat, stretching long legs out as far as she could, which wasn't far.

"I know it's a little small for you." Spinney grinned, glancing over at her friend from time to time. "You need an SUV, or a truck."

"What's that?" Zac asked, her finger taking up camp on the window up and down button. She liked the *whirr* of the window moving.

"Sport Utility Vehicle. My dad drives one, and they're big, so a giantess like yourself can fit better."

"Oh." Zac looked up, seeing the sun visor. Brows drawn in curiosity, she grabbed it and yanked. She was stunned when it flipped down to reveal a mirror. She studied herself, making faces at her reflection.

"You're killin' me, Smalls," Spinney chuckled, shaking her head. "Too damn adorable for your own good."

Zac gave her an innocent smile, but continued to play with all the fun gadgets.

࿇࿇࿇࿇

Abel pulled into town, which was tiny. It supported around two thousand souls, and had one main street lined with ma-and-pa shops. She parked the Jetta in front of the itty bitty all-purpose grocery store and turned to Zac.

"Are you going to be okay?" She watched Zac carefully as her friend looked around at all the activity around them, then nodded numbly. "If you get into trouble, just take my hand, okay?"

Finally, Zac's blue eyes met hers as Zac nodded again.

"I won't leave you, honey. I'm here." Abel reached over and squeezed Zac's hand. Receiving a small, weak smile in return before they got out of the car. Abel led the way into the store where she'd been every summer since she was five years old.

Cartwright's was a small mercantile with a dozen aisles filled with staples as well as any type of camping supply you might need, from camp stoves to gallon jugs of water to biodegradable wipes and everything in between. Zac was all eyes as she studied everything.

"Howdy, Abel. What can I do for ya? And who's your friend?" Mr. Cartwright stepped out from behind the counter to greet one of his long-time customers.

"Hello, Mr. Cartwright. This is Zac, and we're here to fill up our propane tank," Abel responded, after a quick one-armed hug from the kind older man. "You know how it is, big family barbecue." She smiled charmingly at the older man.

"Nice to meet you, Zac." The balding man smiled, brown eyes twinkling.

Zac looked like she had swallowed her tongue, but visibly relaxed when she felt Abel's body heat against her arm.

"Just say hello," Abel whispered. "It's okay."

"Hello," Zac said, her voice tight and rough.

"You know where everything is, girl. You go right on ahead and I'll get this filled for ya." The shopkeeper smiled once more at the two, looking curiously at Zac, then took the propane tank from Abel and pushed through swinging doors that led to the back.

Zac looked around, noting the shelves filled with every type of necessary, and not so necessary, items. Her eyes bulged when she saw every type of syrup imaginable. She hurried towards the shelf and scanned the labels, finally grabbing one of the bottles.

"Strawberry syrup," she read out loud, turning the bottle over to see what else the label had to say.

Spinney stepped up beside her. "You want to try that?"

Zac nodded, turning to see an amused Spinney looking at her. Spinney took the bottle from her and placed it in the plastic shopping basket she carried.

Zac 'oohed' and 'ahhed' at every single thing. She was particularly impressed with a little girl who had on some shoes with little lights that blinked with each step she took. She followed her around the store until the girl's mother gave her the look of death. Zac managed to forget about her fear. She was so excited by everything, but it certainly helped to feel Spinney's presence always near.

"Zac, come here," Spinney said, calling Zac over to the Slurpee Machine.

Zac abandoned her perusal of the potato chip section and wandered over to her friend, eyeing the suspicious looking machine. "Slurpee," she read. "What's a Slurpee?"

"Well," Spinney said, grabbing one of the red and blue stripped cups and sticking it under one of the flavor nozzles. "It's a really cold and yummy treat." She smiled at Zac as she pulled down the lever, the thick red ooze slowly pouring into the cup. "Especially on such a warm day."

Zac was fascinated and leaned down to get a closer look. "Looks like a really long piece of poop," she muttered. Spinney chuckled, outfitted it with a clear domed lid and a red spoon-type straw and handed the treat to an anxious Zac. "Sip slowly, though."

"Why?" Zac asked, bringing the Slurpee up to her nose and sniffing.

"Brain freeze."

Before Spinney could explain that elusive phrase, Mr. Cartwright returned with the filled bottle. "Okay. Ready to go?" Spinney asked, her basket filled with everything she wanted, including a few things for Zac.

"Yeah."

With one last glance around the aisles, Zac followed Spinney to the front where they got into a line, the red straw stuck in her mouth as she relished the new and cold sensations of the Slurpee. She noticed a bunch of magazines lined up in racks, so walked over to them and began to read the headlines. It wasn't long before her attention was caught by something else, which she wandered off to explore. Soon, it was Spinney's turn.

Zac wandered back over to her friend and watched as she handed the guy a little plastic card. He ran it through a slot, then handed it back.

"What is that?" she asked, knitting her dark brows and leaning over her friend to watch the guy punch some buttons on the noisy machine.

"It's a cash register," Spinney whispered. "And this is my credit card." She wiggled the plastic card in front of Zac's face.

Zac took it, the red straw never leaving her lips as she sucked the thick Slurpee. She studied the little card, reading Spinney's name written across it in raised letters and a whole bunch of numbers.

"Visa," Zac read. "'Don't leave home without it.'" She grinned at her recollection of the commercial.

"Yes, ma'am. It's certainly helped me out." She signed the slip and took the two bags from the clerk. "Here you go, stud. Carry that."

Zac took the bags while Spinney handled the heavy propane tank and followed her to the car. The drive back was filled with much less tension than the drive in. Zac glanced over at her friend. "Did you know Tom Cruise is part alien?" she said, allowing the red straw to pop out of her mouth just long enough to share what she'd learned from the magazine.

Chapter Twenty-eight

The days flew by, Spinney trying her best to make both her parents and herself happy. She spent her days with them, sometimes with Zac, sometimes not, but she always spent her nights with Zac. They often spent their time in her lean-to, away from the cabin where they could be alone.

One such night in July found them lying by the banks of the lake staring up into the stars. Zac sighed happily as she wrapped her arms tighter around Spinney, who lay halfway on top of her. Despite Zac's mild freak out a month before, their bond had been getting stronger over the weeks. She could not just hear the hum when Spinney was around, but could feel a pulsing now. It was like the heartbeat of her feelings. And the kisses! They were frequent and getting longer. Sometimes they'd spend an entire afternoon just exploring each other's mouth. It was nice. Spinney said they were the best kisses she'd ever had, which made Zac smile inside.

She wasn't sure what to think other than two things, she wanted to continue, and she didn't want Spinney to go back to school. Her friend had said much the same thing.

Blue eyes, silver in the moonlight, took in the blonde hair spread across her shoulders, the peaceful green eyes that stared out over the water, and a warm hand under her shirt, fingers grazing lazily over her stomach.

Every time Spinney touched her a small shiver would race down Zac's spine. It didn't matter what kind of touch it was. It could be the simplest little tap on the arm to get her attention or the deepest of kisses. Slowly, they'd build back up to where they'd been before Zac allowed her own self-doubt to put a temporary cease fire on their building passions. She dreamed about the green-eyed nymph every night, even when Spinney was lying right next to her, which was most nights.

She brought her hand up, running her fingers through the blonde hair, cool from the late night air. "Spinney?" she said, her voice hushed in the silence of a sleeping shore.

"Hmm?"

"What is sex like?"

Spinney's head lifted, surprise on her face. She stared up into those luminescent eyes, curiosity reflected in them. "Well," she began, resting her chin on her hands that rested on Zac's chest. "It can be wonderful." Her voice was also quiet. "Especially, if you really care about the person. That makes it better somehow."

"Why?"

Spinney rested her cheek against her hands, looking out over the darkened water for a moment. "I don't know. I guess because then there are emotions behind it, too, you know? It's not just about physical pleasure."

Zac thought she understood. "Have you ever been in love?" she whispered, looking into Spinney's eyes, able to feel in that moment what she thought was meant by those two very simple words: in and love, and how their combination gave the words a whole new meaning.

Spinney thought for a moment, closing her eyes as Zac's fingers ran through her hair again. She shook her head. "No."

"Oh." Zac tilted her head to the side slightly, watching the smile that spread across Spinney's lips. Her eyes were still closed. She loved Spinney. She knew that as sure as she knew she had a squirrel that followed her everywhere. "Spinney?"

"Hmm?"

"Can we go to bed and kiss for a while?"

Spinney opened her eyes and looked into the totally serious face of her Zac. She smiled, and pulled herself up. "Come on."

※ ※ ※ ※

Abel pushed to her feet and reached a hand down to Zac. With Abel leading the way, they headed through the dark toward the lean-to. Abel knew the woods now almost as well as Zac did. She could easily find her way in the dark, which was helpful since she had become such a night dweller over the summer.

Once inside the small shelter, Abel lay down on Zac's bed and pulled Zac down next to her. Zac stretched out on her side, her lips immediately going to hers. Abel brought her hand up to bury it in the long dark hair that formed a curtain around them. She heard the cute little whimper that always seemed to escape Zac's lips. She felt it head straight south. Zac had an effect on her that she could neither describe nor reconcile. Never had anyone, especially someone who had no idea what they were doing, touched her so deeply or profoundly. Zac's fingers and lips were like fire, and she craved the burn.

Now, weeks after she'd slowed things down substantially after Zac was so overwhelmed, a slow burn had begun with a fire even more intense than before. By taking a small breather, Zac seemed to have regrouped and gained more confidence in what she wanted. Abel now allowed Zac the lead regarding when and how their intimate moments happened. That too, seemed to give Zac more confidence. She could feel Zac's need building stronger everytime they touched.

Now, as she felt Zac's tongue expertly exploring her mouth, her perfect white teeth nipping playfully at Abel's bottom lip, she grabbed Zac's hand and placed it under her shirt, splaying the long fingers out over her skin. Zac sighed, moving her body a little closer to Abel's, instinct seeming to guide her.

"Touch me, Zac. Don't be shy," Abel whispered into Zac's mouth. She could feel Zac's body almost trembling with need.

Zac met Abel's gaze for a long moment. At Abel's subtle nod, she did as she was told and began to let her fingers move. When she came to the barrier of the underwire of Abel's bra, she stopped. She looked into Abel's eyes once more, uncertainty written all over her face.

"It's okay, Zac," Abel whispered. "Go at your own pace. You're not doing anything wrong." She brought a hand up and brushed some of Zac's hair back, tucking it behind her ear before she briefly caressed the side of her face. She reached down, placing her hand over Zac's, the thin cotton of her tank top between their hands.

Zac gasped slightly when Abel placed her hand directly on the lace-clad breast.

Abel closed her eyes as she absorbed the touch on her extremely sensitive breast. Her fingers dug slightly into Zac's back as she brought their lips together again, searching for Zac's tongue with her own. She had never been so aroused; it was kind of scary. She did her best to hold it in check. Lesson learned where Zac was concerned.

❧❧❧❧❧

Zac squeezed the softness beneath her hand, reveling in finally being able to feel the wonder of what had her attention for months. Yes, she'd had her chance many weeks ago, but the shadows of her own inexperience had sabotaged that situation, and she'd worried she'd lost her chance forever. At that moment, she had no desire to retreat, just wanted to lose herself in Spinney's warmth.

She felt the hardness of Spinney's nipple against her palm and was surprised. She knew there was no way she was cold on the warm night, so figured she must be aroused.

Zac grinned like an idiot.

"What?" Spinney asked.

"You're aroused," Zac observed, pride marking her words. She squeezed her hand once to show her evidence.

Spinney groaned softly, nodding as she arched her back slightly.

"Did I do that to you?"

"Yes," Spinney sighed, closing her eyes again. She brought her hand to Zac's, squeezing herself through her fingers once more. "Yes," she moaned again. She guided Zac's fingers to her nipple, a soft whimper following as Zac lightly pinched the rigid flesh.

Zac felt a surge of arousal spread through her own body and kissed her Spinney with an intensity that surprised them both. She felt herself being drawn even closer by the tightening arms around her neck. Body to body, her hand pinned between them, Zac feasted on Spinney's mouth, making them both moan and whimper with passion.

⁂

Abel's hands left Zac's neck and hair and traveled down her back, over the heated skin that was nearly hot to the touch through her shirt. Her hands sought the roundness of Zac's butt, the fingers spreading out to cover as much as possible, then squeezing, making Zac squeak in surprise. Abel grinned against Zac's mouth that was still on hers.

"You have a really nice ass," she murmured, squeezing for good measure.

"That's a good thing, right?" Zac asked, raising herself up onto her elbows as she looked down into the darkness that was her companion's face.

"A very good thing," Abel purred. "I'm rather fond of it, actually. I like to look at it, touch it. Heck, I'd even kiss it." Abel grinned, knowing that Zac would not get the joke. To her horror, a very long, deep yawn escaped her lips. She was exhausted. Spending all her nights up with Zac, getting only three hours of sleep was catching up with her.

"Tired?" Zac asked, the slightest bit of disappointment in her voice.

"I'm sorry, baby," Abel said, stroking Zac's

cheek. "Can we go to sleep?" She heard and felt Zac's nod before Zac rolled off to lie beside her, gathering Abel's body against her own again. As they settled, Abel realized that Zac's hand was still on her breast, and she also realized that she quite liked that. She turned her head back and reached back with her hand to bury her fingers in Zac's hair. She initiated a slow, exploratory kiss. "I promise," she whispered against Zac's lips. "I'll make it up to you."

❧❧❧❧

Sherry had been tossing something around in her mind for a couple weeks. She had seen and heard some things that she wasn't entirely sure how to compute. First, the little tickle fest she'd heard over the phone before the family had arrived at the cabin. Second, the small kiss she had seen Abel and Zac share at the lake. Then, finally, just last week she went for an early morning swim and had seen the duo on the shore, her daughter lazing against the taller girl, whose arms were wrapped securely around Abel.

She didn't know what to make of it, but had some questions. She had thought about talking to Adam about it, but decided against it. He would not understand, no matter what the situation actually was, or wasn't.

Today Zac had promised to spend some time with Becky alone, just the two of them. Adam was going to take the boys and Rachel into town, so what better time to talk to her daughter?

Abel helped her mother fold a load of laundry. She was quiet and moody as she snapped the wrinkles out of the pillow cases she was folding. Sherry watched her closely.

"Are you okay, honey?" she asked, tossing balled up socks to the small pile on the couch and grabbing a shirt to fold.

"Yup," Abel muttered, placing the folded case on its mate and grabbing for the top sheet. "I don't understand why you don't make the rest of the brood help with this," she muttered.

"They do. You haven't lived at home in several years, Abel."

Abel just grunted, again snapping the clean-smelling material.

"So have you and Zac enjoyed your time together?"

Before she could even register it, the goofy grin was on Abel's face. "Yeah."

"You're certainly attached at the hip, huh?" Sherry prodded, grabbing a pile of Adam's T-shirts, ready to carry them to their bedroom. She indicated that Abel should grab the folded shorts and socks.

"She's my best friend. Of course we're going to spend time together," Abel said, gathering the pile of clothing and following her mother up the stairs.

"I can't remember the last time you stayed in the cabin at night. Is there something to playing Jane to Zac's Tarzan?"

"What?" Abel asked with raised eyebrows.

"Well, you stay out there with her in that little shack of hers. What's up with that?" Sherry asked as she took the socks from Abel's hands, stuffing them in Adam's sock drawer.

Abel shrugged, her gaze dropping away from her mother's. "We enjoy it. It's hot outside, and this way we don't have to use a fan. Besides, I figure I always drag her in here when I'm here, so it's only fair that I try the other side, too. Right?"

"Sure. Sounds good to me." Sherry smiled, though it was only a temporary fix to her curiosity, and they both knew it.

༄༅༄༅

Abel looked out over the water that reflected the stormy sky, which in truth reflected her stormy feelings. She had a lot on her mind, from her mom's suspicions, to her want and need for Zac, to the knowledge that her summer was coming to an end far too quickly.

"I think it's going to rain soon," Zac said, her thumb running over the softness of the back of Spinney's hand. The two stood on the banks of the lake holding hands as Aure explored and sniffed his way to every rock, bug, and piece of vegetation.

"Yeah, I think so." She glanced back toward the cabin, not able to see it, meaning they were out of its view also. She turned to Zac, dropping her hand before snaking her arms up around her neck. "Kiss me," she said, fingers playing with the hair at the back of Zac's head.

Zac lowered her head and placed a gentle kiss to Abel's lips, a teasing touch. Her next touch, however, was far from teasing.

Abel sighed into it, enjoying Zac's step out onto a limb of confidence as she led the kiss. Abel could sense she was feeling more confident with each stroke of her tongue against her own.

Zac's hands moved down along Abel's sides to rest on her hips, hesitating just a moment before she lightly pulled their hips closer together. She broke the kiss, breathing heavily. She rested her forehead against Abel's.

"Spinney," she whispered, so much need in that one word. It was need and it was asking permission all in one.

Abel felt that need clear throughout her body, settling between her legs.

The spell was broken for just a moment as the first raindrop landed on Zac's shoulder. She looked up into the pregnant clouds.

"We're going to get wet."

"Too late," Abel breathed, grabbing Zac and pulling her down for a breath-stealing kiss, the rain forgotten. Abel could feel her body start on fire, and even the rain couldn't put it out. She broke the kiss and took Zac's hand, leading her back to the lean-to. They were soaked by the time they got to the shelter, hair and clothing molded to the skin beneath.

Once inside, Abel turned to Zac, seeing that her clothing was basically non-existent, showing off the gorgeous form beneath. She looked up into Zac's face, seeing the dripping bangs hanging in her eyes and droplets falling from the tip of her nose. She brushed the dark hair back, revealing the stunning face. "You are so gorgeous, so sexy, Zac," she murmured.

Zac said nothing, but the look in her eyes easily matched Abel's in intensity. The air between them was thick and heavy with arousal and need. Abel's fingers found the hem of Zac's soaked tank top and tugged, peeling the sodden shirt up and over her head, dropping it to the floor. Standing there in shorts and bra, Zac watched her green eyes closely.

Abel took in the lean torso before her, her

fingers brushing against the muscles of Zac's stomach. She wanted Zac. She wanted to show her just what she could offer her and how she felt. Abel knew she was in deep. Her heart ceased with every look, with every touch and kiss. She had been honest with Zac when she said she had not been in love before. Not before now.

Bringing her fingers to the cool, wet skin of Zac's sides, she ran her hands up and down the length, noting how Zac's chest was heaving. She knew Zac was as turned on as she was, but she also figured she was probably scared, too.

Looking up into wide blue eyes, Abel smiled. "It's just me, Zac. Your Spinney." She whispered, leaning up and giving her a soft kiss on the lips. "I won't hurt you."

"I know," Zac breathed. She closed her eyes as Abel's fingers worked their way up her torso, fluttering around her breasts.

"You okay?" Abel asked, her breath tickling Zac's skin as her lips left feather light kisses across Zac's collarbones.

At Zac's nod, she continued her perusal of Zac's skin, making her way to her shoulder. She left more kisses there, enjoying the feel of Zac's softness, her smell and the soft sighs that escaped her throat as Abel explored.

"So beautiful," Abel whispered, finally reaching around until she felt the clasps to Zac's bra. Unclasping them with rain-chilled fingers, finally they came loose and the bra came off. Zac shivered as the cold, wet material slid from her body, landing on the dirt floor. Abel took in the sight before her. "Wow," she breathed, unsure if Zac was real or a statue of perfection come to life.

"Spinney?" Zac sighed, her head arching back as wet strands of blonde hair brushing her heated skin as Abel's kisses continued.

"Hmm?" Abel said against Zac's collarbone, her nails trailing down Zac's sides until her hands reached Zac's hips, where they gripped her.

"Are we... are we going to..."

"I'm going to make love to you, Zac." Abel murmured against her neck, her hands reaching around to cup Zac's incredibly shapely and firm behind, which was still clad in her cargo shorts.

"Oh, god," Zac shuddered, her hands fisting at her sides.

"Is that okay?" Abel murmured just before licking a trail up the column of Zac's throat, not waiting for a response as she nibbled her way to Zac's proud jaw. She smiled at the vigorous nod she received. "Good."

Abel knew there was no reason to deny it anymore. She was deeply in love with Zac and needed her. She also knew that this may be their only chance, and she didn't want to live with the regret of not showing her exactly how she felt.

Not entirely sure what she was doing, Abel let pure instinct and desire take over. Never in her life had she been so ready. She looked at Zac's breasts, pale in the growing darkness of the day as the storm continued to pound outside the cocoon of their passion. She noted the erect nipples standing in stark relief. Bringing her hands up, she ran gentle fingertips under the round undersides of the heavy breasts, marveling at the feel.

"So soft," she whispered. Zac's breathing hitching from anticipation, so Abel decided to end the suspense.

She fully covered the softness, eliciting a moan from her soon-to-be lover.

"Spinney," Zac whimpered, "I, I need to sit down."

Understanding, Abel turned her attention to Zac's shorts. Her fingers made quick work of the button and zipper, the cargos falling down long, muscular thighs to puddle at her feet. Abel wanted to take her time to stare, but she knew Zac was hurting, so instead she slipped her fingers down the back of her panties, sending the blue material down to join the shorts.

A moment later, Zac was sitting on her sleeping bag-covered foam mattress, Abel kneeling to untie her boots. She pulled one off followed by the sock, before removing the other, leaving Zac completely naked. On her knees, Abel rested her hands on the sleeping bag on either side of Zac's hips and took her lips in a deeply heated kiss, which Zac returned with equal fire.

Pulling away, Abel stood again and her gaze never leaving Zac's, undressed, allowing her clothing to fall where it would. She gave Zac a sexy smile, thoroughly loving the look on her face as her wide blue eyes scanned her naked body. The funny thing was, Abel knew she had a nice body and had certainly been told so enough times, but none of those other times nor the people who said it in the past mattered. All that mattered to her was that Zac approved, that Zac thought she was beautiful and that Zac wanted her. Though Zac had remained relatively quiet since they'd returned to the lean-to, her eyes said it all, and it made the wet heat between Abel's legs increase exponentially.

Abel lowered herself to the mattress, nudging

Zac to lie back, which she did, her head resting on the fluffy pillow. Abel crawled over to her, not stopping until she rested her body on top of her. They both sighed at the contact of their fully naked bodies pressing together.

"You doing okay?" Abel asked, resting her upper body on her elbows as she looked down at Zac.

Zac nodded, her hands still in fists at her sides. "Can I touch you?" she whispered.

That sexy grin returned to Abel's beautiful face. "You better or I might just cry."

Zac grinned, her hands coming up to rest on the warm flesh of Abel's lower back.

Abel wasted no time finding Zac's neck again. She enlisted her tongue to make Zac moan as she kissed and licked her way up to Zac's ear, where she nibbled briefly on her earlobe before working her way back down, dipping her tongue into the hollow of her throat before steadily exploring her upper chest. She felt Zac's fingers move up her back and finally into her hair as Abel slowly made her way further down.

Reaching the swell of Zac's breasts, Abel felt her nerves coming back. She was beginning to move outside of the box. She lifted her head and looked down at the beautiful flesh, and cupped a breast in her hand. She was admittedly fascinated and thought that Zac's breasts were perhaps the most beautiful and sensuous things she'd ever seen.

Looking up, Abel's gaze met Zac's very hooded eyes. They exchanged a meaningful look, one of Zac's hands coming up to cup Abel's cheek, almost as if to give her permission and encouragement. Abel smiled before she turned her head, leaving a kiss on Zac's open palm. One more glance shared and she returned her focus back to the breast in her hand.

Lowering her head, she closed her eyes and gave the hard dusky nipple a slow moist swipe with her tongue. Zac's throaty groan told her all she needed to know as far as Zac's enjoyment. Encouraged, she ran her tongue over the nipple again, this time remaining, fluttering over the tip before taking it into her mouth, the warm wetness engulfing Zac's breast.

"Spinney," Zac whimpered, her back arching, subtly thrusting her breast further into Abel's mouth.

Abel stroked Zac's side with gentle fingers as she continued to suckle her breast. She couldn't help but compare her previous times in bed with the few men she'd slept with. The truth of the matter was, there *was* no comparison. Being with Zac in that moment, listening to her soft moans and sighs, she knew she'd never share her bed with anyone else again. She had no idea how that would happen, but she knew that much.

After giving Zac's other breast equal attention, she moved her way back up Zac's body until she found her lips again. The kiss was deeply passionate, but Abel also took her time. As the kiss progressed, she ran her hand down Zac's side, over her hip, and finally to the side of her thigh, urging Zac to lift it, which she did. A moment later, Abel's own hips were cradled between Zac's legs. She sighed into the kiss at the extremely foreign sensation. She broke the kiss and buried her face in Zac's neck as she absorbed all that she was feeling.

"Zac." Pressing her hips further into Zac, she felt her wetness. She again ran her hand over Zac's thigh, her nails trailing back up and over her hip. She moaned as Zac whimpered softly and thrust her hips instinctively up into Abel.

"Spinney," Zac whispered, her hands trailing down Abel's back, nails digging slightly into the flesh.

Abel raised her head and they kissed again as she pushed back against Zac. It didn't take long before they started to move together. Her lips found Zac's tantalizing neck again as she moved her hips, Zac's legs spreading a bit further.

"You feel so good," she murmured against Zac's skin. "Does it feel good for you?"

Zac nodded, her eyes closed and fingers kneading reflexively on Abel's shoulders with each gentle thrust of their hips. Her breathing was growing more rapid, as was Abel's.

To Abel's surprise, she felt her climax building. She had no idea that two women in that position could feel so amazingly good, let alone lead to orgasm. She raised herself to her hands for more power and leverage in her hips, as well as to look into Zac's face. No doubt her love would be confused with what was about to happen, as she could tell from Zac's flushed face that she was getting close, as well.

"Spinney," Zac whimpered, voice breathy and high-pitched.

"It's okay," Abel gasped, her climax beginning. "Let it come, Zac." She no sooner got those words out then she cried out, her body convulsing against Zac's. Zac followed a moment later with a loud gasp, her fingers clawing painfully at Abel's back as she threw her head back, her breasts pressing up into Abel's.

Abel pulled her tightly to her, allowing Zac to ride out the intensity of her first orgasm. She rained kisses on Zac's face as she caressed her neck with gentle fingers.

"It's okay," she murmured against Zac's lips. "It's okay."

※ ※ ※

Zac was stunned and struck to the bone at the intensity of her experience. Her entire body continued to quake with aftershocks, and it was only Spinney's comforting words, kisses and touches that kept her feet firmly on the ground.

Finally, she opened her eyes, looking up into her Spinney's beautiful face. They shared a smile before Spinney moved off of her, though they again kissed, Spinney's fingers caressing Zac's stomach and up between her breasts.

"I can't seem to stop touching you," Spinney murmured, her gaze boring into Zac's. "You're so soft, so beautiful."

Zac smiled, her body still buzzing from her orgasm. Spinney's continued touches weren't helping, as–to her surprise–she was feeling her body responding again. "I like your hands on me, Spinney."

Spinney gave her a devilish grin. "We'll get along really well, then."

Zac's eyes fell closed as once again Spinney's mouth found her breasts, but what made her gasp was when one of Spinney's hands smoothed down over her stomach and then between her legs. Zac gasped as those fingers pushed through to her most intimate parts.

Spinney released the nipple from her mouth and raised her head again to look down at Zac, her fingers gently exploring Zac's saturated folds. She let out a long, languid sigh at the contact. "So amazing," she breathed.

"Spinney." Zac's thighs fell open wider as Spinney began to stroke her.

"I'm here, baby," Spinney whispered, leaning down and placing a comforting kiss on Zac's lips as her fingers found the most sensitive part of Zac's body.

Zac whimpered as two of Spinney's fingers rubbed the hard bundle of nerves that became the center of Zac's entire universe. Her hips began to move in time with the circling fingers, the pressure just hard enough to elicit incredible pleasure.

Spinney lifted her head and watched as her hand moved between Zac's legs, her fingers moving faster and adding more pressure. Zac was so wet, her fingers were covered, the flesh softened by Zac's desire.

Zac reached for Spinney, grabbing a handful of her hair and bringing her down for a passionate kiss as her body readied for her second climax. Though it was hard to kiss as she was breathing so hard, she needed to be connected to her Spinney as she fell over the edge, a loud cry erupting from her throat, which Spinney caressed with her free hand, as her other one remained between Zac's legs, pressing down hard on Zac's clit to milk every ounce of pleasure out of the beautiful woman.

≈≈≈≈

Abel watched Zac as she slowly began to come down from her intense experience. She'd never seen anything so beautiful or sexy as Zac's chest heaved, her body splayed out before her like a sacrifice to the gods of pleasure and sensuality. As Zac's moans dimmed to breathy whimpers, she removed her hand.

She discreetly wiped the immense wetness onto a paper towel then ran her fingers all over Zac's torso in comforting caresses as Zac slowly began to calm.

Zac's eyes opened and she met Abel's loving gaze, Abel's hand stroking her cheek. "How are you?" she asked softly.

Zac swallowed a few times before she nodded. "Good."

Abel chuckled at the look of pure amazement and bliss on Zac's beautiful face. "I have to admit," she murmured, "I have truly never seen anything more beautiful or sexy than when you came just now."

"Came?" Zac asked, words still somewhat breathy.

Abel grinned. "It's a term people use for when someone orgasms." She shrugged. "Sex slang, I guess."

"Well, then, with what we did before, well, you know, what you just did, did you came, too?

Abel chuckled. "Yes, I came, but in the way you just said it, it would be come." She leaned down and kissed Zac, her chest nearly ready to explode with love and affection. She caressed Zac's damp bangs out of her eyes.

"Spinney?" Zac said softly, her hand coming up so the backs of her fingers could graze along the side of Abel's left breast. "I want to do that to you, too."

"Oh yeah?" Abel asked.

"Yeah. I want to," her gaze fell to Abel's breasts. "I want to touch you."

"Yeah?" Abel asked, her voice taking on a sensuous timbre. She stretched her body out atop Zac's again, her arousal–never fully sated–flaring up quickly. She initiated a deeply passionate kiss, Zac responding immediately.

Lips still caressing Zac's, Abel rolled to her back, taking Zac with her until their positions were effectively reversed. Now on top, Zac's kiss became almost possessive, her hand cupping one of Abel's breasts and gently squeezing, her palm grazing over the nipple in a slow circle, making Abel moan.

Zac abandoned the kiss as she moved to explore Abel's neck. Abel raised her knees and spread her legs, wanting to feel Zac against her. Zac's drying hair tickled her skin as Zac licked and kissed every inch of skin she came to. Though Zac had never explored a woman's body before nor made love to one, she was a very quick learner. As passionate as she was about learning and 'her Spinney', she was about making love.

Abel moaned softly as Zac's mouth found her right breast. She thrust her hips up lightly against Zac's stomach, which pressed into her wetness. Abel let out a languid sigh, sensations flowing through her body as Zac ran her fingers down over her hip. She moaned into her task as she explored Abel's torso, tongue flicking over her ribs, then teasing her belly button before returning back to her breasts.

"I love these," she murmured against the side of Abel's left breast. "So soft." She flicked her tongue over the hard nipple. "I dream about these every night, Spinney."

"You do, huh?" Abel barely managed to say as Zac suckled her. She was driving her crazy, and Abel wasn't entirely sure if she'd be able to stop herself from coming just from Zac's mouth on her breasts.

"Yes." Zac sucked Abel's nipple into her mouth before gently gnawing on it with her teeth, eliciting a long groan from Abel's throat.

"My god, Zac," Abel whimpered. "If you read

about how to make love in your biology book, I wanna read it."

Zac grinned. "Nope. You just taste so good I can't help it."

Abel groaned at Zac's words. Her arousal was reaching dangerous proportions. "Zac," she whimpered.

"Hmm?" Zac murmured against her throat.

"Zac, I need you inside me."

Zac lifted her head and looked down at Abel, a slightly panicked look in her eyes. "I don't... I don't know how."

"It's okay, baby," Abel whispered, leaning up and giving her a quick kiss before she reached for one of Zac's hands and brought it down between her spread legs. Zac moved off to the side and watched as Abel guided their hands where she needed them, using her fingers to put pressure on Zac's fingers at her opening. "Right here, baby," she murmured, eyes sliding closed. "Please, right here."

Zac pushed her fingers forward, nearly holding her breath as suddenly her first two fingers disappeared. "Oh my god," she whispered, eyes huge.

"Yes," Abel groaned, lifting her hips to meet Zac's fingers. "Yes, baby." She caressed Zac's hand before taking hold of it and showing Zac the rhythm she needed. "God, yes..."

"So soft," Zac whispered. "You're so soft, Spinney."

Abel couldn't even speak as Zac began to gently thrust inside of her, her strokes slow yet firm. Normally, it was extremely rare that she could come simply from penetration. She always had to reach down between her own legs and rub her clit to throw her over the final edge, but she knew that wasn't going to be necessary with Zac. Just the realization alone that it was Zac inside her was bringing her closer to orgasm than any need for clitoral stimulation.

"Faster," she gasped, her hips rising quicker as she got closer. "Yes, Zac. Oh my god, yes..."

Zac's fingers thrust quickly in and out of Abel's body, her own breathing quickening with Abel's.

Abel cried out so loudly that a nearby fox scampered off deeper into the woods. She gasped for breath, aftershocks continuing to ravage her body, which Zac now caressed, much like Abel had done with her moments before.

At length, Abel opened her eyes and looked up to see Zac looking back at her, a very pleased grin on her face. Abel smiled and brought her hand up to cup the back of Zac's neck and brought her down for a lingering kiss before she wrapped her arms around her as Zac moved on top of her again, the two locked in a tight embrace. Breaking the kiss, Zac rested on her forearms and looked down into Abel's face with so much love in her eyes.

"I love you, Abel," she said softly.

It took Abel a moment as, her given name sounded so foreign on Zac's lips. She brought her fingers up to trace those full lips, her fingertips receiving a kiss as they passed. "I love you too, Zac. So very much."

Chapter Twenty-nine

Abel inhaled the early morning air, arms wrapped tightly around her shins. The sun was just coming up over the tops of the hills surrounding the lake, and it was breathtaking.

She felt the small tingling sensation all over her skin from the early morning chill and basked in it. Her days at the cabin for the summer were numbered, and she wanted to be able to absorb as much of it as was possible.

Zac sat next to her, their shoulders brushing. Together they watched the birth of a new day. No words were needed between them. Anything they had to say had been said over and over again during their nights that summer. Through the magic of touch and emotion, they had conveyed all that could be uttered in breath. Their night had been spent making love again and again, only taking intermittent breaks to sleep wrapped in each others arms.

Zac reached her hand out and began to trail her fingers through the golden locks of her Spinney's hair, made even more brilliant from the intense golden rays of the rising sun. A smile spread across her face. "Beautiful," she said, her voice no more than a breath upon the morning.

Abel turned to her, meeting the steady gaze and smiled back. She said nothing, but instead rested her head upon Zac's shoulder. "I love you," she whispered.

"I love you, too," Zac replied, kissing the top of

her head.

※ ※ ※ ※

Zac had been struggling over a single question during the past weeks. She wanted Spinney to stay with her. She knew there was no way this could happen, but it still did not stop her from wishing. She opened her mouth to ask, but quickly shut it again. She could never do that to her, never sentence her to a life of isolation and intimidation. Never take her from what she knew and loved. Never take her from her education and family. Friends. Advantages. Car. Syrup at the ready. None of it.

Instead she held her Spinney closer to her, inhaling her fragrance and counting her blessings for having her as much as she had, even if it was all coming to an end.

※ ※ ※ ※

"Mom, can I talk to you?" Abel asked, her fingers tugging nervously at the hem of her shirt. She watched as her mother knelt on the ground, planting wildflowers around the front of the cabin. Sherry did a little bit of landscaping every summer. Abel always felt that was such a strange thing to do–plant wildflowers in the wild.

"Of course you can, honey," Sherry answered, a quiet sigh following her words.

"Cool," Abel muttered, standing where she was. "Oh, never mind." Abel turned, prepared to bolt when she felt a garden-gloved hand on her arm.

"Hold it. That is the fifth time today you've asked

if you could talk to me, and the fifth 'never mind' I've gotten. You plant your butt right down there and bury those bulbs. While you're doing that, you will talk to me."

Abel nodded, taking the spade she was offered. Plopping down, she used her hands and the tool to gather a little mound of dirt over the planted bulbs. To her it looked just like a little cemetery minus the headstones. She took a deep breath and prepared herself for what she wanted to talk to her mother about. "I want to talk to you about Zac... and me." Abel's green eyes darted up to meet interested ones.

"Okay," Sherry said as she opened another packet of bulbs and began to divide them, then started digging graves, er, holes for them. "Go on."

"Well, you see, as you know, we've gotten very close over the past year." Those eyes flicked up again. "Very close."

Sherry looked up, meeting the gaze and tilting her head slightly. "Uh huh,"

"I love her, mom," Abel said, her voice quiet, nearly a whisper. It was partly out of fear of her mother's reaction and partly out of the fact that it hurt to say it.

"I know, honey." Sherry gave her daughter an understanding smile and patted her hand, leaving a slight dirt smudge. "Oops."

"Yeah, thanks. How did you know?" Abel asked as she wiped the dirt onto her shorts.

"I've watched you two together. It's quite endearing, actually."

"Oh," Abel muttered, looking down as she patted a newly-made pile with the spade. "But, um, do you understand what I mean? By saying I love her?"

"I think so." Sherry sighed, looking out over the beautiful late July day. "Romantically, you mean?"

Abel nodded. "Are you completely grossed out?" She could not meet her mother's gaze, but she felt it.

There was a slight pause before Sherry responded. "I'm not sure what I feel. I have had some time to mull this over, though. I'd been seeing things for a little while, but just didn't know what to make of them, to be honest."

"And now?" Abel asked, giving up the pretense of burying the bulbs and looking at her mother.

"Now, I'm not sure. I could see things getting pretty heated."

Abel ducked her head, peeking at her mother through golden bangs. Sherry smiled and ruffled the bangs in question.

"I do have some concerns, honey. I mean, what will you do once you go back to school? You'll be there, she'll be here. You'll be so busy this time next year chances are good you won't be back. You have to keep all these things in mind."

"I know." Abel picked up a dirt clot and threw it, watching with satisfaction as it exploded against a rock. "I don't know what to do."

"I honestly don't know what to tell you, honey." Sherry looked at her daughter, seeing the worry and despair reflected in those emerald eyes. "What do you want to happen? I mean, what are you hoping for? Expecting?"

"I don't know. I guess if it were up to me, which it's clearly not, Zac would come back to Boston with me. God, I want her there so bad," Abel said as she slammed the sharp tip of the spade into the dirt, stabbing at a clump of clots. "I worry so much about her, you know?" She looked at her mother with pleading eyes.

Sherry nodded. "So do I. But keep something in mind, honey. Zac has been doing this on her own for a long time now. Even when her father was alive, it sounds like it was just Zac."

"I know. But, hell, I don't know," Abel said with a frustrated groan, running a hand through her hair. She looked at her mother. "Are you disgusted?"

Sherry sighed. "No, honey. I'm not disgusted. I worry and don't understand, but I'm not disgusted."

"Please don't tell dad," Abel pleaded, knowing that her father would never understand.

Sherry planted another bulb. "It's not mine to tell. I'm sure you'll fill him in when you feel it's right."

"Thanks, Mom." Abel leaned over and gave her mother a hug, closing her eyes at the comfort and support she felt from her. She was so grateful to have her in her life.

༺༺༻༻

Abel walked toward the lake where she saw Zac swimming with Becky. The brunette and the little imp had gotten so close over the summer. Becky absolutely adored Zac and Abel knew the same was true for Zac. The two frolicked in the water as Abel stood on the shore watching.

"Come on, Becky. Climb on up here," Zac urged as she grabbed the small girl and easily lifted her onto her shoulders. She waded out a little further into the water and then with a playful growl, threw the small, squealing girl into the depths. The five year old giggled as she surfaced. She had always been a little fish, taking to swimming like most took to breathing.

"Hey you, be careful with her!" Abel yelled to the pair.

"Nah, she's fine," Zac yelled back, once again becoming a jungle gym.

"Who said I was talking about Becky?" Abel said with a grin, crossing her arms over her chest. Zac's eyes twinkled as they shared a look, communicating without a single word.

"Come out and play, Spinney," Zac said, dunking Becky.

"Yeah! Come on, Abel!" Becky encouraged once she surfaced.

Finally Abel relented and stripped out of her shorts and shirt, green bathing suit coming into sight. Zac watched, her eyes scanning over Spinney's body, a sexy little grin quirking her lips.

≈≈≈≈

Abel grabbed Zac's hand, holding it tightly in hers as they headed down the hill, down into Spectreville. She wanted to show Zac that it wasn't haunted, and that there was nothing to be afraid of. So many of the things that Bud Lipton had told his daughter were wrong. He had created a woman who was terrified of the simplest things, and Zac had never had anyone to tell her any different.

Zac's hesitance was written all over her face, but she agreed to go anyway. Though she and Abel had been there once before, she was still reluctant.

Abel swung their hands between them as they entered the old, abandoned town. They hadn't been back since the previous year, and she was as struck the second time as she had been the first. The buildings, which had once stood proud housing the timber men, now stood empty and falling apart. It was sad to see their windows and doors drooping like the lids of sorrow-laden eyes.

"So sad that this town was just forgotten, abandoned. Makes me want to cry," Abel said, her voice quiet.

"Yeah. It's said that the ghosts of the men roam around these streets," Zac said, her voice just as quiet. Her eyes were wide, taking in everything.

"Tell me all about this place, Zac," Abel said, her thumb beginning to rub on the back of Zac's hand to comfort her, as she could feel how tense she was. "What did your father used to tell you about it?"

"He said it was filled with evil spirits. He said that if I were to wander over here, they'd catch me and take me away. They'd lock me up in a cave in the hills and no one would ever hear from me again."

The matter-of-fact tone of her voice made Abel so sad. She looked up at Zac. "Oh, sweetie." She reached up and caressed the side of Zac's beautiful face. "You know he only told you that so he wouldn't get into trouble, right? Because he didn't want you to be seen."

Zac looked down at her, conflicting emotions running across her face.

"It's not true, honey. You don't need to be afraid here."

"Do you believe that, Spinney?"

Abel nodded. "With all my heart. I want this place to be a positive place for you, Zac," Abel whispered, sliding her hand to the back of Zac's neck. "Let me show you that it's not bad." She brought

Zac's head closer to hers, closing her eyes as their lips made contact. "Please?" When she felt the small nod from Zac, she deepened the kiss. After long, sensual moments, Abel broke the kiss and took Zac by the hand, leading her into one of the old buildings. As they entered through the arched doorway, she noted the post office sign above it.

༺༻༺༻

Zac followed Spinney to the corner of the small first floor, which was slightly shadowed from the staircase above it. They stopped and Spinney turned to her, snaking her arms up around Zac's neck without a word, she initiated a slow, sensuous kiss, but before Zac could catch up to the sudden change, Spinney was claiming Zac with her mouth, her fingers clawing at Zac's clothes.

Breaking the kiss, Spinney nearly ripped Zac's tank top as she tugged at it, getting it over Zac's head, and tossing it onto the debris-scattered floor. The look in her eyes was nearly frightening. As she clawed at Zac to get her bra off, she actually scratched Zac's skin.

Zac grabbed Spinney's wrists to stop her. "Wait," she panted, pushing her arousal down as her concern rose. "Stop." It took a moment, but finally the crazed look in Spinney's eyes dimmed, the sweet woman that Zac loved returning. "Stop."

Spinney's head fell and the tears came. She brought her hands up and covered her face. "I'm sorry."

"Spinney, what is it? What's gotten into you?" She was stunned when she saw those green eyes that she loved so much look up at her filled with tears and pain. "Oh, Spinney. Don't cry." She wiped one away before it could roll down her soft cheek.

"I'm going to miss you so much, Zac," Spinney cried. She looked pleadingly into her Zac's face. "Please come with me?" she said, her voice a whisper, before beginning to cry harder. Zac gathered her up in her arms and held her. She rocked her, kissing the top of her head.

"I hate this!" Spinney cried, gripping Zac with talon-like fingers. "I hate the fact that I have to leave you! It's not fair." She swiped at her eyes to no avail, the tears kept coming, gathering on the bare skin of Zac's upper chest.

"I know, Spinney. I know," Zac whispered over and over again, her heart breaking right along with her Spinney's.

※※※※

The weeks passed, and the women were even more clingy with each other than ever. They spent their nights awake, talking and making love and their days with the Cohen family. With new understanding, Sherry laid off on her complaints of Abel's time with Zac and let them make their own choices as to how and where they spent their days. Zac acted completely comfortable with just about all of the family now. At times, she even spent time with various members without Abel being present.

As the days of summer marched on, Abel felt her heart getting heavier. She was excited that it was her senior year in college, but it had somehow lost a bit of its specialness. She would have to leave Zac to get that degree. After graduation, it was back for more school. She was torn.

She packed her bags slowly, a soft smile on her lips as she folded her clothing. Each shirt, each pair of shorts and socks, had their own special memory for her. They reminded her of days rolling around on the grassy hillsides with Zac. Stains from food fights or from the dark, rich soil of the forest floor, attested to their antics. She didn't want to leave. Tomorrow morning she would pack up her car and drive away, not to see her love for far too many months. Christmas seemed like an eternity away. Abel was in love. She knew it from the bottom of her soul. She loved Zac so completely, she did not know what to do with the overwhelming emotions attached to it. She needed to talk to Jess.

She grabbed a flashlight, just as a secondary if she needed it, and headed out into the night. She wanted to walk around in the dark, wanted to see the natural beauty that would surround her. This was what Zac saw every single night of her life. This was what drew Zac to the wild, and kept her there. What did it have that a life with Abel didn't?

She looked up into the trees that acted as a canopy, shielding the moon and stars from her sight most the time. She could feel the cool, fresh, night air on her skin and hear the sounds of the night. Birds called to each other and small, unseen animals scampered as they caught sound or scent of her approach. She loved to listen, knowing that although she had come by herself, she was not alone.

She felt, more than heard, Zac walk up behind her.

"What are you doing?" Zac whispered into her

ear, stirring the soft hairs.

"Absorbing. Memorizing. I leave in the morning."

"I know," Zac said with a sigh, wrapping her arms around Abel from behind.

Abel fell back into her, head resting against her shoulder. She sighed with contentment. "Come with?" Abel asked, though only half-heartedly.

"Spinney..."

"I know, I know. I had to try. "

"Are you coming back for Christmas?" Zac asked as she began to run her fingers over Abel's flat stomach through her T-shirt.

"Of course. I'll be here as soon as I can, okay?" She looked back over her shoulder, her eyes meeting Zac's blue that looked silver in the night.

Zac nodded. "Okay."

"Kiss me, Zac." Abel closed her eyes and sighed as Zac's lips lightly touched hers. She turned in the circle of Zac's arms and wrapped her own around Zac's neck. The kiss was slow and leisurely. After many moments, it came to a natural end.

"Come on," Zac said, stepping out of the embrace. She took Abel's hand and led her toward her bluff, where they climbed in silence. "This is my lookout point. Whenever I hear something I come up here. It's how I always know you're coming," she said with a grin.

"Oh yeah? You watch out for me, do ya?"

"Yes, ma'am. Always."

"Good. You keep looking out for me, gorgeous."

"Oh, I will." Zac grinned as she pushed Abel down to lie in the soft grass.

※ ※ ※ ※

Abel could barely see, her eyes were so filled with tears. She looked up at Zac, who swam in her vision and hugged her so tightly she could barely breathe. Zac closed her eyes, a tear slipping out as she nearly crushed Abel to her.

"Please be careful, Zac," Abel begged, kissing the side of her neck and pulling away.

"I will. You, too, okay? Drive safe." Zac placed her hand on the side of the tear-streaked face. "I love you, my Abel."

Abel smiled, once again hearing her birth name. "I love you, too, my Zac." With one last watery smile, she got into her car and drove away.

Zac turned to see Sherry standing in the open doorway of the cabin. The older woman gave her a soft, understanding smile. Zac nodded in acknowledgment then scurried off into the trees. Hiking off toward her lean-to, the tears began to fall in earnest. Her heart had been turned to mush, and it was draining out her eyes. Crawling into the doorway to the lean-to, she curled up around her pillow, which still smelled of Spinney. This made her cry even harder while at the same time comforting her.

She was heartbroken and had no idea what to do with the pain in her chest and hole in her heart. Raising her face to the ceiling, she squeezed her eyes shut, opened her mouth and let her anguish come out.

※ ※ ※ ※

Sherry pulled open the lid to the dumpster, about to toss the bag of garbage into it when she heard the most awful sound. She listened, trying to identify it, then felt pin pricks of emotion behind her eyes. It was an almost inhuman sound. It was a sound of pure devastation that echoed throughout the woods.

"Oh, Abel," she whispered. "What have you done?"

Chapter Thirty

"Abel, honey. Are you okay?" Jessica asked, bracing her hands on either side of the bathroom door. Her roommate had been in there for more than an hour.

"I'm fine," Abel said, though her voice sounded thick from tears.

Jess knew that wasn't the case. Ever since her friend had returned from Maine three weeks before, she had been moody, temperamental and extremely emotional. The two friends shared the same menstrual cycle, so she knew Abel's PMS was long over. Jessica was worried. She thought back to that first night when Abel had gotten back. The woman had been nearly inconsolable. With Jessica's persistence, Abel had finally revealed the rest of the story. Though Jess was not so pleased to be right this time, she figured it had something to do with Zac. She had no idea just how involved it got. Her little friend was in love. And with a woman.

"Damn." She whistled between her teeth. She had no problem with such things, but it was so strange to think of Abel, guy-crazy Abel, in love with a woman. Was she a lesbian now? Jess had no idea. She didn't really care, either. Right now her friend was in pain, and that was all that mattered. "Honey, please let me in." She knocked softly, hearing the sniffling stop. To her surprise, the door opened.

Jess started at the sight before her: Abel's face

was red and puffy, eyes startlingly green from the cry. Her hair was a mess and she just plain looked like hell.

"Come here, bud." Jess took the sniffling blonde into her arms and pulled her to her chest. Abel began crying again. Jessica stroked her hair and rocked her gently. "I know, honey," she cooed. Jess remembered her first heartbreak, but even still, there just seemed no way to help Abel. She had no idea what to tell her friend to make her feel better. So, she wisely chose the road of comforting silently.

Finally, Abel pulled herself together and looked into her roommate's face. With a final sniffle and a deep breath, she said, "I'm going to go to her."

"That's great, Abel. Christmas will be here before you know it–"

"No," Abel said, bringing up a hand to swipe at her tears. "I mean go to her, now. As in, I'm leaving, Jess. You'll have the place to yourself." As she said this, she marched into her bedroom, hers now since their third roommate had graduated and left. She flung open her closet doors and grabbed her suitcases.

Jessica stood there for a moment, stunned. Shaking herself out of it, she hurried after her determined friend. "Whoa! Hang on, chickie." She watched with stark horror as Abel's clothes were thrown into the open bags. "What the hell are you doing?"

"I told you. I'm going. I want to be with her, Jess. I have to be with her." Abel began to rifle through some papers on her desk, tossing some to the floor, others on a pile for the trip to Maine.

"Abel–" Jess grabbed Abel's shoulder. "Please stop and listen to me. Honey, look, you're a senior this year. You're so close to being done." She was relieved when she saw she had Abel's full attention. "You can do so much more for Zac if you're educated or at least know how you're going to get a decent job. What can you do in the woods? At least by finishing school, you can do what you've dreamed of doing for so long, helping other people." Jess searched Abel's green eyes for any sign of understanding and acceptance to her words. She cupped the side of her face. "Don't blow it, Abel. Please think this through."

Abel stared into concerned dark eyes for a moment until finally she sank down to her bed and sighed. "Shit."

Jess sat next to her, laying a hand on her lower back. "Are you okay?"

"I guess," Abel sighed, resting her head against Jessica's shoulder. "I have to be."

"For Zac?" Jess offered.

Abel smiled and nodded. "For Zac."

※ ※ ※ ※

The colors of the leaves and grass would be changing soon. Animals were already beginning to react to the subtle changes in the air. Aure played in the few leaves that were already beginning to fall. He'd see one blowing across the forest floor, his golden butt in the air as he prepared to pounce.

Zac sat on her bluff, chin resting on her hand. She didn't see any of this. Her mind was months ago and miles away when she was headed for Boston on a midnight freight train. She could hear the whistle blasting in her head, almost smell the smoke and feel the cold air blowing into the metal boxcar.

Zac's eyes glanced over at the frolicking dog,

thinking of how he'd handle traveling like that. She'd need to get some sort of leash for him. Maybe a rope? Pack everything, including the tent in its handy carrying case. Pack up her life. Pack up everything she'd known for the past twenty-two years. Pack up her memories, her loves and joys, all that meant anything to her. All but one–Spinney. She sighed again, and stood, calling for Aure to join her. The dog bounded up beside her, tail wagging fiercely as he reached her side.

Without a sound, the two companions made their way through the forest, Zac brushing her hands over the rough surfaces of tree trunks, searching for the squirrel that followed her everywhere via the trees. She smiled when she spotted him right where he normally was–about two trees back, and high above their heads. Aure had long gotten used to the little guy and made no note of him anymore. Zac was glad of this. She thought her dog was going to scare the squirrel permanently away for a while there.

She crested the hill that looked down onto the old town. All was quiet, and though she felt her heartbeat speed up slightly as childish fears began to surface, she held her ground. A piece of litter was blowing through the abandoned streets of Spectreville, swirling in an endless circle, caught in a little vortex between two buildings. Zac could feel Aure's hot breath on her hand as he looked up at her expectantly, waiting for her to do something. She gently patted the top of the golden head and began the descent down. Aure made his way carefully, avoiding rocks and partial roots that stuck out of the ground, his thick tail helping to keep him balanced.

Zac watched as the old logging town got closer and closer. She could hear the howls of the dead moaning quietly on the wind. She kept her mind focused on the task at hand, not allowing her fear to get the best of her. She grabbed a loose branch that lay on the ground, using it as a walking stick, and something for her hand to control, thus taking up some space in her brain. This would make less room for fear.

She reached the start of the street that led into Spectreville. Stopping there, she looked around, taking in the old, dilapidated buildings. She often thought how sad it was to see this once proud, prosperous little town, so dead and half buried in years and mud. Taking a deep breath, she crossed its borders.

Aure followed tail wagging slowly as he took in this new place. His nose was working overtime as so many new smells assaulted his acute senses. He stayed close to his mistress, sensing that she needed him to, though he really wanted to go bounding through this new world. His world had just doubled!

Zac peeked into a few buildings, noting the broken furniture and left-over trash. She hated that transients used Spectreville as their personal dumping ground. Maybe someday she'd clean the place up. She came to the building where she and her Spinney had begun to make love before Spinney had broken down. She could still see them in the corner, a soft, sad smile on her lips. Her Spinney had been so passionate, possessive, and utterly sad that day. It had taken Zac by surprise. She walked to their corner and sat down, running her fingers along the dirt beneath her. Aure sat next to her and automatically her hand went to his head. He whined a little then rested his chin in her lap.

You don't scare me anymore. Zac looked around, noting that indeed her fear ceased to consume her. *I'm free, Dad. No longer a prisoner to your selfish fears, beliefs, and choices. I live for me now. I have to.*

Zac spent half the day in that town, wandering its streets, marveling at all the missed playground that had been at her feet as a kid. She was beginning to see the ghost town as a special place, a place for her and Spinney. She took out her knife from her boot and carved *Zac was here* into the wood paneling that covered a wall in what was once the saloon. Smiling with pride and acceptance, she left that old ghost town, never to be afraid of it again.

Making her way back to the forest, she closed her eyes as she raised her face to the late summer day. It was mid-September and a beautiful day. Just a slight chill in the air, but still T-shirt weather as long as she wore pants. Aure looked up at her for a moment then turned and continued his pouncing on the poor, unsuspecting creatures of the forest. Zac never let him kill anything, but he certainly did play. His long, velvety ears lopped around with every movement. Zac suddenly realized something as the bright colored tent next to the Cohen cabin came into view: this didn't seem like home anymore. It didn't give her the same sense of peace that it used to. Didn't make her feel like nothing could bring her down, or make her sad.

It used to be that all she had to do was look into the lush green of the forest, and all was well. Now, she needed to look into the beautiful green of Spinney's eyes to feel that. She had not felt at peace since her Spinney had left in August. Zac was restless and unsettled. She felt as though all her future happiness rested on the slender shoulders of the beautiful woman.

She shoved her hands into the pockets of her cargo pants as she thought about this. Her earlier thoughts returned. Looking at Aure, she figured he'd travel well, as long as she had plenty of food for him. He loved adventure as much as she did. Maybe...

With a heavy sigh and hanging head, Zac shook these thoughts out of her head. The forest was her home, and always would be. She could wait until Christmas. She had to.

※ ※ ※ ※

Classes were in full swing, and Abel was glad for it. It helped keep her mind on her studies and dedicated to finishing them. It was exciting as newsletters and emails were sent out to seniors with early news on graduation. She'd wanted that for so long, always wanting to follow in her parent's footsteps. Now it was so close she could almost taste it.

Daily, Abel was grateful that Jessica had stopped her from making what would have amounted to be the biggest mistake of her life. Leaving school would have killed a part of her spirit, and she would have resented Zac for it. It was better this way. It had to be.

She plowed away at the first month of school, doing everything she could to ensure her final grades stayed as good as they had over the past three years. She wanted to go to grad school, get her masters in psychology and work with underprivileged youth. Maybe she'd even go further and get her doctorate. She wasn't sure, and decided to wait to see how sick of school she was by the time she finished her first graduate degree.

She tried to keep her mind on school and work only, but Zac filtered in every couple seconds or so. She was literally counting down the days until Christmas break. She tried to get Zac to keep her cell phone so she could call her, but Zac was afraid that Aure would find it and bury it. Besides, Zac didn't like going into the Cohen cabin when they weren't there, so she had nowhere to plug the phone in to charge it. So, alas, she had no contact with her. That was okay – Zac was there in her dreams.

Abel got a sexy little smile on her face as she thought about that. She had to admit, it had been interesting since she'd been back at school. Guys asked her out all the time, and she saw an ex of hers. Nothing. She felt nothing. She was trying valiantly to reconcile the fact that she slept with a woman all through the summer and was in love with her. She wanted to spend her life with Zac. She had no idea how this was going to happen, but still wanted it. Whatever it took.

"What's the daydreamer looking for?" Jess asked, plopping down on the grass next to her. They were in the park across the street from their building. Abel loved to go there and study. Especially now when the air was crisp, but not cold. There were a few people out walking their dogs, as well as one couple with a baby in a stroller. She watched the happy little family of three, a small smile lining her lips. They looked so happy.

"Do you think about that kind of stuff?" Jess asked, noting where her friend was looking. "I mean, if you go forward with this thing with Zac, kids are kind of out of the question, right? I know you've always wanted them."

"Adoption, maybe?" Abel suggested, running a hand through her hair. "Who knows what will happen, Jess. Right now Zac is the most important thing to me. I want to deal with one thing at a time. I mean, who's to say she even wants to be with me that way?" The blonde looked at her friend. "I mean, spend a lifetime, you know?"

"Are you kidding me? You really have to ask that? From what you've told me of your summer and how things went when you left, shit, I don't think there's a question."

Both young women smiled at the couple as they pushed their stroller past them.

"What about you? What do you think you'll do after grad?" Abel asked, turning to look at her friend.

"Other than miss all your life dramas?" Jessica asked. She grinned when she was smacked by a smiling Abel. "Nah, seriously, I don't know. I mean, I'll have my graphic arts degree. I guess get a job somewhere."

"You decided against grad school? I know you were trying to make up your mind."

Jessica sighed as she watched a couple of cute guys start a game of basketball on the park's courts. "Nah. I'm so damn burnt out." She rested her head against the trunk of the tree behind her. "I can't wait to get my career started. Personally, I think you're addicted to school. That's the only bit of craziness I can think of for you wanting to continue."

"Yeah, well, you're just jealous." Abel scooted down until she was lying back in the grass, hands behind her head. "I'll be rich and you, well, won't. Ow! I'm only kidding!" Abel exclaimed, rubbing her arm where she'd just been smacked. "It's just that for what I want to do, this is really the only way to it. I wish I could get Zac to go to school. She's so smart."

"What would she do?"

"She could do anything, and I mean anything. But, I don't know. Something with forestry or animals I'd say. She'd make a fantastic vet." Abel smiled, thinking of her love with the forest animals. Her very own Snow White.

"Then maybe it'll happen my friend. Think positive."

"Thanks, Oprah," she teased. Both grinned, enjoying their day off.

༄༅༄༅

Abel grabbed her backpack, tugging it onto her shoulder. She swore that by time she was finished with school, she would be permanently walking at a slant. Her mother constantly scolded her for not using the straps on both shoulders. Adjusting the bag for balance, she grabbed her hoodie and headed out.

She was happy, acing her first quiz in Models of the Mind. Whistling softly, she headed out into the late September day, thinking about the party she was going to that night. It was Friday, and she didn't have to work until Sunday. *Glory be!*

She strolled out of the building, greeting a few people she passed, many of them friends or acquaintances from the Psychology Club.

"Hey girl, you going tonight?" a tall, lanky redhead asked.

"Yup. I'll see you there, Meryl."

"Awesome! My brother still wants to meet you!" With a flash, the girl was bounding up the stairs, leaving a bewildered Abel by the front door of the building.

"Well, he can keep waiting," she muttered and pushed on. Jessica was waiting for her outside so they could grab lunch together before Abel's senior seminar. She spotted her friend and raised a hand in greeting. "Hey," she said as the two met up. "I am so hungry." She hitched her backpack strap higher onto her shoulder.

"Me, too. Where do you wanna to go?" Jessica asked.

"Hmm. Good question." The friends began to walk, students all around them as the noon rush had started. "How about Arby's?"

"Nah. I'm beef 'n cheddared out," Jessica grumbled.

"Okaaaay," Abel looked around, seeing if anything would inspire her. "Oh! How about that new place they put into the student center?"

"Oh, good call." Jess grinned. They turned in the direction of the large old building when Abel stopped, wrinkling her brow. Jessica glanced at her. "What's up? Come on." Jess began to walk again, but noticed that her friend wasn't following. "Abel?"

The hair on the back of Abel's neck stood on end as she became besieged with a... feeling. She looked around, but saw nothing out of the ordinary. She began to walk again when she felt it even stronger than before.

She felt it. She felt *her*.

"Zac?" she said quietly, unable to shake the feeling that she was near. Her eyes strayed to a large oak when someone stepped out from behind it, the strap of a huge duffel bag slung across her chest. Abel wasn't sure until she saw the golden dog that bolted out from behind the massive tree.

Abel's eyes grew wide and she gasped when Zac raised a hand in greeting and smiled. Abel felt tears pop into her eyes as she dropped her backpack where she stood and bolted. The golden-haired dog ran toward her, tongue flopping out the side of his mouth as he ran at full speed. Abel totally bypassed Aure, needing to get to Zac. She had to make sure it was not a hallucination. She nearly bowled Zac over as she flew into her waiting arms, knocking the wind out of them both. "Zac," Abel breathed, burying her face into the warm skin of her neck. "Oh, Zac."

"I'm here," Zac whispered back, clutching her. "Don't cry, Spinney. It's okay."

Abel squeezed her eyes shut in relief, Zac's warm body against hers. She dreamt of this moment, of seeing Zac again. Abel buried her face into the warmth, a smile on her lips. She inhaled Zac's smell and feel, reacquainting herself with it. Five weeks was far too long to have to wait for this. She could not do it again. Pulling away slightly, she looked up into soft blue eyes. She reached a hand up and brushed a few dark strands out of Zac's eyes. She smiled. "Don't take this the wrong way, but what are you doing here?" she asked, leaning into the touch as she felt a large hand cup her cheek, thumb brushing her tears away.

"Well, you know that feeling we get? That buzz with each other?" Zac asked softly, Abel nodded. "The sound was too low with you being here. I wanted to turn up the volume."

Abel smiled. "You're too cute. How long are you staying?"

"I do what I can," Zac said with a quirky grin. "And, how long can I stay? Spinney, the woods aren't my home anymore."

Abel reached up and covered Zac's hand with her own before bringing it down to cradle it in both hands. She looked into Zac's eyes, studying them, trying to understand. "What do you mean?"

"It's not my home anymore. You are."

Abel felt brand new tears sting behind her eyes and gave into them. Crushing Zac to her, she held on tight, molding their bodies and souls together. She could feel people staring at them, but she didn't care. She had her Zac.

❧❧❧❧

Zac saw a woman walking toward them, a red backpack in her hands, as Zac held her Spinney. Aure, who had been sitting patiently next to the two women, stood and wagged his tail at the newcomer. The woman's dark eyes bore into Zac's before the woman cleared her throat.

Spinney slowly untangled herself from Zac and turned to face her. She swiped at her eyes and looked at her roommate.

"Oh, hi, Jess." She gave her a sheepish smile, a hand still on Zac's arm. "This is Zac. Zac, this is Jess, my friend and roommate. And this big fella here is Aure," Abel said, finally kneeling and saying her hellos to the now-full grown dog.

Jessica took in the tall frame and beautiful face. "Hi, Zac. It's nice to finally meet you. I've certainly heard enough about you." She held out her hand, which Zac took, mindful this time not crush it like she had Adam's.

"Nice to meet you, too, Jessica. Spinney's told me lots about you."

"Spinney?" Jess looked quizzically at Abel.

"Later."

"'Kay. Well, uh, I'm gonna go, Abel. I thought I saw Jennifer over there, so maybe I'll catch up to her for lunch. You two go do, well, whatever." She grinned and handed Abel her backpack. She gave her a quick hug and she was gone.

Spinney turned back to her love and smiled. "Come on. Let's go."

As the two walked toward the parking lot, they couldn't keep their eyes off each other. When they reached Spinney's car, Zac climbed into the passenger seat as Spinney let Aure into the back seat along with Zac's bag and her backpack. Once she took her place behind the wheel Zac glanced at Spinney, who was already looking at her.

"What?" she asked, taking Spinney's hand and entwining their fingers.

Spinney shook her head, the most serene smile on her lips. "Nothing. I just can't believe you're here."

Zac grinned. "Well, believe it."

༄༅༄༅

Jessica finished up her homework, the school library near empty now as it was getting late. Checking her watch, she found that the building would be closing in fifteen minutes or so. She had to go, but wasn't sure if she should go home. She knew that Abel would want some privacy and time alone with Zac, and she wanted to grant them that.

As she packed up her laptop and books, she thought of the unusually beautiful woman who had shown up on campus earlier that day. Zac was truly something, and what pissed off Jess was that she knew Zac didn't do a damn thing to enhance herself: no makeup, no fancy clothes or hairstyle. She was just naturally that gorgeous. Never had she seen someone who turned so many heads, and yet had no clue. Nope, that beauty only had eyes for Abel.

It was kind of cool to see this person that Abel had been crying over for months, but it was a bit surreal at the same time. More than likely, those two had gone back to the apartment and screwed their brains out. Though Jess had no problem with gays, it was still strange to think of it happening under her own roof, especially with her best friend, who she thought had been straight all these years.

Her things packed up, she heaved her backpack onto her shoulders and headed out. She considered going to see Jerome, but decided against it. It was ten o'clock on a Friday night. He was probably already drunk. She decided to risk it and head home.

※ ※ ※ ※

Abel was nearly trembling with excitement as she drove toward her apartment. She held Zac's hand firmly in her own, almost as though she were afraid if she let go Zac would simply disappear and Abel would wake up from yet another dream. Zac's thumb ran over the back of her hand, which helped keep her somewhat calm. Poor Aure was nearly bouncing around in the backseat, as he'd never been in a car before.

Abel pulled her Jetta into the parking lot and parked, cutting the engine. She glanced over at Zac. "This is where I live," she explained.

Zac looked at the large building, ducking her head so she could see all the way to the top through the windshield. She met Abel's gaze. "Can I see inside?"

Abel smiled and nodded. "Of course." She looked deeply into Zac's eyes, trying to read her, trying to wrap her mind around this unimaginable gift she'd been given. "Zac?" she said quietly. "I can't even put into words how happy I am that you're here." She smiled at her. "This has been the hardest five weeks of my life."

Zac squeezed her hand. "I couldn't do it anymore, Spinney. I had to find you."

"To turn up the volume?"

Zac grinned. "Way up."

"Come on. Let's go in."

Abel unlocked the apartment door and pushed it open, allowing Zac and Aure to walk in ahead of her, Zac carrying her duffel bag and Abel's backpack. Closing and locking the door behind her, Abel leaned against the solid wood, watching as Zac set the bags down on the floor. She just couldn't believe that Zac was standing in the middle of her living room, hands buried in the pockets of her cargo pants. Only in her dreams did she imagine this would happen. But, there she was, looking back at her.

Pushing away from the door, she walked over to Zac, never taking her eyes off her. When she reached her, her hands went directly into Zac's hair as she pulled her down for a long-overdue kiss. She'd wanted badly to kiss her on campus, but she wasn't confident enough to show public affection with a woman. She knew in time it would come, as she was a naturally confident and self-assured person, but this new world was still far too new to her.

As the kiss deepened, Abel sighed softly. In that moment, everything was right in the world. There was no war, no hunger, no economic concerns. Everything was perfect, and it all centered around Zac's lips and touch. She buried her fingers in the thick dark hair, desperately needing physical confirmation that she was awake, and that Zac was indeed there.

After many breath-stealing moments Abel broke away from the kiss, needing air. She rested her forehead against Zac's shoulder, her heart racing. She started when she felt something hit her leg. Looking down, she found herself looking into Aure's eyes.

"Hey there, buddy," she said, reaching down and caressing his velvety head. He whimpered and nudged her leg with his nose.

Zac smiled. "I bet he's hungry."

"Oh!" She leaned down and ruffled Aure's ears. "Sorry, sweet boy."

Leaving one final kiss on Zac's lips, Abel hurried into the small kitchen and grabbed two cereal bowls out of the cabinet and set one on the counter as she filled the other one with cold water from the tap. She glanced over at Zac as she entered the room with Aure's bag of dog food. It amazed Abel how, with Zac only being there for a matter of minutes, it felt so natural for her to be there.

"Thanks, babe," Abel said, taking the dog food and filling up the other bowl.

"I like when you call me that," Zac said, leaning back against the counter, her arms crossed over her chest.

"Yeah?" Abel walked over to her, their lips a breath apart. "Babe."

Zac grinned, her hands moving to Abel's hips, pulling them against her own.

"You best be careful," Abel warned with a teasing smile, "or poor Aure isn't going to get fed."

Zac chuckled and left a kiss on Abel's nose before dropping her hands.

Abel decided the best place to put Aure's food and water was in the corner by the small kitchen table. That way it would be out of the way and wouldn't potentially be kicked over. As soon as she put the bowls down, Aure was munching happily.

"Come on," Abel said to Zac, taking her by the hand. "Let me give you a tour."

Zac took in everything with wide eyes as Abel explained where the hand-me-down furniture had come from, when a specific picture had been brought into the apartment and why, or what things Kendra had left when she'd moved out. She was shown the bathroom and where everything was from towels to toiletries, as well as what stuff belonged to Jessica and which were Abel's, therefore Zac's. Lastly, they entered Abel's bedroom.

Abel suddenly felt nervous, though she wasn't entirely sure why. But, as she led the way inside the small room, her heart began to race. The twin bed she'd had when Jessica had shared the room with her had been replaced by a full-sized bed when she'd returned to school.

"I know it's not much, but it's mine," Abel said, indicating the room with its bed, one dresser, and desk near the window. "For the time being, anyway."

Zac looked around. She looked visibly more comfortable being surrounded by Abel's things, many of which were familiar, as Abel had brought them to the cabin at one time or another. She walked over to the Albert Einstein poster that was taped to the closet door and smiled.

"E=mc squared," she said, grinning over her shoulder at Abel, who watched her explore.

"Someone's been reading again," Abel laughed,

sitting on the bed.

Zac moved to the dresser, touching various things that sat on top. She picked up a bottle of Abel's perfume and smelled it before replacing it exactly where she'd found it. "I went to Spectreville," she said, glancing at Abel. "I'm not afraid of it anymore."

"Really?" Abel said, excitement in her voice and in her eyes. She saw Zac's proud smile. "Oh sweetie, that's awesome!" She wanted to go to her and hug her–among other things–but decided to stay put, allowing Zac to get acquainted with the space and with Abel's things. If what Abel hoped was going to happen actually happened, this space would be shared by Zac, too.

"It was pretty neat, I have to admit. Aure was with me. He liked it a lot." She picked up a necklace and brought it up to her eyes to examine the intricate Celtic design of the pendant. "This is pretty."

"My grandmother gave that to me for my birthday last year," Abel explained.

Zac turned to her, necklace still in her hands. "What's a grandmother?"

Abel stared at her for a moment. It never ceased to amaze her, the things Zac knew and the things she didn't know. "Grandparents are my parents' parents. The grandmother who gave me that is my dad's mother."

"Oh." She placed the necklace back on the dresser, exactly where she'd found it, even to the extent of how the necklace was lying on the smooth wooden surface. She walked over to the bed and sat down next to Abel.

"How you doing?" Abel asked, running a gentle hand over Zac's thigh. "You okay?"

Zac nodded, looking around the room again.

"I like your room." She met Abel's gaze. "I like your apartment." She brought a hand up and caressed a soft cheek. "I like you."

Abel smiled. "Well that's good, because I like you, too." She cupped Zac's chin and brought her in for a soft kiss. "A lot," she whispered against her lips.

"Do you still love me?" Zac asked, her eyes and tone serious.

Abel caressed Zac's face with loving, gentle touches. "With all my heart."

Zac leaned in and kissed her, using gentle pressure to push Abel back on the bed. They both sighed into the kiss at the feel of their bodies pressed together. Abel ran her hands down Zac's cotton-clad back only to run them back up underneath the thin material, needing to feel Zac's skin. She had craved the texture and taste of Zac's skin for so long, once again she thought she was having yet another dream.

Zac rested her upper body weight on her left forearm as her right hand reached down and cupped Abel's breast, causing the smaller woman to moan softly. Zac's fingers pinched the nipple, causing it to quickly harden under her touch.

"Zac," she murmured, simply needing to say it, filled with so much need. Zac seemed to understand as her kiss intensified, as did her touch.

Suddenly, Zac removed her hand from Abel's breast, causing her to groan in disappointment, but it didn't last long as Zac wormed her way into Abel's jeans and then panties. Abel's eyes fell closed and she moaned loudly as those talented fingers stroked her saturated sex. Zac dominated Abel's mouth as she brought her to a quick and loud climax.

Abel gasped for air as she clung to Zac, who was

breathing almost as hard as she was. She could tell Zac's arousal was reaching a desperate point. Pulling herself together, Abel forcibly pushed Zac to her back and then slid on top of her. Their kiss was passionate and desperate as weeks of need was unleashed. She tore at Zac's T-shirt, finally getting it off her. Her mouth found Zac's upper chest, her lips, teeth, and tongue claiming the flesh. She moved her way down to bra-clad breasts. Not bothering to reach around Zac and unclasp it, she simply pushed the garment up so she could get to her prize.

Zac whimpered loudly as Abel feasted, her hands buried in blonde hair. "Spinney," she moaned, back arching to offer up all she had.

Abel responded with a moan of her own, her tongue batting at a rigid nipple. It wasn't enough. She pushed up to her knees and tugged Zac to a sitting position so she could reach around her and unclasp her bra, which found its way to the floor atop Zac's shirt. Next, Abel attacked the laces of Zac's boots, the heavy footwear landing with a thud on the floor before they were covered by cargo pants, socks, panties and two T-shirts.

Both naked, Abel laid herself out atop Zac again and once again claimed her mouth. "I want you so bad it hurts," she murmured emotionally, her love for the woman beneath her so deep it was almost painful. That realization made her pause in her frantic need to claim Zac. She lifted her head and looked down into Zac's flushed face. Bringing up a hand, she brushed the hair from her eyes, needing to look into them. "I love you," she whispered.

Zac met and held her gaze for long moments before she smiled. "I love you, Spinney. My Spinney."

Abel grinned and nodded. "Yeah." She knew in that moment she wanted to give Zac the most intimate gift she could. Leaving a lingering kiss on Zac's lips, she began to kiss her way down Zac's body, paying homage to her breasts again before continuing.

As she neared the immense heat between Zac's legs, Abel was surprised she didn't feel nervous. She was about to do something she'd never ever contemplated doing before she fell for Zac. She settled between Zac's spread thighs and used her hands to gently push them open a bit more. She left a trail of kisses over the silky insides of Zac's thighs before she finally met the midnight patch of hair between them. Using gentle fingers, she opened Zac up to her before she lowered her mouth to Zac's core.

Zac gasped and her head fell back to the pillow, as she'd been watching Abel's progress with curious eyes. Her biology book hadn't told her about this! Her hands reached down, fingers running lazily through blonde hair as Abel's tongue ran lazily through her folds.

"Oh my god," Zac whimpered, her hips beginning to move with the incredible things Abel's tongue was doing to her.

As Abel registered the tastes and textures beneath her tongue, she realized how much she loved it. Of course, the sounds Zac was making didn't hurt, either. She felt more and more confident as she explored, using her tongue to bring loud cries of pleasure from Zac. She could tell Zac was getting close, her hips nearly bucking Abel off the bed. She wrapped her arms around her thighs to hold her as still as she could and focused her attention to where she knew Zac needed it most.

It wasn't long before Zac's loud climax echoed off the walls of the small room. She was gasping for breath as Abel placed one final kiss between her legs and moved her way back up, taking Zac in a calming embrace.

≈≈≈≈

Jessica let herself into the apartment, a bag of fast food in her hand. Standing in the entryway, she stopped and listened. To her absolute relief, the apartment was quiet. She flicked on the lamp beside the couch and set her bag of food down on the coffee table before continuing to her bedroom to drop off her backpack and jacket. She chuckled when she heard soft growling on the other side of Abel's bedroom door, followed by the voice she assumed was Zac telling the dog to stop. She used the restroom then headed back to the living room for her late night dinner. She walked into the kitchen to grab herself a beer when she noticed the new addition of the dog's dishes in the corner.

"Guess she's hanging around for a bit," she murmured, allowing the fridge to close. She settled on the couch with her cheeseburger and french fries.

A moment later she heard a door open and close softly. It wasn't long before Abel padded into the room, dressed in a pair of mesh shorts and a tank top.

"Hey," Jessica greeted her friend.

"Hey." Abel plopped down on the couch and snagged a french fry.

"So that's Zac, huh?"

"Yeah."

Jess smiled at the dopey grin on Abel's face. "She's gorgeous. Really hot."

Abel sighed and ran her hands through her sleep-mussed hair. "Yes, she is. I'm so glad she's here. God, Jess, I can't even begin to tell you!" She snagged another french fry. "Her showing up here made my day, my week, my year…shit…my life! But I need to ask you a question," she said, popping the food into her mouth.

"Honey, she can stay here. That's cool. The dog, too. Although, he might get us into a little trouble with the landlord."

"Are you sure? I mean, you won't be weirded out or anything?"

"No." Jess shook her head. "She makes you happy, Abel. That's all I could ask for. Besides, I know damn well if I found my Romeo, you would have no problem with him being here."

"True, but I found Juliet. There is a difference."

"Not to me."

Jessica watched as Abel studied her for a long time, then the sweetest smile crossed her lips. She leaned over and placed a kiss on her friend's cheek. "Thanks, Jess. I can't tell you what this means to me." She took her in a hug before resting her head against Jessica's shoulder. "I love you, girl."

"I love you, too, Abel. Now, scoot so I can eat in peace without wanting to throw up from that goofy ass look on your face. Go back to your girl. I'm sure she's waiting for you." The smile her comment evoked on that adorable face made it all worth it.

Left alone, she realized there was a part of her that was jealous. She was tremendously happy for her friend, but she also wanted to find such happiness. She prayed that someday she would.

Chapter Thirty-one

Zac woke to find herself naked and alone in a strange room in a strange place. Even Aure was gone. Sitting up, she rubbed her eyes and looked around. She felt relief as she saw Spinney's belongings in the room, familiarity for an unfamiliar situation.

There was the massive Einstein poster on one closet door, pictures of Spinney and her family, and some of Zac as well. There were awards, her high school diploma, as well as her cords from graduating with honors. There were some strange gag-type gifts on the dresser top, including a whoopee cushion and some fake black roses, as well as the bottle of perfume and the necklace from her grandmother.

Zac smiled, knowing she was among Spinney's things. She could smell Spinney everywhere–on her own skin, the bedding, the room itself. Getting out of bed, she walked over to the window and looked out. There was a large expanse of grass with some trees out there, and it looked super inviting to her. She knew Aure would love it. Taking a deep breath, she tried to still her suddenly racing heart. Suddenly she was hit with an attack of nerves. What was she doing here? What about all her beloved trees back home? The smells of the forest? The sounds of the animals waking up, or those who had been awake for hours? What about all of that? What about her lean-to, and the land she'd come to see and think of as her own?

Zac shook her head to clear it. She could not

be thinking of such things now. She had made her decision and couldn't-wouldn't-go back on it. That would break Spinney's heart. She could not allow that to happen, no matter what.

≈!≈!≈!≈!

Abel dropped a third slice of turkey bacon in the pan, noting the satisfying sizzle, when she felt arms wrap around her from behind. She smiled and fell back into that strong, glorious body. She had the most amazing memories of that very body from their marathon session of love making that had started up again not long after she'd returned to bed after speaking with Jessica. Zac had declared she wanted to try the neat new trick Abel had showed her earlier that afternoon.

"Morning," she murmured.

"Hi," Zac said into her ear, nibbling on the lobe. Abel felt a small shiver race through her body.

"Stop, you bad girl," Abel chastised playfully, knowing Jess would be getting up any minute. She didn't want to freak her out quite so soon.

Zac kissed the side of her neck and let her go. She saw Aure munching happily on his own breakfast, water sloshed all over the floor from his sloppiness. She grabbed a towel from the counter and cleaned it up after getting her morning bath from her beloved dog, then walked over to a chair and sat down.

"Got any syrup?" she asked.

"Of course, you silly girl. I have been busy this morning." Abel grinned over her shoulder at Zac. "I got syrup, and Hershey's syrup, as well as honey. I'll tell you, babe, I sure hope you have a good exercise regimen in mind to combat becoming a house from what you eat."

Zac gave her a lecherous grin as she scanned Abel's body from head to toe. "I do."

Abel laughed. She was giddy and about to bounce off any wall that would hold still. She filled a plate and took it over to her love.

"Here you go. Eat up." She leaned in close. "Because I'll tell you right now, you need all the energy you can get."

"Okay, save it for the bedroom, girls," Jess muttered, padding into the room, her bunny slippers making flopping noises on the linoleum as she made her way to the coffee maker. Abel stood and gave her friend an apologetic grin.

"Want some breakfast, Jess?" she asked, walking to the counter to prepare her own plate.

"God no. How you can eat that much in the morning always astounds me." Jess sipped the bitter brew then headed back to her room. "Gonna get ready for work. You two have a good day." With the slam of her door, all was quiet again.

Zac looked at Abel. "Is she mad that I'm here?" she asked, eyes wide.

"Oh no." Abel waved it off as she sat down across from her. "She and I talked last night. She just hates mornings, has since I've known her." Abel sprinkled powdered sugar on her French toast. "So I was thinking about something. I have a class today. It's only an hour. What about you coming with me?" She eyed Zac, mindful of her reaction. "You know, sit in with me? You could see what a class is like, maybe learn something new." She hoped that last bit would appeal to Zac's voracious thirst for knowledge.

Zac sat back, chewing slowly on her syrup-drenched food, studying Abel. She sipped from her orange juice. "Okay," she said at length.

"Really?" Abel exclaimed. She jumped up, wrapping her arms around Zac's neck. "I'm so excited! I can't wait to show you around, and introduce you to people!"

Zac smiled, but they both knew she was scared to death.

⁂

Zac swallowed hard. She was nervous as hell. There were people swarming everywhere on campus, going this way and that. Some looked at them, but most went on with their business as though Zac and Abel weren't even there. She eyed them all suspiciously, waiting to see if anyone would do anything stupid. She had agreed to go because she knew that if she wanted to be with Spinney, truly *with* her, in her world, she had to do it on Spinney's terms.

"Come on, honey. It's okay," Spinney murmured as she glanced over at her.

They walked across the expansive and beautiful campus, signs of fall everywhere they looked. Inside, Zac constantly scanned her surroundings. She noticed she was getting looks by both women and men, but wasn't sure why. She ignored them.

"Why are they staring at me?" she whispered to Spinney as they made their way up a flight of stairs.

Spinney grinned at her. "Because you're gorgeous."

Zac met her gaze with raised eyebrows.

They entered into Spinney's *Brain, Behavior and*

Cognition class. A few people were already seated. At the front of the large room a man stood looking over a few pages of paper. He wore ill-fitting khaki pants, a wrinkled button-up shirt, and Birkenstock sandals. He looked up, dark eyes and bushy eyebrows partially hidden behind the large lenses of his glasses.

"Afternoon, Abel," he said with a kind smile, dimples hidden behind his beard.

"Doctor Adams, this is Zac Lipton. She's my guest today."

"Ah." He extended his hand, which Zac took. "It's great to meet you, Zac. Are you thinking of joining our wonderful school here?"

"Oh, uh, I'm not sure." Zac smiled a nervous smile.

"Well, I hope you enjoy the class."

Zac sat down next to Spinney, nearly sitting in her lap, she was so nervous. She eyed the room and the students around her. Many were looking right back at her, mainly the males in the class. They were looking at her the way Spinney's brother, Ben, did.

"I think you're causing quite the stir, Zac," Spinney said with a small chuckle. She leaned over and whispered in Zac's ear. "Are you okay? Do you want to leave?"

Zac shook her head. "No. I'm okay." *I think.*

As the class began, Zac listened to Dr. Adams, not understanding all of what he said, considering they were in the middle of the lesson long before she arrived. But what she did get was fascinating. She watched as Spinney's fingers flew across the keyboard of her tablet, trying to write down every ounce of information.

She watched Spinney, noting the crease that

formed between her green eyes, the way she listened intently, absorbing every word Adams had to say. She noted how Spinney seemed to eat it all up, loving it and tucking it away for future use.

Zac almost felt jealous, jealous of the way Spinney held the teacher in such high regard. It wasn't that she felt threatened. She knew the love she and Spinney shared was solid. But, she wished she had such a passion, the key to something great like Spinney's love of psychology. She knew how much Spinney loved the human mind and the way it worked, the way people interacted with each other and "what made them tick."

Spinney often told her that she would do wonderfully in forestry sciences or maybe even as a vet. Zac had never even contemplated such things. That was for normal people who were smart and driven. Not for her. She was some strange being who had wandered around a forest her entire life. She was someone who was terrified of everyone and everything.

Suddenly, Zac felt a wave of anger pass through her. She stood and walked out of the room, a very stunned Dr. Adams watching her go.

Zac stormed down the hall headed back the way they came. It wasn't long before she heard running footfalls behind her. She was just at the top of the stairs when she felt a hand on her arm, whirling her around to face Spinney, who did not look happy.

"Zac? What are you doing? You can't just get up and leave like that. God, that's rude and inconsiderate to Dr. Adams –" Spinney stopped herself once she saw there were tear tracks down Zac's cheeks. "Honey? What's the matter?" She put a tentative hand on the brunette's shoulder.

"I'm sorry I embarrassed you, Spinney," Zac said, her voice low and flat. "I can go if you want."

"What? Go? No. No, Zac, I don't want you to go. Why would you think that?"

Zac's anger grew as fresh tears began to fall. "I'm sorry I'm not like any of them in there." She pointed toward the direction of the class with her thumb. "They're all normal in there. And smart. Like you." More tears began to slide down her cheeks and she turned away, looking towards the stairs.

"Oh, honey," Spinney whispered, stepping closer. "Please look at me, Zac." She looked into tortured eyes with concern. She reached up and brushed away the tears. "God, I love you so much," she whispered. "Please, don't ever think I think any less of you, Zac. I don't. I swear it. To me, you're so smart. Unbelievably so. And strong. Oh honey, no. You're not like everyone else, but that's what made me fall in love with you in the first place. Don't you see that?"

"No," Zac whispered, gaze falling to the polished linoleum under their feet. "Really?"

"Yes," Spinney said, her hand remaining on Zac's cheek. "God, yes. You…" She paused as she tried to get her thoughts in order. "Zac, what you've been through and the person you are, all those things make me love you more. You are the kindest, most big-hearted person on the planet. The things you know, most of which you have learned first-hand or because of your reading, the things you wonder about and watch, the way you watch the birds outside my window at the apartment, the things you know about all the animals back in the forest, oh, honey. Please, don't doubt yourself."

"But all those people in there, and your strange

teacher. They all have ambition and know what they want. They're all like you, Spinney. Smart and driven and so fantastic. And then there's me. I'm so afraid." The last part was whispered, and Zac's head hung again, tears dripping down to splash on the linoleum.

Spinney gathered her into her arms. She cradled her head against her shoulder and held her. "I'm sorry, sweetie. I'm sorry I put you in this position. We'll go home, okay?"

"You can't miss class, Spinney. I know how much you love it."

"It's okay, Zac," Spinney whispered into her ear. "I know people who can get me notes, okay?"

Back in the car on the drive home, Zac asked, "Does your teacher think I'm an idiot?" Zac asked, her voice quiet, her mood subdued.

"No. I'll explain later. Don't worry about what other people think, Zac. They don't matter. You know who you are, and I know who you are, and just how wonderful you are. That's all that counts. Got it?"

"Yeah."

"Good."

※ ※ ※ ※

Zac lay in Abel's arms, cheek resting against her naked breast. Her head rose and fell with the slow, even breaths Abel took. She was running her fingertips over the smooth skin of Abel's stomach.

"Zac?" Abel asked, absently running her fingers through the long, dark hair.

"Hmm?"

"Do you regret coming here?"

"No," Zac whispered as she kissed the soft skin

under her cheek and lay back down. "I don't."

"What made you decide to come?"

Zac sighed softly, the output of breath washing over Abel's nipple, making it pucker slightly. "Well, it was so hard to watch you leave for school." Zac swallowed at the painful memory. "God, that hurt. I began to hate being there without you, Spinney. It just wasn't home anymore."

"Aww, sweetie." Abel left a kiss on the top of Zac's head.

"I kept thinking about you here, about what you were doing, and how I probably wouldn't see you much anymore. So busy and all. I didn't want that. I wanted to be with you," she explained softly.

"Was it the right decision?" Abel held her breath, afraid to hear the answer. After earlier that day, she felt the heavy weight of guilt. She worried that Zac had left all that she loved and was comfortable with, just to be with her. She worried that Zac would eventually hate her for it.

Zac lifted her head and looked into Abel's very troubled face. She used a thumb and smoothed out the worry lines. "You worry too much, Spinney. Please don't. I want to be with you. I love you."

"I love you, too, Zac." Abel leaned up and placed a soft kiss on her lips. "What would you like to do tomorrow, sweetie? I'm not going to make you do anything you don't want to, or aren't ready for, okay? If you want to stay here with Aure, that's fine. Or I could take you to a park, you guys could wander. Whatever."

"I'm not sure what I'll do. Maybe me and Aure can just wander around campus? Wait for you?"

"I don't have any classes tomorrow, but once

next week comes, will you be okay with that?" Abel asked, reaching up and smoothing back some hair that was curtaining Zac's beautiful face.

Zac nodded. "I think so. Maybe I'll even try another class or two." She smiled weakly. "Maybe."

"Hey, if you want to, I'd love to have you. I'll even sit in the back if you want, so that way if you need to leave, you can." She gave Zac a smile of encouragement. "How's that sound?"

"Good." Zac leaned down and kissed her before resuming her position, getting comfortable as she settled in for sleep.

Abel held on for dear life. She was so afraid to think this was how things would be now. There was the tiniest, niggling voice in the back of her head telling her to protect her heart. She was so afraid that one morning Zac would wake up and decide she wanted to be back home again. She couldn't shake it. But she had to. Zac couldn't know of her doubts. She'd risked so much to come to her, left so much behind.

They had to make it work.

※※※※

Aure stayed with Zac as they wandered around the beautiful campus of Spinney's university. They looked at the various types of flowers and plants that were still in bloom, Zac quietly explaining each of them to the lab, who insisted on sniffing each and every one.

"Come on, you goon." She led the dog further onto campus, loving all the trees that surrounded them. They found a nice little thicket and sat down. Spinney had supplied the duo with plenty of reading material, and Zac was beside herself with it all. She opened the text, one of Jessica's from the previous semester. She began to read all about the history of ancient civilizations and their patterns of war.

She could not understand why people were so stupid and insisted on fighting each other all the time. Though it made no sense, it was fascinating. Suddenly a shadow fell over her book, making Zac squint up at the person. "Hey, Zac."

"Hi, Jessica. How are you?"

"Doing okay. Mind if I sit?" At her nod, Jess sat down, resting her wrists on her bent knees. "So how are things? What do you think of the city?"

Zac glanced over at her unexpected companion and shrugged. "It's very different. But I do like it in many ways. It's nice to be able to actually see what Sp..., I mean, Abel's been talking about all this time." She smiled nervously.

"I bet. Abel talks about you and those woods all the time, too, you know." Jess stared out over the campus, readjusting her sunglasses.

"No, I didn't know."

"Yup. Listen, I've known Abel for four years now, and I care a lot about her. This whole thing with you was a huge surprise to me, but I can see why she fell for you. You're gorgeous and seem like a really sweet chick." She glanced over at the blushing brunette. "Please don't hurt her, Zac. Abel is so fragile. If you hate it here, or don't want her, or whatever, tell her. She can handle it. Just don't fuck with her, okay?"

Zac looked at Spinney's friend, seeing the concern and true friendship and caring reflected on her face. She nodded. "Believe me when I tell you I'd do nothing to hurt Abel. I love her."

"I know you do. And she loves you. You guys will be okay." Jess smiled. "So what's your plan?"

"Other than be there for Abel as much as possible and love her?"

Jess grinned, nudging Zac's shoulder with her own. "I like the way you think. But other than that, yes. You gonna get a job? Go to school, what?"

"Oh," Zac blushed, feeling like an idiot. "I don't know. What does Abel want me to do?"

"Don't know. You can ask her though. She's on her way over here." Jess nodded toward her friend, who was making her way steadily across the autumn-yellowed lawns. An instant smile spread over Zac's face and Aure jumped up, running over to his new favorite person.

"Hey, buddy," Spinney cooed, reaching down to pet the excited dog. She glanced up, glad to see her two favorite people talking and no blood. "Hey guys," she said, tossing her bag down next to Zac. Abel sat and rested her head on Zac's shoulder.

"Hi," Zac said, smiling and giving her a little kiss on the tip of her nose.

Spinney smiled.

"Okay. This is my exit. PDA, PDA," Jess exclaimed, pretending to get up, but was soon tackled by a playful Spinney.

"No ya don't!" she said, looking down at her quarry. "Come to dinner with us."

"You sure? I mean, I don't want to interrupt anything . . ."

"Hush." Spinney pushed to her feet and reached for Zac's hand. "Come on, ladies. Let's eat."

"Can we go somewhere where there's syrup?"

Chapter Thirty-two

Zac sat in the lobby, waiting to be called in. Over the past few weeks, both Spinney and Jess had been schooling her on the art of the job interview. She held her paltry resume in her hands, trying her best not to twist it in her nervous grip. Instead, her foot tapped an endless rhythm that was about to drive the secretary at the Work Force Center crazy.

"Zac Lipton?"

Zac looked up to see an older, balding man in a shirt and loosened tie standing in the entrance of an office. She stood. "Here... sir." She was doing her best to try and remember all her etiquette. Be nice. Be polite. Sell yourself. She followed the man into the office, where he sat behind an old, beat up desk, and indicated that she should sit in the chair in front of him.

"So you're a girl. I have to say, I expected a man with that kind of name." He laughed, his belly jiggling and coffee-stained teeth glinting off the heavy overhead lighting.

"I'm all girl, sir."

"So I see. Okay." He leaned forward, his elbows resting on the table. "Down to business. I have to say, Zac, can I call you Zac?" At her nod, he continued. "There isn't much here to work with. Where have you been? Living in a cave or something?"

"Well, more like half-cabin, half-cave, actually."

The man threw his head back and laughed once again, slapping the desk with a meaty palm. "You're funny, kid, I like that."

Zac smiled, uncertain what was so funny, but remembering Spinney's words about politeness she remained silent.

"Well, since you don't really have an iota of experience, how are you with physical labor?"

⁂

Abel flipped the page of *Maxim* magazine she found abandoned on the bench outside the Work Force Center. Brows rose in surprise as she began to read and look at the pictures in the racy mag. She had trouble concentrating. She knew Zac really wanted to be able to help out, and decided that a job was the place to start. Abel thought it was an excellent idea, though she still worried.

Zac had started to get better and slightly more comfortable around other people. She was totally cool with Jess now, and in fact, they got along very nicely. More than once, Abel had come home from school and found them laughing and cleaning up after one of their numerous food fights. She wasn't sure why Jessica insisted on having those juvenile fights, but they both seemed to enjoy it, so be it.

Abel turned another page, shocked at the rather skanky picture of a popular young singer that she liked. Sighing, she tried to get interested in the article but it wasn't working. Finally she gave up and set the magazine aside, beginning to understand why the person had left it there in the first place. She tapped her fingers to a distant beat in someone's idling car, her head beginning to bob as she checked her email on her phone.

"Care to dance?"

Her head popped up, startled and slightly embarrassed. She saw a grinning Zac standing there, hands on her hips. She looked great in the new black slacks, blue button-up shirt, and loafers Able had bought her for her job hunt.

"Why yes, I would," Abel said, standing and taking Zac's hands in hers, singing in a really bad voice as she led Zac all over the front of the building. Passersby on the sidewalk grinned at the pair. "So?" Abel asked, bringing their impromptu dance to an end.

"I'll be working on the docks," Zac said, grinning from ear to ear.

"What? You got a job?"

"Yep. Helping to unload boats."

"Zac, that's great!" Abel exclaimed, grabbing Zac in a massive hug, so proud of her. "That's wonderful! When do you start?" She put her arm through Zac's as they walked along the street, headed for the blue Jetta.

"Monday. I've got a week. That is, I start Monday, provided my drug test comes out okay. Have you ever had to pee in a cup? That's not fun. I just kept thinking of when I have to pee in coffee cans when I travel the rails. Got real good at my aim."

Abel glanced up at her love, brow raised and her nose pulled up in a grimace.

"What?"

༄༅༄༅

"Twenty bucks an hour!?" Abel exclaimed, then

groaned, again. "That is so not fair!"

"What? Is that a lot?" Zac asked, grabbing the milk and juice out of the fridge.

"I've been at the grocery for four years and still only managed to get them to raise me to eleven!" She slammed the cabinet closed.

Jessica snickered at the two.

"Hey, I don't know. So, that's a good thing?" Zac asked, looking between the two.

"Yes, that's good. That's very good considering you're a human crane." Abel plopped the tuna casserole she'd made onto the table.

"Whoa! Down girl," Jess said, picking up a stray piece of tuna that leapt out of the hot pan on contact. "Probably pretty hard work."

Abel plunked her own defeated self into her chair, arms crossed over her chest, and pouted at Zac. "You're buyin' me nice stuff, then."

Zac leaned over and whispered into her ear, making her giggle and blush.

"Okay, ew," Jess groaned as she grabbed plates and silverware, handing the pair a set. "Congrats, Zac. I'm proud of you even if Stimpy here isn't."

"Hey, I am too," Abel protested, throwing her balled up napkin at her friend.

"Oh, thanks." Jess straightened it and stuffed it in her shirt like a bib.

"Give me that back." The blonde pouted again.

"Finders keepers, losers weepers."

"I am not a loser. Just because I'm poor."

※ ※ ※ ※

The leaves changed and the temperatures

dropped. Winter was coming, and it was coming fast. One thing Zac found she definitely liked better was being inside during storms. She loved that she could curl up with Spinney any time she wanted to, plus she stayed warm.

Aure loved his three mistresses. Heck, he was in doggy heaven all the time now. With somebody always there to take him to the park across the street and toss the ball for him or just let him chase the few squirrels out of the trees, what could be better?

Zac was settling into her job at the docks. It was backbreaking work, but she was able to work alone often. Being with people all the time was strange for her, and took a great deal of getting used to. At first, her co-workers scared the crap out of her, but she was used to them now. She even liked a few. There was a guy named George who was rather nice to her.

Abel's second-to-last semester was flying by and she seemed ready for it to end for Christmas break in two weeks. She had gone all out to make Zac's first Christmas in the city a good one. They would go to the cabin for the actual day itself, to spend with her family, but she wanted to have a special holiday with just the two of them and Aure at the apartment, especially since Jessica was going home for the Christmas break, so they'd have the place to themselves.

One fall day, the two had driven to a tree lot and bought a beautiful six footer. They tied it to the top of the Jetta and drove home. Getting that tree into the building had been a task at patience. Luckily they lived on the first floor, but still, the tree did not want to go through the front or back door. Finally with a mighty push, it popped through, only taking about half the paint from the doorway with it.

"Extra decoration," Zac proudly announced referring to the paint-tipped branches.

They had waited until Jess had gotten home with the decorations, then the three had set to trimming it. They put tons of colorful balls on it made of glass, garland and popcorn strings. This, they found, was an extraordinarily bad idea. Aure went behind them and ate it off as soon as it was placed. He even managed to get the higher strings.

Three yelling women chased him out of the room to figure out what would replace it. More garland and lights. Later that night, Zac once again stood next to Abel as she lit the first of the eight candles on her menorah and recited the song of Hanukkah. Zac watched her as she sang, her voice low and sweet. She saw the way the burgeoning flame from the candle lit up her profile with its delicate, beautiful features. The way her green eyes looked gray in the orange hue, yet her blonde hair seemed to glow with a light of its own. Zac was transfixed. She didn't even notice when Abel finished her song and turned to look at her.

Without a word, Abel grabbed Zac's hand and pulled Zac to her. She leaned up and kissed those soft lips that she grew to love more and more with each passing day. She stepped away from the kiss, but not the circle of Zac's arms. "I love you, Zac. So much."

"I love you, too, my Spinney," Zac whispered, kissing the tip of her nose.

"I'm yours."

"I know. Happy Hanukkah." Zac reached to the shelf nearby and handed Abel a small, wrapped package.

Her eyes lit up. "For me?"

"Who else?" Zac grinned. Shyly, she clasped her

hands behind her back as she watched. Like a little kid, Abel tucked into the wrapping paper like nothing else. Zac had never been able to buy her-or anyone- anything, so she was excited.

Abel unwrapped the small gift, finding a small, long, white box beneath. She glanced up into shy, uncertain blue eyes before looking back to the box. Carefully opening it, she saw a simple, but very beautiful, white gold bracelet tucked into velvet.

"Oh, Zac," she breathed.

"Jess said you like white gold a lot," Zac shyly offered.

"I do. Put it on me."

Quickly Zac took the bracelet and the proffered wrist, clasping the piece of jewelry. "Do you like it?" she asked, watching as Abel studied the bracelet.

"Oh, yes." Abel looked up at Zac, her heart so full it brought tears to her eyes. "Thank you, Zac. Thank you so much." She grabbed the beautiful woman in a massive hug and laid one on her. "I love it. And I love you."

"I'm glad, and I love you, too."

༄༅༄༅

The drive up to the cabin was beautiful. Fresh snow had fallen over the past couple of weeks, enough to stop traffic, but too much for Abel to feel comfortable letting Zac drive. She'd passed the written test and was now the proud owner of a driver's permit at the ripe old age of 23. Zac sat in the passenger's seat, looking excitedly out the window, Aure panting over her shoulder.

"Going home, boy," she said, reaching back to

wiggle one of his ears.

Abel glanced over, feeling that comment like a dagger. She said nothing. It was not made to her. Instead, she focused on the welcome she'd receive from her family. Back in October, she'd called her mother and told her the wondrous news. Sherry had been overjoyed and supportive, even though Abel had voiced her concerns about what her dad would think. Sherry had done her best to convince her daughter that it would all be fine. Abel was happy to see her family, and the smile on her face attested to that.

"What are you smiling at?" Zac asked, taking Abel's hand and placing it on her thigh.

"Oh, just thinking about my mom."

"She's pretty amazing."

"Yes, she is."

༒༒༒༒

Abel woke and looked around the room. She saw her and Zac's stuff piled near the wall, but no Zac and no Aure. Slightly irritated, she got up, the cold air sending a chill across her naked skin. Quickly pulling on her clothes from yesterday, she headed downstairs. She loved waking up wrapped up in Zac. Where did she go?

There were no food smells as she reached the second floor landing, and the house was quiet and dim as the sun hadn't fully risen, yet. Hurrying faster, she was about to start down to the first floor when she glanced out the back window. Twenty yards from the house, she spotted two figures, one dark, one light. Zac was bundled up, and she and the dog were playing in the snow.

Abel folded her arms across her chest, feeling hurt and left out. She knew she was feeling very sensitive right now. She was so worried that Zac would come back to the cabin and realize she wanted to stay. She almost packed more clothes for Zac for that very reason.

Dog and human frolicked, throwing up snow as they pranced around. Aure could vaguely be heard barking, a white puff accompanying each one. Zac grinned like a fool and threw snow into the air, which the dog swiftly jumped up to try and catch.

Abel couldn't help but smile at the show, even as her heart sank. Why didn't Zac wake her up? Did she not want her with them? Did Zac want to be alone? Did she regret that she had left the forest in the first place?

She swiped at a tear she felt slip from her eye and headed back upstairs.

※ ※ ※ ※

Zac inhaled the cold air, letting it fill her lungs to capacity. Aure had pooped out on her, so she was letting him take a rest. As he did, she turned in a slow circle, taking in the trees and land that she knew so well. She could be blind and she'd still know where every single tree stood, and how to get around them. She could find all the hidden little holes and caves, all the bumps and ruts in the path. It felt good to be around such familiarity.

She strolled through the snow, so white, clean and crisp. One thing she didn't like about Boston was the snow didn't stay pure. Far too soon it was ruined by dogs, traffic exhaust, or the throngs of people. She could never take snow from the ground and eat it like she did in the forest. To prove her point, she grabbed a handful, chewing on the wetness.

As Zac looked around, she realized that she felt different being here than she had three months ago, or even this time last year. She felt more at ease with herself and less afraid. Before, she always had this strange feeling of anxiety or anticipation lurking in the back of her mind. Now that she had faced so many of her fears–had a job, had walked the streets of Boston alone as well as with Spinney and had even driven a car–she felt like she had conquered so many of those anxieties. She knew now that there wasn't a Boogie Man waiting around every corner, and in fact, some cops could be really nice. Like when that guy in the SUV had knocked her over as he pulled out of his parking space, that cop had been so nice and helpful.

"You lied, Dad," Zac said into the cold morning air. "You lied to me so many times." *No longer.* She didn't believe him anymore. He was dead and so were all of his selfish, selfish lies.

Zac grinned, feeling so free and happy. She put her arms into the air and spun around in a circle where she stood.

༄༄༄༄

Abel stood at the window in her bedroom and continued to watch Zac's excitement at being home again. She couldn't keep the tears from streaming down her cheeks, knowing that she was losing Zac. They had had three of the most amazing months, and it was coming to an end.

Her heart was breaking.

※※※※

Abel sat on her parent's bed, hands clasped in her lap. "Dad, why are you mad at me?" she asked, watching her father pace back and forth, hands shoved into his pockets.

"I'm not mad at you, Abel," he said, although his clenched jaw seemed to say different.

"For some reason, I don't believe that."

He stopped his pacing and faced her. "Why, Abel? Why a girl? Aren't there plenty of nice, good-looking guys there at your school? Wasn't that why you chose BU over Stapleton, because it was co-ed?"

"Yes dad, but–"

"But what? You have the pick of the crop, honey." He walked over to his daughter, and placed his hands on her shoulders. "Honey, you're a beautiful, intelligent young woman. Any man would be honored and lucky to have you."

Abel sighed, trying to keep her own anger under wraps. "That may be, Dad, but I don't want them. I only want Zac."

Adam stared down at her, brows drawn as he took in what she said. "You do, huh?"

"Yes. Please understand that. There is nothing you can say or do to change that. Please don't make me choose." Abel looked up at her father with pleading eyes. They had been close when she was little, but ever since she'd started making her own decisions, he'd had problems with it. She hated to admit that perhaps her father was a bit chauvinistic. He'd been her hero, and she was so disappointed that perhaps he'd fallen off that pedestal.

Adam sighed and took his daughter in a hug. "I love you, honey. I want you to be happy. Okay? Does Zac truly make you happy?"

She nodded.

He sighed, but held her a little tighter. "I don't understand, and I have to be honest and tell you, I don't approve. But, alas, I have nothing to say in this." He released her from the hug and sat down next to her. "It's your life and it pisses me off that I owe your mother ten dollars."

Abel pulled away, looking up at his smiling face.

He shrugged. "Teach me to bet against you."

"Jerk." Abel grabbed him in another hug, happy to be safe in her daddy's arms. Okay, maybe he hadn't fallen too far.

∽∽∾∾

It was the day after Christmas, and Abel and Zac would be heading home the following morning. Christmas had been a huge success. Although, ever since Abel woke to find Zac missing from their bed, she'd been quiet and reserved. Now, she stood in the living room staring out the front window. Zac was outside playing with Abel's siblings. She had to smile at the giant snow creature they were making.

"Did you enjoy Christmas, honey?" Sherry asked, walking up behind her daughter.

Abel nodded. "Yeah, it was great. You outdid yourself with dinner." She patted her still satisfied stomach.

"Good. Glad you approve. So, what's up?"

Abel glanced at her over her shoulder. "What do you mean?"

"I know you, my sweet. You can't hide your emotions from me." Sherry's green eyes, so much like those of her daughter, bored into Abel's.

"Nothing. Really mom, it's nothing."

"Mentiroso."

Abel rolled her eyes. "I am not a liar, Mom." Abel glared at her mother then returned her gaze to the scene beyond. Rachel was screaming as Ben forced snow down her back.

"Maybe not, but you are lying. Come on," she said softly, putting her arm around Abel's shoulders. "Talk to me."

Abel let out a sigh. She felt so tired. "I'm so afraid that Zac is going to want to stay here," she finally said, her voice quiet.

"Why do you say that?"

"She's out there all the time, Mom," Abel said, indicating her smiling love not thirty feet away. She looked up at her mother with pleading eyes, hoping that she'd understand. "It's like she can't get enough. And so often now, she goes off by herself with just Aure. As if she doesn't want to spend any time with me." She looked down, realizing how childish that sounded.

"Honey, she was with you all day. She was at your side, and rather solicitous of your needs, for that matter." She snorted. "Hell, even I was jealous! You think your father would ever do that?"

Abel smiled, running a hand through her hair. "Yeah, she was. But, at the same time, I don't know, it's just a feeling I get."

"A feeling or a fear?" Sherry challenged. "Have you asked her?"

"No!" Abel looked terrified at the idea.

"Why not?"

Abel turned to face her mom. "I'm so afraid of what she might say," she whispered. "You know, the 'If it's not said, it's not thought,' mentality." Abel hugged herself. "I now it's childish, but I love her so much, and I've been happier in the past few months than I ever have. It would kill me if she left."

"Well, honey, until you decide to talk to her, I'm afraid you're stuck in your rut of indecision and doubt." She leaned over and kissed her daughter on the top of the head. "I love you, honey. Know your family is here no matter what happens, okay?"

≈≈≈≈

Later that night, Abel lay in bed, listening to Zac get ready in the bathroom. She was amazed that Zac was staying with her in the house. She fully expected her to want to stay in her lean-to. She already had once this trip. The bathroom door opened and Zac quickly made her way over to the bed, climbing in and automatically taking Abel in her arms.

"I've gotten spoiled in Boston," Zac said, inhaling the scent of Abel's hair.

"In what way?" Abel asked, readjusting her head on Zac's strong shoulder as she wrapped an arm around her, tucking her fingers under Zac's opposite side.

"The apartment being so warm, smaller space easier to heat up." She grinned, leaving a kiss on Abel's head. "But then again, being colder here means more snuggling." She wiggled her body contentedly. "I love it here, babe," she breathed, her voice full of wonder and happiness. "I love having you here with me, smelling the fresh, clean air again, seeing all my old haunts. I was thinking we'd go into Spectreville tomorrow before we leave if you're game."

"Oh, okay." Abel felt her eyes stinging again, and swiped a hand at them. "We can do that." She did her best to keep her voice steady and calm.

"Great!" Zac pulled Abel even closer, oblivious to the tempest of emotions in her Spinney.

≈!≈!≈!≈!

Zac held Spinney's hand in a death grip as they walked through the forest, bundled up to no end, but that didn't matter. She had to see it one last time. She had to absorb as much of her old life as possible so she could say goodbye. She had to say goodbye, and was getting ready for just that.

≈!≈!≈!≈!

Abel watched as the trees passed, seeing a memory at each one. She wanted so badly to know how Zac was feeling, and what she was thinking. She didn't dare ask. She could not stand the thought of hearing that Zac decided to stay in Maine, and that she'd be driving home by herself. The thought of that big bed alone was too much to bear.

The irony wasn't lost on her that, one of the most amazing things between them was their connection. No matter where they were or what they were doing, they were always able to feel each other, know what was going on inside, but now, when she needed that connection more than ever, it seem to fail her.

Zac could feel the weight starting to press upon her. They'd be leaving in a couple of hours, and a sense of sadness began to fill her. She was anxious to get back to the life she had begun to build in Boston, but at the same time, she was afraid to leave her comfort zone once again. She was filled with so many mixed feelings, but total resolve.

Over the past few days, she had fallen back into her old world. She had been in every nook and cranny of the woods and had even stayed in her lean-to one night. She'd desperately missed her Spinney that night, but she truly wanted to see what life was like again in the woods without her. It had been devastating and she had barely been able to sleep. She'd never known that kind of loneliness before.

Even so, Zac was grieving. She was hurting inside, feeling a part of herself die slowly. It was painful, yet she was so hopeful. With Spinney at her side, she could do anything, and she knew that her love was worth all the pain in the world. Saying goodbye to her world was not easy. She felt guilty, like she was betraying her father, but she knew he had betrayed her long ago. He had filled her head with so many lies, lies that held her back from a normal life.

As she held Spinney's hand a bit tighter, she smiled, thinking of all that she wanted to do once she got back to the city. She wanted to go to school and get her GED. She had read about it on the internet, which she had figured out how to use, and spent hours scouring over the endless information on it. She wanted to do so many things for and with Spinney. She wanted to make her proud of her, and wanted to make herself proud, too.

"It's beautiful here, isn't it?" Zac asked, feeling her chest expand with pride in her new-found decisions, strength, and courage.

"Sure is. Will you miss it?" Spinney asked, her voice a bit tight.

"God, yes. It's going to be so hard." Zac's voice was quiet and filled with reverence for her surroundings. No matter where she ended up, she would always love her beloved forest. She'd even miss her little squirrel buddy, who, to her dismay, she had not seen since returning. "I'll miss it very much."

"I'm sorry, Zac. Really, I am."

"It's okay," Zac said, squeezing her hand, not understanding that Spinney's heart was breaking wide open. "I love you."

"I love you, too, love."

Zac didn't see the watery smile that accompanied the sentiment.

≈≈≈≈

"Good luck, honey. We're here for you," Sherry said softly to her daughter as they stood next to the packed Jetta.

"Thanks, Mom. I'll call you later."

"Okay. I love you."

"I love you, too."

With final goodbyes, hugs and kisses, Abel and Zac climbed into her car and drove into the falling snow.

Zac was quiet on the drive. She tried to do her best not to cry, feeling that final tear in the strings of evolution. She also tried not to look in the rearview mirror. She didn't want to see a final look at her past gone. She only looked forward out the windshield and into her future.

"Are you okay?" Spinney asked, her voice quiet and unsure.

Zac nodded. "Yeah. Fine."

"Want to talk about it?"

"Nothing to talk about."

She sighed, turning up the radio to absorb the silence.

Chapter Thirty-three

Abel rolled over, a deep, sleep-induced sigh escaping her lips. She immediately reached out for the familiar warm body, only to find a cold mattress. Opening one eye, she saw the empty space next to her. Listening, she realized that she didn't hear the soft snoring of Aure, either. She sat up, nearly throwing the covers to the floor in her haste. Panic filled her hazy brain as she realized that both her love and their dog were gone.

As she jumped out of the bed, tugging on any clothing she found, she just knew that they had gone, hopping the rails to make their way back to Maine. She grabbed two shoes, just happy that there was a left and a right one, not caring if they matched. Grabbing her keys off the side table, she was about to bolt out of the room when she glanced out the window. There, across the street in the tiny park, were two figures. They sat under one of the only trees, one with his head in the other's lap.

Icy fingers wrapped around Abel's heart as she slowly made her way across the snow-covered street, mismatched, too big shoes flopping against the pavement. As she got closer, she saw Zac sitting there, chin resting on a raised knee.

"Zac?" Her voice was quiet against the even quieter early-morning chill. She pulled her jacket a little closer to her body.

"What are you doing up?" Zac asked, raising her

head to look up at her love. "What are you doing out here?" Abel indicated the park around them.

"Just thinking," Zac said softly, resting her head back against the tree at her back.

"Oh," Abel said, not sure what else to say as she shoved her hands into the front pockets of her jeans, sighing in a puff of white. "Listen Zac, I've been doing some thinking, too." She looked down, her long, blonde hair falling to cover her face. "I saw the way you were back at the cabin. I know how much your heart is still there." She glanced up, but could not look at Zac. "I'm sorry I've kept you here, Zac. I know you can't stand the craziness of the city when you love the peaceful quiet of the forest so much." Her voice began to tremble.

"Abel –"

"No! Please just let me get this out." Abel glanced very briefly at Zac, but once again her gaze fell to the snow-covered grass at her feet. "I'm not going to keep you here against your will. I know you long for the wild, and probably Aure does too. If you want, I would be…" she swallowed, "happy to drive you back to Maine. Just say the word, Zac." She was on the verge of outright crying. "I'll do it. For you. I love you that much." She could not hold it in. "Just tell me." She turned and began to quickly head for the apartment building.

Zac stared after her, mouth hanging open. "Abel?"

Abel stopped, her back still to Zac. She was so upset, she hadn't even realized that Zac was using her given name, only the second time in their entire relationship. "Yeah?" she managed through her tears.

"Do you love me?"

Abel turned, fuming. "Of course I do, goddamn it! That's why I'm willing to let you go, Zac! I want you to be happy, and if it's back in the woods, then so be it. It would kill me to see you unhappy, especially if I were the cause. I saw the way you looked out into those trees, such longing." Abel took a breath. "Oh, Zac. I'm so sorry I've made you so unhappy here."

Zac pushed to her feet and took a few steps towards her. "Abel...Spinney...I'm out here because Aure needed to pee." The dog looked from one to the other. "Spinney?" she said, her voice soft.

"What?" Abel wiped at her eyes, the tears just not stopping. She was confused.

"Can we get a house plant?"

"Wait, what?" Abel wasn't sure she'd heard right. She was even more confused now. "A house plant?"

"Yeah." Zac grinned, that cute little crooked one that Abel loved so much. "We can water it together, watch it grow, have to replant it in like six months, yell at Aure as he tries to eat it, you know. A house plant."

Abel turned to fully face Zac, her head cocked to the side, trying to absorb what she was being told. "You and me? Where?" She took a tentative step forward.

"What do you mean, where? Here, you goof, and of course you and me. I don't want crazy Jess anywhere near any plant of mine."

Without warning, it all hit Abel at the same time, and with a squeal of relieved delight, she ran to Zac and bowled her over. Zac fell back into the snow, squirming under the onslaught of kisses that were being rained all over her face.

"I love you, I love you, I love you, I love you!"

Abel managed between each one.

"I love you, too," Zac laughed, trying to avoid being kissed in the eye, or having Aure's tongue end up in her mouth as he joined in the kissing fun. Finally, Abel let up, looking down into the beautiful face of her love.

"You mean it? You're not unhappy here?"

"God no! You're here, Spinney. I could never be unhappy where you are."

"But at the cabin..."

Zac reached up and cupped Abel's cheek. "Honey, I was saying goodbye. I knew my life belonged with you and Aure here. It wasn't home anymore. I love it there, always will, but it's not where I belong anymore. I'm with you. Only with you."

Abel wrapped her arms around Zac's neck and held her close, eyes squeezed shut in utter relief and love. "Mine."

"Yours. And Aure's. And the houseplant's."

Epilogue

So you see, Abel found me, saved me and inspires me every day. I did eventually get that GED and obviously found my way to college. After four years I wasn't ready to stop, so here I am, asking you, good sirs, to find it in your hearts to let me into your master's program.

The wild is in my blood, and my love for it is indisputable. Just ask Abel. It's my dream to save and preserve what has so generously been given to us in the form of the forests of the world, all that cannot protect itself. My sworn duty is to protect, preserve, and learn. My desire will never die, but rather grow with the foliage around me.

You can take a girl out of the wild, but you can't take the wild out of the girl.

"I always loved that line," Abel said, grinning as she handed the old papers back to Zac.

"I guess they did, too, huh?" Zac asked with a grin as she filed her entrance letter back with all her old papers and grades.

"How do you feel? Leaving here?" Abel asked, looking around the bedroom they'd had in the small townhouse for the past ten years.

"I'm sad to leave Boston, but I can't even begin to say how excited I am to start the new job." Zac grinned from ear to ear.

"I bet, baby. I'm so proud of you." She wrapped her arms around her love's neck, smiling up at her and bestowing a small kiss on her lips. "I just wish Aure could be around to see the cabin now. He'd be so excited."

"I know." Zac rested her head against her Spinney's forehead. It had been a sad day for her last summer when they'd had to bury the old dog. He'd lived to be seventeen, so she couldn't really complain. But still, she missed him.

"But, we'll be getting lots and lots of animals there. No limit." Abel placed a kiss on Zac's forehead before stepping out of their embrace.

"The old cabin. Crazy. I can't believe your folks sold it to us."

"Hey, I'm not going to complain. I guess it was just so hard for dad to keep driving there every year, you know? Got tired of it," Abel said, continuing to pack up their things.

"Yeah. Oh, let the remodel begin!" Zac clapped her hands together happily.

"Yeah, yeah. Speak for yourself, Ranger Rick," Abel said, slapping Zac on her very shapely behind.

Zac stuck her tongue out at her, only to have it caught between straight, white teeth.

Zac's tongue between her teeth, Abel grinned sexily up at her.

Zac purred, squeezing the smaller woman's own shapely behind, packing could wait.

About the Authors

Kim Pritekel was born and raised in Colorado, where she still lives. She considers herself incredibly fortunate to do what she loves most for a living and to have an incredible woman by her side.

You can also find Kim's other books at -

www.sapphirebooks.com

www.kimpritekel.com

Alex Ross lives in Manhattan with her partner and their two cats. When not writing or editing, she enjoys exploring all over the world, hiking, rock climbing, reading, and is about to start grad school to get her MBA.

Contact her at alexleaross@gmail.com.

Check out Kim's other books.

After Shadow - ISBN - 978-1-939062-10-9

Clara always knew she was different, but just how different she was was to be seen. She will be forced on a journey to places that, though nightmarish to some, make perfect sense to her. While living a life in darkness and shadow, massaging the ghosts we all want to hide from beneath the covers, she will discover her own light of day. But, can she discover her heart?

Shadow Box - ISBN - 978-1939062-07-9

One 3 a.m. incident would change everything forever.

Tamson Robard spent a childhood with a weak mother, desperate to land a man in order to escape a horrific secret that Tamson can't even fathom. Tamson ran away as a teenager, but is now a grown woman. Other than drugs, her only friend is a guardian angel, Penny, whom she confides in, sharing feeble hopes and unending pain.

Together, the two will discover buried truths that will lead them through tears and to death's door. Can the collision of Erin and Tamson's worlds save them both?

Connection- ISBN - 978-1-939062-24-6

Julie Wilson lives a charmed life as a beloved teacher and aunt in the small town of Woodland. Close to her brother and guardian of two adorable Yorkies, she loves her life, the only negative being ex-boyfriend, Ray who can't seem to understand the phrase, "We're done." Believing that's her only problem, Julie has no idea what hell awaits her during a normal summer afternoon.

Remmy Foster is the quirky, friendly drifter who has never found roots after a difficult childhood, as well as the difficulties her very special gift brings into her life. Though she may call it exploring, the truth is she's running from ghosts that haunt her every step.

After a chance meeting with Julie while hitchhiking, Remmy will be thrown head first into darkness she could never have foreseen, regardless of her abilities. As the clock ticks, life and death is on her shoulders to make the right connection.

Warning - Some scenes may be too intense for some readers.